Bittersweet

Books by

Cathy Marie Hake

FROM BETHANY HOUSE PUBLISHERS

Letter Perfect

Bittersweet

CATHY MARIE HAKE

Bittersweet

BETHANYHOUSE
MINNEAPOLIS, MINNESOTA

Bittersweet
Copyright © 2007
Cathy Marie Hake

Cover design by Jennifer Parker

Scripture quotations are from the King James Version of the Bible.

Published by Bethany House Publishers
11400 Hampshire Avenue South
Bloomington, Minnesota 55438

Bethany House Publishers is a division of
Baker Publishing Group, Grand Rapids, Michigan.

Printed in the United States of America

Paperback: ISBN-13: 978-0-7642-0166-0   ISBN-10: 0-7642-0166-2
Hardcover: ISBN-13: 978-0-7642-0333-6   ISBN-10: 0-7642-0333-9
Large Print: ISBN-13: 978-0-7642-0332-9   ISBN-10: 0-7642-0332-0

Library of Congress Cataloging-in-Publication Data

Hake, Cathy Marie.
   Bittersweet / Cathy Marie Hake.
     p. cm.
    ISBN 978-0-7642-0333-6 (alk. paper) —ISBN 978-0-7642-0166-0 (pbk.) —
ISBN 978-0-7642-0332-9 (large-print pbk.)
   I. Title.
   PS3608.A5454B58   2007
   813'.6—dc22   2006038413

The Bible speaks of us all being part of the body of Christ, all of us having functions that are infinitely varied, specialized, and essential. Bethany House Publishers is much like that. Behind every author there are editors, copy editors, book cover artists, marketing gurus, print setters, binders, secretaries, and booksellers. We all need each other so we can work together to serve the Lord.

This book is dedicated to the wonderful team whose dedication and hard work enable me to tell a story.

The story is dedicated to the Lord.

CATHY MARIE HAKE is a nurse who specializes in teaching Lamaze, breastfeeding, and baby care. She loves reading, scrapbooking, and writing, and is the author or coauthor of more than twenty books. Cathy makes her home in Anaheim, California, with her husband, daughter, and son.

Bittersweet

CHAPTER ONE

Sacramento, California
September 1860

Laney McCain fought the urge to lick her fingers. The Fry's chocolate bar had come all the way from England, and it seemed wrong to waste even a dab of something so wonderful. Behind the cover of her hankie, she buckled to the temptation. One . . . two . . . three quick licks. Both bitter and sweet at the same time, the last little taste left her craving more. She smiled down at her neighbor, Dale O'Sullivan. "We're going to have to go back to that candy place!"

"Right now?" Greed lit the six-year-old's eyes.

"Yeah!" his brother Sean agreed.

"No." Laney used her hankie to clean Sean's chocolate mustache.

Dale hastily licked his own mouth clean and grinned. "I got it all, Miss Laney!"

"Yes, you did." She straightened up and scanned the crowded California State Fair pavilion as she tucked the hankie back up her sleeve. "You boys stay close. Here, Sean. I'll carry the pail now."

"Do you know where we're 'posed to go?" Dale grabbed a fistful of her skirt.

"No, but I see a gentleman over there who's wearing a name tag. We can ask him." Laney approached the bewhiskered man. "Excuse me. I have grape jelly and canned veg—"

"You're in the wrong place." Vexation creased the man's brow and lent a surly edge to his voice. "Produce is over in the west side of the pavilion. Tallow, lard, and preserved meats are here. Milk, butter, and cheese are on the south side. Grains and starches are north."

Sean O'Sullivan scratched his bony elbow and asked, "Are potatoes produce or are they starch?"

"Don't get smart with me," the man snapped.

Laney wrapped her left arm around Sean's shoulders and drew him closer. Her fingers made contact with the black strip of mourning crepe on her ten-year-old neighbor's upper arm, so she slid her hand higher and patted him while drawing his little brother closer to her on the other side. "I wondered the selfsame thing. I guess it doesn't matter much since I don't have potatoes."

"Guess not." Sean shrugged—a tense move that tattled on how upset he was.

"Your mother's over there with Hilda. See? They're entering their tubs of lard."

"Uh-huh."

"Since I need to go over to the far wall with my jelly, Sean, why don't you go tell your mother that Dale and I will meet you all outside by that bench where we ate our chocolate?"

Sean looked up at her, his blue eyes filled with a mixture of sadness and anger. "Yes, Miss Laney."

"That's very helpful of you."

A moment after he left, the grumpy man *harrumphed.* "Didn't notice the lad's armband. Didn't mean to upset him."

Laney cast a meaningful look down at Dale, then tried to sound chipper. "I convinced the O'Sullivans to come to the fair with me. Two of your brothers and your mother came along, didn't they, Dale?"

"Uh-huh. But Galen stayed behind to work."

"Right smart idea." The old man bobbed his head knowingly. "Treat your servants well and they work harder."

"The O'Sullivans work harder than anyone I know." Laney smoothly set his false assumption straight by adding, "It's a pleasure to have them as our neighbors." *And someday I'd like to be more than just their neighbor. It's proper to have a year of mourning; that's long enough to let Galen see that*

I'm not just his best friend's baby sister. He'll finally see how much I love him and his family.

Laney pulled the blue gingham cover off her pail and entered her jelly and vegetables in the competition when they reached the correct booth. A sense of accomplishment washed over her. Even six months ago she hadn't known how to cook anything. She'd only tried to make jelly once before—with disastrous results. Thanks to Mrs. O'Sullivan's gentle guidance, Laney now knew her way around a kitchen.

As she and Dale left the booth, he tugged on her sleeve. "Miss Laney?"

"Yes?"

He crooked his finger at her, so she leaned down. "Do you got any extra of that grape jelly?"

"Back home I do. Why?"

He looked crestfallen. "Never mind."

"Are you hungry?" When he shook his head, Laney drew Dale off to the side and sat on a small bench. Taming her hoops took a fleeting second, and then she reached and pulled Dale onto her lap.

"My shoes'll make a dreadful mess of your pretty new dress."

"A little dirt never hurt anyone." She curled her arms about him. "Now suppose you tell me why you wanted to know about the jelly."

"I thought maybe if I put some on Hortense,

nobody'd want her." He blinked and hung his head.

"Ahhh," she said softly, then cuddled him closer. "I see." Laney smiled, recalling her first jelly-making experience, which had ended with her discarding her work into the pig sty. Her brother, Josh, thought the hogs had contracted some ailment upon seeing the purple splotches on their skin.

Laney threaded her fingers through Dale's unruly red curls. All around them, the fair went on. *But Dale's little world is falling apart.*

Dale finally tilted his head back. "Galen says I've gotta be brave."

Her heart leapt at the mere mention of Galen's name. "If anyone knows about being brave, it's your big brother." Laney slowly stroked her hand up and down Dale's skinny back.

"'Farmers raise crops and livestock to sell. It's our job,'" the little boy quoted, but his voice quavered.

"There's no denying that you've taken fine care of Hortense. I remember when she was just a tiny piglet."

Dale nodded. His hair caught on the pin-tucked bodice of her gown.

For a few more minutes, they stayed silent. Laney spent the time plotting what to do so Dale wouldn't have to lose his pet. "I must say," she told him as she gave him a squeeze, "I think you've been exceedingly brave. Your big brother and mine could probably take a lesson or two from you. I've never seen a pair of grown men act the way they did at the railway station!"

Dale perked up and giggled. "Hortense sure and enough gave them a hard time, didn't she?"

"I can't say who behaved the worst: my brother, yours, or Hortense."

"You can't blame Hortense. She'd never seen a train afore."

"That's a very good point in her defense. Josh and Galen had no excuse. Then you"—Laney tapped his freckled nose—"just crumbled that cookie and made a trail that had her walk right up the ramp and into the livestock car. That was very clever."

"Not really. I didn't have a cookie to eat, then." Glum as could be, he added, "If I'd kept my cookie, maybe Hortense would still be back home."

Arguing about that would be pointless, so Laney whispered, "There's nothing keeping us from getting cookies now. I saw some enormous ones at a booth just outside the door—right next to the candy place. We could get a few chocolate bars to share and a couple of cookies." When Dale's eyes brightened, she shifted her gaze around the pavilion a few times, then leaned closer. "I think . . ." She paused for a moment to stretch out the suspense.

Dale squirmed. "Whaddya think, Miss Laney?"

"I think"—she gave him a squeeze—"Hortense would enjoy a cookie, too."

His jaw dropped. "You'd buy a cookie for my shoat?"

"Hortense isn't any ordinary pig."

"No, she isn't." Dale couldn't resist boasting, "Hortense is very smart."

"There's only one problem, though."

"There is?"

"Yes." Laney nodded her head solemnly. "I don't know which Hortense likes best: sugar cookies or gingersnaps."

———

"What a darlin' lass you are." Galen O'Sullivan patted the spirited mustang's neck. "Aye, you are. Itchin' to run, too. Well, you'll be on your way soon." He led the mare out to the fence and scanned the horizon.

For months he'd been managing the Pony Express relay station. The riders were impressively punctual, the horses even-tempered, and the news from back East fresh instead of weeks old. If only the Pony were profitable.

Four-and-a-half months was a long time to board, feed, and groom horses without compensation—and that didn't take into consideration that Galen needed to stop in the middle of his farming chores to saddle up the exchange mounts and cool down the traded ones.

Then, too, he'd needed to do a lot of doctoring recently. The riders obeyed the order to ride hard and push the horses to the limits of their endurance. That kind of use invariably took its toll. Of the three horses that belonged to the Express, Galen usually had to keep one out of the rotation for medical reasons.

"You stay here, lass. I'll fetch a dipper for the rider. He'll be by anytime now."

Galen went into the cabin and grimaced. He'd been busy trying to handle everything on his own. The house showed it, too. Instead of being orderly and redolent with the aromas of Ma's good cooking, the place would send any woman into a swoon. An unmade bed, dirty dishes, and a crusty-looking pot on the cold stove all declared Galen's lack of domesticity.

Pumping water into a bucket, he tried to recall where he'd last seen the dipper. The day Ma and his brothers had left for the fair, he'd used cups. The next two days, he'd used the bucket and dipper. That morning he'd caught water in a mixing bowl and drunk from the rim. After all, Ma always allowed her sons to lick the bowl when she mixed up a treat. Surely she wouldn't deny a thirsty son his fill of water!

But she'd have a conniption if he offered a rider water from her mixing bowl.

The distant drumming of hooves warned Galen he'd better hurry. A few minutes later, he shoved a quart-sized Mason jar at the rider. "Water."

"Thanks." He drained the whole thing.

"Ma's at the fair in Sacramento. This'll have to do." Galen handed the rider a large pear from his mother's orchard. Though it wasn't part of the business arrangement with the Pony Express, Ma refused to allow any man to come across their land without offering hospitality. She usually had a sandwich or a baked treat ready for the riders.

"You here alone?"

"Aye." Galen yanked the leather *mochilla* from the lathered mount and slung it over the saddle of the waiting mare. All four pockets of the carrier were full. That must be a good sign— that business was picking up.

"Talking to yourself yet?"

Galen laughed. "Aye."

The rider nodded sagely. "You can even answer yourself. If you start arguing with yourself, that's when you know you're Bedlam-bound."

"I'll keep that in mind."

"Bet Miss McCain's been dropping by to bring decent grub."

"She's in Sacramento at the fair, but even if she hadn't gone, it wouldn't be fitting for her to come here."

"She's a proper young lady. No one would ever imagine her misbehaving. She's here so much, she's practically like family already. When are you finally going to pop the question?"

"I'm not. She's like a kid sister—nothing more."

The rider shook his head and swung up into the saddle. "She's got her heart set on you."

"What do you know? You come by a couple of times a week for a few minutes."

"I know a woman in love when I see one. You're going to break her heart."

"She'll grow up and forget her foolish notions. I'm sparing her feelings by ignoring a young lass's passing fancy. Off with you now. God go with you."

Galen watched as the horse and rider disappeared from sight. Turning back toward his fields, he heaved a sigh. *Lord, I've already got far too much on my plate. You promise you won't give us more than we can bear. Well, I'm at that point. I'm worried about Ma. She's mourning Da somethin' fierce. And try as I might, I can't fill his shoes by playing father to my little brothers.* Tending both the farm and the Express with Colin's help this summer had taken all their effort. Now with Colin going back to school, Galen knew he'd be stretched to the limit. *That's everything, Lord— my family, my finances, my farm—everything's in disarray. Can't you please help me out?*

He grabbed the lathered horse's reins and walked him for a gentle cooldown, then rubbed him, soothed him, and finally allowed him a small drink from a pail. "That's it for you, boy-o. Though you're wantin' more, 'twould make you founder. In a little while I'll let you drink to your heart's desire and feed you well."

Galen weeded and watered the huge garden surrounded by Ma's fruit trees. The McCain ladies—Laney and Josh's bride, Ruth—had been helping Ma garden, pickle, preserve, and such for months now. Their companionship helped keep Ma going, especially after she lost Da. That being the case, Galen knew he couldn't very well tell Josh to keep his kid sister at home. He'd learned to ignore Laney's attention.

He worked well into the evening, then did more by lantern light in the barn. Finally Galen went into the house. It was far too hot to bother lighting the stove to cook anything. The end of the loaf of bread Ma had baked and left for him was stale. He ate it along with a hunk of jerked meat and a pear.

Before falling into bed for the night, Galen filled the big half barrel they used as a bathtub. After shaving in a few curls of lye soap, he gathered up all of the dishes and dumped them in to soak overnight.

Loud rumbles from his stomach woke him the next morning. Galen thought of all the eggs he'd gathered over the past four days, then looked at the soaking dishes and promised himself he'd rinse them and set them out to dry so he could have eggs tomorrow morning. For now he settled for a hefty wedge of cheese from the springhouse and more fruit.

Round about noon, whilst weeding the garden, he heard a sneeze and straightened up. "Rick Maltby! What brings you here?"

"A guilty conscience." Rick lifted a pasteboard box. "And a mercy meal. I figured by now you'd be starving."

"Close to it." He motioned to a shaded spot. "Meet you over there."

"If you don't mind, I'm—" the town's lawyer sneezed again—"a-a-allergic to something out here."

"We can go into the house on one condition."

Maltby sneezed again. "Anything."

"Give your word that you'll never mention what you see."

"What are you talking about?" Maltby let out a typhoon of a sneeze. "Out with it, Galen. My hay fever is—"

"Come on." Galen strode toward the house. "The house is a wreck. Ma'd wring my neck if she ever caught wind of my letting things go."

Maltby chortled.

"It's not funny in the least." Galen glowered at his so-called friend.

"Yes it is. I'm relieved I'm not the only grown man who hates the thought of disappointing my mother!" Once he stepped into the cabin, Maltby let out a long, low whistle. "That's quite a collection."

Galen gathered the dishes from the towel he'd spread on the table that morning. Stacking them in the cupboard, he changed the subject. "So you've a guilty conscience?"

"I do." Maltby sat down and shoved the box across the table.

Finished putting most of the dishes approximately where he thought they belonged, Galen sat down and pulled off the lid. The sight and scent of fried chicken made his mouth water. He forced himself to rise again.

"What're you doing?"

He tore his gaze from the box. "Getting us plates."

"I've already eaten. I figured you'd just save some for supper."

Galen sat back down and rubbed his hands together. "I'm not sure what to pray first— thanksgiving for the food, for you being such a fine friend, or that Bill was cooking at the Copper Kettle today."

Rick didn't crack a smile. "I'm not feeling as if I've been such a good friend to you, Galen."

Galen froze and looked at the food with nothing short of horror. "Ethel was cooking?"

"Bill cooked. If Ethel had, I wouldn't have brought you anything."

Relief flowed through Galen. "You brought

me good food; that proves you're a grand friend."

Maltby let out a long sigh. "I approached you and your father about running the Pony Express relay from your farm. I've recently heard the company is in arrears insofar as their payroll is concerned."

"That's not your fault. Da and I prayed together and made the decision to manage a station."

"You could cite your father's death and the company's failing to meet their obligations as reasons to sever the contract. I'm willing to represent you at no cost."

"That's generous of you, Rick, but I'm giving them a fair chance. I won't welsh on a deal. Da's passing is no excuse for me to back out of a business agreement."

"But the Pony is failing to pay up."

"I can't deny wishin' they'd cough up the money. Still, I'm noticing the mochillas are full these days. Maybe they needed a little time." Galen shrugged. "Perhaps 'tis the farmer in me. I understand there are times when we can't see growth because the plant has to set down roots first."

"The offer stands—at any time, if you want my help, it's yours."

Galen inclined his head in acknowledgment. "As for hard feelings about money—forget that. 'Twould be a sorry excuse of a man who ruined a friendship for the sake of greed." Galen pulled out a perfect golden brown drumstick and waved it a few times. "But don't put that comment to the test if you're thinkin' of reaching for a piece of chicken."

For the first time since he'd taken a seat, Maltby smiled.

Decent food and someone to talk to went a long way toward perking up the day. After Maltby took his leave, Galen went back out to work. Late in the afternoon, he squinted off into the distance. What he saw curdled his blood.

CHAPTER TWO

Shoulders, back, and legs aching, Ivy Grubb stretched and squinted at the sun. "I'd best go put supper on."

Her twin, Ishmael, nodded. "I slung the snake o'er yonder."

Gritting her teeth to keep from whimpering, she walked toward the yard-long headless rattler. Others said snake meat tasted good, but Ivy hadn't ever gotten past her revulsion enough to eat any. Her stomach lurched at the sight, but Ishmael's hunger kept her resolve strong. She stared down at the hideous reptile. "I'd rather stay hungry, myself, Mr. Snake, but my brother's belly is growlin' like a winter-waked bear."

"What's holdin' you up, gal?" Pa shaded his eyes and scowled at her. "Got us that fine meat, jest a-layin thar. 'Tain't gonna slither its own way into a fryin' pan."

"Yes, Pa." Ivy shuddered and lifted the snake.

"And mind how you skin 'im. I tole Ishmael to make it into a belt or hatband. No use wastin' somethin' that'll put cash money in my hand."

After dumping the snake by the ring of stones that served as her kitchen fire pit, Ivy grabbed two buckets and hiked over to the small creek. Sluicing water over her filthy hands, she tried to ignore her rippled reflection. On Ishmael, white-blond hair looked fine. On her, it looked as washed out as her one and only dress. Just as scraggly, too. " 'Tain't like nobody's gonna ever pay me any heed, no how," she muttered.

The creek wasn't deep enough to submerge the buckets, so she tilted each, then poured the contents of one into the other. Having a bucket and a half beat having just two piddlin' halves.

The water here tasted cool and sweet. Pa had decided since corn grew well for lots of folks in the area, this would be as good a spot as any to stop. Ivy didn't know whose land it was. She didn't bother to ask, either.

For the past six years, Pa had been dragging her and Ishmael from one town to the next. The first two years she'd kept hoping they'd finally set down roots and Pa would stop fiddling with his still. Four years back, Ivy gave up that false hope. Pa was jug-bit. 'Twas a sickness, and no one knew the cure. Plenty of folks were more than willing to buy corn likker, but there was always someone who sent the law after them. As a result, she and Ishmael tramped along with Pa to wherever he took a notion to go.

Cagey as could be, Pa had things down to an art—they couldn't draw attention to themselves, so instead of chopping a lot of logs to build a habitation, they lived in a tent and immediately cleared the land to put in a crop of corn. Folks who noticed figured the Grubbs were like many farmers—barely eking by.

Pa always promised they'd build a cabin and stay, but more often than not, the only thing he and Ishmael constructed was a lean-to. The lean-to wasn't for shelter; it served as a shield so folks couldn't see what he was up to.

Ishmael and she tended the corn and gathered wood. A little went for cooking but most fired Pa's still. In the end, it never mattered that they hadn't built a cabin. Seven places in six years taught Ivy the only things she could rely on were Pa's lies, having to pull up stakes and move on, and that Ishmael was the only good thing in her life.

Their first day there, Pa had spent his time pitching the tent—though why it took him from sunup to sundown that first day to do that simple task didn't bear any scrutiny. Pa didn't much like having to work. Depending on the day, he'd rub his back or knees or elbows and carry on about how his rheumatiz was kicking up and nobody'd ever know just how much he endured. That suffering was his reason for brewing moonshine—nothing else helped with the pain. He reckoned he was doing a great service by providing his white lightning to plenty of other folks who also suffered.

Over the years Ivy had come to the conclusion that Pa could rightfully claim only one affliction: selfishness. Folks with rheumatiz ended up with knotty hands or scraggly, twisted limbs or a gnarled back. If they didn't have those, their joints popped and cracked or got all swoll up. Pa—well, if work needed doing, it was one of his "bad" days. Once the work got done, he'd suddenly improve.

Ivy worried that poor Ishmael would probably end up worse than a knotted oak by the time he reached his middle years—what with Pa always making him do the hard work. The way her own back ached might be nasty, but Ishmael never let her do the hardest labor. He loved her.

A gal couldn't have a better brother.

A quick glance at her brother made Ivy wince. He stooped and wrapped his big hands around a stone the size of one of Pa's kegs. Ivy fought the urge to go help him. Pa would wallop both of them if she didn't get supper fixed soon.

"Haaa-ehhh!" Ishmael hefted the rock and headed toward the side of the lean-to. "Pa, I got another one!"

"Set it yonder and fetch least four more what're bigger afore we eat."

Four? Ivy started to skin the rattler. *I've gotta time this right. Pa's a-wantin' chow now, but Ishmael's gonna catch what-for if he don't haul four more stones.*

"My belly's achin', gal!" Pa exited from the side of the lean-to and scowled at her. "You ain't even started the cook fire yet."

"I brung buckets of water, Pa. I'm bein' mindful like you tell me to. If'n the fire takes a mind to blaze hot, I cain stop it afore folks catch wind of it at a distance."

"Wind's fixin' to shift." He tilted his head back and sniffed like a hound dog. "Reset the fire ring to the far side of the tree."

"Yes, Pa." Glad to have a task that she could dawdle over to give her brother a little more time, Ivy cast a quick look at Ishmael. He'd started toward another big rock. "Ishmael, betcha I have my rocks moved afore you do!"

He flashed her a grin. "Don't count on it."

"Cut out your jawin' and get busy." Pa went back to tinker with his copper tubes.

Ivy relocated the stones and created a new cooking pit. The location Pa instructed her to use didn't seem quite right. A mess of leaves and twigs covered the ground. She scuffed her feet as she walked in an attempt to clear the area.

Ishmael sauntered over and pretended to assess another big rock. "Gimme the snake. I'll skin 'im for you."

"I'll do it. I'm lollygaggin' so's you'll have time to haul the rocks."

"I've been dawdlin', thinkin' you needed more time to cook!"

Ivy laughed. "Poor Mr. Snake. He gave his life for your supper, and now we're both makin' him wait to be served."

Ishmael chortled softly as he set his big foot on a stone and shoved against it to loosen it from the ground. Ivy watched him lift the large hunk of granite, and then she used the flint to start the fire. A hundred times or more, she'd thought of leaving Pa, but she couldn't ever leave Ishmael.

The wind shifted—but not the way Pa had predicted. Sparks hit some leaves, and fire shot across the ground outside the fire pit. Twigs, the pile of firewood, and a lightning-struck ghost tree all ignited.

Ivy jumped into action and tossed the water bucket onto the spreading flames. Ishmael grabbed the shovel and set to work. Pa bellowed loud enough to wake the dead and ran to save his precious copper tubing.

"Wet a blanket!" Ishmael called to her.

Ivy did as he bade, and they managed to put out the fire. Pa finally left his still and came over. "You near kilt me! Stupid gal. I—" His eyes narrowed. "That's my blanket!"

Ivy looked down at the heavy cloth in her hands. The olive-colored wool was now muddy and mottled with ash. Singed edges and burnt holes made it clear the blanket couldn't be salvaged.

"My blanket!" he hollered again. "You went and ruint it."

"I'll trade you, Pa." Ishmael stepped between her and Pa. "You cain have mine."

"You swapped Ivy last winter. A spider web is thicker than yourn. My old bones cain't take the cold. Gal, what yore a-holdin' is what's yourn now. Don't matter what it is, you spoil ever'thang."

Ivy chewed on her lower lip.

Pa muttered a stream of cuss words and went back behind the lean-to.

A short time later, Ivy knelt over the frying pan and poked at the segments of snake so they'd turn. "Better we et you than you try to et us," she muttered. Her stomach cramped from hunger, but she couldn't convince herself to eat the meat.

Holding the frying pan's handle securely, Ivy

stood and called, "Come and get—" The words died on her lips as a redheaded man on a scrappy little mustang raced into camp.

He pulled back on the reins and surveyed the place. "You're trespassing."

"Didn't see no fences," Pa said as he sauntered out from behind the lean-to. "Just tryin' to set down roots and provide for my own. Times are lean, but we're doin' our best. Why don't you come down offa that horse? Join us. My daughter's got supper ready."

"Rattler," Ivy said as she jostled the pan to keep the snake from burning. *Don't rightly know whether I'm tellin' him what's for chow or warnin' him 'bout Pa.*

The man frowned at her. "You and your brother—"

"That'd be me." Ishmael dusted his hands off on the sides of his britches. "I recollect you. You was the feller in town 'bout two months back. You gave me and Ivy them jars of food for holpin' you tote a mess of 'em into the grocery."

"I am." The man nodded curtly. His face remained harsh. "But this land is already claimed."

"Cain't blame us. No fences. Nobody improvin' it." Pa got his poor-pitiful-me look. "Thunk we was finally set."

"My family owns clear to the ridge." The man swept his hand to encompass a sizable area.

"We've been here for years and have the legal claim."

"But we ain't hurtin' nuthin' or nobody." Pa managed to sound like somebody just shot his best coon-huntin' hound.

"This is my land. You have to leave."

"Ow!" Ivy grabbed her skirts with her left hand and transferred the frying pan over to that hand. "Sorry. Seems snakes ain't any better at waitin' when they're dead than when they're alive."

"Go on and serve it up, lambkin," Pa said.

She started dishing up the chunks. Pa rarely even called her by her name. Most often it was *gal* said in something akin to a snarl.

"And," Pa tacked on, "be shore to make up a plate for the gentleman."

Pa knows we only got three plates. Good thang I didn't get my mouth all set for eating tonight.

"I've already eaten." The stranger's tone sounded downright polite, all things considered.

"Hope you don't mind us diggin' in. We've worked up a powerful appetite, and food's scarce." Pa took the plate with the most on it and sat in the dirt.

Ishmael accepted his plate and murmured, "Thanks, sis."

"Shore you don't want none, mister?" Ivy held the plate up to him.

"No. Thanks."

She went back toward Ishmael and tilted her

plate so all of the snake rolled onto his. Shoving her other hand into a patch pocket she'd sewn on her skirt, she declared, "Good thang I found this here wild onion today. Niver could abide snake."

Ishmael patted the spot beside him. "Have a sit-down. You've been workin' hard all day."

While every last one of Pa's actions and words carried the intent of making the stranger give in, Ishmael was just acting the same as always. Ivy sat next to him and took a small bite from the onion.

Pa smacked his lips. "Mister, it ain't too late for you to have yourself a taste of this."

"You need to leave by tomorrow."

"Awww, now." Pa put aside his plate. "You just done went and ruint my appetite. And why? Why, I ask you? I'll tell you why. For no good reason. As a matter of fact, us bein' here is a holp to you. Until yore ready to work this section of land, we're willin' to work to improve it. Take a gander at what we done in just a little while."

The man's face stayed cold as sleet as he stared at the charred mess and ashes. "I'm doing just that."

Pa looked affronted. "We was fixin' to rich-up the soil. Ever'body knows mixin' ash with the ground gives it better growin' power. I got a buildin' and a crop both put in, too."

"Used the last of our seed on that corn." Ishmael poked another piece of snake with his knife and lifted it to his mouth.

"Shouldn't have." Pa shook his head. "But my boy took a mind to put in a crop. I done tole him, if it's not knee-high by the Fourth of July, you're in trouble." Regardless of his claim to have lost his appetite, Pa snatched up his plate again and gulped down another bite.

Ivy held her tongue. It wasn't right, Pa blaming Ishmael, when the truth was Pa had insisted on planting the crop.

"We're in Californy." Ishmael's voice sounded calm as could be, even though Pa wronged him by telling such a lie. "S'posed to be sunny here later."

Pa shook his head. "I'm tellin' ya, mister. I'm sore afraid I'm gonna have to watch my kids go hungry all winter."

Niver bothered him afore now. Long as he stays roostered on his shine, he don't feel cold or hunger.

"If there's a late fall, it might still yield," the man said as he finally dismounted. "Several farmers actually plant a second crop."

"Mister, you gotta let us stay on here," Pa said.

"Leastways through the winter." Ishmael's comment took Ivy by surprise. He usually let Pa do all of the fancy talking when things were bad. Her brother cast a worried look at her, then stood up. "We don't got much, but you could either have us sharecrop or I could come over to that place of yourn and work."

"Now, thar's a fine plan!" Pa slapped his leg. "My son already proved hisself to you that day in town. He's a hard worker and got a strong back. The gal and me—we'd keep thangs goin' here. Why, by spring when you're ready to do your plantin' and such, you'll be beggin' us to stay on so's you cain have my son's holp."

The man stood in silence.

Ivy's heart plummeted. Ishmael's offer might have tempted him, but Pa went on and on, making it sound like the Grubbs were doing the man a favor by squatting on his land. *Pa, shut up!* Only Pa wasn't a man to pass up an opportunity to hear himself talk. He kept right on. She took another small bite of the onion.

When the man had heard more than enough of Pa's palaver, he turned his attention to Ishmael, then glanced at her. "I can't afford to pay a hand."

Ivy blinked and looked down. She hoped he'd assume the tears in her eyes were from the onion.

"Don't matter none to me," Ishmael declared. "You letting us stay here—that's good enough for me."

"But we keep all of our yield," Pa tacked on.

"There's still a lot of work to be done around here." The man's eyes narrowed as he looked at Pa.

"The gal and me—we'll manage."

Ivy bobbed her head and rose. To be able to

settle here without worrying that they'd be shooed off at any moment—this man was fulfilling her most ardent dream. It didn't matter that she'd be doing the work and Pa would barely lift a finger. Wasn't any different than it had always been.

The man shook his head. "I can't agree to that."

Her hopes crashed, and the onion in her belly burned.

"Two full days a week, and three half days." The man nodded. "That's what I ask in return as rent for your temporary use of my land."

Pa gargled a wad of spittle and spat it at a dandelion off to the side. "Two full days and *one* half day."

Oh, Pa. How could you spoil this?

Ishmael forced a chuckle as he scrambled toward the stranger. "When you get to know Pa, you'll learn he's got hisself a rare sense of humor." He stuck out his hand. "Two full days and three half days are a fair deal, seein' as you're lettin' us keep the crop. Mister, you got yourself a farmhand."

"I remember your given name is Ishmael. What's your last name?"

"Grubb." Since he'd finished eating, Pa finally set aside his plate and got to his feet. "I'm Ebenezer Grubb. You got yourself a fine worker in Ishmael. Ivy's my daughter."

The man turned toward her once again and

nodded his head to acknowledge her. "Miss Grubb. I'm Galen O'Sullivan."

"Mr. O'Sullivan." Nobody ever used fine manners toward her. His gentlemanly greeting left her feeling unaccountably shy . . . but sad, too.

He and Ishmael made arrangements for Ishmael to show up to work the next morning, and then he took his leave.

Pa did a funny little jig once Mr. O'Sullivan rode out of sight. "Boy howdy! It's 'bout time thangs went right for me. I got me a right good deal here."

Ishmael looked down at her. "I'll work hard for the man, sis."

"I knowed you would, Ishy."

Ishmael turned to Pa. "It still don't seem right, repayin' his kindness by runnin' a still on his land."

"What he don't know won't hurt him." Pa waggled his finger at them. "Keep your yap shut and work hard. Ain't no reason for you to ruin my good fortune."

Ivy turned away and looked at the cornfield. Pa hadn't lifted a finger to clear the land, plant, water, or weed. Come harvest, he wouldn't strain himself to help, either. He never did. But he'd spend time nursing that dumb old still and drink part of the profits.

Ishmael waited till Pa went back behind the

lean-to. "Sis, I'll work my fingers to the bone for that farmer."

She gave her brother a weary smile. "Pa don't know that the best deal he ever got was havin' you for his son."

"Hey, now. You an' me—we was born together. You cain thank I'm the best deal Pa ever got, but shore as I'm a-standin' here, I got the real prize that day. You're the specialest fortune I ever got."

Her nose wrinkled. "Yore one sorry man, Ishy, to consider someone who reeks of onion as a prize."

———•———

"Boys!" Laney tried to maintain a modicum of dignity and grace, but with Dale and Sean each pulling on her hands, she did well to keep her hoops in some semblance of order. She feared at any moment she'd lose the battle and provide all and sundry with an immodest view of her ankles.

"We can't be late, Miss Laney!" Sean said as he tugged on her hand again.

"We've time aplenty yet," Mrs. O'Sullivan said. "If you drag her much farther, her legs are goin' to be worn down to nubbins and she won't be tall enough to watch."

Colin chuckled. The sound made Laney smile, for he'd barely spoken or smiled since the day his father died. Bringing the O'Sullivans to the state fair was working even better than she'd dared hope.

They halted by the fence and watched as a man spread grease all over the squealing pig.

"It's bigger around than you, Miss Laney!" Dale declared.

"Dale!" Mrs. O'Sullivan's brows knit. "You can't be likening a lady to a pig!"

Laney's brother and sister-in-law walked up. Ruth tried to hide her giggles while Josh glanced at Laney's sash. "Galen's sunk fence posts that are half again your size."

If only Galen would notice! Laney couldn't help thinking.

"Joshua McCain"—Mrs. O'Sullivan managed to sound both exasperated and entertained at the same time—"how am I to teach my sons their manners with you setting a bad example?"

"She's right." Ruth agreed. "You need to be truthful. The fence posts are at least twice Laney's size."

Hilda, the McCains' housekeeper, mumbled, "Though it's not for want of good hot food."

Dale pressed against the fence and stared intently at the shoat. "I'm gonna win this greased pig chase. I gotta."

"None of us won the pie-eating contest, but we had plenty of fun anyway." Josh ruffled Dale's carroty curls. "You'll have a great time trying, regardless of who wins."

"Having fun doesn't matter." Dale looked up at Josh. "I need to win."

"Now, whyever do you need to win?" Mrs. O'Sullivan asked.

"'Cuz when I win the money, I'll give it to you and I can keep Hortense."

"The winner doesn't get a cash prize, boy-o." Mrs. O'Sullivan stooped down to Dale's height. "Whoever wins gets to keep the pig."

"I don't want another pig. I want Hortense."

"But you're going to be brave." Colin gave his little brother a stern look. "We farmers know the animals we raise are meant to be food, not pets. There'll be another litter during the winter. You'll find a new piglet to love."

"But it'll be a different piglet." Tears glossed the little boy's eyes. "I'll still love Hortense and miss her."

Mrs. O'Sullivan reached for her youngest son. Fresh grief ravaged the recent widow's features. "You're sad, I know. Sorrow comes when you love deeply and lose."

Laney blinked back her own tears and made up her mind. She'd concoct a plan to rescue Hortense.

Chapter Three

"Boys and girls!" A gentleman stood in the center of an adjoining area that was blocked off with bales of hay. "Anyone participating in the greased pig chase needs to come listen to the rules."

A moment later, Dale stood in the center of a clump of small children, listening intently. "Oh!" Mrs. O'Sullivan looked distressed. "I didn't have Dale change into his old shirt."

Laney made a dismissive gesture. "So little Dale will be as grubby as his big brothers. After the pie-eating contest, they're a sight!"

"I'm no better." Josh looked down at his shirt. "Ruth said she'd get me a new shirt, and I need one badly."

"Can I tell her now?" Sean nudged Josh.

"Yep."

"Ma, Mr. Josh said if Colin and me got as much pie on our shirts as he did, he'd get us new shirts, too."

"Joshua McCain!" Mrs. O'Sullivan and

Hilda both said in unison.

Laney loved the impish sparkle in her brother's eyes. He shrugged and said in a blithe voice, "Hey, we men have to stick together."

"As much pie as you're all wearing," Laney said as she started to giggle, "you'll definitely stick to something!"

"Release the pig!" someone shouted.

Laney turned her attention back to Dale. All of the other children raced after the squealing pig. Many of them fell into a tangled knot of arms and legs, but the pig popped out and ran willy-nilly around the enclosure.

"What is Dale doing?" Laney watched as he sat cross-legged on the ground.

Above all of the pandemonium, she heard him. "Soooo-eeee! Sooo-eee! Pig. Pig. Pig."

The little pig dodged several children and headed for Dale. One little boy dove and grabbed hold of a hind leg, but the pig slid out of his grasp. He shot off into the direction he'd come, squealing loudly.

"Dale's one smart little guy," Josh said.

"Aye, that he is," his mother agreed.

A couple more children managed to grab hold, but the pig slithered away. Dale remained in the same spot. "Sooo-eee!"

Laney stood on tiptoe and held her breath as the pig veered toward Dale. Two boys descended on it and each grabbed a leg.

"Turn loose!" the director shouted.

"Why?" Sean craned his neck to see the boys grudgingly release their holds.

"Only one person can touch the animal at a time," Mrs. O'Sullivan explained. "If two grab him, they both have to let go."

Laney tossed caution and propriety to the wind. She cupped her hands around her mouth and called, "You're doing fine, Dale!"

He cast a happy smile in their direction, then beamed as the pig came toward him. "Soooeee!" The pig trampled across one of Dale's legs, and Dale collapsed around him.

"Five, four, three," the director counted.

"Two, *one!*" everyone joined in.

"He won!" Colin wheeled around and threw his arms around his mother. "Ma, he won!"

Someone fashioned an odd-looking halter that went around the pig, wiped much of the grease off, then handed the end of the rope to Dale. Dale trotted out of the enclosure. "Lookee, Ma!"

"Now aren't you a sight! Why don't we go put him in the pen with Hortense?"

Colin jogged ahead. "Hey! There's something on Hortense's pen!"

Sean joined him, then hollered back, "Hortense got an honorable mention!"

Dale led his pig into the pen. "Hortense, I caught you a friend!"

A man sauntered over. He looked at the pigs,

then nodded. "Good-looking shoat you have there."

"Thank you." Dale beamed.

"Couple of good hams and a bunch of pork chops from her." The man didn't notice how Dale's smile twisted into horror. "The going rate is—"

"I'm sorry." Laney stepped forward. "I've already decided to buy this shoat. As you said, she's very good-looking. The judges obviously agree, as well. That being the case, I thought she'd be an excellent investment."

Mrs. O'Sullivan looked completely flummoxed.

"Dale's latest acquisition is a male." Laney tried to make her plan sound reasonable. "This could be the start of a business venture for him."

Hilda rubbed her jaw. "Of course, you'd have to board Hortense over at the O'Sullivan farm, Laney."

"Yes. Yes, I would. But I can go visit her."

"Now, wait a minute," the butcher growled. "The man in charge of this place told me this shoat was for sale. There weren't all that many hogs here this year."

"Which is why this would be a sound business venture." Laney smiled at him. "Why, next year, we'll probably have several pigs for you!"

The man walked off, muttering under his breath.

"I getta keep Hortense?"

"You're going to board her—much like Galen boards the horses for the Pony Express." Laney did her best to make her voice sound serious. "Business deals are very important, you know."

Eyes wide, Dale blurted out, "We'd be partners?"

"Exactly. A business between two people relies on their honor and integrity. Neither one of them slacks off or gives up."

"Never, ever?"

"Never, ever," Laney confirmed. "No matter what."

"That's right." Hilda narrowed one eye and stared at the pigs. "I'll bet Laney would be willing to make a deal with you, Dale. In exchange for Hortense's board, you could—"

"Have all of the piglets!" Laney leaned forward. "Would you be willing to do that for me, Dale? I know I'm asking a lot of you."

"If you're asking my son for a partnership, it needs to be a mutually beneficial agreement." Mrs. O'Sullivan's jaw rose a notch. "Dale, any partnership needs to be fair for everyone. If you do this, Miss Laney ought to own half of the piglets."

"Half," Dale said, looking up at Laney.

"I couldn't agree to such an arrangement." Laney shook her head. "And it's not ladylike for me to haggle," she added.

"Three quarters." Hilda suggested. "That's

fair. Dale keeps three quarters of the piglets; Laney gets one quarter."

"Miss Laney, which quarter do you want? A forequarter or a hindquarter?"

"That's not what Miss Hilda meant, Dale." Colin grinned at his baby brother. "She means out of every four pigs, you get three and Miss Laney gets one. They weren't talking about butchering them all!"

"I didn't know. 'Sides," Dale said, giving his newly won pig an assessing look, "I'm a farmer and I'm s'posed to grow things up to be food."

———•———

Crack! The eggshell shattered, half of the pieces sliding into the skillet with part of the egg. The other half glued themselves to Galen's slime-coated fingers as the other portion of the egg oozed down the outside of the skillet.

The rooster crowed as someone knocked on the door.

"Come in!" Galen shouted as he tried to figure out how to clean his hand enough to use something to flip the measly half egg before it burned.

The door creaked open. "Good mornin', Mr. O'Sullivan."

"Ishmael." He grabbed a dish towel and began to wipe his hand. "And the morning's not starting out so well. Do you know how to cook?"

"Not really. Sis usually sees to that. Your

breakfast's startin' to smoke."

Galen grabbed the nearest implement and tried to flip the egg. The tines of the fork poked through and shredded it. "Scrambled eggs," he muttered to himself as he started to stir the blackening mess. Most of it clung to the skillet and smoked more. In desperation, he flipped the skillet over a plate and two stinking pea-sized blobs fell onto it.

"Must've been quail eggs." Ishmael didn't sound as if he was joking.

Galen stared at the mess inside the skillet. "The sad truth is, it was a chicken egg. Looks like you're the only Grubb I'll have today."

Laughter rippled out of Ishmael. "I don't mean to make fun of you, Boss, but you've got a right clever mind to come up with a joke like that."

"If I'm so clever, why can't I fry an egg?"

"Thought you was trying to scramble it."

Galen glanced at the pathetic plate and then held the cast-iron skillet for the new farmhand to inspect. "I was trying to salvage it."

Ishmael cleared his throat. "From the looks of your land, you're a fine farmer."

"But a more miserable cook you'll never find." *Ma's teased me about how I need a wife to take care of me. For the first time, I'm thinkin' that's not so much of a joke.* "Cooking makes no sense to me. Ma always cracks the eggs straight into the pan, and they slide out perfectly. What

I wouldn't give for a good plate of her bacon and eggs."

Ishmael swallowed.

Here I am moaning about wanting bacon and eggs, and this man is truly hungry. "Get on over here, Ishmael. Two grown men can't let a bunch of eggs get the better of them!"

Three eggs and a huge mess later, Galen yanked the plate of charred blobs from Ishmael and dumped them into the swill bucket. "Those aren't fit to eat."

"They were tolerable."

"Maybe I could put water on to boil, and we can just drop in the eggs."

"Sometimes when we have eggs, Ivy puts 'em in the pot and boils 'em at the same time as she's a-boilin' the coffee."

"We can do that!" Galen pumped water into the coffeepot. He thought for a minute. "Hand me that kettle there, will you?"

"This one?"

"Yeah." Galen filled it with water, too. "If I'm making eggs, I'm making enough to last for tomorrow." He started to gingerly place eggs in the kettle and had to dip out some of the water when he'd put in a dozen. With the extra room, Galen popped in the rest from the egg basket.

"Want me to make the coffee anyway?"

"Better. Otherwise, I'll be surly the whole day long." Galen put the eggs on to boil and sheepishly admitted, "I drank stone-cold leftover coffee for the past two mornings."

"Coffee niver lasted long 'nuff for me to try it cold." Ishmael squinted at the cupboard. "Where d'ya keep the beans?"

"Blue canister. Bottom shelf."

"Here, found it. I'll scour that skillet so's I can roast—"

"No need to roast the coffee beans. Ma's started buying this new stuff. Osborn's Celebrated Prepared Java Coffee. Just toss some into the grinder, and we'll be set."

Ishmael whistled under his breath and opened the canister. "A name like that makes a feller feel like he's getting sommat extry special. How many cups d'ya wanna brew?"

"The pot holds eight."

"You wanna make a whole pot?" When Galen nodded, Ishmael grinned. "Reckon on drinkin' it cold again for a few days?"

"We'll polish it off by noon. I'm planning on getting a lot done today." Galen pretended not to notice how Ishmael painstakingly counted out seventeen beans and put them in the grinder. "Tell you what: why don't you go gather eggs while I finish the coffee and eggs?"

"Shore." Ishmael took the empty egg basket from the table and left.

Galen shook the coffee beans out of the grinder and into the scoop Ma used to measure them. They filled the scoop only halfway. He added more, quickly spun the handle on the

grinder, and dumped the grounds into the coffeepot.

A short time later the men sat down to
breakfast. Looking across the table, Galen
stated, "I'll ask grace."

Ishmael's brow furrowed as he glanced
around the cabin and squinted at the loft. "I
thought you was on your lonesome. Is Grace up
thar, abed?"

"Saying grace is the same thing as asking a
blessing or praying before a meal."

"I ain't niver been churched. Whaddya want
me to do whilst you tend to grace?"

"Just bow your head and close your eyes.
When I say amen, that means the prayer is
over." Galen rested his elbows on the table and
folded his hands.

"That's a good notion—keeps a body from
wantin' to swipe a mouthful since nobody's
looking." Ishmael promptly thumped his elbows
onto the table and clenched his hands so tightly
together his nails went white.

*Lord, this man doesn't just lack his daily bread;
he knows nothing about the Living Water. Is that
why you brought him here?*

"Dear heavenly Father, we thank you for
providing this meal. Bless it to our bodies and be
with us as we work today. We'd like to ask you
to keep watch over our loved ones and keep
them safe. In Jesus' name, amen."

Galen reached for his coffee.

Ishmael gave him a puzzled look. "I thought you Christian folks prayed to God. Didn't know you talked to the departed. Bet your pa's pleased you ain't forgot him."

Peeling the shell from an egg, Galen carefully considered his words. "My da passed on about two months back." His voice broke, and he cleared his throat. "We're all missing him something fierce, but I wasn't speaking to him when I prayed. God is my heavenly Father."

"So who's your heavenly mother?"

The question stunned him. *It's logical. I've never thought of that before, though.* "God created us. Because He is the Creator, we call Him our father."

Ishmael wolfed down an egg. "Guess that makes sense."

Galen bit into an egg and shoved the kettle full of them toward Ishmael.

"Thanks."

They'd both eaten two, and Galen took a third. "Keep going. I was serious when I said I'd work you hard."

"I'd rather set one aside and take it home to my sis if you don't mind."

Galen plucked three eggs from the kettle and put them on his new hand's plate, then took two more for himself. He lifted another from the kettle and turned it so a big crack faced Ishmael. "I must've done something wrong, because most of the eggs are cracked. They won't keep, so I figured on sending them back home with you."

Color flooded Ishmael's face.

"I came from Ireland," Galen said in a pensive tone. "Probably didn't need to tell you so. I've never lost the accent. Anyway, times were hard. Potato famine. Ma and Da both did without more often than not so us kids could eat— but even then, two of my brothers were so weak, the cholera killed them. I don't have much money, Ishmael, but God's blessed my family with an abundance of food. I couldn't look myself in the mirror each morning if I hoarded something someone else needed."

"I'm beholden to you."

"Nonsense. With Ma and the boys gone, I'm not using up the eggs, and I'm not taking them to town for the mercantile to sell. They'd spoil."

"When'll your kin come back?"

"Two or three more days." Galen tapped his foot on the floor as a thought flashed through his mind. "Your dad and sister have a lot to do, especially since you're working here, but I'd dearly love to surprise Ma and have some stuff done. What are the chances that I could have Ivy come over for the morning the next two days? It'd be only half the day, and she could take home some truck like tomatoes and pears as payment."

"Boss, you ain't got no idea what kind of deal you jist made."

Chapter Four

Galen opened the door to leave as the cock crowed. Ishmael stood there with the pail full of milk, and his sister cradled something in her skirt, which pulled the hem higher, baring her shins and ankles. Galen quickly jerked his focus back onto Ishmael. "The two of you got an early start."

Ivy barged in and filled the wire basket with eggs from her skirt. "You got yourself a goodly flock of layin' hens. Ishy tole me 'bout yore eggs yestermorn. I cain cook 'em any way you fancy."

"Over easy?"

Her wispy pale blond braid bobbed above and below her waist as she nodded her head. "Jist tell me whar yore lard is."

Lard! Galen turned toward Ishmael.

Recognition of the ignorance they'd shared yesterday twinkled in Ishmael's eyes. He pressed his forefinger to his lips and turned away.

"Ma keeps the lard beneath the sink. Says it stays cooler there."

"Don't mean to horn in on another woman's kitchen, but as your mama's away, I could whip up a batch of drop biscuits to go with the eggs."

"That would be great!"

"Niver seed me such a fine stove. Oven on it's huge. Could handle a pan of corn bread, too." Ivy pulled out the lard, then opened the jar next to it She sniffed and let out a loud sneeze. "Thunk 'twas flour, but 'tisn't."

Ishmael moseyed over and read the label. "Bo-ric acid." He pointed at a cupboard shelf. "Coffee's in the blue thang. Already roasted, no less. Reckon that's whar the missus stores her edibles. Boss, I'll go muck the stable whilst we wait for vittles, 'less thar's sommat else you planned for me."

Galen didn't want to leave a strange woman alone in the house—but it wasn't right to be alone with her, either. He thought for a moment. "Go ahead and muck. Ma's knives are getting dull. I'll sit out on the porch and sharpen them till breakfast's ready." He pulled the whetstone from the back of a drawer and set to work.

Soon aromas wafted from the cabin out onto the porch. Galen tried to concentrate on the blades, but Miss Grubb kept singing snatches of tunes he'd never heard. Her voice could curdle milk.

"Cuckolds all in a row," she warbled. A second later, she stood in the doorway. "Mr. O'Sullivan, sir, vittles are 'bout ready. D'ya like your biscuits dry, or would you have me plop a dollop of lard in their middles?"

"There's butter in the springhouse. I'll fetch a block."

As he returned with the butter, Galen heard Ishmael through the open window and door. "Boss prayed afore we et t'other morn. Jist close your eyes and fold your hands like so. Onc't he says amen, that's the sign 'tis time to dig in."

"I recollect them colored folks sangin' that word whilst out a-pickin' cotton. Member? 'Amen. Amen. A-a-men, amen, amen.'"

Her voice and timing were both off, but Galen knew the spiritual she meant.

"Don't make no sense," Ivy mused. "Them slaves wasn't 'bout to git their fill of vittles. They was prickin' their fingers on them pickery cotton bolls."

"Churched folk got their own notions. Don't gotta understand it, sis. Jist foller along. This feller is pure hickory. Won't hurt us none to respect his odd ways."

Galen waited a few moments before going inside.

Ivy glanced over her shoulder, then grabbed a plate. "Perfect timin'. Eggs are done." She flipped three eggs onto his plate. "Here you be."

"Thank you." Galen accepted the plate and set it on the table along with the butter. He frowned at the other two plates.

"Sommat a-wrong?" Ivy asked.

He lifted the plate that held a solitary egg and slid it onto the other that held two. "My littlest brother is six, and he eats two eggs. Seeing as none of us is six, I expect you'll need to fry up some more."

"How many d'ya normally gobble?"

"He et five yestermorn," Ishmael said.

"With the biscuits today, these three will do me just fine."

Ishmael sat down and Ivy turned back to the stove. She rubbed a blob of lard in the skillet and quickly fried a pair of eggs. When she came toward the table, she gave Galen a wary look. "Sommat a-wrong?"

"What makes you ask?"

"You're a-standin' thar, starin' at me."

"It's considered bad manners for a man to take a place at the table until the ladies are all seated."

"Niver lernt them kind of thangs." A self-deprecating little huff exited her. "Then again, ain't nobody ever mistook me for a lady, neither."

"You ain't no tart, sis."

Galen felt a pang for her. Poor and plain, she'd not been afforded even the most common of courtesies. "Riches don't make a woman a lady, Miss Grubb. A caring heart and hands are what count. As your brother just attested, you have sound morals. It's plain to see you love your family, and you're kind to cook for me, too."

"Nice of you to say that, but your manners make me nervous. I'd rather have you et whilst the eggs're still hot." She sat down.

Galen took his seat and cast a dark look at her plate.

"My belly cain't holt three—not if'n I holp myself to a biscuit. Ain't had me flour-built bread in ages, so I aim to save room for that treat."

She wasn't complaining or trying to call his attention to what she'd done without. Her voice rang with the same cheery tone Laney's did when Ma surprised her by baking her favorite pearsnapple pie. Galen smiled, then said, "In my home, we start each meal with a prayer."

Ishmael promptly stuck his elbows on the table and clasped his hands. Ivy copied him.

Galen clasped his own, bowed his head, and closed his eyes. "Beloved Lord, thank you for this meal. I ask you to bless the hands that prepared it and to strengthen us so we can accomplish all we need to do today. Envelop those we love with your tender care and bring them back to us safely we pray. In Jesus' name, amen."

Ishmael grabbed his fork, but Ivy studied her clasped hands. "Don't reckon they look no diff'rent. Niver had nobody ask God to bless my hands. How's a body s'posed to know if that God-feller listened?"

"God always listens to His children."

She sighed and attacked her eggs with a fork. "You ain't a child. You're a man."

"Mr. O'Sullivan explaint it to me yester-morn." Ishmael's voice took on a behave-yourself undertone. "Christians figure since God made 'em, He's their pa."

"Seems to me you got thangs backward. A child don't tell his pa what to do. Why should that God-feller be listenin' to you 'stead of you listenin' to Him?"

"I do listen to Him. He speaks to me through the Holy Bible. In church, the minister preaches and I learn more about the Lord. I also have very dear brothers and sisters in Christ who have given me wise counsel."

"Don't thank I'd be happy with that many folks tellin' me what to do. D'ya mind if'n I use a dibby-dab of that butter?"

"Help yourself." Galen scooted the dish closer to her.

"What did you wanna get done today?" Ishmael asked as he sopped his biscuit in egg yolk.

Galen outlined his plans. It was a bittersweet thing to do. Da used to do the same thing each morning, and since his brothers weren't old enough to handle a grown man's share, Galen hadn't carried on the tradition. Part of him withered in grief while the other part felt great relief in knowing they would achieve far more than had been accomplished in a single day for the past several months.

Ivy slurped coffee, then set down her mug. "Onc't I wash up the dishes, I cain meet you in the barn and—"

"Miss Grubb, I didn't expect you to join us." Galen shook his head. He'd purposefully chosen chores that required brute strength.

"I got a strong back."

"Actually, I planned on you tending Ma's garden. It's quite sizable, and without her and my little brothers here, weeds have sprung up all over. You're to harvest whatever's ripe, then weed until noon. At midday, I'll divert water from the stream so everything is watered."

"Gardenin' ain't work—'tis a pure pleasure. You got buckets or baskets to hold the truck I pluck?"

"There's a wheelbarrow in the barn. You can pile baskets and bags on it. At noontime, I can help haul the harvest back here."

She beamed. "Is it true you got yourself a pear tree?"

"Several. Ma makes pear butter and pear-snapple pies, and she dries pears so we have 'em all winter long. I'm sure you'll want to take some home with you so you can dry them, too."

"Can't recollect the last time I et a pear." Ishmael finished the last crumb from his biscuit. "Sounds like a golden reward for our work today."

Galen thought about taking the last biscuit. Instead, he nudged the plate toward Ivy. "Your brother and I dug right in. Your biscuits are good."

"Well, have that last 'un."

"I've had plenty."

"I'm full up, too, sis." Ishmael cracked his knuckles. "Why don'tcha tuck the straggler in your pocket and nibble on it later?"

Suddenly Ivy sniffed and popped up. "Corn bread's done." She pulled a pan out of the oven and set it aside. "I got beans a-soakin'. Come suppertime, all you need to do is change off to fresh water and bile 'em. You'll have yourself a stick-to-your-ribs meal."

"Appreciate that."

Once Ivy went to the garden, Galen and Ishmael used a pulley to haul feed into the hayloft until it bulged with cured, healthy hay for the coming winter. One of the barn doors sagged and had become difficult to move. Ishmael held it in the correct alignment and Galen rehung it.

As they finished, Ishmael looked at a fallow field. "We a-gonna plant anything thar?"

Galen nodded. "That field's ready to hold barley again."

"You got plenty of land. Good to let a plot lie fallow now and again so's the soil don't weary. Bet that's why your crops thrive."

"God's been gracious."

Ishmael shrugged. "Don't know 'bout that.

Seems to me you've worked dreadful hard." He scanned the farm. "Ain't seen such bounty—and Pa's drug us clear 'cross the country."

"Where did you come from?"

"Crooked Leg. Dependin' on who you ask, 'tis in 'Bama or Tennessee. Anyhow, been over six years since we was there, though. Want me to walk that field and clear the stones whilst you hitch up a horse and ready the plow?"

Galen nodded. He took the hint and said nothing more about the Lord. Long ago, Da told him the soul was like a field—until the rocks were cleared and the soil turned, seed went to waste. Trying to douse a man with living water before the Holy Spirit had wooed him only mired everyone down. The best thing a Christian could do was set a good example and let God use him in whatever capacity He willed.

"Any time you want my holp, you jist holler." Ivy stared at the crate at Ishmael's feet. Cabbage, tomatoes, and pears filled it. Beside the crate, a burlap bag bulged with string beans, broccoli, and apples.

Galen O'Sullivan smiled. "I'll be sure to tell Ma you're a hard worker. Could be she'll want a day's help from you."

His red curls were as different as could be from Ishmael's straight tow hair, but the kindness glowing behind their eyes was alike. *This here feller's one I cain trust.*

Ishmael hefted the crate. "I'll be back tomorrow."

"See you then."

Ivy reached for the bag.

"Hang on, sis." Ishmael set the crate down. "This here crate has handholds. You and me can tote a side each, and I'll get that bag."

"Okay."

"We're used to workin' side-by-side," he said to their boss. "Twins're thataway."

Galen nodded in acknowledgment.

As Ivy held her side of the crate and headed toward "home," she cast her brother a look. "I coulda toted that poke. 'Twasn't too heavy for me."

Ishmael sauntered along. He always matched his stride to hers when they walked together. Just as he shortened his stride, Ivy attempted to lengthen hers a bit so as to meet him halfway. "I reckoned havin' Boss watch us working together would set in his mind that he can ask you to come holp at all manner of thangs."

"You're cleverer than a fox."

"You've got a fine mind, too. Sharp. Noticed how you chose truck that's good for eatin' now, but some of it cain be dried up for later."

"Ain't so much my choice. I took what he had on hand. Jist so happens to be the season whar lots cain be stored up." She sighed. "I'm sorta thinkin' on us stopping afore we reach Pa.

Mayhap we could hide away a little of this for later. He done et so much the last few days, I'm afeared he's a-gonna gobble through all this afore I cain squirrel any away."

"Someday, sis, we'll have a place as nice as the O'Sullivans. I know Pa makes promises he niver keeps, but I mean it. You and me—we was borned together, and I always sorta reckoned we'd stay together. When I find me a wife, she'll love you, and yore welcome to stay with us. You got my word on it."

"Ishy, you got my promise straight back— if'n I ever get a man what'll jump the broom with me, he'll know yore kin and be glad to have you."

As they continued walking, Ivy sighed again. "You got me started a-dreamin' of a good future, and that's a bad notion. We're like gophers—diggin' ourselves in and outta holes all our lives. Like as not, we're gonna get throwed outta 'nother eight places afore we get shot by the law or starve to death."

"You got us a fair garden planted here. We'll be eating more'n we have in a long while."

"Ishy, I'm sore afraid we're gonna wake up tommorry and find out Pa sat hisself down and et most of this here food that O'Sullivan man paid me."

"He couldn't."

"Could, too. You brung them boilt eggs home and he et nigh unto all of 'em. Me and you—we each got one. I reckon he'll gobble his way through all this."

Ishmael chuckled. "Even half of half of it, and he'd wind up with a bellyache."

The daily drudgery and hunger had left her numb . . . but a day of helping at the O'Sullivans' farm, of seeing a sound roof and verdant lands, jolted Ivy out of her daze. Desperation made her dare to broach a subject she'd never dared speak aloud. "I been ponderin', Ishy—other folks claim land. How'd they do it, and why don't you and me jist find us a parcel of land and do it, too? Cain't be that all the land is already took up."

"Cain't, Ivy." He gave her a sorrowful look. "Plenty's the time I spent dreamin' on that very notion. Didn't venture to say nothin' to you on accounta we cain't do it."

She set down her side of the crate. "Why not?"

Ishmael lowered his side of the crate and carefully released the bag so nothing would spill out. As he straightened up, he gave her a mournful look. "Wouldn't work for us to break off from Pa. Wouldn't have no seed or mule or plow. Wouldn't have no ax, neither."

"There's gotta be a way. We could hire on at some farm or ranch. I could cook and clean whilst you worked with the critters. We would save up every last bit of money till we could buy those thangs."

"I ciphered it. More often than you'd guess. But I cain't make it work."

"You keep workin' on that, Ishy. I ain't givin' up. Neither of us is scairt of hard work. It shames me to have that nice O'Sullivan feller pay us with so much good food and let us live on his place, when we're smilin' and pretendin' nary a thang's wrong. We're liars—bald-faced liars. I don't care what it takes. I want more outta life than shiverin' under a thin blanket inside a battered old tent, a-wishin' my belly wasn't empty."

CHAPTER FIVE

The train's going to be crowded," Laney said as she looked up and down the station.

"It's nigh unto impossible to read signs." Hilda shot a man a dirty look for bumping into her. "Between all of these election posters and banners, you'd think this was Washington."

"It's an important election," Laney said. "The future of our nation weighs in the balance."

"If it's so important, why is someone trying to get votes when he can't even spell his name?" Sean pointed at three different posters. "Abraham. Abrm. Abram. If he can't decide how to write his name, how will he ever decide how to lead America?"

"Well, now, in the Bible God changed Abram's name to Abraham." Mrs. O'Sullivan threaded her fingers through her son's unruly mop of red curls. "And Abraham ended up being the father of Israel. He was a good and wise man."

Dale wrinkled his nose. "If men are s'posed to vote and it's a secret, then why do they talk so much about it?"

"They're trying to talk others into voting for the candidate they want to win." Laney winced as two men argued in strident tones over whether Bell or Breckinridge ought to withdraw so the other would have a better chance of winning. "I'm going to relish the peace and quiet when we get home."

Josh's wife, Ruth, nodded. "Me, too. I have a new appreciation for the wide-open spaces of the Broken P. But getting home might not be so easy. I'm wondering how this many people will ever fit on the train."

"Board!" the conductor shouted. Josh sauntered over and assisted the ladies up the train's steep steps.

Laney waited until Dale scooted toward the

window, then gathered the golden skirts of her traveling dress and carefully arranged them so they wouldn't obstruct the aisle.

"This is about as backward as things get," Mrs. O'Sullivan said as she took the seat on the other side of the aisle. "We were supposed to go home with less than we brought."

"Except for the library books," Ruth said. "You were all so helpful. We got a wonderful start on that library I'm going to open. I couldn't have gotten half as many good books without your opinions and advice."

Dale bounced up and down on the wooden seat. "But best of all, 'stead of going home with no pig, now I have two!"

"Hortense is Miss Laney's shoat now," Mrs. O'Sullivan reminded him.

"Yeah, but she said she was sharing Hortense with me. And I'm going to share Snout with her."

"Snout?" Laney tilted her head to the side. "Snout. I'm not sure that's a name a pig can be proud of."

"Since when were pigs proud?" Hilda tried to adjust her hat so the brim didn't hit the window.

"Snout is Hortense's beau. He has plenty to be proud of." Laney looked at Dale. "In fact, since he's such an important pig, I'm going to call him Mr. Snout."

"Didja hear that, Ma?" Sean laughed. "Wait

till I tell Da—" His mouth snapped shut and
tears filled his eyes.

"Here now." Mrs. O'Sullivan pulled her son
close. She rocked back and forth as she whispered in a voice thick with tears, "'Tis hard, I
know. Twenty times a day at least, I catch myself
thinkin' to tell him something."

The train's engine started chuffing, and a
shrill whistle rent the air. Anticipating the fair
had made the trip to Sacramento exciting;
returning home to an empty place at the table
sobered everyone. The short train ride back to
Folsom didn't take long; it took forever.

When the train finally pulled into the station,
Laney scanned the area and tamped down a
flood of disappointment. She'd secretly hoped
Galen would come to town to fetch his mother
and brothers . . . and see her. *It was a ridiculous
hope. He's been home alone, trying to run the farm
and the Pony Express relay all by himself. He didn't
have time. I can't expect him to see me as a grown
woman when I dream up impossible situations.*

Josh helped them all down from the train.
"Go on over to the Copper Kettle. I'll arrange
for wagons from the livery and load up our
things. Dear—" he gave Ruth a firm look—"you
know what to do before you order for me."

Ruth nodded. "Ask who's cooking."

"If Ethel's at the stove, it's a waste of money
to stay in town for a meal," Hilda stated.

"A waste of food, too," Sean piped up. "I

heard she burns everything."

"Gossip is beneath you, son," Mrs. O'Sullivan said. "Besides, you couldn't cook any better."

"I wonder how Galen's managed." Laney grinned. "He's hopeless when it comes to food."

"Oh, he's good at eating it," Mrs. O'Sullivan said, a smile tugging at her mouth. "He just can't cook."

Laney took Dale's hand. "Let's go. Josh, please be careful with those special boxes."

"You got special boxes?" Dale tugged on her hand. "We're partners. You're not s'posed to keep secrets from me."

Laney leaned down toward him. "Shhh. It's a Christmas surprise."

"Ohhh." Dale's eyes grew huge. "I got a peppermint stick big around as Ma's broom handle last Christmas!"

"I'm more interested in meat and potatoes than sweets," Hilda said as she trundled up the boardwalk.

As they walked up the hilly main street, the Copper Kettle's door swung open. Lester Pearson from the mercantile exited and said under his breath, "I'd best warn you—Ethel's cooking today."

Hilda stopped so quickly Sean bumped into her. She looked from Laney to Ruth and back. "I could rustle up sandwiches at the Broken P."

"There's no bread at home." Ruth straightened her shoulders. "We'll do as Josh said."

Laney leaned over and whispered to Sean and Dale, "That means we're supposed to order sandwiches along with pie for dessert."

"Pie!" Sean perked up.

"The boy ate an entire pie all to himself the other day at the contest. You'd think he's had enough," Hilda huffed.

"Colin ate two whole pies." Sean cast a look at his older brother. "And he got sick from it."

"That was a few days ago." Colin opened the door to the diner. "I'm ready for more now."

Josh joined them. They'd all eaten ham sandwiches and started dessert when Ethel exited the kitchen. "I declare, I don't understand," she told the group. "I fricasseed four chickens today, figurin' folks'd snap it up. Only one order for it. And my pork chops! I baked up eight big fat ones with radish and raisin stuffing in a molasses sauce. With you having sandwiches, all that good food's going to waste."

"That's a shame," Josh said.

Laney nodded. "Ethel, if you can box up the chicken, we'll take it with us."

"We will not!" Hilda half shouted.

"Of course we will." Laney blotted her mouth with the napkin.

"We will?" Ruth gawked at her.

"Yes, we will."

Ethel bustled back toward the kitchen. "I'll get the chicken ready to go." She reappeared soon thereafter and stacked several pasteboard boxes on a nearby table. "They didn't understand, Laney, but I do. When you're sweet on a man, he's on your mind night and day."

Laney wanted to crawl under the table. She'd tried hard not to be obvious about her attraction to Galen; a lady oughtn't pursue a gentleman.

Blind to the embarrassment she was causing, Ethel prattled on. "You've been worried about Galen O'Sullivan."

Ruth burst out, "We've *all* been concerned."

"No need for that. My niece packed a fine meal for Rick Maltby to take out to him just the other day. Myrtle is helpful like that—going to make some man a fine wife. She thought to take more meals out to him, but it's just not done. A gal can't be too careful about her reputation." Ethel patted the top of the uppermost box. "Anyway, no reason for anyone to fret over Galen. My good food will fill him right up."

Hilda eyed the boxes. "That's enough to give ten men a royal bellyache."

"I figured on ten," Ethel said, completely oblivious to Hilda's meaning. "There are the eight of you here, and Galen back on the farm. He'll be hungry enough to eat for two. Just to be sure you'll all be full, I boxed up my famous chocolate applesauce cake."

"Oh, you really didn't have to do that," Mrs. O'Sullivan said.

"But we appreciate it all the same." Laney smiled.

As Josh stacked the boxes in the back of one of the rented buckboards, he gave her a wary look. "Laney, this is a bad idea. Try feeding any of this to Galen, and he'll get sicker than a dog. He'll never forget—"

"Or forgive you," Ruth inserted.

Hilda gave the boxes a dark look. "Elaine Louise McCain, what possessed you to take four fricasseed chickens?"

Laney popped open her pretty paper parasol. "It was the better choice."

"I suppose all things are relative," Ruth said slowly.

"Ethel's a nice woman but a terrible cook." Hilda shook her head. "Her food's not fit for—"

"*Human* consumption," Laney supplied as she sashayed toward the mercantile. "I'll go see if we have any mail waiting for us."

Galen gathered the weary horse's reins and watched the rider speed off on the fresh mount. Walking the mare to cool her down, he called over to Ishmael, "You'd best put your hat on. That field's supposed to grow barley, not beets."

"I reckon I'll slap my hat on my head onc't my face gets as red as that hair of yourn."

"That was at least half an hour ago."

"Whoa." Ishmael stopped at the end of the

row he'd just plowed. He rubbed his sleeve across his damp forehead. "Boss, I got a twin sister who frets over me. No need for you to take up whar she leaves off."

"She's not here to talk sense into you."

"Yeah, well, anytime you take a notion in your head that you or your ma need some extry holp, I'll bring Ivy back."

"I'll keep your offer in mind. After I cool down this beauty, I'll take a turn with the plow."

"No need. I ain't had to stop onc't on account of the blade clogging. I heard tell of these steel moldboard plows, but niver got to use one." Ishmael stuck out a bony finger and drew a line in the air. "This'un cuts on through the earth, deep and sure."

"It does." Galen didn't remember seeing a plow back at the Grubbs' place. They owned one very sorry-looking mule. Had Ishmael prepared the ground with nothing more than hand tools? "I don't mind lending my plow out to folks who treat it with respect. In fact, a neighbor will be over early next week to borrow it. He uses my John Deere plow, and in return he lets me use his McCormick reaper."

"Don't mean to boast, but I'm good with a reaper. Come harvest, you'll find that out."

Ishmael didn't take the opening and ask to use the plow, so Galen let the matter go. "If you're half as good with the reaper as you are with a plow, I'll be satisfied."

"I promised I'd work hard for you, and I will. It feels good, turning your soil. It's rich—mighty rich. Niver saw me such a wiggle of worms whilst turnin' over the ground."

"The birds like it, too." Dozens of sparrows and chickadees dotted the earth, hopping to and fro, feasting on whatever insects and seeds surfaced as Ishmael turned the ground.

"Got a scarecrow handy?"

"Nope. Haven't gotten around to making one. Ma always has my littlest brother help her with that chore. It's a family tradition." *I sure miss them.*

"Your family shore has a heap of traditions."

Galen nodded and led the horse off. Since Da passed on, something came up nearly every single day that underscored his absence. Silly things that never registered suddenly became important—Ma still hugged and kissed them all good night, but now Galen squeezed Colin's arm and ruffled Sean and Dale's hair ere they climbed the ladder to the loft. Da always left the porch humming or whistling. Even though Galen's heart weighed heavy with grief, he forced himself to whistle just so Ma and the boys wouldn't be robbed of that tiny thing.

Jesus, the pastor said at Da's funeral that you lost your earthly father. Joseph had already taught you carpentry, but you were known as Mary's son. You know what it's like to love and lose your daddy. You carried on and provided in Joseph's stead.

Even on the cross, you took care of your mother.
Help me meet my family's needs—those of their bod-
ies, their minds, and their hearts. I can't do it on my
own. I've got to rely on you.

"Hey, Boss!"

Galen left the horse in a stall and went back outside.

Ishmael pointed. "Somebody's a-comin'."

Galen pivoted to the side. He stuck two fingers into his mouth and let out a loud three-toned whistle. The whistle came back with the notes reversed.

"It's them—my family!"

The group disappeared in a crook in the road, then reappeared.

"How come so many are a-comin'? I thought you got yourself a ma and three youngers."

"The neighbors are with them. My best friend, Josh, gave me his word that he'd keep watch over my family."

"But they got two wagons."

Galen laughed as yet another wagon followed the second. "Josh's wife, Ruth, is opening a library. It looks like she bought every book in the state of California!"

"Hoo-oo-eee! Lookee thar. They have stuff loaded onto every last wagon!"

Galen shook his head. When Josh McCain stopped the first wagon in the yard, Galen raised one brow in silent query.

"I brought them all home, safe and sound."

Josh's housekeeper, Hilda, stopped the second wagon. "Facts are facts, so I'm not boasting. I took first place for the best bucket of lard, and Laney got second for her grape jelly. Your mother could fill a washtub with all the ribbons for her vegetables and preserves and such."

Colin pulled the third wagon up next to the second. "Guess what we brought back!"

Seated in the bed of that wagon was Laney, holding a picture-pretty parasol above her and casting shade on her delicate complexion. The skirts of her traveling dress formed a puddle of sunshine all about her, but the way she held Hortense's head in her lap and the shoat kept making earthy grunting sounds spoiled the effect.

Galen folded his arms on the edge of the buckboard and addressed his youngest brother. "Dale, you were to sell Hortense."

"I did! Miss Laney bought her!"

Turning his attention onto Josh's pesky kid sister, Galen scowled. "Just what are you up to, Laney McCain? That shoat weighs as much as you do."

Chapter Six

That was hardly a flattering comparison, but I'll ignore it." Laney scratched Hortense between the ears, and Hortense let out happy little grunts. "I've gone into business. Dale is my partner."

"Yeah! And lookit, Galen! I got a boy pig. I won him in a greased pig chase." Dale cranked the pig's head toward him. "Mr. Snout, that's my brother Galen."

Galen wrinkled his nose. "What am I smelling?"

Hilda laughed so hard, she snorted.

Laney nudged Hortense, who obligingly trampled off her skirt. "We brought home fricasseed chicken."

Galen whooped. "Hey, Ishmael! Get over here! They brought us dinner!"

"Who's Ishmael?" Ma twisted on the seat.

Galen reached up for her. "Our new farmhand." He helped her down but didn't turn loose right away. Instead, he gave her a good long hug and whispered to her, "It's good to have you home."

Ishmael reached over the wagon and hauled Hortense out. "I reckon you'll want her over in the sty."

"I'll take Mr. Snout," Galen muttered. He cast a longing look at the pasteboard boxes from the Copper Kettle. "What's in those?"

"Fricasseed chicken," Sean told him, and he and Dale burst into giggles as they scrambled down.

"Good thing there's lots of it. Ishmael and I'll sluice off at the pump. We've built up quite an appetite."

"It's not for you, Galen." Colin swiped Mr. Snout from him.

"Why not?"

Galen glared at his brother—partly because he'd just denied him good food, but mostly because Colin took his excuse for not helping Laney out of the wagon.

"Because," Laney said as she rested her hands on Galen's shoulders, "I bought the chicken for the pigs."

"You bought chicken for the pigs!" He swept her down to the ground. *The lass is daft!*

Laney didn't turn loose of him yet. "I couldn't buy the pork chops for them." She smiled and said in a tone that sounded perfectly reasonable, "That would make them cannibals!"

"Ethel cooked it," Ma said.

"We're sitting down to dinner anyway." Galen shot a look over at the sty. "Ishmael's our new hand. He, his sister, and his da are half starved. You're all going inside and eating that meal . . . like it or not."

"Already know I'm not going to like it," Hilda grumbled. "Don't know why I gotta suffer for Laney's plan going awry."

"Galen?" Sean tugged on his sleeve. "Why don't we just send the chicken home with him?"

"Because I like Ishmael," Galen snapped.

Folding his arms across his chest, Josh crooked a brow. "Thought you and I were friends. Never for a minute thought you'd try to wrangle me into eating Ethel's food. We just choked down her sandwiches. That's bad enough. No use adding insult to injury."

"You'll be eating again now." Galen refused to back down. "I won't slop hogs with better food than my neighbors eat."

"I suppose I could manage a bite or two." Laney casually brushed hoof-shaped smudges from her gown.

"I can, too." Ruth patted Laney's arm. "And we can count on Josh. Can't we, dear?"

Josh groaned. "Galen, this is a true test of love and friendship."

Under other circumstances, Josh's desperation would tickle Galen. He shoved aside a flash of amusement and summoned his resolve. "Don't think I haven't noticed you failed to commit to eating a bite."

"My sister meant well."

Laney's but a child, and a cosseted one at that.

"Galen," Josh repeated, "Laney meant well."

"I've heard the road to hell is paved with good intentions." Galen's jaw jutted out stubbornly.

"Can't say as I'd know for certain." Ma threaded her hand through the crook in his arm. "But this much I do know: Good intentions surely paved the road to indigestion this time."

Laney waited out on the porch so Mrs. O'Sullivan and the boys could enter first. Hilda tutted and pointed at Laney's skirts. "Brush off that dirt. Kelly's too busy to have to sweep up extra grime."

Josh stood there, still holding the door open for Hilda. All four boxes formed an ominous stack in his arms, and Hilda's eyes narrowed. "Cowboy, there's times for brawn and times for brain. You got 'em mixed up just now. Instead of holding the door open and balancing those boxes, a smart man woulda arranged an accident and dropped every last one of 'em."

"That wouldn't be honorable."

Hilda gave Laney a baleful glare. "Someday maybe you can talk some sense into your brother. Sparing women and children from needless suffering is more important than anything else."

Once their housekeeper huffed into the house, Josh winked at Laney and whispered, "She's still sore over me getting cherry pie on my shirt."

Laney flashed a smile at him, then rustled her skirts to dislodge a few tiny particles of dust. "There. Do I look passable now?"

Josh didn't bother to look at his sister's clothing. His jaw tightened ever so slightly, and he shut the door. "Laney Lou," he murmured, "forget it. Galen isn't interested in you. Don't make things harder on him. Life here is already tough enough."

Laney shook her head. "I understand, Josh. Propriety demands a full year of mourning. I can wait for his feelings to develop."

"They're not going to." Her brother tacked on in a lower voice, "Galen's never done anything to encourage you. Stop coming here to pester the man."

She stepped closer and whispered, "Hilda refuses to allow Ruth and me to do anything at the Broken P, and you know it. Mrs. O'Sullivan, on the other hand, has patiently taken us under her wing. She's teaching us all of the practical skills the finishing schools back East ignored. Galen's little brothers are adorable, and I love each of them. I would come here regardless of my feelings for Galen."

"This isn't the time or place, and Galen's not the right person." Josh stared at her intently.

"Don't set yourself up for heartache."

Laney didn't want to respond to his assertion. Instead, she said, "I need to go in and help get the food on the table." The sigh Josh heaved ought to have blown the door open. Since it didn't, he obliged.

Laney slipped inside, and her heart lurched when she realized Galen's mother had gone straight to her husband's side of the bed. She stood there with her head bowed.

I'm so selfish, thinking of my future when they're hardly able to make it through each day.

Sean slid past Laney and clutched his mother's hand. "Da's-not-here-an-ny-more."

Laney started toward them, but Josh dumped the boxes of food onto the table and held her back.

"He's not." Mrs. O'Sullivan pulled Sean closer, and Dale sidled up to her, as well.

Laney closed her eyes to hold back her tears and fished up her sleeve to find a hankie. Rumbling voices and boots on the porch announced Galen, Colin, and another man. Laney opened her eyes and inched to the side.

The trio entered the cabin and Galen took in the scene. He led Colin over to the bed, his arm wrapped around him. "The bed's as empty as my heart. Havin' you all home—that softens the hurt."

Mrs. O'Sullivan turned and burrowed into Galen's arms. Colin, Sean, and Dale held fast to him, as well, creating a knot of misery.

Laney longed to go over and comfort them, yet she didn't. Couldn't. It wasn't her place. Her heart and mind warred over what to do.

Josh half pushed Laney and Ruth toward the table, ordering in a gruff whisper, "Set the table and serve up the food. The new man and I'll go fetch the other things from the wagons."

Laney turned back to her brother and said in the barest whisper, "Bring in sugar and flour."

He blinked his understanding and left.

Ruth took a stack of plates from the cupboard and pressed them into Laney's hands. "Keeping busy," she whispered.

Laney nodded. When Ruth's mother had died, Mrs. O'Sullivan had claimed staying occupied helped a person through the early months of grieving. They took her advice to heart yet again. Ruth lit a fire in the stove and started coffee.

Josh came back in with two valises balanced atop a full crate. The farmhand trailed in with a twenty-five pound bag of sugar over one shoulder and another one of flour on the other.

"Please set those down by the window," Laney said to him.

"Yes'm."

Galen cleared his throat. "Ma, this is Ishmael Grubb. He'll be coming over two full days and three half days a week. I'm allowing his family to sharecrop the far southern corner of our land, but they'll keep the crops and we'll have his labor. Ishmael, this is my ma, Mrs. O'Sullivan."

"Ma'am." Ishmael set down the bags and fumbled with what to do with his hands. "I'm shore sorry that man of yourn is dead and gone."

Mrs. O'Sullivan manufactured a pained smile. "Thank you, Mr. Grubb."

"I need to say something." Laney let out a shaky breath. "Cullen O'Sullivan is gone, and knowing he's with the Lord is great consolation. But—" she looked at the O'Sullivans, her gaze resting on Galen last—"he's still here in the best of ways. Cullen O'Sullivan lives on through Galen, Colin, Sean, and Dale. They're his legacy, and as long as we remember him and his sons carry on the family name with the same honor, a very special part of Mr. O'Sullivan is still with us."

Galen didn't say a word, but the grooves bracketing his mouth eased.

"Ooch, now Laney, if that's not just like you. You've said a very beautiful mouthful, you have." Mrs. O'Sullivan looked at each one of her sons in turn. "I've still the present to live in and a future to look forward to."

"And friends to share it with," Ruth added.

"Doesn't feel very friendly to me, dishing this up." Hilda had lifted the lid on one of the boxes and was staring at the contents with undisguised dismay.

"I'm sure it's fine," Galen said.

Hilda snorted and turned the box upside down over a plate. Everyone watched, but nothing happened. Suddenly, *thump*! A huge wad of mashed potatoes plopped onto the plate. Grayish bits of the pasteboard box formed unappetizing scabs here and there.

Ruth upended the next box over a serving platter. About two dozen pebble-sized hunks of brown chicken rained down. "I think the rest are stuck to the box."

Mrs. O'Sullivan reached for her apron. "You men give us twenty minutes, and we'll have a fine meal ready."

"What—" Galen surveyed the remaining boxes, and Laney marveled they didn't burst into flames from the angry spark in his eyes. He turned that gaze on her and asked in a deep, nail-in-the-coffin tone, "—is in the other two boxes?"

"One is chocolate applesauce cake." Laney tried to act downright cheerful even though the combination sounded utterly revolting. After all, Galen had demanded they eat Ethel's food, and she'd do her best to support his vile plan.

Ruth opened the last box. "Half is chicken. The other half is potatoes."

"Let's set that one off to the side." Mrs. O'Sullivan turned to Hilda. "Some seasoning and eggs, and those mashed potatoes will turn into delicious potato pancakes. I'll whip up some white gravy. Laney, boil noodles. Ruth, be a dear and grate some cheese for me."

Ishmael began to back away toward the door. Mrs. O'Sullivan wagged her finger at him. "If you're sneaking away, I'll still expect you back for lunch. Aye, I will, Ishmael Grubb. And whilst you escape, take those bags you toted in along with you. The sugar and flour are for the Broken P."

"Kelly," Hilda said to Mrs. O'Sullivan, "Laney brought three flour and three sugar. Altogether, I don't have storage at the Broken P for more than four sacks. You've got to keep those two sugar."

"Lester sold every last jar of jelly and jam I took in to the mercantile, Ma," Galen said. "Could you use the sugar to put up some pear butter?"

"Why, yes."

Laney smiled. *Everything's going just as I hoped it would!* "Ruth and I will be happy to come help."

"Me, too," Hilda tacked on.

"You ladies have done so much for us already." Galen shook his head.

He started out with a word of praise, but that stubborn look on his face and the way he's shaking his head . . . Laney blurted out, "Your mother has been exceptionally gracious, Galen. She's taught Ruth and me so much. We're both very grateful."

Galen turned away from Laney and said to his mother, "I'm thinking Ishmael's twin sister could help you."

Laney couldn't move. Galen's words and action tore at her.

"Wow!" Dale stared up at Ishmael. "You got a twin?"

"They can't be twins if she's a girl." Sean wrinkled his nose. "Twins gotta both be boys or gotta both be girls."

Ishmael hunkered down in front of the boys. "Now that ain't quite the truth. Twins cain be a matched set, or they cain jist be two borned at the same time."

"Like when Gertie farrowed. Hortense and Peasley and—"

"Sorta like that."

"Dale!" Mrs. O'Sullivan sounded as if she couldn't decide whether she was shocked or amused. "Mrs. Grubb isn't a sow. Please don't take any offense, Mr. Grubb."

Ishmael grinned. "After seein' jist what a fine shoat Hortense is, and with Mr. O'Sullivan saying how Dale dotes on her, I'd say he was payin' a compliment. I reckon if'n my ma was still alive, she'd be tickled."

Galen ruffled Dale's hair. "With twins, there are only two babies."

"Oh. So do they look alike?"

Laney dreaded hearing what Ishmael's twin looked like, but she also desperately wanted to know. She waited to hear his answer.

Ishmael rose and a slow smile crossed his face. "Me and my sis—we both got pale hair and sky eyes, but on Ivy, it's beautiful."

"Miss Grubb and I came to an agreement," Galen said, looking to his ma.

Laney's heart dropped clear down to the toes of her slippers. Not only did Galen indicate he'd rather have Ivy Grubb come help his mother; Ivy was beautiful.

Chapter Seven

I'm letting my imagination run away with me. Galen's too methodical to be swept away by a pretty face in just a matter of days. But I would have said the same thing about Josh, and he's besotted with Ruth.

Oblivious to how his words alarmed Laney, Galen continued on. "Miss Grubb's come over and kept up your garden, Ma. She weeded and made sure to pick beans, tomatoes, and pears so you wouldn't have to set to work till tomorrow."

Galen's mother has had to teach me about

gardening. Ivy already knows so much, she can take care of that on her own. A farmer like Galen needs a wife who can work by his side and do those practical things. I didn't learn them fast enough. Laney's stomach clenched.

Weak laughter bubbled out of Mrs. O'Sullivan. "I should have guessed you'd found some help, Galen-mine. You were never one for cleanin' the house, and my stove's gleaming brighter than a diamond-dust mirror."

"Elaine Louise," Hilda said, tugging at her. "You're to put on water to boil and make noodles. Stop daydreamin' and be useful."

Laney nodded. She didn't trust herself to say anything. Her faith and prayers hadn't made any difference. Galen still treated her like she was Josh's bothersome baby sister instead of seeing her as a mature young lady who'd be a good wife, so he'd grown interested in someone else and given her his heart.

———•———

Ivy winced as she hefted the pail from the stream. She'd burned her hand last night—something she hadn't done in ages. The calluses on her hands usually protected her, but she'd been distracted by Pa. By morning a blister as big as a robin's egg had formed in the crease of her hand. The rope handle of the pail grated across it.

"What's takin' you so long?" Pa hollered at her.

"I only got two more rows to water," she called back. Under her breath, she muttered, "If'n yore in such an all-fired hurry, you could holp me out."

"Stop by me so's I cain have a drink." He didn't even bother to look up at her. He kept shaving his knife across a small branch, making wood form curls that fell into a huge pile around him.

She backtracked and switched the bucket to the other hand. Pa stabbed his knife into the side of the stump he sat upon and crammed that hand into the bucket.

Yanking his hand back out, he snarled, "That ain't cool 'nuff."

"I'll use it to water the corn and fetch another."

He pushed the bucket, causing water to slosh all over her skirt. "Yore as stupid as yore ugly. How many times do I gotta tell you, a gal's s'posed to put the men in her life first?"

Ivy trudged back to the stream. The thin, soaking wet material of her skirt stuck to her legs. She dumped out the water, then chose a shady spot to refill the bucket. As she knelt, she studied the faded red and blue marks on the material. B-E-S-T.

"That spells *best*," Ishmael had told her years back as she'd used the flour sacks to stitch the garment. "And that's what you are, sis. Yore the best sister a man e'er got."

Fine quality flour came in pretty calico; middlings were sold in simple white sacks with some lettering across them. A quick glance, and folks could tell how her clothes marked her as mangy-dog poor. Nobody but Ishmael could look at her one and only dress and think of something nice to say.

"What's keepin' ya?" Pa spat loudly. "I'm so parched, I cain barely e'en spit!"

Pa's sore as a billy goat with a boil on his tail. Ishy don't know how lucky he is to get away.

"Gal!" Pa let out a stream of curses.

Ivy hoisted the pail and headed back to her father. "Here. It's cool as cain be." She held out the bucket, and Pa slurped as much as he wanted. "You shore got a pile of shavings thar, Pa."

"Yup. They're gold in my pocket."

Gold? Ivy gave no reply. Pa couldn't just take a handful of dried leaves and twigs to start the fire for his still. He insisted on using shavings from an east-pointing branch from an oak tree— at least today he did.

"Don't stand there the whole livelong day. Ain't like yore purdy 'nuff for a man to wanna take a second look. We've gotta get us some corn right quick. All I got is one jug left, and it's half gone."

She headed toward the far corner of the garden and emptied the bucket on the corn. It took five more trips to finish watering the farthest little patch where the water didn't manage to seep when she diverted the flow from the stream into the irrigation ditches.

During that time she watered her worries, and they grew. At best, Pa tended toward being surly. When he ran out of his oh-be-joyful, he turned impossible. *The corn won't be ready yet, and he'll run out of his likker. Ishy always holped me when Pa took a bad turn like that. With Ishy a-workin' at the farm down yonder, how'm I a-gonna manage Pa?*

"Hey."

Ivy wheeled around and spied her brother over several rows of corn. "Ishy! What're you doin' home?" He didn't look sad in the least, but Ivy couldn't help blurting out, "Yore s'posed to be working for that O'Sullivan feller. Did he—"

"Stop frettin'." Ishmael carefully weaseled his way toward her. "His kin came home. I'll work a full day tomorrow 'stead of today. And lookee what I got here."

Ivy tilted her head to the side. "A box?"

"A box from a real diner. This is store-bought food!"

"Cain't be. Nobody's fool 'nuff to put vittles in a paper box."

Ishmael chortled softly. "Depends on what kind of vittles, but the gal in town at the diner don't have much horse sense. Took Mr.

O'Sullivan's ma and three other gals a chunk of time and work to fix it up afore we et."

"Don't make no sense. Why'd anybody pay lots of cash money for food they had to take home and cook up again?"

"No explainin' the peculiarities of others." Ishmael lifted the lid on the box.

Ivy looked inside and resisted the urge to poke at the contents. "What is it?"

"Taters and fur-ick-a-seed chicken."

"I don't see no seeds on the chicken."

"Me, neither, but I didn't ask. Miz O'Sullivan mixed up a batch of white gravy and we poured it o'er the chicken and a mess of noodles."

"Why'd they leave the eyes in the mashed—"

Ishmael chuckled again. "Those ain't the tater peels or eyes. Part of the box stuck. They picked off the pasteboard, mixed eggs and cheese with the taters, and fried 'em up."

Ivy's mouth started to water.

"Tasted right fine. Miz O'Sullivan said she was too tuckered out from travelin' to have to do the same all o'er again with this box. The other gals—they're from the ranch next door—they said they was plumb wore out, too. The McCain gals—one's Joshua McCain's wife and t'other's his sis—well, when Mr. O'Sullivan tole them how good yore breakfasts was, they asked if you'd be willin' to take this on. Elsewise, they was gonna jist drop the box into the pig sty!"

"They couldn't!" Ivy glanced back at the box. "Then again, cain't say as I blame 'em if'n they're dead on their feet. That food's a rare mess."

"Miz O'Sullivan stuck a hunk of cheese in my pocket." He shook his head. "Niver woulda thunk I'd do it, but I fed the cake to the pigs, sis."

Ivy gawked at him. "A cake?"

"If you could call it that. 'Twas burnt on the outside and mushy like muddy grits on the inside. Soon as Boss's ma cut into it, it run all over. Ever'body started a-roarin' like 'twas a grand joke. One of the boys stuck his finger in it to sample it. Grabbed for a cup of water to wash out the taste."

"That's a cryin' shame."

"Sis, if that gal cain get herself a job in a diner cookin' sommat that sorry, I'm shore one of these days when—" He stopped and shoved the box into her hands. "You got a future, Ivy. Yore a fine cook. Someday, you'll be a-cookin' in one of them fancy town diners and folks'll come from far and wide to get a taste."

He picked up the bucket and scanned the field. "I'll get up early tomorrow and water afore I hie on over to the O'Sullivans'."

"You don't need to."

They walked back toward the fire pit. Pa sat there, scowling at a curl of oak and going on the second round of cusswords.

"That's a powerful lot of oak." Ishmael's

voice took on an edge. "Thunk you finished doin' the shavin's yesternoon."

Pa shook his head. "Didn't hardly sleep a wink last night. Couldn't figger out why. This mornin' it all come to me. East of the Mississip, I did branches growin' west. We're clean on the west coast. I reckon that means the shavin's ought to come from a east-growin' branch. The one I did yesternoon went the wrong way. Had to put that matter to rights today."

Ishmael shot a look at Ivy. "D'ya got any wood for supper tonight?"

"Not much. Used up most of the deadwood I collected these past days. Pa's been claiming what he wants for the still." Her father had taken almost everything she'd gathered. She pointed at a pitiful little tangle of wood. "That thar's what I got left to cook with."

Ishmael set down the bucket and picked up the ax. "Since Pa favors the oak for his still, I'll be shore to find some sycamore or cottonwood this time."

"I'm a-gonna need plenty of oak when the time comes." Pa tossed down the last bit of the branch he'd been using. "And I need one straightaway. A beetle-bug crawled 'cross jist now."

"You already have plenty to use as tinder." Ishmael focused on the pile of shavings. "Fact is, Pa, that's a powerful lot there. Bet you worked all day on it."

"Ain't no good now. The beetle-bug ruint it. I'll jist make a new supply tomorry. You find me a good east-facin' oak branch now."

Ishmael let out a long, mournful sigh. "Sorry, sis. Guess we ain't a-gonna have that good supper after all."

"Huh?" Pa finally bothered to look at her. "Why not, and whatcha got thar?"

"Don't matter what she got, Pa." Ishmael studied the ax blade. "You always say we gotta put the still first."

Pa's face pulled to the right, the way it always did when he was fixin' to concoct an excuse. "I reckon you cain chop wood for a cook fire. I was about done with that branch afore that blasted beetle-bug took a mind to scurry here, so this tinder'll be good 'nuff."

Ishmael nodded gravely. "You know best, Pa."

"Gal, tote all these careful-like to the lean-to. Don't you go breakin' none of my special curlies."

"Ain't that nice of you, Pa?" Ishmael smiled so big, Ivy could see his back teeth. "Lettin' Ivy move them light little curlies while us men go drag back the heavier wood. It's right gentlemanly."

"Now hold on. My back's twinged the whole livelong day."

"Don't doubt that atall," Ivy said.

"I'll rig a travois for the mule," her brother

said. "That'll spare your back, Pa."

Pa settled back. "Then you won't need me."

"Till I get wood," Ivy said, striving to keep bitterness from her voice, "I cain't very well get supper goin'."

Pa shrugged. "It's jist past midday. Ishy's got plenty of time."

Ivy turned away. *No use trying to get Pa to do any work. If he put half the effort into doing chores as he did to avoiding them, life would be a lot easier. Well, it'd be easier for me and Ishy. Pa don't care none 'bout that though.*

"Whoa. What in thunderation d'ya thank yore doin'?"

Ivy turned and saw Ishy fill his big hands with the silly little oak shavings. "I figgered if I had time, I oughtta holp Sis."

"That's woman's work."

"When we bartered my labor for the right to work this land, you said you and Ivy would work the fields here so's you'd bring in the crop. Every crop we've ever had, it's taken Sis and me both to grow it. Ivy's a-doin' man's work. Heavy work. Ev'ry day."

"Ain't my fault my rheumatiz is so bad. The gal's got a strong back. She jist gotta step lively 'stead of lollygaggin' and dawdlin'. Took her half of forever to tote water to that far-back section whar she's planted t'other vegetables."

"I recollect a few years back when we had us the same trouble. We dug a second little valley in the dirt and used a board to coax the water to trickle from the stream into that other field for a little while each noon after waterin' the corn."

"I ain't a-digging. Tole you my back's painin' me sommat fierce."

Ishmael took off his shirt and knelt. "Sis, you go on and search for a willow tree." He scooped several curls onto his shirt. "I'll move these shavin's real careful-like. Then, whilst I go fetch wood, you cain comfort Pa with some willow bark tea or a poultice."

"Ain't no willows hereabouts," Pa grumped.

"Prob'ly are some upstream a ways. Sis is good at findin' stuff. It'll take her a spell, but yore worth it. Ivy, go and take yore time. Be shore to find a good willow—one what's bark is better'n the bite of Pa's pain."

Ivy smiled at her brother. "You shore, after talkin' like that, you don't want me to find a dog-wood?"

"Don't you have a fresh mouth with yore brother!"

"Now, Pa. Sis was jist funnin' me. Yore back must be dreadful sore for you to miss the twinkle in her eyes."

"My rheumatiz ain't niver been this bad." Pa glowered at her. "What're you waitin' on? Go fetch me the willow bark."

"I won't get jist any willow, Pa. I'll be shore to find powerful strong bark." She set down the box of town-made food, picked up the bucket, and headed out.

A short while later, Ishmael sauntered up to her beneath the boughs of a willow. "How full's yore bucket?"

"Half the way. Reckoned I'd dry up some bark on account of Pa's gonna want some sometime when I cain't hike off after it."

"That's right clever of you. Whar ya gonna keep it?"

"Member that cigar box I found? I reckon it'll come in handy for the medicinal yarbs I'm finding." She ducked between some of the hanging branches and spied the mule about fifteen yards away.

"I drug a big old fallen limb back already. Figgered the mule could drag the rest. Listen up. It vexes me how Pa swiped the wood you gathered, but argufying ain't gonna change that. I'll take 'nuff back to camp to last you a few days, and I'll drag in some oak to make Pa happy— but off a ways, I'm fixin' to make a few secret stashes whar I'll put more firewood for you. Thataway, you'll have what you need on the days when I work over at the farm."

"Thankee, Ishy."

"No need to thank me. I prob'ly oughtta be thankin' you. Whilst I'm workin' at the farm and gettin' fed, yore here havin' to do all the work with nothin' from Pa but complaints and criticizin'."

"I'm used to it." Her stomach growled loudly. "But I aim to go back now and have me my fill of some of that store-bought food."

"You'll have to fix it up plenty to make it taste decent, but if anybody cain, 'tis you."

They led the mule back toward camp. Suddenly Ishmael stopped.

Ivy leaned forward to see past him, and she bit back a cry.

Pa sat on the stump. If the pasteboard box wasn't in his lap, Ivy would have sworn he hadn't bothered to move at all. A stranger sat by him. They were both eating.

CHAPTER EIGHT

ⓒome on." Ishmael pulled on the mule's bridle.

Ivy wasn't sure whether her brother was speaking to her or the beast, but she trudged ahead. The food hadn't looked or smelled appetizing in the least, but hungry as she was, she'd have gladly eaten it anyway.

Pa looked over at them. His jaw jutted

forward. " 'Bout time you got back, gal. You been gone half of forever. Didn't care that I was back here starvin' and hurtin'."

"I gathered willow bark for your spinebone pain, and I found some yarbs to flavor supper."

"Don't know why you thunk you'd be able to improve on it. 'Twas fixed by someone who knows how to cook. 'Bout time I et sommat that didn't make me wanna puke."

"It was filling." The stranger leaned forward and squinted at Ivy.

"Was?" Ishmael's voice rang with outrage.

"Mr. Smith and me had us a business dinner. Nuthin' a-wrong with that." Pa shook his fork at Ishmael. "You et at yonder farm, so you got no reason to whine." He dropped his fork into the box. From the way it rattled, Ivy knew they'd eaten every last morsel.

"Sis had plans—"

"Well she cain jist go change 'em. She oughtta be thankin' me. Now she don't have to cook for us men. I spared her havin' to work. Soon as she brews me that willow bark tea, she cain rustle up sommat to keep her own slats apart."

The stranger turned his attention on Ivy. His mouth bowed upward in the sorriest pretend smile a mouth ever made, but pure old meanness turned his eyes a flat gray color. "She's as scrawny as I heard."

Ishmael growled, "Don't be talkin' about my sis thataway."

"Truth's the truth." Pa waved his hand back and forth in the same way he'd want to swish flies off his plate.

Ishmael tugged the mule forward another step, blocking Ivy from view. "And who was talkin' 'bout Ivy?"

"Now, Ishmael," Pa brayed, "don't get all het up."

The mule hedged sideways, so Ivy saw the stranger hitch a shoulder. "Plenty of us men like a woman we can span with our hands."

"Another feller come by today," Ivy said in an undertone to Ishmael. "Had blacker hair'n this 'un, but I reckon they're brothers or cousins."

"Mr. Jones here . . ." Pa started.

"Called 'em Mr. Smith not three minutes ago," Ivy whispered.

". . . is my new partner," Pa went on. "Until I get 'nuff corn to ferment, he's gonna bring me some corn and sugar."

"That's right." Mr. Jones or Smith—whoever he really was—stood up and dusted off the seat of his britches. "I'll be back tomorrow."

"Day after tomorrow'd be better. After-noon." Ishmael's voice carried great certainty.

"Sooner we start, the better," Pa said. "Tomorra sounds right fine."

Ishmael shook his head. "Pa, yore back's been dreadful bad. No use in makin' it worse. Day after tomorra, I'll be here all afternoon and evenin'. You'll need my holp unloadin' the supplies Mr.—"

"Johnston," the stranger filled in.

"Mr. Johnston brings by."

"No need to wait." Pa's voice sounded cranky. "The gal's got a strong back."

"Pa, Mr. Johnston hisself said Ivy's scrawny. If she tries a-totin' a bag of sugar and drops it, it could bust open. Day after tomorra is best."

"He cain come whene'er he wants," Pa snarled. "Gal, stop lollygaggin' and brew me that willow bark."

Ishmael pushed Ivy away from the stranger and toward the stream. "And go fetch a fresh bucket of water. Test the water a couple of places so's you bring back the coldest, sweetest thar is."

Ivy headed as far off as she could. The black-haired man earlier today had been handsome and sleek as a raven that just took a bath. He'd had an easy-going, friendly manner about him—a far cry from this man. Pa's new partner made the hair on the back of her neck prickle. Lots of the folks Pa trucked with were shifty-eyed, but none ever felt menacing like this one did.

Footsteps sounded behind her. She tensed and whirled around.

"It's me, sis." Ishy drew closer. "That feller's gone. Here. This is the cheese what Boss's ma give me to have you fix up the taters. You go on an et it."

"Wanna share it?"

"Nope. I et till I nigh unto busted my seams."

Ivy bit into the wedge and tamped down a moan at how the flavor burst in her mouth. "Ishy, it's wondrous good."

"You still got that sheath for yore knife?"

"Uh-huh." She swallowed and waited a second so she'd be able to savor the flavor of the next bite.

"You ain't been wearin' it. From now on, you keep yore knife on you all the time. Don't reckon as I b'lieve in God, so ain't a devil, neither—but that thar man what jist left, he shore puts me to thinkin' mayhap the devil's real after all."

"Worthless, lazy, no-good," Pa was muttering in the distance. Then he bellowed, "I'm sufferin', gal! You kept me waitin' far too long."

Ivy hurriedly scooped a little water in the bucket. "I'll wear my knife from now on. You cain be shore I will."

"Ishmael and I are planting the barley today." Galen stood at the washstand in the kitchen, preparing to shave. He looked in the mirror to see his mother's reaction.

"I wondered why you didn't plant it yesterday after you harrowed it."

"Need a scarecrow." He turned around. "Think maybe you and Dale can see to that?"

"Sure as I live and breathe, we can." Ma started some coffee. "Once was, I'd already have a scarecrow waitin' on you."

"You and the boys were away. 'Twas time well spent."

She went on. "When I dyed my dresses, the pink one didn't take right. Instead of wasting good clothes, I aim to make the scarecrow a lass instead of a lad this year."

"A lass? That would be different." He shrugged. "I suppose there's no reason why not."

Ma nodded. "That's what I thought. There's something else."

Galen waited for her.

"Sick as he was, your da wore his nightshirt these last months. Last eve, I set out to store a few things of his in my trunk. . . ." Her voice faded out, then came back in a plaintive half whisper. "Galen-mine, you look so very like your da."

Galen blindly set down the razor, then crossed the cabin and held his mother.

She burrowed into his arms. Once she'd seemed every bit as indomitable as his father. Now he realized that for all her strength, she also had her frailties.

Ever since Da passed on, Ma had started encouraging Galen to take a wife. He'd dismissed the thought because his first sweetheart ran off with a butcher from Sacramento, and then Josh up and claimed Ruth when Galen fancied her for himself. Those two experiences left him guarded. *No more. I'll start paying more heed to the young ladies at church. God said it's not good for a man to be alone. I'll have a helpmeet and fill our home with children. My wife will help Ma, and babies will keep them busy and content.*

"I don't think I could bear seein' you wear Cullen's shirts."

Galen held her tight. "Don't worry, Ma. I don't need Da's shirts."

"I know. But I wondered if—" She sucked in a breath, then said in a rush, "Would you be upset if I gave them to Ishmael? We buried Cullen in his Sunday-best shirt, and the other two are just ordinary work shirts—and well worn, at that."

Lord, you know this was what was on my heart this very morn. Galen dipped his head and pressed a kiss on her morning-mussed hair. When had it gotten those silver strands?

She stroked small, comforting arcs on his back. "If the thought troubles you . . ."

"Ma, Da would be pleased to know someone else could use them. Ishmael looks so different, it won't bother me." Even in the midst of her pain, she still thought of others. He needed to do likewise. "What about the boys, though?"

"I'll tell you what I think," came a voice from up in the loft.

"Sean Michael O'Sullivan, you've been eavesdropping?" Galen gave him a stern look.

"Not on purpose." Sean looked down at them. "Miss Laney said 'twas a blessing to be either a giver or a receiver. Mr. Josh got us new shirts, so maybe it's our turn to be givers."

Dale sidled up by Sean. "Besides, a scarecrow will be okay in a dress, but Ishmael would look silly in it!"

The door opened and shut as Colin returned from the outhouse. "What's so funny?"

Dale piped up, "We decided Ishmael shouldn't wear Ma's dress."

"So we're giving him Da's shirts instead," Sean finished.

"No!" Colin's head swiveled from side to side.

Galen wasn't sure whether it was a violent shake of negation or if Colin was trying to decide whom to blame and whom to appeal to as he looked from Ma to Galen and back. Galen turned loose of Ma and stepped forward. "Letting go is hard. It takes practice. Trust us on this, Colin. Ma and I both feel it's the right thing to do."

Footsteps sounded on the porch, and then someone rapped softly on the door.

"Yes?" Galen rasped.

Ishmael barely opened the door a crack and whispered, "Milk pail's not in the barn."

"We've gotten a slow start this morn, Ishmael. I'll send Sean out to milk the cows, and you can muck the stable."

" 'Kay." The door shut.

Ma looked at Colin, but she said nothing.

"We'll work things out here, Ma," Galen promised.

"Dale and I'll go gather the eggs." She reached over and squeezed Colin's hand. "None of us'll breathe a word to Ishmael yet. I won't do anything that'll hurt any of my dear sons."

Everyone else slipped out of the cabin, but Colin didn't budge an inch. Anger sang from his tense body.

Lord, grant me wisdom.

"You can't give away Da's shirts!"

Galen looked over at the washstand and let out a long, slow breath. *Be with us, Lord. The valley of the shadow of death is far darker than I imagined.*

Galen wrapped his left arm around Colin's stiff shoulders and half dragged him to the washstand. "The cotton of a shirt is insubstantial. It tears and rots away." He opened the washstand drawer and slowly curled his hand around something. "You're a man now, Colin. Aye, you are. I'm thinkin' Da would be wantin' you to have this." He pressed the item into Colin's hand.

"Da's razor." Surprise and reverence mingled in Colin's voice.

"Aye. And a fine one 'tis. The one I use belonged to Grandda. Proud I am to have it. This one—Da's—was made to last and be passed on." He reached over, wedged Colin's jaw in his hand, and turned it from side to side. "Time's come to let go of your childhood, Colin. We're going to shave now."

He'd already stropped his razor, but he did it again for show. "Now you do yours."

Colin smacked the razor up and down the

strop with more zeal than skill, but that didn't much matter. He squinted as he checked the edge of the razor and nodded as though he knew exactly how it was supposed to look.

"Hot water works best. Ma always sets a full pot on the stove in the mornin', so fetch it."

Bringing the water toward the washstand, Colin asked, "How much do I put in the mug?"

"Just a wee bit. Barely cover the soap."

Colin slopped in a little too much and winced.

"Since we're both shaving, we'll use it." Galen forced a smile. *I did the same thing the first time I shaved, and Da said the selfsame thing to me.*

"Nothing smells like McGillicutty's," Colin murmured.

" 'Tis the finest." Galen relaxed at the familiar recitation of what Da always said about his shaving soap. "Now work that into a fine lather, then scrub it onto your face in brisk circles."

Soon they stood side-by-side, faces covered in a white froth. "Watch me. Hold the razor just so. Keep your forefinger firm, then lift your chin and pull your face to the side so the skin's taut, then shaaave."

Intent on faithfully copying every nuance, Colin managed the first stroke fairly well. By the third stroke, his confidence got the better of him and he managed to nick himself. "Ouch!"

Galen yanked open the drawer, grabbed the styptic pencil, and put it beside the mug. "The alum in that styptic stops the bleeding but stings like a wasp."

A grunt was about the only response—until Colin used the pencil. He grimaced and chuffed air in and out for about half a minute. "That'll teach me to be more careful."

"Aye." Galen continued to demonstrate how to shave and warned, "Many's the time you'll shave your mustache and get McGillicutty's up your nose. Pull the razor away, else you'll sneeze and cut yourself."

Colin finally finished wiping the last specks of soap from his face. "Well?"

Pretending to be critical, Galen rubbed his thumb across his brother's chin. "I'd say you're owning a fine razor now. It did a grand job."

Colin looked at their father's razor. "It served Da well. I won't ever forget watching him shave."

" 'Tis the memories that make us strong. In the years ahead, you'll use his razor and recall the wise and good things he said and did. We'll share the memories, and that'll keep Da alive in our hearts and minds. Other things we have to let go of, Colin."

"You're talking about Da's shirts."

" 'Tis true, I am. And there'll be other things, as well."

"But why?"

"I keep telling myself I can let go of things because I have a wealth of memories that no one can ever take away. We found pleasure in remembering what Da said each morn about McGillicutty's. Such a simple thing, that—but good."

Sean came back in, and Ma and Dale returned just moments later. Worry tightened Ma's features as she stared intently at Colin and Galen.

"Now, Ma," Galen said, his arms bent akimbo. "You had no cause to worry. Colin barely even nicked himself."

"Colin shaved?" Sean's eyes bulged.

"Of course he did." Ma finally smiled. "I'm thinking 'twas about time, too. He's turned into a young man right before our eyes—and a handsome one at that."

"Aye, he's not hard to look upon, but that's just the outside." Galen served him a manly slap on the back. "On the inside, where God looks, Colin's striving to have a pure heart."

"As well he should." Ma scanned all of them, then headed for the cupboard. "But I'll not stand for empty-headed sons. If we don't make haste, you lads'll be tardy for school!"

While bacon sizzled on the griddle, Ma set six places at the table. It looked wrong and right all at the same time. She cleared her throat. "I'm scramblin' eggs, Galen. Won't take but a few minutes. You'd best summon Ishmael so he can wash up."

"I'll fetch him." Colin headed outside.

While Sean and Dale washed up, Galen

went over and murmured, "I hope you don't mind, Ma. I gave him Da's razor."

Ma poured the eggs into the skillet and made a funny little sound. She blinked to keep from crying. "Since Colin has his father's chin, 'twas fitting."

Galen watched as she pushed the eggs around and they turned into fluffy yellow clouds instead of the charred mess he'd made. Odd, how such little things made life seem almost normal.

"Galen-mine, I'm glad you worked it out." Ma leaned into him. "I wasn't sure how to comfort Colin. Giving him the razor was a grand plan."

"I think Da would have wanted it."

"That he would."

After they all sat down and Galen said grace, Ishmael didn't reach for any of the food. "Miz O'Sullivan, ma'am, Colin asked me if'n I'd like his daddy's shirts."

Ma nodded.

"I won't take 'em if'n spying me in 'em will stab yore heart."

"Take them. Please." Ma passed him the bowl of eggs. "These, too."

"I think Da would have wanted it," Colin said.

"For Ishmael to have the shirts, or the eggs?" Dale asked.

"The shirts." Sean plucked three rashers

from the platter and shoved it toward Ma. "We all think Da would have wanted them to go to good use."

"That he would," Galen agreed.

CHAPTER NINE

"Galen."

"Yes, Ma?" He looked at his mother over the gelding he'd just unsaddled. She held a lumpy flour sack.

"You mentioned the Grubbs are staying on our land, but I don't remember where."

"South corner, by the stream. Why?" He saw tears welling up in his mother's eyes and went around to her. "What's wrong?"

"I can't bear the thought that the Grubbs are hungry." The tears sketched down Ma's cheeks.

Galen pried the sack from her, set it down, and pulled her into his arms. At breakfast and lunch, Ishmael had obviously been trying not to eat too much, but when Galen or Ma offered him more, he accepted with alacrity and wolfed down the food.

"We know what it's like to be hungry." Ma's words came out hushed and choppy.

"Aye, we do." They'd lost two of his little brothers to the great potato famine before coming to America. He'd thought Ma had come to peace about it. That was years ago, and she'd said God generously gave her three more sons to replace the two she'd lost. But Da's death seemed to be raking up that sadness all over again.

"Ma, I hired Ishmael's sister to come over twice while you were gone. She took home fruit and vegetables as her pay."

Ma pushed away and dried her face with the hem of her apron. "Well and good, but I'm going to take over more and ask the lass to help me put up pear butter."

"No."

"But you're the one who suggested it."

But I don't want you going there. I don't trust Ebenezer Grubb. Ishmael has proven to be gentle-spirited and reliable, and Ivy worked hard when she was here; but their father is fast-talking and shifty-eyed. Why am I letting someone I don't trust live on my land? Galen tried to put his thoughts in order. "We'll just ask Ishmael to invite her over."

A tune carried in the breeze. Galen's head swiveled toward the source. Ishmael kept whistling as he propped up the scarecrow. The song was one they'd sung at Da's funeral.

"'Asleep in Jesus.'" Ma slid her hand into

Galen's as she named the piece. "You were humming it after breakfast today. 'Tis consolation, thinkin' on how Cullen's resting against the bosom of the Prince of Peace."

Ishmael learned the tune from me. He doesn't know it's a hymn, but it's a start. That might well be why they're here—for us to lead them to the Lord.

"We're supposed to give secretly, Ma. I'll take the bag and drop it off. Choose a day when you want to make pear butter and tell Ishmael before he leaves tonight. He'll ask Ivy."

"I suppose 'tis best."

Ma went inside, and Galen hid the bag. He finished caring for the mustang and set it out to pasture.

"So, Boss," Ishmael called to him, "whaddya want me to do now?"

Galen tilted his head toward the pigsty. "Reinforce the bottom boards all around that. Dale keeps climbing on it to visit Hortense and Mr. Snout."

"Snout?" Ishmael threw back his head. "Hooo-ooo-ie! I mis-heared him. I been thankin' he gone and named that pig Mr. Snot on account of how the critter's coloring goes white on the bottom part of his nose."

"You'll have to tell that to Dale. It'll tickle him."

"I'll be shore to. Long as I got a hammer in my hand, I could walk yore fences and check to be shore they're standin' strong."

"I did that after you left yesterday." Galen needed to keep Ishmael busy for awhile so he could go drop off Ma's bag. "After you see to the sty, chop firewood. I'm behind on that, and we'll need plenty for the winter."

"Got stuff ready to be cut, or do I need to go chop down trees?"

"One day next week, we'll go chop down a few trees. I recently dragged several large branches over. You can hack them into manageable lengths."

Ishmael knew where the tools and nails were; he'd helped rehang the barn door. He gathered the necessities and went over to the sty.

Galen grabbed the bag and sneaked away. He couldn't take a horse because it would be obvious. Instead, he set out at a fast pace. When he approached the Grubbs' camp, Galen slowed and looked for a likely place to leave the food. He didn't want to be seen, but he wanted Ivy to find the bag.

"Oh, my stars and garters!"

Galen wheeled around.

Ivy stood about four yards away with her hand pressed to her heart. It didn't escape his notice that she had a knife in that hand. "Mr. O'Sullivan, you pert near scairt me outta my skin."

He pressed his finger to his lips and shook his head.

"Ain't much of a secret. I already spied you."

He set down the bag and looked over his shoulder.

"Oh." Her voice dropped to a mere whisper. "You don't want Pa to know you brung that?"

He nodded.

"Whate'er 'tis, thankee, Mr. O'Sullivan."

Galen smiled and left without uttering a single word. By the time he got back to the farm, the sound of the ax rang in the air. He walked through the cornfield they'd already harvested and decided that for another two weeks he'd still be able to coax beans from the vines that climbed the stripped stalks.

Last year Da tried to help strip the last of the beans, but he'd been too weak. Galen stood in the very spot where Da's legs gave way. He'd known his father was frail, so he'd been working alongside him and caught him.

"Son, let me sit on my land. Time's come for us to talk, and there's no better place than this." Galen fell to his knees as the memory crashed over him. *"We're surrounded by life, son—but seasons change. Our precious Savior will be taking me home ere we see another harvest. Your ma and your brothers—I'm entrusting them to you. God will give you strength to carry on."*

"Galen?"

The panicky edge in Sean's voice yanked Galen back to the present. He strove to sound calm. "Aye, boy-o?"

"So you're not hurt or sick, are you?"

Galen rose and grabbed Sean, then tipped him upside down and shook him until he giggled. "I'm hale as a horse. Aye, I am." He pretended to drop Sean, jerked him back up and set him on his feet. "But you're growing big as can be. One of these days, I'll pull with all my might and you won't budge an inch."

"Does that mean I getta pick the corn tomorrow, too?"

Galen closed one eye and tilted his head to the side. "Hmm."

Sean stretched tall and puffed out his scrawny chest.

"Close, but I'm thinking you'll take on that job next season. You and Dale need to be picking the beans in this field while Colin, Ma, and I harvest the last of the corn."

"Aww, Galen!" Sean kicked the dirt.

"And you'll weed Ma's flower garden, too."

Sean folded his arms across his chest. "Da wouldn't make me do woman's work."

"Da would paddle your backside for saying that." This was the first time one of his brothers had challenged his authority. *They'll not grow up to be the kind of men God and Da would approve of if I'm not firm. Da entrusted me with the boys on this very spot. 'Tis fitting that I'll be making my first stand here.*

Galen glowered at Sean. "A man—a real man—does what needs to be done. Adam and Eve were the first farmers, and the only job God gave to the woman that was hers alone was to bear children."

"Huh-unh." Sean shook his head. "Eve had to sew the leaves into clothes."

He's testing me. Galen leveled a stern gaze at his little brother. "Making clothes isn't a woman's work. God himself made clothes for Adam and Eve when He cast them from the Garden of Eden."

"Are you teasing me?"

"Our Lord is to be praised and worshiped. I'd not treat Him or His Holy Word lightly. 'Tis in the second or third chapter of Genesis."

The slightest squint still narrowed Sean's eyes, and his head cocked a little to the right.

He's trying to figure out how far he can push me. Galen's jaw hardened. He lowered his voice and spoke very distinctly. "The next time you try to shirk a chore because you think 'tis beneath you and expect Ma to do it, you'll be doing that chore while suffering a sore backside."

Sean's jaw dropped open.

"We're a family, and we work together. Whatever work needs to be done, we do." He crooked a brow. "Are you hearing me, Sean Michael O'Sullivan?"

Sean nodded very slowly.

More than once, Da had said God tempered His power with wisdom. Galen took that lesson to heart. He'd made his point; best he dismiss

Sean now. "Go on and change out of that new shirt and put on your old one. There's plenty of daylight left."

Sean didn't scamper away. "Galen? I came to tell you my horse is going lame."

Galen folded his arms akimbo. "Change and meet me in the stable. We'll look at her together." Once Sean left, Galen bent forward and smacked the soil from his knees. *Don't know why I'm bothering. My brothers are going to keep me on my knees, Lord. If you'd spare me a good measure of wisdom and a bushel of patience, I'd appreciate it. Oh, and while I'm asking for things, if you could see clear to having that horse be hale, I'd be thankful.*

Ten minutes later Galen held the mare's hoof between his knees and guided the dull knife in Sean's hand. "See here? That pebble worked its way in and is hurtin' the poor beast. Pry it out gently. Aye. Better to take your time and do a good job than to rush."

"It's hard not to hurry. Lightning is hurting!"

"Not when she's not putting her weight on this hoof. There! You got it out."

"I did it!" Sean beamed. "I made Lightning better!"

"Aye." Galen turned loose of the mare's leg and straightened up. "But you were right to have me come check her. Have you ever noticed how Josh and I often look at a horse together?"

"Yeah."

"There are plenty of good reasons. A second opinion or evaluation can often bring to light something one man might miss. Then, too, hurt beasts aren't always docile, and horses are big and powerful."

"Like when Mr. Lufe's stallion bucked?"

"Exactly so." Galen slid the knife into his belt. "Eddie Lufe was smart enough to have someone with him, else he might have gotten hurt. Never mistake being brave with being foolish."

"I won't, Galen." Sean stooped down to pick up the little pebble. He stood up, admired it for a moment, then stuck it in his pocket.

"Go round up Dale. I'll have the two of you carry some wood in for Ma." Minutes later, Galen held Dale and Sean off to the side until Ishmael finished splitting another piece. Just as the ax descended, the log tumbled. The ax struck and most of the log shot off to the side while a big chunk flew up and hit Ishmael.

"Argh!" Ishmael dropped the ax and covered his eyes with his hands.

Chapter Ten

Galen parted the boys and ran over to the stump. He spun Ishmael around and shoved him to sit right where that log had once been. "Let me see."

Ishmael didn't remove his hands. He rocked back and forth. "Dad burn it!"

Grabbing his bandanna from his back pocket, Galen barked, "You lads go tell Ma he's hurt and I'm bringing him in." He didn't bother to look to see if they obeyed. Blood poured from Ishmael's nose and through his fingers. Galen wrenched Ishmael's hands away and smashed his bandanna to the wound running from Ishmaels eyebrows to his hairline. "It's your forehead. Can you see now?"

The farmhand's eyes opened. "Wouldn't hurt . . . so much . . . if you weren't so ugly."

"If you weren't already bloody, I'd punch you for that. Here. Stand up. I'll help you into the house."

Ishmael stood. "Dad burn it! Dad burn it!"

Galen clenched Ishmael's arm. "You're hurt, but mind your tongue. Bad enough you cursed with my little brothers here. I won't have you speaking that way around my ma."

Ishmael reached up and took over holding the bandanna to his head. He gritted his teeth, and that was the full extent of his reaction.

Galen led him across the yard and up the porch. Colin stood in the doorway. "Do I need to go fetch Doc, or do you want me to hitch up the buckboard to drive him in to town?"

"Let me have a look at it first." Ma already had towels on the table and one in her hand. "Half of this mess is nothing more than a bloody nose. Ooch, now. A chunk of skin's missin' from your forehead, Ishmael Grubb. It's none too deep, but it's wide enough to make you glad the dear Lord gave you a thick skull to protect your brain."

"What do you need, Ma?" Galen admired the way she always stayed calm in an emergency.

"I'm wanting to stop the bleeding and clean him up."

"We've got a styptic pencil with our razors." Colin dashed toward the washstand.

"Nay, Colin. Some purple loosestrife would serve far better. Ishmael, pinch your nose here to stop the bleeding. Galen, hold this towel to his head. I'll fetch some loosestrife."

Ma left and returned with three stalks of a purplish-pink flower. "Wouldn't you know they're dusty?" She rinsed them, then stripped the flower petals into one of her smaller mixing bowls. After adding a small splash of water, she crushed the petals with a wooden spoon and mixed them to form a paste.

"Boss, I left yore ax out thar."

"Colin will see to it." Galen glanced at Colin, who nodded and left.

"Ma," Dale called down from the loft where he'd gone so he could see better, "whatcha gonna do with that?"

"I'm making a paste."

Dale giggled. "You're going to paste him back together?"

" 'Tisn't funny when someone's hurting." Galen gave his littlest brother a stern look.

"Don't mean to be quarrelsome, Boss, but I was a-thankin' the selfsame thang."

"Loosestrife stops bleeding and has healing properties." Ma took the towel off Ishmael's forehead and started smoothing the paste on him.

"Ain't niver wore posies afore. My smeller ain't good with my nose messed up, so I cain't tell if'n these got much of a scent, but they're shore puttin' a halt to the burnin'."

About ten minutes later, Ma fussed over Ishmael as she gently cleaned off the paste. "It's going to be sore for a few days, I'm afraid. I hope it won't scar."

"Do you think Doc would want to stitch him

together?" Sean asked, leaning over the loft railing.

"He wouldn't," Ma said with great authority. " 'Tis wide and shallow, and you only stitch when a wound goes deep. Galen, his shirt's a rare mess."

Galen silently crossed the cabin and got one of his father's shirts. *Lord, you knew this need before the accident even happened. Thank you for preparing the boys—and especially Colin—this morn.*

"Much obliged for the doctorin', Miz O'Sullivan. I'm beholden to you."

"Nonsense. It's thankful I am that you'll be just fine. Your head'll ache a day or two, so I'll get you some willow bark. But don't drink any willow bark until tomorrow. If you have it tonight, that wound might start bleeding again."

"No need for any, ma'am. Sis got some on account of Pa's rheumatiz sometimes kicks up."

Galen stood next to Ishmael. "As soon as Ishmael changes, I'll be sure he gets back to his family."

Ma took the hint. "Good. I'm needing something from the springhouse. Ishmael, if you need anything, send your sister here."

"Won't be any call for that, ma'am."

"Oh—and on Monday, I'd like to finish putting up pear butter. Will you please ask your sister if she could help?"

"I'm shore she'd be tickled, ma'am." Ma left,

and Ishmael changed into one of Da's shirts. "I'm steady as a hunnert-year-old rock, Boss. Don't have no need to be watched home like a boy on his first trip home from the school-house."

"Your wits are addled if you think I'd let you saunter off."

Galen and Ishmael started back toward the south corner of the farm. Ishmael waited until they were halfway to his place, then stopped.

"What's wrong?" Galen asked.

"Cain't rightly say as I know. That's why I'm a-stoppin' here. I ain't a fine gentleman, but I niver stooped to bein' raw-mouthed. Pa cusses, and I'd druther he didn't—specially when Sis is around. But you got yore hackles up and I cain't figger out why. All I said was dad burn it."

"I understand you didn't mean to curse." *I was wrong, Lord. I expected a man who knows nothing about you to act like a Christian.* "I'm sure you must not have known what that saying really means."

"It meant I done sommat stupid and got myself into a fix."

"You got hurt; it was an accident. There's not a man alive who hasn't had a log shift as his ax was arcing down. But your words—they have a meaning you didn't know. *Dad* is slang for God. Remember how I said He's my heavenly Father?"

"Yup. So you thunk I was a-wantin' your God to burn my head?"

"No, Ishmael. Christians believe after this life, a man's soul either goes to heaven or goes to hell. Hell is an eternal fire. When a soul is sent to hell, we say it is damned. *Burn it* is just another way of saying the same thing."

"So when I say dad burn it, that's the same as . . . Well, shut my mouth! Niver knowed them was cuss words."

"Now that you do, I need to know you won't use them. The boys deserve a good example, and Ma is a lady. I don't want my family hearing foul language."

"Cain't honestly say I'll niver again say it, but I shore will try not to. Is that good enough?"

Galen smiled. "I appreciate your candor. Aye, 'tis good enough. You don't work tomorrow or Sunday. We take the buckboard to town on Sundays for church. You're welcome to join us."

"Nah. Cain't see much need for gettin' churched so late in life. This old dog ain't gonna learn a new trick."

Galen didn't want to pressure him. Folks had a tendency to dig in their heels when someone else tried to strong-arm them into doing something. A nonchalant hitch of his shoulder felt like the best response to Ishmael's comment.

Ishmael shoved his hat far back on his head. "Onc't upon a time, I knowed a buck whose boss made him rise up early every Sunday morn jist to be shore he'd be at church. You ain't mullin' over makin' me sit on a hard bench and listenin' to a preacher-man rant and rave 'bout God, are you?"

Galen shook his head. "Whether you attend is your choice. The invitation's always there, Ishmael—for you and your family."

His farmhand merely shrugged.

"How's your head?"

"I got me a real hard head, Boss. You don't gotta worry none."

"You'll ask Ivy about helping Ma put up the pear butter?"

"Shorely will. But I'm a-tellin' you here and now, you cain count on her. Fact is, Sis ain't had a chance to swap howdies with a woman in a long while. She'd do jist about anything to spend time with yore ma."

———◆———

"What're you a-singin', little bird?" Ivy looked up at the songbird on the branch overhead. "Yore cheery as cain be. I reckon yore a-trying to sing for your supper. Well, I ain't sharin' none of this. Yore fatter than I am."

"Sis?"

"Uh-huh?" Ivy rubbed the back of her hand across her cheek to banish a vexacious itch. She turned and let out a yelp. "What happened to you?"

"A log I was a-choppin' decided to hit back."
Ishmael grinned. "Didn't knock any sense into
me, so you cain stop lettin' your hopes soar."

"That's gotta smart."

Ishmael gently touched the wound on his
forehead. "Ain't bad a-tall. And lookee here.
Ain't this a fine shirt I got on?"

"If it wasn't for that nasty scrape on yore
head, I'd say yore right handsome."

"The O'Sullivans gave me the shirt. It
belonged to Mr. O'Sullivan before he died."

" 'Less I seed a ghost today—" she frowned
as she shooed away the persistent little bird—
"Mr. O'Sullivan's still alive and kickin'."

"I meant his father. You saw Galen
O'Sullivan today? When?"

"Wasn't s'posed to know 'twas him. He
snuck through the trees and give us a poke full
of vittles." Ivy snapped the ear of corn in half
and slipped it into the kettle. "Gonna have us
some nice sweet roastin' ears tonight."

"Sounds toothsome."

"You shore yore head's alright? It looks
dreadful bad."

"Ain't nothing more'n a scrape. What's been
goin' on round here today?"

Ivy didn't want him worrying about her. Ishmael didn't need to know that Mr. Smith or
Jones or Johnston—or whatever name he made
up—made her hackles rise. She shoved her braid
back over her shoulder. "That feller and the man

what come earlier both showed up. Brung a heap of corn and four bags of sugar."

Ishmael's eyes went dark and the muscle in his jaw twitched. "I don't cotton to them comin' round when I'm not here. You give 'em wide berth."

"I got my knife, and I ain't afeared to use it. Put yore mind to rest." Ishmael knew her too well. If she didn't change the topic, he'd ferret out her fear. Ivy flashed him a smile. "You'll niver guess what was in the poke Mr. O'Sullivan brung."

"Roastin' ears sound mighty fine to me."

"Yup. Me, too. Pa done et most of the pears and apples I brung back, but we got more now. And a bag of rolled oats so's we'll have us some stick-to-yore-ribs breakfasts."

"Don't make any tomorrow or the next day."

Ivy gave him a disgruntled look. "Why not?"

"'Cause I'm here. All the days I work, I get a strappin' breakfast and lunch. On the morns when I'm at home, I cain do without. It'll make me feel better when I walk o'er to the farm, knowin' you'll have a warm belly full of oats."

Ivy playfully bumped into him. "You been workin' with horses too much. Yore makin' me sound like one!"

"Boss shorely has hisself some fine horse-flesh. Four are his own, and t'other three belong to the Pony Express."

She nodded. Ishmael never tired of telling

her about those horses. He'd never dared to admit it, but Ivy knew he wanted his own mount. What man didn't?

"It's downright gratifying, sis, watchin' them O'Sullivan young'uns ride off to school."

"Ishy, deep in yore heart, d'ya ever begrudge them even a little?"

Ishmael looked surprised, then tried to hide the wince that expression caused. "Down to my toes, I'm glad them boys got a sound future a-waitin' them."

She shook her head. "Sometimes I wonder that we're kin atall."

"Cain't get no closer'n bein' twin-born."

"But yore glad for them kids. Me? I cain't holp thinkin' t'ain't fair." She cast a look at the tent. "Ever'body else gots a roof o'er their head. I spent my first dozen years with a tin roof what leaked like a fishnet, and the last eight years with canvas that ain't no better. I ain't had a day of book-learnin' and niver e'en onc't sat on the back of a horse or mule or donkey. Most of the time, I'm so hungry my belly button's scrapin' my spinebone."

With each flaw she cited, the corners of his mouth tightened. Ishmael cleared his throat. "Thangs are gonna be better now."

She shook her head so adamantly her braid bounced from shoulder blade to shoulder blade. "No they ain't. Might be we're lucky a little while. But folks'll run us off and we'll trudge on.

Dreamin' on sommat that won't ever be jist stomps on my soul. I done a real stupid thang that day, a-talkin' with you 'bout how someday one of us would get hitched and have a house and all. Onliest thang that did was make my innards go spleenacious."

"Ain't nothin' awrong with lookin' to the future, sis. Things cain change."

"They won't. Onliest way we'll ever see a better life is for you to steal some rich girl's heart."

"That ain't so."

She poked at the ears of corn as they bobbed in the boiling water. "Is too. Pa tells more lies than truth, but he's right 'bout me. I'm ugly and stupid. Not a man in the world will give me a second look."

"The right buck jist hasn't happened to cross your path yet." He curled his fingers around her arm. "You got a sharp mind, sis. Book-learnin' ain't the onliest kind of smart. As for looks—if'n my face wasn't so catawomptuously chewed up at this here minute, I'd take offense. Folks say you an' me favor each another."

"Only because we're towheaded, blue-eyed, and rawboned."

Ishmael flashed her a grin. "The both of us got good, strong straight teeth."

"Yore back to makin' me sound like a horse again."

On Monday morning, Laney carefully tied a cocoa-colored velvet ribbon at the throat of her pin-tucked blouse, then stepped back from her looking glass. A frown sketched across her face as she surveyed her reflection.

"Elaine Louise McCain," Hilda bellowed from downstairs, "I'm leaving in five minutes. If you aren't outside by then, you're staying home!" Hilda had a habit of bossing everyone. She'd been with their family since Laney was a tiny child, and she'd scrubbed and scolded her way into Josh and Laney's hearts. When Daddy and Josh bought the Broken P and sent Laney away to school, Josh wrote how Hilda stormed about the place, seasoning the meals with her opinion. Even now, with Josh married and Laney all grown up, Hilda managed to assert herself.

"It's me," Ruth said as she tapped on the door and let herself in. "Aren't you ready?"

"No. I need help. I can't pull my stays tight enough." She tore off the ribbon and swiftly unbuttoned the shirtwaist. "You'll have to help me." With a speed she'd never achieved before, she unbuttoned her skirt, untied the tapes to her petticoats, and let them all wilt into a pile on the floor.

"They're fine."

"No they're not. I look like a crumpled

handkerchief. Please, Ruth, help me." Laney wound her arms around a bedpost.

Ruth untied the laces and started tugging them. "It's ridiculous for you to wear this so tight. It'll be hot and you'll end up swooning."

"I'm much—" Laney took a little gasp as the whalebones cinched tighter—"heartier . . . than . . . you think." She took another little breath and clung to the bedpost like a limpet. Ruth managed to yank the laces so violently, Laney bobbed back and forth with each move. "I've never . . . swooned."

"There's a first time for everything." Ruth pulled again.

Laney drew in a pitiful little breath. "This won't be it."

"Make sure of it." Ruth stopped tugging and started tying.

Hilda's muttering and trundling footsteps warned she was coming.

"Hurry!" Laney grabbed her shirtwaist and shoved one arm into a sleeve.

"Here!" Ruth pushed her to stand in the center of the petticoats and skirt. Yards upon yards of fine cotton, cotton flannel, and wool engulfed Laney.

Hilda's mutterings grew louder, and Ruth hissed, "We don't have time."

"Just tie all of them together!" Laney desperately fought with a stubborn button.

"Easier said than done," Ruth grumbled.

"Your skirt is dragging the petticoats back down." The woolen petticoat slid back down to the floor with her skirt. "You'll just have to make do." Ruth pulled the waist tapes and knotted them.

"Elaine Lou—" the bedroom door swung open—"eeese." Hilda's stormy expression suddenly changed. "I shoulda known. It's going to be too hot to wear that third petticoat—and wool, at that! That fancy finishing school's idea of what's proper doesn't work out here."

Hilda crossed the room and nudged Ruth out of the way. "While you're half dressed, we may as well cinch you in a little more."

Chapter Eleven

Laney refused to look at Ruth. If she did, she'd burst into laughter.

"Awww, girl." Hilda looked at the incredibly huge knot Ruth had tied to hold up the petticoats, then patted Laney's cheek. "You're nervous about seeing Galen. Well, don't you fret. Hilda's going to help you."

"Thank you," Laney said at the same time Ruth said in a disbelieving voice, "You are?"

"You bet." Hilda wrestled with the knot when suddenly it came free and the petticoats all tumbled into a pool about Laney's feet again.

"Hilda," Ruth began in a wary tone, "what did you mean about helping Laney?"

"Ruth, you're so head-over-heels in love with Josh, you can't see the forest for the trees. I've known for some time that Laney's been sweet on Galen. Other folks are pairing them up, too—like Ethel at the diner. Even if the woman can't cook a lick, she still realizes what a fine couple Laney and Galen will be."

"Galen's in mourning," Ruth pointed out. "So is Laney."

"Did I say they had to buy a ring and run down the aisle tomorrow? No, I didn't." The housekeeper picked a tiny speck of lint off Laney's chemise. "But I know the look a man gets in his eye when he's decided it's time to marry up."

Panic surged through Laney. She rasped, "Galen?"

"Mm-hmm. Galen minded himself during church, but before and after the service yesterday, that man surveyed the young women."

"Hilda!" Ruth protested.

The housekeeper's face puckered. "You can go ahead and think since I'm an old maid I don't know a thing about love, but you'd be wrong.

Those of us on the outside watch how attraction sparks between everyone else. Seen it a hundred times over. Those who fall in love don't see anyone else—and that's how you are now, Ruth. You're too besotted with Josh to have noticed. Well, I spotted the way Galen studied all the unmarried gals, and I knew then and there that Laney's time has come."

"Oh, that." Ruth made a dismissive gesture. "Galen was returning the dishes to folks who took over food for the family."

"Everyone provided meals immediately after Cullen's death, but it's been two months now." Laney tried to fasten her last button, but her hands shook. "All of those dishes were ones he's received recently, and every last one came from a girl who'd swoon to have him court her."

Ruth gave Laney's stays a telling look. "Swoon?"

Hilda towed Laney to the bed. "Hold fast. I'm going to shave off at least another inch and a half."

"She'll swoon," Ruth warned.

"And what's so bad about that?" Hilda arched a brow. "A strapping buck like Galen likes to feel manly and show off his strength. Laney, just be sure to sway a little and fade toward the floor. Don't keel over like a dying cow."

Laney wound her arms around the bedpost

again. "They taught us that at Lady Gene-vieve's."

"Well, well." Hilda grinned. "Maybe all that money wasn't such a waste after all."

"Hilda, it's a mistake for us to play match-maker." Ruth separated the petticoats and folded the wool one. "These things have to develop on their own."

"A helpful nudge never did any harm."

"I'm just saying there's no reason to rush things. Mrs. Landon—or was it Mrs. Penley?—well, whoever it was taught me that a woman never pursues a man. Men like to be in control."

"Men like to believe they're in control," Hilda countered. "We women just let them think they are."

Ruth tugged on Laney's wrist, jarring her from her the bedpost. "Laney, I don't want you to be hurt, and that's what's bound to happen. Galen's never once hinted that he has tender feelings for you."

"And that's why we're going to open his eyes," Hilda inserted.

Laney nodded, but Ruth held her wrist so tightly her fingers were starting to go numb.

"I want the man you marry to love you for who you are," Ruth said. "If all it takes to attract him is a tiny waist, then he's not worthy of you. It's not what style you're wearing on the outside; it's who God made you on the inside that matters."

"I know that." Laney patted Ruth's hand. "Galen is honorable."

Ruth's hold loosened and her features no longer looked strained.

"Hilda and I talked it over. We're convinced Galen hasn't realized that I'm more than Josh's little sister. Once he understands that I've grown up, he'll allow himself to fall in love with me." Laney turned back to the bedpost and clung for dear life as her mind whirled.

Hilda yanked harder on the laces. "Galen's a man in need of help. From the sounds of it, that new farmhand's sister is something else. We can't let her sashay in and steal Galen away."

"I'm afraid . . . she already . . . might have." Laney let go of the bed and turned. The room tilted wildly, then leveled out.

"Here, now. Just two petticoats. Can't very well have you sweating like a pig before Galen scoops you into his arms."

———•———

Galen glanced up as a buckboard approached, then cringed as a terrible sound rent the air.

"Mrs. O'Sullivan!" Laney called out, scrambling to her feet.

"Nothing's wrong," Josh assured the group as he strode over to the wagon. "Ivy's singing."

"Saints preserve us," Hilda exclaimed as Galen helped her down. "Sounds like a cat with turpentine under his tail."

Galen fought the urge to agree. Ever since Ivy and Ishmael had arrived at dawn, Ivy had hummed the same set of notes over and over again. Galen thought she was warming up by doing her scales. If so, the scales went to an ear-splitting sharp and traded keys halfway up and halfway back down.

"Old man Tucker was a fine old man," Ivy now sang at an impressive volume.

"I thought it was old *Dan* Tucker," Ruth said.

"It is—or is supposed to be." Galen helped her down.

"Washed his feet in a fryin' pan," Ivy continued on.

"Face," Laney told Ruth. "It's not feet, it's face."

"That's gotta be Eddie Lufe's kin in there, slaughtering that song." Hilda grimaced as she grabbed a big wicker basket.

"Ishmael's twin sister." Galen had hoped in vain that Ishmael would come over and help Laney down from the buckboard but realized he would appear rude if he didn't assist her now. As he cupped his hands around her waist, Galen frowned.

"Is something wrong?" Laney leaned close, and the fragrance she wore wafted over him. Fresh. Lemony.

Galen inhaled again and noted that his fingers met in the back. Slowly, he lifted her. *I've always thought you were a half-pint, but you're not. You're tiny, but . . . but you're all woman.* Slower still, he set her down and shook his head to clear his thoughts.

Laney looked up at him with big brown eyes. "Nothing's wrong?"

"No." He smiled at her. "Don't go in quite yet."

Laney moistened her lips.

He'd asked her to stay here, but now Galen realized he didn't have a reason. Other than staring at her. A man could get lost in her velvety eyes . . . unless he caught sight of her sweet mouth. *Why is everything about Laney McCain suddenly fresh . . . different . . . womanly?* Galen grasped at straws. "I haven't congratulated you yet. I heard your grape jelly won second place at the fair."

Her lips bowed upward. "Thank you. It was the grape jelly I learned to make here. Your mother deserves some of the credit."

"Ma took ribbons for things that you helped her with."

"She deserved them. So do you. It takes the finest quality of produce to make superior preserves. The O'Sullivan farm is flourishing under your care."

He acknowledged her praise with a nod. Ivy started slaughtering another song, and it suddenly struck him that dainty little Laney was completely unprepared for Ishmael's twin.

"Laney, it feels awkward, but I'm asking you to be kind to Ivy." When he saw how his words carried an unintended meaning, he tried to soften the gruff order. "I want her to feel welcomed."

Hurt flashed across Laney's face for the second time in as many seconds, but she gave him a wobbly smile. "I'm sure she's a very nice young lady."

"She's different." Galen spied Ishmael out of the corner of his eye and lowered his voice. "I can't explain it now. It's ... well ... complicated."

Ishmael reached them, chuckling. "Good thang my sis is purdy 'cuz she shore cain't sang."

"Good morning, Mr. Grubb." Laney dipped her head politely. "I'm positive Miss Grubb has several other accomplishments."

"Yup." Ishmael smacked his hand against one of the sugar sacks in the buckboard. "That last name of ourn suits her. Sis wrestles up the best vittles you'll ever et. No offense to that mama of yourn, Boss. She's got a way with food, too."

"Laney," Ruth called over from the porch. "The men will bring in the supplies. Let's go meet our new friend."

"I'll bring in the spices." Laney went up on tiptoe and claimed a basket.

Laney's never afraid to pitch in and help. He watched as she walked away, her skirts swaying gently from side to side. Galen forced himself to turn away from that feminine sight and hefted a fifty-pound bag of sugar. "Grab a couple of bags, Ishmael. We've got a full day ahead of us. If I have my way, we'll time it so we can come home for lunch."

Galen followed Laney into the house. Though Laney had a kind heart and polished manners, Galen worried Ivy would shock her.

Ivy was sitting on a bench with her back to the table. Her legs were spraddled wide beneath her skirt and peeled pears bobbed in the huge washtub between her bare feet. She finished peeling the pear she held, then stood as she wiped her hands on the apron Ma had loaned her.

Ma called from over by the stove, "Ivy, these are our neighbors from the Broken P Ranch: Hilda, Ruth, and Laney."

"Ma'am," Ivy said to Hilda, "yore daughters're both purdy as yearlings."

Hilda shook her head. "I'm the housekeeper, Miss Grubb."

"Oh, blast and bother!"

Galen tensed. He'd rebuked Ishmael for saying *blast*. Now Ivy used that same crude word in the presence of four ladies.

Ivy prattled on, "You don't gotta get all

fancy-like with me, Hilda. Yore their servant, not
mine. I'm plain old Ivy."

"Housekeeper is Hilda's official title, but
she's like family to us," Laney said.

"I agree with Ivy," Ruth declared. "We're all
neighbors. We ladies ought to dispense with the
formalities."

"That suits me more'n fine. Which one of
you is which?"

"Ruth recently married my brother," Laney
explained as her hand barely grazed Ruth's
sleeve, "so she and I are sisters-in-law."

"So yore Laney. It's good to clap eyes on
you." Ivy stuck out her right hand.

Galen held his breath for a split second, but
Laney smoothly moved forward and shook
hands. He suspected she'd never shaken hands
with anyone. Ladies didn't, but Laney graciously
chucked the fancy finishing school manners.

"Your brother has spoken well of you."
Laney's smile didn't fade in the least, even
though Ivy's fingers had to be sticky with pear
juice and her handshake would have done a
horse trader proud.

"Mmm. You must got on some purr-fume.
You smell better'n possum pie."

"Thank you."

Ruth stepped up to shake hands, too.

Galen set down the sugar sack. He'd worried
in vain; Laney was acting as sweet as could be,
even though Ivy's greetings would make any

other woman's hair stand on end.

"Whar d'ya want me to put these?" Ishmael looked over the jelly jars at Ma.

"In the corner, please."

Galen headed back out for more supplies. The ladies from the Broken P had come with a staggering supply of jars and sugar. They'd done the same thing throughout the summer, helping Ma make jellies and jams and put up vegetables.

Galen struggled with the whole situation. Josh always refused to accept any of the money for what Galen sold to the mercantile in town. Josh pointed out that his family got all the fruits, vegetables, and nuts they needed from the O'Sullivans.

Josh also said the jars, sugar, and spices the Broken P sent over were paltry pay for the cooking lessons Ma gave Laney and Ruth. Finishing schools had taught them social graces but left them wholly ignorant about how to get a decent meal on the table. If that weren't enough, Josh claimed perhaps the most important result of the Broken P women coming to help was that the time Hilda spent with Ma seemed to improve his housekeeper's grumpy disposition.

Galen wasn't fooled. Josh knew money was tight and made up all those excuses. Galen's pride rebelled at that.

"Onliest time I ever seed this many jars in one place, 'twas in that store in town," Ishmael commented as he hefted another load from the wagon.

Galen nodded and grunted as he grabbed another bag of sugar. Back in the house, Laney and Ruth now bracketed Ivy. All three were peeling pears.

"Son, I'm wanting more pears."

"I'll be happy to fetch them, Ma, but you'll have to give me a few minutes. When I brought in the pears, I set a bushel or two of apples in front of the rest."

"Apples!" Hilda spun around.

Laney's eyes sparkled. Their eyes met, and she cast a meaningful glance at Hilda. "Remember last year, Galen?" Laney's smile took on an impish tilt. "Your mother and Hilda made a wonderful batch of apple-pear butter."

He rubbed his jaw and pretended to ponder a moment. "Now that you mention it, yes, I do remember."

"I haven't had any since I've come here." Ruth feigned great concentration in choosing the next pear to peel. "Why is that?"

"How do you expect a body to recall?" Hilda bristled. "That was almost a year ago."

"Trifling details like that don't matter." Ma stirred a pot on the stove. "Galen-mine, when you bring in the pears, you might as well bring in some apples, too."

"Sure, Ma."

Laney compressed her lips to try to keep

from laughing. She made a tiny sound and turned it into a fairly convincing-sounding cough.

Ivy smacked Laney on the back. "You okay?"

Laney practically doubled over from the blow.

"Laney!" Galen stepped close and knelt beside her. He couldn't fathom what possessed Ivy to be so rough. "Are you all right?"

Laney managed to straighten up. Eyes huge, she nodded.

"Knowed that'd work. A good wallop stops a body from choking."

"I . . . appreciate . . . your concern," Laney said faintly.

Ivy looked as pleased as could be. "No need to give me yore fancy thankees. You woulda done the same for me."

Galen rose and kept watch over Laney. Gradually, the color came back into her cheeks. Her voice almost sounded normal when she said, "I'm so glad you just happened to mention the apples, Galen."

"If'n you chop up apples real fine, you cain dry 'em right quick. Then, when you make oatmeal, toss some of the apple in with cinnamon if'n you got any. Makes your mouth wanna sing 'Holly Knew Ya.'"

"Oh, I love that song." Laney carefully slid

her peeled pear into the washtub so it wouldn't splash.

"Mayhap you cain teach it to me." Ivy dropped her pear in and splashed them all. "I only heared it onc't, but it sounded real grand. Cain you tell me who that Holly gal was?"

"It's not a girl's name, Ivy." Ma left the stove. "It's *hallelujah*. It's a special word Christians use to praise God."

"Oh. I reckon I jist made a fool of myself."

"Not at all," Laney jumped in, not hesitating a single second. "Last Christmas we sang that chorus at church. Would you like to come this Christmas?"

Galen felt a surge of pride. After the way Ivy was acting, a petty woman could have demeaned her or been chillingly polite. Laney showered Ivy with her kindness and took the very first opportunity to extend a warm invitation to worship.

Ishmael shifted uncomfortably. "We ain't the Sunday-go-to-meetin' type."

"The invitation's always open." Galen caught himself just before he gave Ishmael a solid thump on the back. Ivy might see his example and think it was okay to hit Laney or someone else again. Instead, he gave Ishmael's shoulder a good-natured jostle. "Come on."

"There's a song that has holly and ivy in it," Galen heard Laney say as he stepped out onto the porch.

"Oh, I know that 'un!" Ivy started right in, "The holly and the ivy, when they are both full growed—"

At least she has the lyrics right even if she's tone deaf.

"Of all the bears that are in the woods," Ivy warbled, "the holly scares 'em off."

"Boss, don't worry none. Sis'll keep a close eye out for that little McCain gal. She looks sorta weakly."

"Actually, Ishmael, I'm discovering Laney has a lot of hidden strengths."

CHAPTER TWELVE

I s there enough room for me?"

Laney's heart raced as she looked over her shoulder at Galen. She couldn't tell whether he'd asked her or Ivy.

"Shore." Ivy scooted away from Laney.

Galen sat between them on the porch step and balanced his plate across his thighs. "Looks like you ladies are getting a lot done."

Never before had Galen taken a place beside

her. In fact, Laney had noticed he usually waited until she'd been seated before he'd take a place as far from her as he could. His nearness left her breathless. *It's him. It's not my stays. If it were my stays being too tight, I would have been dizzy all morning long. I'll wear them this tight every day for the rest of my life if that's what it takes to be by Galen's side.*

"Good thang we chopped down that second tree." Ishmael straddled the porch rail as if he were riding a horse. "These gals are liable to burn every last twig in yore fancy cookstove by the day's end."

Galen lifted a slice of bread laden with pear butter. "I'm thinking I'd gladly chop a tree a day if this is the result."

"The aroma of cooking pears is wonderful." Laney pinched the ends of a beef rib and lifted it from her plate.

"Onliest thang that smells half as good is that purr-fume Laney's got on herself."

Galen turned to Laney. "I'm partial to it."

Laney smiled at him, but confusion assailed her. *Is he agreeing that the pear butter smells good, or is he complimenting my lemon verbena?*

"Just you wait till this next batch." Hilda said as she plunked into a chair next to Mrs. O'Sullivan. "Apples will smell heavenly."

Miss Genevieve would have kittens over seeing me eat with my fingers. Laney smiled to herself and took a bite. Miss Genevieve probably never had the joy of sitting on porch steps and eating a rib. The taste more than made up for the mess, and being beside Galen certainly rated as sufficient reason for casting away most of the trifling rules of propriety.

Conversation flowed along. Between nervous hope and being laced in so tightly, Laney didn't have much of an appetite. She'd barely managed to nibble one side of her rib.

"Hold still," Galen said as he pulled a fresh bandanna from his pocket.

Laney flushed, realizing his intention. *He's never going to see me as being mature when I wind up with food on my face.*

He wiped her left cheek. "There. How much am *I* wearing?"

"On yore shirt, yore hands, or yore face?" Ivy asked.

Ishmael chuckled. "What does it matter, Boss? You still got another rib to et. You'll wind up with more on you, so no use a-wipin' up the mess twice."

"Yup." Ivy bit into her rib and shook her head side-to-side to worry off the last morsel.

Galen frowned at Laney's plate. "Aren't you hungry?"

"After tasting pear butter all morning? I couldn't eat another bite."

"She only et one side of her rib."

Heat filled Laney's cheeks at Ishmael's

observation. "Ruth, it tasted wonderful. You seasoned them perfectly."

"Shore did," Ivy agreed. "No use letting good food go to waste."

"You're right." Galen took the last rib from his own plate, put it on Ivy's, then snatched Laney's leftover.

"Mr. O'Sullivan, yore workin' hard out thar." Longing crept into Ivy's voice. "You oughtta have the big 'un."

"Nope." Galen lifted the other half of Laney's rib to his mouth. "This one suits me just fine."

As soon as they finished eating, everyone went back to work. Hilda gave Laney a smug smile. *It's not just my imagination? Is Galen really noticing me?*

The afternoon flew by. Galen's brothers came home from school, did the chores their mother assigned them, then sat out on the porch to read or do schoolwork.

"Ma," Colin called to her, "When's supper?"

"Soon, soon." Mrs. O'Sullivan continued to stir the huge pot on the stove. "Hilda, can you pull the roast out of the oven? I don't want this last batch of pear butter to burn."

"Wait just a minute." Laney tore a generous chunk of bread off a loaf. Hilda had brought enough dough for four loaves, and Mrs. O'Sullivan already had six rising when they arrived. Since the stove was lit, it only made sense to bake at the same time. All day long, they'd baked bread. "Here, Ivy. Go taste this batch."

Ivy didn't demure. She grabbed the bread and scrambled over to Mrs. O'Sullivan's side.

Mrs. O'Sullivan spooned pear butter onto the bread. "I'm wondering if we have enough cinnamon in this. What do you think?"

Ivy didn't wait for it to cool. She blew on the food, then popped it into her mouth. "Ohhh." Mouth full, she chuffed in a few breaths, then started chewing and talking at the same time. "This here's the best batch yet. Didn't thank it could get any better'n the first pot this morn, but saddle me and call me a donkey if'n every batch don't get better'n the one afore it."

Hilda waved the potholders in her hands at Ivy. "The roast is going to burn if you don't move."

"Cain't let that happen!" Ivy got out of the way.

Ruth motioned to Ivy. "Come with me to the springhouse. I'm not sure what Toledo, our farmhand, brought over in those buckets, but he seemed anxious for Hilda to have it," she said with a smile as they stepped out the door.

Hilda opened the oven, and the mouthwatering aroma of meat overcame the sticky sweetness of pears and apples. "Here's a spot, Hilda." Laney snatched a few jars from the corner of the table, and her housekeeper set the roasting pan down with a resounding thump.

"Laney," Mrs. O'Sullivan said, "I'm thinking the way you declared Ivy to be the official tester was clever."

"We had to do something. The day we returned from the fair, Galen said the Grubbs were half starved. I thought he might have been exaggerating." She paused, then added, "But he wasn't."

"Nay, he wasn't."

"What can we do to help?"

"'Twas my hope that you'd ask. I wouldn't hurt your feelings for the world, so I'll say it straight out. Some days, I'll ask Ivy to come work. It lets us send food back to her family and allows the Grubbs to keep their pride. Don't be gettin' upset that I don't want you gardening with me for awhile."

Though saddened, Laney nodded. She loved being with Galen's mother. *But that doesn't compare to Ivy's need.*

"We should still get together." Hilda yanked her apron bib to center it once again. "What about sewing?"

"Sure and enough, we can do that." Mrs. O'Sullivan banged her wooden spoon against the rim of the pot. "Why not later this week?"

"That would be wonderful. Thank you." Laney gazed at the stack of green sacks. As things turned out, these sugar sacks didn't match the other sacks for the quilt Ruth had hoped to make, but Laney decided they'd make lovely cushions for the window seat in her bedroom. *It'll allow Galen to see how I can tend to housekeeping matters. I might not know everything about running a kitchen, but I'm more than able to sew.*

Ruth and Ivy returned. Ruth seemed utterly fascinated by the contents of the bucket she held.

"Set that aside," Mrs. O'Sullivan said. "This last batch is ready."

Jar after jar went over to the stove. Fragrant brown goo filled them, then Ruth and Hilda set them on the table. Laney ran a knife around the inside edges to banish any air pockets, and Ivy put on the lids.

"Ma?" Dale called from the porch, "Do we get to lick the pot now?"

"Son, you'll have a bellyache if you do."

Galen's chuckle filtered into the cabin from the porch. "I'm thinkin' they won't, Ma."

"I know they won't," Ishmael added in a playful tone.

Ivy asked no one in particular, "When did the bucks come back?"

"Ishmael and I worked up an appetite," Galen declared from the porch. "These boys out here would have to fight us for a taste."

"You're not too old for me to paddle you for teasing your brothers, Galen Cedric O'Sullivan!"

Laney and Ruth looked at each other and

silently mouthed, "Cedric?"

Galen filled the doorway. "It's a good thing I'm a forgiving man."

"The smell of good food always tames the beast," Hilda said in a wry tone.

Ishmael shouldered his way past his boss. "Ready, sis?"

"For what?" Ruth set the last jar down on the table.

"To go." Ivy pointed at the jar. "Soon as that'un's got a lid, I'm ready."

Ishmael and Ivy—especially Ivy—need to stay and eat, Laney thought. *But Galen's starting to notice me a little, and he's been interested in Ivy.*

"Go?" Ruth said in disbelief. "You can't go now. It's suppertime."

Ivy shrugged. "Pa had to rustle up his own lunch. I gotta go."

Hot pear butter slid down the knife and hit between Laney's thumb and forefinger. Twisting her hand so the knife pointed downward, she thought, *It serves me right for being selfish.* "Supper's almost ready. What if—"

"This is nonsense." Mrs. O'Sullivan waved her hand as if she were trying to shoo away a pesky fly. "We'll make a plate for Mr. Grubb and send it with you."

"That's right neighborly of you." Ishmael hooked his thumbs into the waist of his britches. "Much obliged, ma'am."

Laney ran the knife around the jar. A big air

bubble surfaced and popped, and the level in the jar dropped. *Just like my hopes and dreams for Galen and me?*

"Good thang you got that ugly old pocket of air outta thar. 'Twould have spoilt the whole jar if'n you hadn't." Ivy sealed the lid.

I don't know what to think, Lord. You promise to grant the desires of our hearts if we walk uprightly. But I've been claiming that promise and now I'm jealous and selfish. I don't know what to do.

"Since you're done with that . . ." Galen robbed Laney of the knife and grinned as he licked the pear butter from it.

A short trill of laughter bubbled out of her.

"Simple pleasures are what make life worth living." He took another long lick, then sighed. "A spoon would have had more on it."

Ruth lifted the bucket of meat and carried it over to Galen's mother. "Ivy recommended we bring these back."

Mrs. O'Sullivan peeked in the bucket. "Ah, yes. The tongue."

Laney shuddered. "Tongue?"

"Aye." Mrs. O'Sullivan pushed the tongue to the side and lifted another huge, thick, hideous-looking thing from the bucket.

A funny buzzing sound filled Laney's ears.

"This here," Mrs. O'Sullivan said as she held the big maroon thing that dripped blood, "is liver."

The cabin started to tilt.

"Laney!" Hilda squawked.

A dark haze spun wildly about Laney, and she felt strong arms catch her.

Chapter Thirteen

Mr. O'Sullivan managed to catch Laney before she hit the floor. She draped over his arms like a soggy dishrag. "Want me to put her on your bed, Ma?"

"And where else would you be putting her?"

Hilda pumped water onto a clean dish towel. "Here."

While he stretched Laney out on the bed and patted her cheek, his ma wiped her own hands on the towel and came over. "Out with you boys. Don't go too far. Supper's in a few minutes."

Once the door shut, Hilda took over another wet cloth. Mrs. O'Sullivan pushed it away. "That won't make a spit of difference. I've been marveling all day she hasn't done this—she's laced far too tight."

Ivy stood back while they loosened Laney's beautiful clothes. She wasn't just wearing a pretty skirt; she had not one, but two under-skirts, as well. "She must be a-swelterin' in all them layers."

"She normally wears three." Ruth imparted that scrap of information in a distracted tone. "Is she—"

"She'll come around in a minute." Mrs. O'Sullivan yanked on laces. "Once she can breathe. It's pure nonsense, a lass cinching her-self in like this. I aim to scold her if you don't, Hilda."

Hilda shook her head. "She has tender feel-ings."

Something akin to the sound of a day-old kitten's mewling came from Laney as her eyelids fluttered. "She's comin' round."

"Oh," Laney whispered as her eyes opened. "What—"

"You swooned, Laney Lou." Hilda fussed over her like a hen over her first brood. "Just lie still a minute."

"It's no wonder you did." Mrs. O'Sullivan managed to sound firm, yet caring. Ivy won-dered how she did that. "Your stays were far too tight. There's a difference between being prop-erly clothed and being vain. You know better than this."

"Sorry," Laney said in a whispery tone.

"She's never fainted before." Ruth waved a

piece of paper over Laney's head as if it were a fan.

Ivy stood on tiptoe and stared at the garment Mrs. O'Sullivan had loosened. It didn't seem possible that something that silly would make anyone keel over. "Mayhap she needs her blood built up. Liver's good for that. I could slice that 'un along with a mess of onions and fry it up right quick."

"She doesn't like liver," Hilda fretted.

"Elaine Louise McCain—"

Uh-oh. Mrs. O'Sullivan don't call someone by a whole string o' names 'less she's fixin' to bring 'em up short.

"You'll eat liver tonight." Mrs. O'Sullivan fiddled with the strings coming from the back of Laney's rich-lady clothes. "A generous serving of it."

"I'll start on it," Ivy volunteered. She didn't wait but went straight to work. *Cain't imagine what'd be like havin' folks make a big fuss over me. Ain't niver seen such a to-do over nuthin'. Don't make sense that a body wants to bind up so's they look like they're starvin'.*

At supper Laney obediently took a serving of liver. Ivy couldn't tell whether she'd finally gotten some color in her cheeks because she wasn't strangled anymore or if she was embarrassed. Ruth sat on one side of her, and Mr. O'Sullivan made sure to sit on the other side—

like it was going to take both of them to keep her upright.

"Ivy, we'll make up a plate for you to take home to your father. Would he rather have liver or roast?" Mrs. O'Sullivan asked.

"Liver, ma'am," Ivy lied. She didn't dare look at Ishmael. He was gone most days and didn't know how mean-drunk Pa was nearly all the time. With the still fired up and going, Pa managed to wet his whistle liberally. Ivy didn't want Ishy to know how bad things were. He already fretted about the "partners" who came to fetch the who-hit-John whilst he was away at the farm. He couldn't do anything about it, so she made a point of pretending everything was fine.

"Liver?" Mrs. O'Sullivan sounded vaguely surprised.

Ivy nodded emphatically. "Liver." Remembering what her brother had said earlier, she tacked on, "Much obliged."

"You've been a tremendous help today. We wouldn't have gotten this much done without you." Mrs. O'Sullivan patted her arm. That little action made Ivy's heart skip a beat.

"You gals shore got a bunch of work done," Ishmael said with a smile. "I thunk 'twas crazy to be totin' in that many jars this morn, but hooo-ooo-ie, you done went and filled every last one of 'em."

"Did you go through all of the sugar, too?"

Galen craned his neck and gaped at the neatly folded sugar sacks over by the windowsill.

"Twenty-five pounds of sugar in each batch, Plowboy," Hilda said. "Now pass me the corn."

"O'Sullivan corn is the sweetest-tasting I've ever had," Laney said.

"Not from the looks of yore plate." Ivy stared at the single skimpy spoonful of each item Laney had taken. "Hilda done tole us you don't like liver. If'n yore tryin' to fool us by nibblin' itty-bitty forkfuls so's all you had to take was three measly bites of liver, 'tain't a-gonna work."

"I'm afraid I've made a mess of things."

"No you didn't." Josh pointed his chin toward the other side of Laney's plate. "Please pass the butter."

Ivy seriously doubted Laney'd ever gotten messy. Why, at lunch, she'd had the tiniest speck of sauce on one cheek when everyone else had big smears across their face. Even after a whole day of working in the kitchen, Laney's apron looked just-washed fresh. At least Ruth had stuff slopped all over the front of hers.

"Miz Ruth," Ishmael said, "you'll be able to start workin' on that quilt you were talkin' 'bout now that you gals emptied out all them sugar sacks."

Ruth spread pear butter on a slice of bread. "Laney feels this green won't work—she has such a good eye for color." A few crumbs fell from Ruth's bread and sprinkled the bib of her apron. She set down the bread and impatiently flicked off the crumbs. "I've changed my mind about the pattern again, though. After looking at all of those quilts at the fair, I decided not to do any appliqué on this one. I'm starting to lean toward the flying geese pattern."

Laney set down her cup so gently the coffee in it didn't even slosh. "I think the quilt would be very handsome if you simply changed the green to browns. Galen, didn't your mother make you one last year?"

He nodded. "You've a good memory, lass."

"She sure does." Ruth took another bite of the bread.

Ivy watched crumbs tumble onto Ruth's apron bib again. *If'n I didn't know better, I'd reckon she ain't one of them rich gals. She spills and flubs pert near as much as me.*

Mr. O'Sullivan took stock of his plate. All the food had gone around once, but he'd managed to wolf down a lot in a few minutes. "Please pass the meat."

"Liver or roast?" his ma asked.

He grinned. "Both. I have to make up for what Laney doesn't eat."

Laney tilted her head to the side like a little bird choosing the tune she wanted to sing. "All of this talk about sewing makes me want to do more. Could we visit Friday to sew together?"

"Ma," one of the littler boys piped up, "your pink dress is on the scarecrow. With all the green sacks, there's gotta be enough to make a new one. All your dresses are ugly black ones now. Are you gonna make a pretty dress for yourself, then?"

Mrs. O'Sullivan's eyes welled up with tears, and she shook her head.

Laney turned to Ivy. "Ruth and I just made new dresses for ourselves. Would you like the sugar sacks?"

"Yeah, sis. You'd look fine in green."

Scarcely able to breathe lest she say anything to make them snatch back their offer, Ivy gulped. *Here I was thankin' Laney's a spoilt brat with her fancy manners and rich-lady clothes. And she up and give me purdy green material so's I cain have me a real dress!* Ivy ignored most of the conversation bouncing around her. *This gotta be the bestest day of my life. I et near to busting my seams, and I'm a-gonna get me a new dress!*

"Sis, we'd best get home."

Ivy popped to her feet.

"You worked hard today, Ivy," Mrs. O'Sullivan said, waving at all they'd put up. "Take a dozen jars back with you."

"Thankee, ma'am. If'n 'tis all the same to you, cain I tote six home tonight and take t'other after we sew on Friday?"

On the way home, Ishmael held the jars like a litter of kittens in his arms. They clanked and jangled. "Have a care, Ishy. Don't want none of 'em to break!"

"Why'd you only take half tonight?"

" 'Cuz Pa's gonna splavocate 'bout me goin' back on Friday. I cain't come home empty-handed, and if'n what I bring back is a new dress, I'll be switched."

"All that food on the plate thar'll help convince him that you goin' to the O'Sullivans' is all right."

Ivy nodded, but she doubted it. Suddenly, she wished she'd told the truth and had roast to give Pa instead of liver.

***

Galen approached the McCain stable, the rising sun warming his shoulders. "What's wrong?" Josh called out as he hurried toward him.

"Nothing. Nothing a-tall." Galen dismounted.

Brows furrowed, Josh asked, "What would pry you off your land in the middle of your morning chores?"

"Not what. Who." Galen rested his hands on his hips. "Laney."

"Aww, Galen." Josh heaved a loud sigh. "I'm sorry. I'll ask Ruth to—"

"Nay, Josh. I've been a fool." He paused, then said, "I opened my eyes and realized our wee little Laney blossomed into a lovely young lady."

Josh dusted his hands off on the sides of his

britches. "She has. I'm not even sure when or how it happened."

"I'm counting my blessings that another man hasn't swept her up. I realize this may surprise you, but I'm asking your permission to court your sister."

Instead of readily agreeing, Josh chewed on his lower lip.

Galen's mouth went dry. *All this time, I thought he was doing me a favor by discouraging his sister. Could it be he doesn't think a poor farmer is good enough for Laney?*

CHAPTER FOURTEEN

Listen up, Galen." Josh folded his arms across his chest and stared at him. "I don't want you to pay attention to Laney if it's just going to be a fleeting fancy. I know the reason behind a courtship is to see if the gal and guy suit one another, but Laney's already wearing her heart on her sleeve for you. If you're not dead certain you're planning to marry her, don't mess with her now."

"I didn't think it wise to ride over here and ask to court her and also seek your blessing on our marriage all in the same day. But 'tis the truth, I'm aiming to marry the lass." He nodded once to emphasize his point. "I love her."

"This is quite a change of mind."

Galen shook his head. "Nay, Josh. To say 'tis a change of mind would mean that my affections could change with the wind. 'Tis a change of heart—and once my heart accepted the truth, there's no going back. I've always considered Laney to be a child. In the midst of all life's brought in these last months, she's shown maturity and strength. Instead of wanting to avoid her, I've longed to seek her company. She's the woman for me, Josh."

"You're sure?"

"Knowing Laney's felt fond of me all this time—well, 'tis clear where her heart lies. Once I came to my senses, I saw what a wondrously fine young lady she is."

Josh crooked a brow. "My sister was trained to be a fine lady. But even with your mother teaching Laney, I'm sure she has a lot to learn."

"Even so, she's not afraid to work hard. But before you think I'd wed her to have help about the farm, you should know 'tisn't the labor of her hands I've considered. A more loving woman I'll never meet. We'd make each other happy, and God willing, we'll grow old together."

A sly smile spread across Josh's face. "If all

you wanted was help around the place, you could always ask Ivy Grubb."

"I'm wanting Laney to be my bride. She and Ma are more than welcome to have Ivy over to help out around the house and garden."

"I'll talk to Laney," Josh said.

Galen looked his best friend in the eyes. "Don't. Don't breathe a word of this to anyone. I'd rather Laney see the change in my heart. That's the kind of wooing that will convince her of my sincerity."

"I won't tell Laney, but I don't keep secrets from my wife."

"Fair enough. But just as I've gotten your word that you won't say anything, I assume Ruth will hold this in confidence, as well." When Josh nodded his agreement, Galen dared to be bolder still. "I'm not feeling patient in the least. Seein' as you've already established I have honorable intentions, come Christmas, I'll be asking Laney to marry me."

"You're supposed to ask for her hand, not to tell me you're claiming it."

"Joshua McCain, I love your sister from the top of her pretty head clear down to the hem of her dress. My plan is to sweep her off her feet. I'm trusting the Lord to make her mine, but I'd surely appreciate it if you'd stop hanging on to that sweet little left hand of hers." Galen grinned. "I'll even wait till Christmas Day so you can get used to the idea."

"Was that Galen I saw talking to Josh?" Hilda asked Toledo as she reached for the milk pail.

Laney stopped refilling the sugar bowl. "Galen's here? Now?"

Toledo stayed on the veranda by the kitchen door and nodded.

"Does it ever occur to you to talk?" Exasperation tinted the housekeeper's voice. "Compared to you, a hermit is downright chatty."

Ruth smiled but didn't say anything.

Two loaves of zucchini bread sat in the center of the kitchen table. They looked like a good excuse to tempt Galen into coming in. "So Galen's talking with my brother?"

Toledo started to nod and stopped. "Yep." He winked at Hilda.

"You rascal." She tried to take possession of the pail.

He pulled it backward. "No use you lugging this when I can set it on the table."

Eyes wide with shock, the housekeeper stood there and stared at him.

Laney slid up next to Hilda. "I'll go offer him some coffee."

"You do that, Miss Laney," Toledo said with a chuckle.

She'd managed to get halfway across the yard when Galen and Josh came out of the stable. Josh had an arm slung around Galen, and the two of them seemed to be deep in conversation. Josh looked up.

Skidding to a stop, Laney suddenly felt embarrassed. A woman shouldn't pursue a man. She knew better. But this wasn't exactly pursuing Galen. After all, he'd come to their ranch. She would simply extend the Broken P's hospitality.

Galen followed Josh's gaze. Even from this distance, the power of his blue eyes made her heart skip a beat. He studied her for a moment. "Good morning, Laney."

"It's a pleasant surprise for you to pay a visit. Is everyone at home okay?"

"Right as rain. I needed to discuss a matter with your brother."

Josh slapped him on the back. "How about some coffee?"

"Sounds good."

Laney slipped her hands behind her back and pinched herself. It hurt, so she knew she wasn't dreaming this. Feeling giddy, she told Galen, "There's fresh zucchini bread to accompany the coffee."

"And will I be lucky enough to taste some of your grape jelly on it?"

"Grape jelly on zucchini bread?" Josh let loose of Galen and looked at him as if he'd taken leave of his senses.

"She won second place at the state fair with

that jelly. I'm sure it'll taste grand on anything."

Josh jabbed him in the ribs. "Hilda's bucket of lard took first place. Do you plan on smearing it on your food, too?"

"Nope, but if I ever need to fry eggs, I'll remember her lard."

As they entered the kitchen, Ruth plunked mugs down on the kitchen table. "Toledo, stay and have coffee."

"Don't mind if I do." He pulled out a chair. "Here you are, Miss Hilda."

"I have to get the coffee, cowboy."

"I've got it." Josh snatched the pot from the stove. He set it on the table while pulling out Ruth's chair.

Galen did Laney the courtesy of pulling out a chair for her, too. With the other men performing that same nicety, he had to, she supposed—didn't he? But why, then, did he sit beside her? Mind awhirl, she turned and blinked at him. "I forgot to get the jelly."

"That's okay. It'll be a good reason for me to come by again."

Hilda started pouring coffee. "Laney's grape jelly is the best I ever tasted. She earned that red ribbon, and I'm betting she'll win the blue next year."

"That reminds me," Ruth said as she added a third spoonful of sugar to her coffee. Since she normally used less than one spoonful, Laney wondered what had put her sister-in-law in such a dither. As she added a fourth, Ruth said, "We got the grapes from Eddie Lufe's vines. Laney, you ought to take him a few more jars of your jelly."

"He doesn't like grapes."

Galen shot Laney a long look. "You know what Eddie likes?"

"Pie. He loves pie." As soon as she babbled the words, Laney wished she could shut up, but nervousness kept her talking. "Not that I know him all that well. It's just that he's been here a few times. I don't think there are many things he won't eat. But he brought over crates of grapes and said he didn't like them. Since Josh gave him a good deal on that stallion, maybe Eddie was trying to find an excuse to come over and see if Josh had another horse to sell."

"Not many men could command a stallion like that." Toledo took another piece of zucchini bread. "He's spirited."

"Eddie," Ruth laughed, "or the stallion?"

"How can you tell the difference?" Hilda's voice took on a wry edge. "Lufe's a huge horse of a man. I will say this, though: the man appreciates good food. Does a cook's heart proud to see a man taking his fill of the meal she made."

"Then pass that bread over here," Galen said as he motioned. "I don't want Hilda feeling I don't appreciate her baking."

"I didn't make that. Laney did."

"Then I'll take two pieces."

"Did you see that? Did you hear him?" Laney clutched Ruth's arm and watched as Galen rode away. "God's answering my prayer!"

"Laney, don't do this to yourself. Galen is a good man, and he's a fine friend. You need to be satisfied with that. Just because he was amiable over a cup of coffee doesn't mean he's smitten with you."

Laney turned toward her sister-in-law and rasped, "Why do you say things like that? You know how I feel about Galen. I—"

"The Bible tells us where to set our affections, Laney. 'Set your affection on things above, not on things on the earth.'"

"Galen isn't a thing, he's a man—a wonderful man. You love my brother. How can you tell me not to carry those same feelings for Galen?"

Ruth took her hand and led her over to the wicker chairs on the side veranda. She let out a loud sigh and plopped into one of the chairs. Laney perched on the edge of another.

"You can't force anyone to love you, Laney. My mother learned that lesson the hard way. Father sent her away, even though she stayed true to him until her dying breath. I don't want you to experience that kind of heartbreak."

"Galen wouldn't send me away. He's honorable and would keep our marriage vows."

Ruth leaned forward and curled her fingers

around Laney's hand. "I love you dearly, Laney. I never want to say or do anything that would hurt you. You know that, don't you?"

"You're my dearest friend as well as my sister. That's why I don't understand why you act as if I should stop being true to my heart's most ardent desire. Psalm thirty-seven says, 'Delight thyself also in the Lord: and he shall give thee the desires of thine heart. Commit thy way unto the Lord; trust also in him; and he shall bring it to pass.'"

"Laney," Ruth said, drawing out her name slowly, "you can't just decide you want something and tell God to give it to you. If your heart truly seeks God's will, then you'll be satisfied with whatever decisions He makes. You have to commit yourself to *His* plan, not one you cook up yourself. That verse doesn't promise God will fulfill our whims and wishes."

"Galen is not a whim or a wish."

Ruth squeezed her hand. "I haven't said anything until now. I hoped you'd outgrow the fancy you held toward Galen. The fact is, the only feelings he has toward you are those of a Christian brother."

"You can't know that."

"But I do." Ruth's normally lively features turned somber. Instead of speaking freely, she searched to find the right words. "The very first time you and I went to pay a visit to them, Mrs. O'Sullivan asked you to fetch some butter from the springhouse. I don't want you to think anything unkind was said. The O'Sullivans adore you—but Galen made it clear that he didn't see you in a romantic light. I would be a horrible friend if I fostered any hope on your part when I know he cannot return your affections."

Tears stung her eyes. "That can't be true. You saw Galen today."

"I did. And I've seen how Hilda is trying to play matchmaker for the two of you. You can't make someone love you, Laney. Galen is a wonderful friend. Accept his friendship, and allow God to bring some other man—the right man—along."

"Today was different. He was different."

Ruth nodded. "And maybe that's because Hilda's right about his deciding to take a wife. If he's decided on someone, he'd no longer feel the need to discourage you because you'd finally accept that he's out of reach."

Everything inside of Laney revolted at that thought. She stared at Ruth in disbelief. "Today—"

"No, Laney. Galen wasn't flirting with you today. He was in a good mood—that's all. You've been home from Miss Genevieve's Finishing School for well over two years now, and Galen still hasn't given you a scrap of encouragement. You have to stop this."

Tears slid down Laney's cheeks. "I don't know how to stop loving someone."

———•———

"So you ladies are going to sew today, are you?" Galen brushed a kiss on Ma's cheek.

"Aye, that we are." She handed him the small pot of hot water from the stove.

Galen went over to the washstand. Pouring hot water into the shaving mug, he listened to his brothers waking up in the loft. The last thing he needed was for them to overhear him revealing his innermost thoughts to Ma. *Ma's smart. She'll see how things are between me and Laney. Aye, she will. And 'twill likely make her happy as a lark. She already loves my Laney as if she were a daughter.*

As he wiped the last speck of shaving soap from his face, Galen heard Ishmael and Ivy coming up the steps. Ishmael tended to clomp as he walked. Ivy managed to match her twin's loud gait. Then again, she wore men's boots.

Laney would die of embarrassment before she'd sit spraddle-legged the way Ivy did the day they made pear butter. We all pretended not to notice how Ivy's skirt hiked up and her boots stuck out when she sat that way. Laney notices every little detail. It won't surprise me if, after she helps sew Ivy a new frock, she'll find a way to put her in the right shoes, too.

The Grubbs didn't even knock because Ma called out, "Come on in!"

Ivy flung the door open and tromped in.

" 'Mornin', ya'll. I'll gather the eggs soon as I grab up the basket."

"Milk bucket's in here, too." Ishmael followed on his sister's heels. Just as quickly as they arrived, they left.

"Dawn's barely broken." Colin scrambled down the ladder from the loft. "What are they doing here so early?"

"Getting to work." Ma banged her wooden spoon against the side of the oatmeal pot. "I'm needing you to stop by the mercantile and sell the eggs this mornin', so shake a leg."

After breakfast, Colin rode ahead to the mercantile. Sean and Dale saddled up and would meet him at school. Just as they left, Hilda, with the girls at her side, drove the Broken P buckboard right into the yard. Ishmael took charge of the horses, and Galen assisted Hilda down. Manners dictated he assist the eldest woman first. Besides, he'd save helping Laney for last so he could hold her back a few moments and pay her some special attention.

"Ruth." He reached for Josh's wife.

Her eyes widened in surprise. "No. I mean—well . . ." She groped around the buckboard. "I seem to have lost my needle case."

"Ruthie, you asked me to keep it in my reticule." Laney sounded subdued. Even sad.

Galen reached for Ruth again. "If I were a wagering man, I'd bet you're thankful Laney is so organized."

"I'm thankful for Laney in more ways than I can count."

"Betcha you cain count dreadful high, too," Ivy said as she tromped up. "Maybe e'en to a hunnert!"

Galen reached for Laney. She didn't lean toward him or brace her hands on his shoulders. Instead, she braced her hands on his forearms as if to keep as far from him as she could. His hands spanned her waist. He gently lifted her out and set her down as close to himself as her skirts would allow.

Laney didn't look at him. Instead, she murmured, "Ivy, Ruth is undoubtedly the smartest woman I've ever known."

Galen didn't turn loose of her. "Are you all right?"

Her shoulders rose and fell—a dainty, dismissive move. "A lot has happened. I'm having melancholy thoughts."

Taking one of her soft, small hands in his, Galen said, "A penny for your thoughts."

She fussed with her sleeve. "My thoughts aren't worth a penny."

"Nonsense." He dared to crook his forefinger and tilt her chin upward. Finally, she looked at him. The confusion and sadness in her deep brown eyes tore at him. *I've been wallowing so much in my own grief I've barely acknowledged that she lost her da not that long ago, too.* He cleared his throat. " 'Tis hard, letting go of one you love."

CHAPTER FIFTEEN

L aney blanched and blinked back tears.

"We're . . . friends, Laney. If e'er you want to talk, let me know."

Pulling free from him, she straightened her shoulders and nodded. "You're most kind."

At lunch, Ivy plopped onto the bench where Galen had hoped Laney would sit. "Laney, you was right when you said Galen's kind. Niver had a buck show me manners like he does."

Ma's mouth bowed upward. "I despaired of teaching all of my boys manners. The first time Galen shook hands with someone, 'twas the captain of the vessel that brought us to America. Soon as Galen finished shaking hands, he promptly confessed he'd been hiding a frog in his pocket and hoped he hadn't given the ship's captain warts."

"If'n he did, he coulda gotten rid of 'em. All he needed to do was rub a cut onion on the wart, wrap that onion in a yeller dishcloth, and bury it by the light of a full moon."

"Would that work?" Ruth sounded completely earnest. "I mean, since there's no soil aboard a ship, they do burials at sea. I wonder if you drop the onion into the water . . ."

Galen watched Laney slip into place beside Ruth. "What do you think, Laney?"

"I think—" she looked at her sister-in-law instead of him—"Ruth never ceases to delight me with how she can look at matters from such clever and unique angles."

Ruth laughed. "It's too bad you weren't one of the head mistresses at those finishing schools. They didn't think of me in those terms at all. Maybe if they had, I wouldn't have been shown the door."

"Galen-mine, why don't you ask the blessing?" Ma folded her hands.

"Hold up a minute here." Ivy leaned over the table. "I wanna know what kinda door you got showed. Musta been sommat real special if'n they showed it off."

"Being shown the door is a fancy way of saying they asked me to leave," Ruth confessed.

"You was in school and they done kicked you out?"

Ruth nodded.

"Galen is going to pray now." Laney clasped her hands. "If we don't eat lunch and get back to sewing, it'll take us forever to finish Ivy's dress."

"Aye, we've all work a-plenty to accomplish. With the good Lord's help and our diligence, the important things will all be done." A short, heartfelt prayer, a quick meal, then Galen needed to return to work. Instead, he dawdled like a schoolboy to steal a few more minutes with Laney.

"Boss, these gals—they done a heap of work today. Lookee thar at what all they got started. Why, another day or two of them all workin' and Ivy'll have a fine dress to show for it."

"Ain't nobody gonna show me my dress. I double dog dare anybody to try to send me through a door and leave my purdy green dress behind. I'm keepin' it!"

"Of course you're keeping it." Laney took a sip of water and refrained from showing any outward signs that Ivy's adamant assertion reflected blinding ignorance. "Next week, if Ruth reminds me, I'll bring over my button jar. Wouldn't it be nice to use some pretty buttons on the bodice?"

"I cain't pay you no cash money for 'em."

"Laney wasn't asking you to," Ma said as she stood up and started clearing the dishes. "She's sharing with you."

Ivy grinned. "I'm much obliged—'specially if'n you got some like the one at yore throat. That one's so purdy, makes me wanna cry."

Laney reached up and grazed her fingertips across the item. "Oh, this isn't a button. It's a cameo—a piece of jewelry. It belonged to my mother."

"Hmm." Ivy leaned across the table and squinted. "Yore ma shore was a purdy woman."

"That's not her mother, Ivy." Ruth looked at the lovely piece. "It's a shell someone carved and made into a beautiful picture."

"Aye, 'tis beautiful." Jumping at the opportunity to compliment Laney, Galen went on, "No wonder Ivy thought that comely woman was Laney's mother. I've thought on occasion that their features are much alike."

Laney tucked her chin and looked down at the cameo. "Thank you."

Pleased at how he'd praised her beauty, Galen rose. "We've work waiting for us, Ishmael. Let's get going."

———

"That was a fine meal." Galen laid his napkin on the table. When Josh had asked him to join them for supper after church, he had happily accepted.

"We're glad you could share it with us." Josh patted Ruth's hand. "Aren't we?"

"Galen's always welcome. Galen, your mother mentioned she'd enjoy a new book to read. Why don't we all walk over to the cottage, and you can find a few to take home to her?"

"Good idea." Josh nodded. "You saw the books we brought back from the fair. What you probably don't know is, Ruthie's been ordering books. And books. And more books. That little yellow cabin that once was her father's place is now chockfull of crates of books."

"The library is in honor of my mama. I refuse to skimp on it." Ruth shot Josh a smile. "And you have no room to complain. Just the other day, you handed me a list of books you thought we ought to add." She turned to Galen. "My husband should be glad that cabin is there. Otherwise, I'd be filling up the parlor."

"You still might," Josh teased.

"Laney's been a big help to me. Galen, I'm sure she could help you find something interesting for your mother to read."

"I'm not sure what she'd like. Laney, you and Ma both crochet. Maybe you could help me pick out something with patterns for her."

Laney searched for a way to avoid going. Being around Galen hurt—and of all people, Josh and Ruth ought to understand. They'd counseled her to leave Galen alone because he'd never love her. And now instead of helping keep Galen away, Josh had invited him over for Sunday supper.

"I'm not going," Hilda said with a sniffle. "No use in my getting any more books when I'm only halfway through the one I got."

"Ruth can assist you," Laney told Galen as

she stood and started to stack plates. "I'll help Hilda in the kitchen."

"Nonsense." Hilda brushed Laney's hands away. "You young people go on ahead."

Just as they stepped off the porch, Ruth stopped. "I forgot to tell Hilda something."

"We'll wait for you," Laney said.

"Oh, go on ahead. I'll catch up with you."

Josh walked on one side of Laney and Galen took the opposite side. *I'm glad I'm wearing my Sunday-best gown. Three petticoats and a crinoline give me an excuse to stay back a little.*

"Hey, Toledo!" Josh waved. "I need to speak with you about something important." He strode off and threw over his shoulder, "I'll join you soon."

The cottage was only a stone's throw away. If Laney refused to accompany Galen, it would be rude. After all, he was a guest at the Broken P and Ruth had offered him access to the library books. As long as the door remained open and Josh was close by, she couldn't very well demure and bring up proprieties.

"I recall the first step on the cottage porch being a mite loose the last time we were here." Galen threaded her arm through the crook of his elbow. "Here."

"You're most kind." Just walking beside him made her heart patter faster; looking up into his clear blue eyes left her longing to be his bride. And looking at him was a mistake. A huge mistake. He studied her quietly, and Laney could feel the heat of a virulent blush start at her throat and sweep up her face. She quickly compressed the sides of her hoops and skittered sideways between several boxes. "I seem to recall seeing some books on handwork back here."

"Where?"

Galen's deep voice near her ear made her jump. "Oh! Um . . . in this box." She patted the crate.

"Let's set you aside." He cupped his big hands around her waist and effortlessly lifted and moved her. As he set her down, he grinned. "I don't want to drop the crate on any of your dainty little toes."

"I hope I'm not putting you through any unnecessary work. Ruth and I tried to repack books of the same variety in crates. Since the lid's back on that one—"

"Prying off a few lids is no problem." He pulled that crate from a shoulder-high stack and used a crowbar to open it. As he removed the lid, he cast a long look at her. "You were right. I'm seeing books on sewing and such."

"Good!" Relief flooded her. They'd grab the first one, and she could dash off.

"I'm wondering about flowers. You know how Ma loves flowers. Let's find her a book of patterns that show how to crochet something pretty."

"Your mother's flower garden is always a joy."

A sad smile crossed his face. "This past year she didn't have much time for that. Had it not been for all the help you and Ruth gave, Ma's flower patch would have been nothing but weeds."

"We're always willing to come help her. I do hope you'll feel free to mention her needs to us."

"You've a generous spirit, Laney. You've helped with everything from baking to weeding whilst Da's health failed, and afterward, you took my family off to the fair so they'd not wallow in their grief. You even bought Hortense for Dale."

"That was a business decision." Laney pulled a book from the box and started to leaf through it. "Hortense and Mr. Snout make a nice couple." As soon as she spoke the words, Laney wished she hadn't. She'd just dithered her way into sounding like a matchmaker for hogs! Well, Miss Genevieve taught the girls at her finishing school to laugh off slips of the tongue and divert attention. "You must be proud of Dale. He's been very responsible."

"Aye, he's trying hard. He knows full well you rescued his pet and wants to make you glad you're his partner." Galen chuckled. "You're such a refined lady, it ought to stretch my imagination that you'd care a whit about Hortense. But it doesn't. You see the needs of others and step in to help. Take Ivy, for instance. That green dress—"

Laney leafed through the book. She held it out to Galen when she found a page with an illustration of a crocheted dresser scarf that featured roses all about the edges.

Galen shook his head. "Ma could crochet roses in her sleep. Those camellias Ruth got for her—she surely does treasure them. Could we find a camellia, perhaps?"

"I'm afraid they'd look much like roses."

"Hmm. What's your favorite flower?"

"I like the scent of lilies of the valley, but daffodils always cheer me up."

He reached into the box, rummaged past a few books, and pulled out another. "Let's find both. It'll be nice for Ma to have a choice."

They continued to search and made small talk. Galen shuffled closer so he could lean over the pages she showed him. "You're sworn to secrecy, Laney. The men of Folsom would think I've gone daft if they knew I fretted over a crochet pattern."

She laughed.

"Having any luck?" Josh asked from the doorway.

"Oh, look! Isn't this charming?" Laney showed him an illustration. "And it mentions that you can use colored string for the flower petals and stems."

"That's grand!" Galen set aside the book

he'd thumbed through. "In fact, I'm so sure that's what Ma would want to make, I won't need another choice for her."

Ruth came over, and Galen admired the sheer volume of books she'd acquired for the library she was starting. Not long thereafter, he mentioned needing to get home and left.

Ruth, Josh, and Laney went back home and sat in the parlor as they usually did on Sunday afternoons and evenings. Josh picked up a newspaper. "This advertisement says the mercantile just got a shipment of veterinarian medicaments. I'm going to need to restock for the winter."

"Oats." Ruth patted his arm. "Be sure to pick up a few bags of oats. I like to give Maxie a treat after I ride her. It's just a pity oats don't come in pretty sacks."

Josh smiled. "Are you already scheming to make another dress for Ivy? Galen mentioned the other one is almost done. Laney Lou, he's pleased you gave those green sugar sacks to Ivy. That flour sack dress is all she owns."

"It was good, you making sure Ivy got those sacks." Ruth bobbed her head. "Mrs. O'Sullivan tells me the Grubbs haven't ever stepped foot in a church."

Josh turned to the next page in his newspaper. "Galen and his mother are trying to be solid Christian witnesses. I agree with him. We shouldn't do a bunch of preaching; let the Holy

Spirit do the rest. We'll follow Galen's example and simply love them."

Slowly, Laney rested her teacup on the saucer and set it on the table. *Am I mistaking Galen's simple kindness as interest? Was I right originally when I thought he might have a tender spot for Ivy?* Her thoughts whirled and fear's bitter taste banished the honeyed sweetness of the tea as Galen's words swept through her mind. *"She's different. It's complicated. . . . Love them. . . ."*

CHAPTER SIXTEEN

"Careful now," Josh directed as Galen and Ishmael fit the third stained glass window into its place. When Ruth discovered her inheritance was to be immense, she'd wanted to use it for good causes. The library was one of her many projects; these stained glass windows were another. While on their wedding trip, she and Josh commissioned an artist to make them. A few months ago, they'd taken an afternoon away from the fair to go and approve of the designs.

"Oh, Ruth. This one's my favorite," Laney

whispered as the men eased the last window into place

"I've been impatient to have them here. Now I'm glad Josh insisted on hanging all of them on the same day. I would have pestered the artist to hurry up if he'd sent the first one when it was done."

"Niver thunk glass could be so heavy," Ishmael said just before his hand slipped.

"Whoa!" Galen braced the window and nudged the final corner into place.

"Glad you men were available to help me today," Josh said.

"I was coming to town anyway." Galen carefully tapped another finishing nail into the wood molding to keep the window in place, then started sealing it with glazing compound. "I've not missed voting even once, and if ever I wanted to let my voice be heard, sure and enough today's election is the one."

"The nation's future rests on the results," Josh said from nearby.

"Them men all speechifyin' and posters hangin' ever'whar, and newspapers all spoutin' off differ'nt opinions . . ." Ishmael shook his head. "It stretches the imagination that anybody cain make sense of it all and figger out who to vote for, for president."

"Aye, you said a mouthful there, you did." Galen wiped a small spot on the window. " 'Tis rather like this stained glass. When a man gets this close, he can't see the whole picture—just bits and pieces. I had to step back and ask God to shine the light on it."

Laney looked up. "That image you just painted with your words—it makes more sense than just about anything I've heard or read."

"I agree." Ruth shoved back one of her irrepressible curls. "And I agree with Josh—we're fortunate that Galen and Ishmael could come help with the windows. It's certainly been a blessing that Galen knows all about glazing," Ruth added. "I didn't know we needed to seal the edges. Did you, Laney?"

"No."

"It doesn't take long." Galen daubed the compound into place and smoothed it down the side with his thumb.

Laney wasn't sure why he'd given her the job of holding the glazing compound. She'd needed to stand quite near him as he scooped out what he needed and applied it to the edges of all three windows. Truth be told, the can would have fit on the ledge. Instead of pointing out that fact, Ruth had pushed the can into Laney's hand and nudged her into helping. *She told me to stay away from Galen, and here she is pushing me at him.*

"I'm needing a wee bit more, Laney."

She held the can up to him. "There's not much left."

"Just enough." He scooped out what

remained with a chisel and worked it into place.

Ishmael chuckled. "Niver thought I'd be glad to be inside a church, but here I am."

"You and Ivy are welcome to join us for worship any time." Laney smiled at him. "Don't you think she'd look beautiful in her new green dress sitting in a pew with the light shining through the windows you helped hang?"

"S'pose that might make somebody else perk up, but it ain't ticklin' me. My sis gotta be one of the purdiest gals in the world. Don't make no difference what dress she gots on or whar she is."

"I'm done here." Galen cleaned off his hands with a damp rag, then set it across the handle of his wooden toolbox.

Laney stepped back and looked at the window. "Have you ever seen anything so beautiful?"

"Nay, lass. I've ne'er seen anything half as lovely." Something about his voice made Laney turn her attention to him. Galen wasn't looking at the window.

He's looking at me!

A slow smile lit his face. "Lovely beyond compare."

Ruth bustled closer. "The children all have such sweet faces!" she exclaimed, gently touching her finger to the nose of one of the children in the glass.

Josh tapped a small brass plate below the window that bore the verse the artist based the window upon. He read it aloud. " 'Suffer little children to come unto me, and forbid them not: for of such is the kingdom of God. Luke 18:16.' "

"That feller thar, sittin' in the midst of that passel of kids, shore don't look like he's sufferin' none."

"Jesus loves children," Josh explained. "That's just an old-fashioned way of saying He wanted children to be allowed to be with Him."

Galen continued to look at Laney. "You love children, too, don't you, lass?"

She could scarcely believe this was happening. A man didn't ask a woman questions like this unless . . . well, unless they were courting. Not trusting her voice, she nodded.

"Ma always said she would have gladly embraced a dozen babes if the Lord had seen fit to bless her with them." Galen drew closer and dropped his voice. "Have you e'er thought on how many you'd wish for?"

Heat filled her cheeks and she whispered, "It's in the Lord's hands. I'd dearly love several, though."

Galen grinned. "Fond as I am of children, I'd enjoy a houseful of them."

"You got plenty of good food and a sound roof. Them kids'll be lucky."

Laney jumped at Ishmael's voice. She'd completely forgotten anyone else was there.

Galen smiled. "Speaking of food, Ma sent along a picnic lunch. She remembered hearing

Ethel at church Sunday, boasting about a new recipe."

Ruth laughed. "Hilda did, too. She sent along lunch. We're going to have enough to feed half the town."

To Laney's delight, Galen made a point of sitting beside her on the quilt out in the churchyard. "You'd better have more of an appetite than you usually do, Laney. Ma sent fried chicken and biscuits."

"My favorites!"

He gave her a sly wink and pulled a jar from his basket. "Look here, will you. Ma sent apple-pear butter."

"It's a good thing we're sharing baskets!" Ruth announced as she promptly swiped it from him. "Hilda's been hiding ours from me."

Laney and Galen looked at each other and started to laugh. Her heart overflowed with happiness.

———————

"There you are." Galen hoped Laney heard the pleasure resonating in his voice. Her smile made him think so.

"Here's her parasol," Sean said as he shoved it into Galen's hand. "We'll see you at home." Sean swaggered toward the horses tethered to the next tree.

Normally, he rode to church in the back of the buckboard with Ma and Dale. But today

Laney would be Galen's Sunday supper guest. Her beautiful full skirts took up considerable space. And though Galen would far rather have Laney ride up on the seat beside him, he let Dale scramble into that spot. If he gave Ma a tiny bit of time on the trip home with Laney, then Galen could have her all to himself for a nice stroll after the meal. Galen opened Laney's Sunday-best parasol and handed it to her. "M'lady."

"Thank you." She leaned a little closer. The refreshing, tangy scent of her lemon verbena wafted over him. "Aren't we blessed to have such beautiful weather? I missed California's sunshine when I was away at school."

"Aye," Ma said. "But keep using that parasol. You're fair and the sun's harsh."

Galen didn't bother to look at the creamy fabric contraption with swirling lace about the edges. He'd seen it countless times. He couldn't get his fill of looking at Laney. "Aye, lass. You're fair, indeed."

A fetching blush filled Laney's cheeks. "Thank you."

They'd gone no more than a mile out of town when Dale scrambled over the seat and wiggled in beside Laney. Ma shot Galen a secretive smile. He grinned back. *Everyone loves Laney. In the midst of my family—'tis where she belongs.*

"Ma's making ham for lunch," Dale said.

"But don't worry, Laney. It's not from one of our pigs. When I take you to the sty, you can count to be sure."

"I don't need to count, Dale. We're partners. I trust you."

"Hortense and Mr. Snout trust us, too. That's why they aren't ham or bacon or pork chops."

Immediately following lunch, Dale made a pest of himself. Ma had asked Sean and Colin to wash the dishes, so Dale invited himself to go along on the walk. To Galen's dismay, Ma agreed. "Aye, our Dale. You take Laney over to see how well you're caring for your pigs."

I want to take my lass on a leisurely stroll. Alone. 'Tisn't romantic in the least to have a wee little brother tag along, and to stop by a reeking sty. Instead of wooing Laney, I'll be scaring the lass away!

"But once you've swilled the hogs, you come back home to me." Ma smiled. "I've not forgotten how you and I each won a game of draughts this week. Today, I aim to play the third—and win it."

Dale adamantly shook his head. "I'm gonna beat you, Ma. Just you wait and see!"

"Don't keep me waiting too long."

Galen winked at Ma. She'd had a plan all worked out. *Aye, and I should have known. She loves my Laney so. 'Tis a joy to know the two women I love get along so well.*

Galen's gaze traveled back to Laney. Her smile had faded. Truth be told, she looked woefully sad. *Why? All this time, she's wanted me to court her. Now that I'm doing that, she'd rather have my pesky little brother come along? It makes no sense.*

Once Dale showed off how well he'd been tending Hortense, he scampered back to the house. Galen dared to take Laney's hand and thread it through his arm. That ought to let her know straight off that he'd come to his senses and cared for her. Perhaps she'd come to lunch today thinking 'twas more for little Dale's happiness than a subtle foray into a carefully thought out wooing. The way her lips parted showed her surprise. Galen didn't say anything. Sometimes words got in the way. Best he show her his love. Words hadn't ever been his strong suit. He looked deep into her eyes and smiled.

Her face lit up, and the corners of her mouth lifted.

They wandered past the fields. "Your father would be so proud of you, Galen. He already was, but to see how you've kept the farm so nice and the crops are thriving—it's been difficult, but you're more than equal to the task."

"Thanks, Laney. I want to do Da proud. Ma and the boys need to see things are still safe and good. I don't want them worrying about whether the harvest will be enough to cover our needs."

"You've surpassed that goal. Farming's a hard life. I look at other farmers, and they always look like they're battling the earth and weather. You . . . you don't. It's as if . . ." A nervous laugh bubbled out of her.

"As if . . . ?"

"It might sound fanciful, but you work *with* your land, not *against* it. The way you tend it and coax it—how could it not yield gracious plenty?"

"Hard work isn't all it takes, Laney. God's been good to me. Nevertheless, I think of how the Bible talks of years of plenty and years of want. I'll pray and work night and day to be sure my family's got what they need." *And I hope someday soon that will include you.*

"There was a time before Josh married Ruth that he'd wondered about traveling east to enlist if there's a war. The other day, he said he'd not go."

Galen heard the unasked question in her voice. "I pledged to Da that I'd be here to care for Ma and raise up the boys. I've no doubt that the North and South will be battling. It's a war that's been long brewing and cannot help but come. Me? I'll pray for those who fight, but I cannot forsake my vow and leave my family defenseless and in need."

Laney's strained look lessened but didn't vanish. "Lester Pearson was boasting in the mercantile the other day that the war will last three weeks or less. He predicts the South will whup the Northern oppressors.'"

Galen smiled grimly. "Don't forget how he says the South will 'be eating on the White House lawn and drinking tea in Boston.'"

"I didn't hear him say that. Probably because Mr. Darlden took exception to Lester's opinion. He said the only thing the South might 'whup the North' at was a game of draughts."

"Is that why you looked so sad when Ma mentioned draughts?"

She nodded. "Lester and Mr. Darlden used to be friends. Now they're barely civil to one another."

Galen nodded. " 'Tis a sad thing when friends let a difference of opinion part them."

"Politics, religion, and finances—the three things Mrs. Genevieve exhorted us all to avoid discussing. She was the headmistress at the finishing school."

Galen nodded.

"I'm not sure why, but it seems to me those are the three things men discuss the most!"

"Some men." He led her toward the edge of the path. "There are those of us whose favorite topics are God's grace and our family."

"I knew I liked you." As soon as she spoke, she looked stricken.

Galen laughed. He pulled his arm free, stooped down, and picked a few pretty wild-flowers. Standing, he gently put them in her hand. "And I like you, too."

"Don't make no sense, that Jesus feller jist lyin' there and lettin' 'em pound Him onto a cross."

"He did it out of love," Galen said.

The day they'd installed the stained glass windows in the church had done more than shed light into the church. It had brought to light Ishmael's ignorance and staggering innocence when it came to spiritual matters. In the two weeks since then, Ishmael had asked about God every other day or so. Their conversations were startling. Things Galen grew up "knowing" and never questioned as well as other things he'd never thought about all cropped up.

"That don't make sense. Only them disciple fellers treated Him good."

"He did it for everyone; not just His followers."

Ishmael shook his head. "Cain't fathom that. Now for somebody special, I s'pose a buck could take the blame. If'n 'twere for Ivy, I'd let 'em kill me."

"Jesus said that very thing. He told His followers that regular people would lay down their lives for a loved one—but when we belong to God, we are to be different. We have to love one another and be willing to make sacrifices even for our enemies."

Ishmael stopped working and stretched his back. "Whar I come from, a smart feller lets his enemies die off. Pa done taught me early on that a man's gotta take care of hisself. Ain't nobody else gonna."

"As I said, Christians believe differently."

Ishmael cracked his knuckles. "That Jesus of yourn—He shore had some addlepated notions."

Galen accepted Ishmael's opinion; it stood to reason that he'd consider something so contrary to human nature as illogical or foolish. "Christ urged us to love our neighbors as much as we love ourselves."

"Well, you got yoreself some fine neighbors. Them McCains are nice as cain be. Liking them ain't so hard for you."

"We are blessed to have them as our friends and neighbors." Galen waited half a beat, then went on, "But Jesus used a story to show us who our neighbors are."

"Back home in Crooked Leg, we had old Cletus Bantley. He shore did love to spin a fine yarn. Bet him and yore Jesus woulda had themselves a fine old time together."

Galen smiled. "I'm sure they would."

"Too bad Sis ain't here. Nobody savors a tale more'n Ivy."

"What about Thursday? Are Ivy and your father coming for Thanksgiving?"

"Pa says it's a Yankee holiday." Ishmael rubbed his nose with the ball of his thumb.

"You can tell your father California started celebrating Thanksgiving ten years ago, so it's not just a Yankee celebration." Galen chuckled. "As a matter of fact, Laney and Ruth are stalwart supporters of Sarah Josepha Hale. She's the editor of *Godey's Lady's Book* and writes passionately about making Thanksgiving a national holiday."

"Pa ain't so sure we're gonna stay one nation. Truth be tole, Lincoln gettin' hisself elected has Pa mad as a gypped whore."

Galen cocked a brow.

"Whoops. Sorry, Boss. 'Tis jist a sayin'."

"Not one I want to hear."

Ishmael nodded sheepishly. "Niver thunk much 'bout them kind of sayin's. I'm tryin' to mind my mouth."

"I appreciate that."

Ishmael scuffed his boot in the dirt. "Ain't niver spent time or money on one of them gals, neither. Even if I had the money, don't reckon I would. Don't seem right somehow."

"It isn't," Galen agreed.

"If Pa comes to supper for Thanksgivin', he's liable to spout off some stuff that ain't polite. And he'll have plenty to say 'bout how the election was shady."

"Feelings are running high about the results. We can turn the conversation onto a different topic."

"Pa ain't easy to sway when he sets his mind on something."

"He's never tasted my mother's cooking."

Ishmael chuckled and shook his finger at Galen. "Whoa-ho. That's whar yore wrong. Three times now, yore mama sent Ivy home a-carryin' a supper plate to Pa. Onc't I remember Pa on that, he'll be champin' on the bit to come."

"I'll tell Ma to count on him coming."

"Ivy, too. I reckon you could recite that story Jesus tole 'bout neighbors. I'll tell Ivy yore fixin' to spin a tale. 'Twill give her sommat to look forward to."

"You do that."

"Boss? You know Ivy's come over twice to sew." Ishmael grimaced and stared down at his feet. "If Pa knowed she was jist comin' here to get herself a dress, he wouldn'ta let her. It shames me to admit it, but he's dreadful hard on her. We let Pa think them jars we toted back was pay for her holp two of them times. T'other time, you sneaked a gunnysack of vittles by that tree. Ivy done tole me you done that three times now, but you didn't want Pa to know, so we ain't tole him."

"Ivy wasn't supposed to see me that first time."

"Then how was she a-gonna know them vittles was thar?"

Galen grinned. "My plan was to set the bag

somewhere she was sure to find it. The Bible tells us to give quietly—so subtly that the left hand doesn't know what the right hand is giving."

"Yore Bible-book shore has some fanciful notions. But the last time you put a sackful of vittles thar, I strung 'em up from a tree. That next day, when we was a-walkin' back home, I got it down so's Pa would reckon lettin' Ivy go away for a day now and then was a right smart plan."

"I see."

"Don't think you do." Ishmael sighed. "Pa got hisself a rare bad temper. Ivy and me, we learnt early not to rile him. We didn't 'zactly lie to him. We jist let him draw his own conclusions when Ivy brung home stuff."

"I won't lie, and I won't ask Ma to lie, either." Galen frowned. "Is Ivy safe?"

"Safe as she's ever been." Ishmael finally looked back up. "And happier, too. Yore ma and neighbors—they've been real nice to Sis. Pa don't thank Ivy's worth much, her bein' a gal. But that worked in her favor this time. He didn't 'spect she oughtta earn much, so her comin' home with vittles for later and a plate of meat— well, that more'n satisfied him."

Lord, how do I handle this? Give me wisdom. Galen looked off in the distance. The boys were starting off to school, and Ma made sure she hugged and kissed all three of them. *How would I feel if Ma only loved some of us and was mean to the others? What would I do to protect them?*

"Mayhap 'tis best that we jist not come."

Galen made a show of folding his arms across his chest. "You think your father is difficult? Just you try tellin' Ma you're not accepting her hospitality." He shook his head. "You're a braver man than I am. I'd rather walk through a swarm of angry bees than disappoint Ma. I'll have a talk with her, and we'll be careful with what's said so Ivy is safe."

The sadness fled Ishmael's eyes, only to be replaced with a mischievous gleam. He poked his tongue out into his cheek and ran it back and forth for a long count, then nodded. "I'll take yore word for it, Boss. If anybody's a-gonna be riled, best it not be the cook!"

Ivy pinched the edges of the pie closed and carefully lowered it into the Dutch oven. Ishy had snared her two fat squirrels. With the flour and lard the O'Sullivans had given them, Ivy had turned those squirrels into a masterpiece. She could hardly wait till tomorrow. From all the chatter about Thanksgiving while she'd been sewing over at the O'Sullivans, she knew there'd be plenty of food. Pride led her to make something to take, too.

Folks always told her she baked the best squirrel pie they ever ate. She looked forward to putting on her beautiful green dress and carrying that pie into the O'Sullivan place. Oh, it would be a fine moment.

A shadow fell over her. Ivy looked up and tried not to let her fear show. "Pa's back 'hind the lean-to," she told the black-haired man.

"I figured as much." Pa's partner waved toward the right. "I brought more corn."

Ivy nodded. One or the other of the partners managed to come by with corn or sugar or both a couple of times a week. Every other time, they'd come with a wagon to tote away the jugs—but never on a schedule, so she couldn't guess when one of them would show up.

Mr. Whatever-his-name-was-today hunkered down close beside her. She flinched as he ran a finger down her cheek. "You're filling out. Looks nice on you. Real nice."

Trying to be subtle, Ivy felt for the knife she kept in her belt sheath.

"Hey, thar!" Pa came around the lean-to.

The man slowly rose. "I brought more corn. From the looks of your field, you're ready to harvest now."

"Yup. Gal, I tole you to start round the edges whar the sun ripens the field. Got enough sunlight to pick a bunch."

Glad to have an excuse, Ivy scrambled away.

The stranger led his heavily-laden horse around the lean-to. Pa was urging him to continue bringing more corn and sugar, blaming Ivy's poor farming and complaining that the late start on the crop made for a low yield.

Pa cain lay blame whare'er he wants, so long as he and that feller keep outta my hair. She walked the first row of corn and harvested the ripest ears. Some still needed a few days. Before turning the corner to do the next edge, Ivy tiptoed over and checked on her squirrel pie. She rotated the Dutch oven and replaced the coals on top of it.

Judging the time, Ivy decided she'd best set supper to cooking. The most recent gunnysack of vittles that nice Mr. O'Sullivan had left still had food in it. She kept track and tried to stretch each bit so's they'd have enough to fill 'em and still last awhile. She measured out some black-eyed peas and rice into the only other pot she owned. Ishy liked hoppin' John, so he'd be happy when he got home from work.

The sounds of Pa and his partner drifted toward her every once in awhile. Ivy wished that man would go. About half the time, he'd lollygag round and join Pa in sampling the corn whiskey. He didn't get mean drunk like Pa, but he'd knock back enough to be tipsy. Ivy wished his brother or cousin—whichever he was—had come instead. He just got down to business and left.

After adding more ears of corn to the heap she'd started, Ivy checked on the squirrel pie. It was close to being done, so she thought to take it away from the fire and just let the heat the

Dutch oven held finish the job. A hasty glance at the lean-to left her giddy with relief. She popped to her feet and started to sneak away with it.

"Gal!" Pa's voice made her freeze. "Whar d'ya thank yore goin'?"

Chapter Seventeen

Here. Let me help." Laney hated getting up from the Thanksgiving table. Ever since the day she'd come to make pear butter, Galen had made it a point to have her sit beside him. Today he'd done the same thing. She would gladly stay next to him much longer, but she couldn't allow her hostess to do all of the work. "Please excuse me," she murmured.

Galen rose and moved so she could get to the other side of the bench. "Ladies, everything tasted wonderful."

"Shore did." Ivy started rolling up the sleeves of her new green dress. " 'Tis a wonderment the table didn't start beggin' for mercy onc't we started piling all them heavy plates and bowls on it."

"Hilda, why don't you and Mrs. O'Sullivan go rest?" Ruth put her arm around Laney. "We'll clear the table and clean up."

"Really?" Sean asked excitedly.

"Boy-o, don't you be gettin' too excited." Galen gave his little brother a stern look. "Ma told you and Colin that you're to wash the dishes."

Laney tried not to look amused at Sean's crestfallen expression. Galen managed his brothers well. *I ought to praise him about that. It can't be easy trying to be both brother and father to them.*

"It's pure nonsense, me not helping clean up." Mrs. O'Sullivan's forehead wrinkled as she looked at the table.

"We insist," Laney said.

"Yup. We shore do." Ivy pulled one of Mrs. O'Sullivan's aprons on over her dress.

"At least let me take the rest of the milk and cheese out to the springhouse."

"One trip," Ruth allowed.

Mr. Grubb stayed at the table, and Laney didn't reach for any of the bowls or platters near him. Everyone else had eaten plenty and enjoyed lively conversation. Mr. Grubb had made a few terse comments, but he'd mostly just sat there and continued to eat. And eat. And eat.

After having seen Ishmael and Ivy, Laney had expected Mr. Grubb to be mere skin and bones, but he wasn't. Though lean of limb, he boasted a fairly generous belly. Witnessing how he ate, Laney suspected he took his fill of whatever meager meals Ivy cooked before his children got much.

It seemed rude to be clearing the table, but he hadn't shown a single sign of stopping any time soon. Josh, Ishmael, and Galen stayed at the table to be companionable, but they'd long since given up their plates.

Hilda didn't bat an eye. She set a hand on Josh's shoulder, then leaned over and dragged the turkey platter toward herself. Mr. Grubb glowered at her, and she glowered right back.

Twice more, Hilda and Mr. Grubb went through a silent battle. Hilda won those, too. Laney, Ivy, and Ruth all stood off to the side, gaping at the war. Mr. Grubb's bushy eyebrows beetled, and the left side of his unkempt mustache raised in a soundless snarl as Hilda hooked her thumb inside the rim of the bowl of mashed sweet potatoes.

Then Hilda surprised them all. She pushed the bowl straight in front of him, bumping his sopped-clean plate to the side. "Seeing as how you're appreciating those, you go on ahead and eat your fill." She gave him a toothy smile. "Would you like a little more brown sugar on them?"

"Don't mind if I do." As Hilda added brown sugar, he motioned for her to keep spooning in more and more.

My gracious! There have to be almost two cups

*of sweet potatoes there, and he's going to eat them
all straight from the serving bowl!*

A moment later, Hilda stood back and rested
her hands on her hips. "Does my heart good,
seeing a man who's unafraid to eat."

Mr. Grubb shot a dark look at Ivy. "Ain't
often I getta et anything decent. The gal ain't got
a scrap of talent for cookin'. Made squirrel pie
yesternoon that set like an anvil in my belly."

*He has that big tummy from eating her food.
How can he complain? He's dreadfully mean.*
Laney reverted to what Mama and Miss Genevieve taught her to do when her expression
would transmit her opinion: she dipped her head
and lowered her eyes.

"The squirrel pie come from Ma's recipe."
Ishmael's shoulder hitched in a tight shrug. "Sis
always did what Ma showed her—to make it and
let it sit overnight so's the flavor comes up."

The muscles in Ivy's jaw twitched.

*She baked that for today. He ruined it just to
spite her. What a dreadful man.* Laney shot Galen
a pleading look.

"The hopping John that Ivy brought tasted
wonderful," Galen countered. Laney watched
how he folded his arms on the table and leaned
forward a little. "As a matter of fact, if I hadn't
seen her bring it in, I would have said Ma
made it."

Josh forced a chuckle, "And I would have said
Hilda had. They've probably swapped recipes."

Galen slapped his hand on the table for emphasis. "That's among the grandest compliments I can give a woman—that her cooking is as fine as Ma's. Isn't that right, Laney?"

"Definitely." Laney turned to Ivy. "Remember how you suggested fixing up oatmeal by adding dried apple bits along with cinnamon? We tried it. It's delicious."

The scraping of his spoon against the bowl didn't cover Mr. Grubb's rude snort.

"We all have different tastes." Hilda's tone sounded too hearty. Laney stepped back and watched as her housekeeper bobbed her head. "Yeah, different tastes. Mr. Grubb, there—he's a meat-and-'taters man. Isn't that so?"

Mr. Grubb nodded as he shoveled the last bite into his mouth. He pushed the bowl away, rubbed his belly, and let out a loud belch.

"All full up?" Hilda asked.

"Uh-huh." A self-satisfied smile flashed across his face. "Couldn't wedge another bite in sidewise."

"I suspected as much," Hilda said. "That's maturity showing."

"Maturity?" Mrs. O'Sullivan gave them all a puzzled look as she came in the door.

Hilda picked up the bowl and tilted it. "Mr. Grubb finished off your mashed sweet potatoes."

"Did he now?" Surprise and shock mingled in Mrs. O'Sullivan's expression.

"Every last little bit," Hilda declared as she pushed the bowl into Colin's hands. "Good, healthy food. A mature man appreciates it."

Laney couldn't keep from gawking. Hilda was being downright chatty. Once or twice when a ranch hand had dared to burp in her presence, she'd walloped him upside his head and singed his ears with her opinion of his manners. But Hilda was nattering along and praising Mr. Grubb like a woman who fancied a man to be her beau!

"These young fellows," Hilda said, scanning the men, "they're still children at heart. I know exactly what they've been thinking and planning." She folded her arms across her chest and gave Galen, Ishmael, and Josh an assessing look. "You've been waiting to have something sweet."

Josh leaned back and gave her a scandalized look. "Hilda, you would have been offended if I didn't save room for some of your pie!"

"Pie?" Mr. Grubb's eyes widened. "I don't see no pie."

Hilda swished her hand at him. "They're in the pie safe. Laney and Galen carried them in earlier. Don't feel bad about already being full. I'm sure Kelly feels like I do, glad that you were so satisfied with the supper we made. We're not offended; you've paid us quite a compliment."

"Absolutely," Mrs. O'Sullivan said as she bustled around. "Ivy, your father seems a bit disappointed. If you could come help me tomorrow, perhaps we could send you home with a pie."

"I'm done scraping the plates into the bucket," Dale announced. "Miss Laney, are you going to come with me to feed the hogs?"

"Ya ha ha ha!" Mr. Grubb slapped his thigh as if he'd heard a hilarious joke.

"Of course I will, Dale." Laney turned her back on the rude boor. "It's been a whole week since I've seen Hortense and Mr. Snout. How are they doing?"

"Miss Laney, I've been takin' real good care of 'em. You'll see how big they are now!" When they reached the sty, Dale tugged on her hand. "Well?"

"Hmm?" Laney blinked at him.

"You said you'd help me. The bucket's too heavy for me to lift all by myself."

"Mercy me! I didn't think about how heavy it must be with all of those Thanksgiving scraps. You must be very strong or you wouldn't have been able to carry that bucket out here all by yourself!"

Glowing from her praise, Dale nodded. "I'm getting big muscles."

"Of course you are, but I'll help you now. After all, we're partners." Careful to stand over by the side where Galen had thoughtfully placed a sheet of tin so the slop wouldn't splash on her, Laney helped Dale raise the swill up over a fence slat.

"Now wait a minute!" Dale turned loose,

climbed up on one of the lower slats, and hollered, "Soooo-eeee!"

Laney let out a rueful laugh. "Dale, Hortense and Mr. Snout are already here."

"I know. But I do that cuz it lets everybody know I'm doing my job." He helped her tilt the bucket into the trough.

"One look at them and it's clear you've been doing a fine job. Look how fat they are!"

Wiggling with glee on the fence slat, Dale laughed. "See? Hortense is almost as big as Gertie."

"How can that be? Wasn't Gertie Hortense's mama?"

"Yup!" Dale finally hopped down. "But I told you I've been taking good care of her! Just yesterday, Ma said Hortense is so big we're gonna have to call her a gilt instead of a shoat!"

"You're quite a farmer, Dale. I'm very impressed."

"I'm gonna grow big and fat, too." He patted his stomach. "I left room for two pieces of pie!"

Laney couldn't keep her laughter from escaping. Joy surged through her. *Today, of all days, is a day to be thankful to the Lord.*

"They won't eat the pie without us, will they?"

"I wouldn't think so."

Dale started to trot. "We'd best hurry, Miss Laney. That man said he's full, but he could change his mind!"

Laney lengthened her stride and matched pace with him, laughing with glee.

"We're back!" Dale announced as they entered the cabin.

The men had moved the benches over by the window to catch the late autumn sunlight. Galen and Josh rose at once. Ishmael copied them, but Mr. Grubb didn't budge. Silverware clinked and water splashed as Colin and Sean washed the dishes.

Laney rested her hand on Dale's shoulder. "This young man is doing a marvelous job."

"Aye, he's conscientious," Mrs. O'Sullivan agreed from the side of her bed, where she and Hilda sat knitting.

Laney continued to look at Galen. The odd feeling that she'd interrupted something washed over her.

"I've been reading the parable of the Good Samaritan."

"Oh!" Laney finally stopped staring at Galen's handsome blue eyes and glanced down to see he held his Bible.

"Miss Laney, come have a sit down." Ishmael pointed at the end of the bench where he'd been seated. "Mr. O'Sullivan's sharin' a fine tale from the Bible."

"Thank you."

Galen scooted over. "There's room here by me." Warmth filled Laney. Galen wanted her by his side. She gathered her skirts and sat down between him and Ivy. Galen looked into her eyes. A long, slow smile lifted the corners of his mouth. " 'Tis good to have you here."

He couldn't have said anything to make her happier. "It's been a wonderful day. I'm glad you're reading from the Word."

" 'Tain't jest one word. 'Tis a story made up of lotsa words." Ivy elbowed her. " 'Tis a dreadful good tale. A feller was a walkin' somewhar and thieves done beat him up sommat fierce. Nobody wants to holp him now. I cain hardly wait to hear how it turns out."

Of all the people he could go to, Dale leaned against Laney, and she lifted him onto her lap. "Please go on, Galen."

" 'But a certain Samaritan," he started, "as he journeyed, came where he was: and when he saw him, he had compassion on him, And went to him, and bound up his wounds, pouring in oil and wine, and set him on his own beast, and brought him to an inn, and took care of him. And on the morrow when he departed, he took out two pence, and gave them to the host, and said unto him, Take care of him; and whatsoever thou spendest more, when I come again, I will repay thee.' "

"Ain't that the beatenist?" Ishmael leaned against the table. "He done paid for a man he don't even know!"

"So did that Samaritan feller track down them thieves and string 'em up?" Ivy's enthusiasm made her every bit as wiggly as Dale. "I shore do love a tale when folks get their come-uppance!"

"The Bible doesn't tell us what happened," Galen said. "This was a parable—a made-up story Jesus used to make folks think. Listen to this verse: Jesus asked, "Which now of these three, thinkest thou, was neighbour unto him that fell among the thieves?""

"Dunno." Ishmael's forehead creased. "That story thar didn't say whar any of 'em lived. Jist said they was happenin' along."

Ivy's nose wrinkled. "Was it s'posed to be a riddle?"

"'He that shewed mercy on him.'" Galen pointed to the verse in the Bible. "That's the answer the man gave to Jesus. 'Then said Jesus unto him, Go, and do thou likewise.' So what we're to do is think that everyone is our neighbor, and we're to be kind and helpful whenever an opportunity presents itself."

Mr. Grubb snorted. "'Twas easy 'nuff fer that Sam feller to holp. He got money and a strong mule. He even had hisself wine. I reckon folks who got so much cain holp out, 'cuz plenty of us ain't able to." He jerked his chin toward Ishmael. "We got work waitin' back home."

"I'll cut some pie." Ruth headed for the pie safe. "Ivy? Ishmael? Did you want pumpkin or pecan?"

"Pecan!" Ivy lit up.

Ishmael chortled. "Yore askin' a gal from the South if'n she'd like herself a slice of pecan? Might as well have asked a beaver if'n he likes birch!"

"Oh, I ain't et pecan pie in six years or better," Ivy said as she joined Ruth at the table. As soon as Ruth cut a generous slice, Ivy grabbed it right off the server and bit into it. "Mmm! Oh, it's wonderful good!"

"It's my grandmother's recipe," Hilda told her as she set aside her knitting. "If you'd like, I'll write it down for you."

Mr. Grubb snorted. "Ain't no use. The gal cain't read a word."

"That doesn't matter," Laney burst out.

"Shore does," Mr. Grubb said, giving her a dark look.

"You read, don't you, Ishmael?" Galen asked.

"Some. Not as much as I wish."

"I'm starting a library for the town." Ruth didn't bother to ask Ishmael what kind of pie he wanted. She cut another huge wedge and served it straight into his hands. "You're welcome to come to the Broken P and borrow books any time."

"And until you can read, I'm sure Ishmael will read aloud to you." Laney took a deep breath. "Josh read aloud to me all the time until Ruth taught me to read this past year."

Pain shot across Ivy's features. She dipped

her head and muttered, "Yore funnin' me."

"No, Ivy," Laney said quietly. "I'm not."

"We're all very proud of the hard work Laney put into learning." Galen's voice resonated with warmth.

"See?" Hilda waggled a knitting needle at them. "I'll be sure to write my recipe down for you, Ivy. Until you learn to read, your father or brother can read it to you."

"It's past time we left," Mr. Grubb announced as he slapped his knees and rose.

He can't read, either. The realization stunned Laney. He'd belittled his own daughter, which was horrid in and of itself; but he'd done it over something he lacked himself.

In less than a minute, Mr. Grubb had said good-bye, made sure Ivy had hold of the pot she'd come bearing, and pushed his children out of the O'Sullivan home.

"I'm looking forward to your help tomorrow, Ivy!" Mrs. O'Sullivan called from her doorstep.

"I'll be here. You cain count on me!" Ivy's voice faded as she added, "Thankee for the grand day."

"Ma?"

Mrs. O'Sullivan turned around. "Aye?"

Sean was drying a platter. "Ishmael and Ivy are nice, but their da—I tried hard to like him, but it didn't work. He's greedy and mean."

"He rubs me the wrong way, too," Galen agreed with a grimace. "We'll have to be good neighbors and pray for them."

"It strains my mind," Ruth said, "to think that in this day and age, someone hasn't heard the gospel."

"Our example will say far more than our words." A wry smile tilted Galen's mouth. "Ishmael watches me like a hawk."

"Aye, that he does." Mrs. O'Sullivan stared out the window. "A while back we heard Ishmael whistling a hymn Galen left the house singin' that very morning."

"Speaking of hymns . . ." Laney slipped past Galen and went to the far side of the bed. She'd waited a long time to share this surprise with the O'Sullivans and now pulled out the gift hidden in her knitting bag.

"This is for your family. Because, well—" All of the tender things she'd thought up and practiced saying fled her mind. She slipped her knitting bag into Mrs. O'Sullivan's hands. "Today is Thanksgiving. We want to give thanks that Cullen O'Sullivan was such a big-hearted man."

"What have we here?" Mrs. O'Sullivan pulled out the book.

"*The Sacred Melodeon*," Galen read aloud.

Mrs. O'Sullivan's mouth formed a tremulous smile. "This is so kind of you. My Cullen always loved to sing hymns."

Galen nodded somberly.

"Our Galen whistles or sings every morning now when he goes out to work." Dale stood on tiptoe to get a better look at the book.

"Open it," Laney urged.

"In memory of Cul—" Mrs. O'Sullivan's voice broke as she tried to read the inscription.

Looking up at Galen, Laney said, "I wanted to do something special because your father was such a wonderful man of God."

Galen's hand found hers and squeezed it. "What a thoughtful gesture. We'll treasure it."

Josh slapped Galen on the back. "My sister's tongue-tied for the first time in her life. What she's trying to tell you is that the church now has hymnals in your father's honor."

"Oh," Sean said with a frown. "Mr. Lufe won't make up his funny words anymore."

"Now that," Hilda said with great enthusiasm, "is something we can all truly be grateful for!"

———————

"Pa's gonna be happier'n a dog with two tails," Ivy declared the next day as she set the second hot pumpkin pie on the table.

Mrs. O'Sullivan smiled. "My own da used to use that same expression. It brings back many a pleasant memory."

Ivy nodded. Try as she might, she couldn't come up with a single time with Pa that brought happy thoughts to mind.

"The laundry ought to be dry in a little bit." Mrs. O'Sullivan went over to the pie safe.

Ivy held her tongue. If Mrs. O'Sullivan

wanted to put the pies in her safe, she could—
but they'd store better if left to cool awhile first.

"You and I are going to sit out in the sunshine and finish this off." Mrs. O'Sullivan turned
around, a pie tin in her hands.

"Hilda's pecan pie!"

"Grab us each a fork. We'll sit together and
eat straight out of the tin."

"You don't have to ask me twice!" A minute
later, Ivy sat beside Mrs. O'Sullivan on the
porch steps and took a bite of the pie.
"Mmmm!" She closed her eyes. "It's even better
than I 'membered." Her eyes opened. "And
that's sayin' a mouthful!"

Mrs. O'Sullivan stuck her fork in and took a
bite. "There's something different about her recipe. We'll look at the ingredients together and
figure out how she manages to make it so good."

Ivy stared at the way her dress draped over
her bony knees. "You don't mind readin' to
me?"

"And why would I?"

Boom! The ground shook.

Ivy sprang to her feet. Mrs. O'Sullivan did
the same. They turned toward the sound, and
Ivy started running.

Chapter Eighteen

Ishmael and Galen both streaked past her on bareback as she ran toward home. Ivy held the stitch in her side and forged ahead. By the time she reached the clearing, Josh McCain and three of his men had arrived, as well.

The lean-to was gone. Its logs littered the area and burned like torches. Parts of the still lay strewn about, most of them sparking. A ball of flames consumed the mule cart Pa had used for storing the full jugs. Dried leaves crackled and blew in the wind that continued to fan the flames higher.

Pa wasn't anywhere to be seen, and their mule was missing, too.

"Mind the horses!" Josh shouted at Ivy as he shoved the reins into her hands.

Ivy managed to drag the horses over to the rope Ishy used to hang food. It took every last bit of her strength to tie them all.

The area filled with acrid dark gray smoke. Ivy strained to see what was going on. The men hollered at one another. As he had before, Ishy used their shovel to scoop dirt over the flames to extinguish them. Ivy longed to go help, but she didn't dare leave the horses.

Just as thick as the smoke, fear and sadness blanketed her. *Pa's done it now. He's blown up the works, and Mr. O'Sullivan's gonna be hoppin' mad. He'll drive us from his land, and we won't have nothing at all to take with us this time.*

It took forever, but the men finally had matters under control. Galen O'Sullivan stomped up to Ishy and roared something at him. Ivy couldn't make out the exact words, but that didn't much matter. Another feller went over and told them something. Mr. O'Sullivan and Ishy both turned and looked at her.

Mr. O'Sullivan shoved back some of his hair and said something more.

Ivy didn't want her brother to suffer alone. Pa ought to step up and be a man. Seeing as he wasn't, Ivy determined the horses were calming down, so she went to stand by her brother's side.

Ishy clamped a hand around her waist and dragged her up tight against his side. He was trying to protect her from his boss's wrath, but Ivy wouldn't allow it. She pushed away and faced him. "Soon as Pa comes back, we'll be gone."

Galen O'Sullivan looked at her, then next at Ishy, and clamped his mouth shut.

Ishy yanked her back to his side.

"Yore nice shirt is burnt," she blurted out.

"Sis—"

"I—"

Ishy covered her mouth with his other hand. "You gotta listen to me."

She nodded, and he took his hand away.

"Pa ain't comin' back."

———◆———

"Well?" Galen looked around the small circle of men in the pastor's parlor.

"It's a difficult situation," the pastor said slowly.

"We've looked at the situation from a dozen different angles, but nothing is clear." Galen finally sat down.

Rick Maltby, the only attorney around, folded his arms across his chest and leaned back. "Let me get this straight: The Grubbs are illegal squatters—"

"*Were* illegal squatters." Galen wanted to be scrupulously honest. "I came to an agreement with them."

The sheriff shook his head. "It's cut and dried as far as I see. Those people operated an illegal still."

"They didn't; their father did," Galen clarified.

"The twins knew about the still, and the girl was growing corn for it." The sheriff bashed his fist into his open palm. "That implicates her, if not her brother."

"Galen told us their crop was just now ready for harvest." Maltby pinched his lower lip and tugged on it thoughtfully. "It could be argued that Ivy Grubb didn't support her father's illegal enterprise."

Galen wasn't sure whether Rick truly felt he could support such an argument or if he was trying to nettle the sheriff. The two of them had been at odds ever since they discovered one supported Breckinridge while the other voted for Lincoln.

Josh frowned. "Where did Mr. Grubb get the corn and sugar for the whiskey he's been producing?"

"I'd like to know that myself." The sheriff leaned forward. "We've had a rash of thefts recently. The thefts began around the time the Grubbs arrived. If they're not guilty, then I suspect whoever was supplying the corn and sugar might have been financing his partnership with what he stole."

"We can ask Ishmael. He might be able to tell you who it is." Galen heaved a sigh. "He's worked hard for me."

"Their father died." Pastor Dawes spoke in a quiet voice, and Galen couldn't tell whether he'd muted his voice because of compassion for Ishmael and Ivy or because he knew Galen would be sensitive about the subject of death. The minister added, "Their loss seems like punishment enough."

"O'Sullivan gave them jobs." The sheriff stood and paced back and forth. "The thanks they gave for all of his generosity was to practically set fire to the whole farm with a still!"

"Galen can't do everything." Josh leaned forward and rested his forearms on his thighs. "The farm alone is more work than he can handle. Add on the Pony relay and it's far too much. Ishmael is a hard-working man. More than once, Galen's said he's a godsend."

"God isn't in the habit of sending moonshiners to act as His agents," the sheriff snapped.

"The Almighty's used anyone or anything He chose," the pastor countered. "He used the harlot Rahab to help the children of Israel, and Balaam's donkey spoke."

"Ishmael and Ivy have almost no knowledge at all regarding the Lord." Galen rubbed his hand across his forehead.

"Then we're making a huge mistake." Pastor Dawes drummed his fingers on the arm of his chair. "We're measuring the Grubbs against Christian values and standards. Especially if they've had no training, they've lived merely to survive and couldn't see past each day's challenges."

"What they did was illegal," the sheriff gritted out.

"Christian values are the cornerstone of our

legal system." Maltby stuck out his hands and moved them up and down as if he were comparing the weight of two items. "Justice and mercy have to be balanced. Someone who's come from the backwoods and never stepped foot in a church—such a man deserves consideration."

"From what I see," Pastor Dawes said slowly, "there are two issues at hand. The first is whether the Grubb twins should be brought up on legal charges."

The sheriff scowled. "Most of the evidence of the still probably burned, so I might not be able to indict the Grubbs. Even if I bring them in, Maltby here is soft-hearted and sounds like he'll find any loophole he can to get them off."

Maltby nodded.

Pastor Dawes faced Galen. "Then the other issue is, what is to become of the Grubbs?"

"Ride 'em out of town," the sheriff asserted. "The faster, the better."

"I thought that yesterday when we were fighting the fire," Galen confessed. "Then they found out their father was dead. I realized my original response was spiteful, yet vengeance belongs to God."

Maltby spoke up. "That doesn't mean you're supposed to turn the other cheek and keep them here."

"That's the first thing you've said I can agree with." The sheriff scowled at Galen. "They've deceived you already. How can you be sure your mother and little brothers are safe?"

"Ishmael and Ivy Grubb are raw, but they're not dangerous in the least."

"Josh, you've met them," Maltby said. "What's your opinion?"

"Ishmael's a hard worker. He's respectful of Mrs. O'Sullivan and good to the boys."

The sheriff hadn't stopped pacing. He wheeled around. "And Ivy?"

"Backward," Galen said, "but we can't hold that against her."

"Ruth and Laney have spent time with Ivy." Josh straightened up. "Their impression is that she worked herself silly and got nothing but grief from her father."

"Pa don't thank Ivy's worth much, her bein' a gal." Ishmael's words echoed in Galen's mind. *"Pa got hisself a rare bad temper. . . . It shames me to admit it, but he's dreadful hard on her."*

"There's a difference between pitying someone and begging for trouble," the sheriff said, staring at Galen.

"You asked us for our counsel." Pastor Dawes looked at each of them in turn. "Since the legalities—"

"Illegalities," the sheriff muttered.

"Are a matter that won't need to be addressed," the pastor said as if he hadn't been interrupted, "what you have to do is determine whether to allow the Grubb twins to remain on the farm or ask them to leave. We started out this meeting with prayer and asked for wisdom. We'll be ending it the same way. You don't have to account to any of us for the choice you make. It's between you and God."

"Not exactly." The sheriff cleared his throat. "If I find out either of the Grubbs is behind the robberies, you could be accused of harboring criminals."

Josh scoffed, "That's absurd."

"Actually, it's true." Maltby shifted uncomfortably. "Because you know Ishmael and Ivy's character is questionable, and it's been ascertained that the thefts coincided with their arrival, you could be viewed as an accomplice of sorts if they're implicated in any way."

"Mark my words," the sheriff said, smashing his fist into his other hand again, "you're courting trouble if you keep them on."

After they closed in prayer, Galen stopped at Lester's mercantile to pick up Ma. They stayed silent the whole way home. *Lord, what am I to do?*

"What are those?" Ma asked as they pulled up close to the house, pointing to a dozen or so odd ridges in the earth.

Galen helped her down, then followed the marks around to the far side of the house. The woodpile was much larger than it had been that morning. Most of the new wood was charred on one surface. Etched into the dirt in front of the pile were two stark words: *Sorry Boss.*

Ivy refused to look off to the side where the men had buried Pa yesternoon. All things considered, they'd been downright civil, digging a hole and such. Ishy hadn't let her see Pa. He'd taken the worst of their three blankets and wrapped Pa in it. Mr. O'Sullivan offered to say a prayer, but Ivy refused. It didn't seem right, talkin' to God over the grave of a man who insisted He didn't exist.

Pa was gone but Muley had returned. Ivy walked alongside the beast, gripping the rope halter tighter than ever, letting the stiff hemp fibers dig into her palm. It didn't banish the memory of the soft dirt she'd held for a moment before dropping it into the grave.

"Anywhar you wanna go in particular?"

Ishmael's question made her look over Mule's head. Ivy merely shrugged.

"Up till now we always headed west. Could be we should go south. Winter's a-comin', so we'd be ten kinds of fools to aim for somewhar cold."

"You gotta point." They continued on. Birds sang as if everything in the world was good. The only other sound was the dull scraping of the travois Ishy had fashioned out of their tent. By sheer luck, the tent hadn't caught fire. The meager belongings Ivy could salvage comprised two bundles on the travois.

"I'll take care of you, sis." Ishmael wiped his brow and slapped his hat back on his head. "We got us Mule and an ax. Even got us a little food and the pots."

She pasted on a smile so he wouldn't know how tired she was. "'Twixt yore snares and my gatherin', I reckon we cain get along."

"Only till I find work. Good, honest work. Either in a town or mebbe as a farmhand again. That kind of work suited me jist fine."

"You ain't the onliest one what cain work. Could be the farmer's wife might need some holp."

They didn't dream aloud about claiming land. The fire had destroyed their plow and all of the corn. *A crop of goose bumps is all I'm ever gonna call my own.*

The sound of a horse coming made Ivy tug on Mule's rope. "C'mon, you flea-bitten sorry bag of bones."

Mule whinny-brayed a protest.

Ishy nudged against the beast and rumpled its stiff mane. "Gotta move, Muley." The animal's long ears twitched. "Jist a few steps now."

Whether it was the coaxing tone or the pressure, Ivy didn't know. Didn't really care, either. It worked. Mule plodded over at an angle.

Ivy and Ishmael both turned back to make sure the travois would be out of the horseman's way. Ivy blinked. She couldn't believe her eyes.

Mr. O'Sullivan pulled back on the reins, and

his horse obediently halted. Mr. O'Sullivan even tipped his hat to Ivy.

He shore is a strange feller. Acts mannerly even when we done him wrong.

"Ishmael."

Ishy cleared his throat. "Boss, we know we done wrong. You ain't been nuthin' but good to us, and we kept Pa's secret. Weren't no way to return yore kindness."

"It wasn't."

The shade from the brim of his hat made it impossible to see his expression, but his clipped words made it clear he'd just as soon wallow in a sty as to waste his breath on them.

"You said yore land went to the ridge." Ishmael slapped Mule to set him in motion. "We'll be offa yore property in a few more minutes."

"We had a deal."

Ivy looked from Mr. O'Sullivan to her brother and back. He'd already hollered at Ishmael yesterday. Probably was fixin' to lay into Ishy again. *No matter whar we go, folks're always the same. They find out what Pa was up to and they tear into us till they're shore we're gone.*

"We had a deal," Ishmael agreed, "but Pa—"

"My deal was with you, not your father."

Ivy and Ishmael traded a startled look.

"Don't mistake me. I won't put up with any more deceit. If I so much as find one drop of moonshine, I'll have the law on you. But I won't hold you responsible for your father's behavior."

Mule's rope slithered from Ivy's hand. The rough fibers rasped, proving this whole scene was real, not a dream.

"Christians rely on God's grace and forgiveness. We confess our wrongs, and He forgives us. You've been man enough to apologize, Ishmael. I'm giving you a chance if you choose to take it."

"I cain still work for you, and Ivy and me are okay to live on your land?" Ishmael sounded as incredulous as Ivy felt.

"That was our deal. Either you stick with it or you move on. Your choice."

Ishmael swiped his hat off and rushed toward Mr. O'Sullivan with his hand outstretched. "Much obliged, Boss."

The men shook hands, and Ivy's knees began to shake.

Mr. O'Sullivan sat up tall in the saddle. "You'll need today to set up your camp. I'll see you in the morning."

Ishy waited till his boss rode off, then tossed his battered hat into the air. "Yeehaw!"

* * *

Excuses. Silly little excuses that fooled no one. But how wonderful they were! Laney watched as her brother and Galen stood by the mare and talked about it while Laney waited astride the other horse. Josh—bless him—was the one who had concocted this excuse. No doubt, it was with Ruth's help. They'd started finding ways to allow Laney and Galen to be together. Nothing thrilled her more.

"She's a bit fractious," Josh was telling Galen. "I'd appreciate it if you'd ride her and let me know. I wouldn't want to sell her to the Darldens for their son yet if she still needs more training."

Galen chuckled. Laney loved the rich, happy sound that came from him. He shook his head. "That boy's just like my brothers. I'm thinking 'tis usually the boy rather than the horse that requires more training."

Josh cast a glance at Galen's paddock. "I'll ride Nessie home. You can trade me back when you come by."

"You have to give me Nessie back." Galen gave him a friendly shove. "I know you always did take a liking to her."

"She's one of the sweetest horses I ever broke. It's a pity all girls aren't as biddable."

"Joshua McCain!" Laney gave him an outraged look.

"I'm sure he meant mares, lass."

"I'm sure he didn't."

Josh didn't look penitent in the least. "I live in a household of women. Ruth, Laney, and Hilda gang up together. You don't know how lucky you are, Galen. The men in your house outnumber your mother."

"Aye, that we do." Galen grinned. "But then

again, Ma's been known to hold her own quite nicely. Still, she'd be happy to have me take a wife so she has someone to back her up."

Galen's words echoed in Laney's mind. He swung into the saddle and rode alongside her. "This mare's got some frisk to her."

"She's spoiling for a run. Josh made her plod the whole way here."

"I've never seen you ride at anything faster than a slow trot."

Laney flashed a smile at him. "I'll beat you to the ridge!" She took off before he did. Before long, Galen's bark of laughter caught up with her. A heartbeat later, they rode side-by-side up to the ridge. Once there, their horses pranced and pawed, then wended back and forth between clumps of trees.

"You ride well. 'Tis a pleasant surprise."

"Thank you. I like the feel of the wind in my face." Laney reached up and adjusted her hat-pin.

"It fans your color higher." Galen studied her face. "Aye, and it makes those little curls wisp around your face. The only other times I've seen them is when you've been here to do some canning or make jelly."

Laney reached up to smooth them back.

Galen's hand shot out. He stopped her and gently kept her hand in his. "Don't. They're dar-ling." Slowly, he turned loose of her hand. "There are many facets to you, Laney," he said, his voice gruff. "I'm liking each one I see."

"Hey, thar!" Ivy walked out from behind a tree. "What're y'all doing out here?"

"We're taking a ride." Galen's hand rested on the pommel. "Josh is thinking of selling this horse, but he wanted my opinion as to whether she was tame enough for a youngster to handle."

"Anybody worryin' o'er whether a kid oughtta ride a beast might think on gettin' a mule. They're strong and steady. Muley of ourn, thar's one hard-workin' beast. Ain't much to look at, but sometimes looks ain't what matter most."

"You're right," Galen agreed.

"What do you have there?" Laney nodded toward the bucket Ivy carried.

"Pine nuts. Mighty fine tastin' when you know how to fix 'em."

"I've never had them, but I can tell from your voice that you love them. By the way, Ivy, since the O'Sullivans had us all over to their home for Thanksgiving, I wanted to invite you all to Christmas at our place."

Ivy gave her a wary look. "You ain't a-gonna make us go to church first, are you?"

Laney saw the small shake of Galen's head and took his cue. "Ivy, you're always welcome to join us for worship, but coming to supper is all I'm asking."

"I'll talk to Ishy."

"You go on ahead and talk to your brother."

Galen turned to Laney. "The O'Sullivans will be happy to accept your hospitality. I can't think of a nicer way to spend the day."

"Well, y'all have a nice ride." Ivy turned and walked off.

"Shouldn't we offer her a ride?"

Galen shook his head. "Nay, Laney. The Grubbs are living in a tent. It would embarrass Ivy for you to see how she lives."

"A tent! Galen, that's dreadful. They must be cold!"

"Ishmael said they've lived in a tent for years now. Pointed out they'd done so in far colder places, too. I gave him a length of gutta-percha cloth to put over the tent to keep any rain out. When we put out the fire, their blankets were ruined. Ma gave me some new ones to drop by. With Ivy helping in the garden and taking home produce and our sending supper plates over with Ishmael, they're doing okay. It's not great, but they don't want charity. It's a tough balance between helping them and hurting their pride."

"Then we'll convince them to come for Christmas. I already have a shawl for Ivy. Ruth and I are making her a dress. It's our tradition to have a new outfit for Christmas. It will be easy for me to use that as an excuse."

"Laney, you've a generous spirit. Ma's done well, taking care of necessities here and there, but Ivy—well, she could use a young woman to guide her."

"Your mother has been wonderful, teaching me things I needed to know. I won't end up teaching those same things to Ivy, but it's the same sort of situation. I'll do my best to help her and still be mindful of her pride."

They turned the horses and rode a bit farther. When Laney's riding skirt caught on a shrub, Galen halted. "Whoa there." He leaned over and freed her. One brow hiked. "You mentioned a new outfit for Christmas."

Laney nodded as she imagined Galen's reaction to the dress she'd finished hemming last night. She would wear it on Christmas—first to church, with the hoops beneath it in order to be stylish. The sleeves were cut sparingly as a contrast to the full skirt. The base color reminded her of toasted almonds, and raised dashes of cream lent it a wonderful texture. A high-necked bodice of a slightly darker brown contrasted with the rest of the ensemble—but on Christmas Day when she got home, she would remove the hoops and suspend the textured outer skirts up in the back to form a series of pretty swags. She'd sewn an underskirt of the same material as the bodice. The way her gown transformed from picturesque to practical would impress upon Galen how she could adapt to fit into his world.

"Are you going to tell me about it?"

Laney playfully shook her head. "You'll have to wait to see it."

Galen opened his mouth to say something, but he shut it. A long moment later, he said, "Some things are worth waiting for."

CHAPTER NINETEEN

Galen reached down and pressed his hand on Dale's knobby knee. Dale ceased swinging his leg and gave him an apologetic smile. *Da used to have to do that with me,* Galen thought. *Aye, and I recall him praising me for sitting still in church when I grew tall enough for my toes to touch the floor. Sean's just about there himself. I'll make a point of commending him at Christmas dinner today, I will.*

Da's absence hit Galen afresh. On Christmas Day a year ago, Da had been too frail to stand long, so Galen and Ma had sat on either side of him while everyone else stood to sing the carols. Ever since Da's death, Galen strove to fill in for him in every possible way. Today, he didn't. Instead of sitting beside Ma as he had since the funeral, Galen intentionally arranged for Dale and Sean to sit on either side of her.

"Now if you'll all rise and take up your hymnals, we'll sing, 'It Came Upon a Midnight Clear' and follow it with my favorite, 'Good Christian Men, Rejoice.'"

The hymnals. Da would have been delighted by them! He loved music so. Memories, sweet and painful, assailed Galen.

After the music, Pastor Dawes said, "We have a few special surprises. If the adults will please be seated, we'll begin."

Dale and Colin jostled past Ma and joined Sean in the aisle. Laney and Ruth slipped out of their pew, too. *Such a lovely gown my lass is wearing! I'll be sure to let her know how I admire it.* Laney reached down and took Dale's hand. Galen didn't know what they were up to, but Laney's tenderness toward little Dale warmed Galen clear down to his toes. She'd be a good mother.

Da told me I'd know deep in my heart when the right woman came along. Aye, Galen did know— and right Da was.

In a matter of moments, all of the children left the sanctuary. Laney and Ruth accompanied them out and shut the door, keeping whatever they were doing a secret. But Galen grinned. He'd been keeping a secret himself. A thin band of gold rested in his shirt pocket, right over his heart. In the past few weeks he'd been tempted on many occasions to speak out of the abundance of his heart, but he knew once he confessed his love he'd ask her to marry him in the very next breath. Today, he would take his beloved Laney on a walk and propose.

Galen slid across the pew and draped his arm along the back of it. As he crooked his arm to encircle Ma, he felt the elbow of his shirt give way. His best shirt had grown threadbare, but he didn't want Ma to have to sew him a new one. She already worked too hard.

After a pause, Laney and Ruth opened the doors again.

"Awww," the ladies of the congregation all breathed softly.

Galen tore his gaze off of Laney and grinned at the sight of Mary and Joseph. One of Josh's striped shirts hung from Dale's shoulders. Even though it was belted at the waist with a length of rope, the garment brushed the floor. A towel covered Dale's head, and he gripped a staff in one hand.

Pretty little Greta Newman wore a pale blue shift, and a length of white cloth draped over her dark hair. She gently cradled a blanket-wrapped doll in her arms, and her sweet smile revealed a missing tooth.

Dale's left arm shot up in the air, and he wiggled his hand until the rolled-up cuff fell back to his wrist. Then he cupped Greta's elbow and led her down to the front of the church.

All of the other small children trooped in, each of them wearing white paper wings. Bumping and whispering, they arranged themselves all around Mary, Joseph, and Jesus. Laney stood off to the side and directed them as they sang "There Came a Little Child to Earth."

Burlap sack-clad shepherds arrived next. Then Sean, Colin, and a third boy entered wearing fancy velvet robes and crowns. Instead of going down the center aisle, they formed a procession around the side of the church and sang a song about three kings of the Orient Galen hadn't heard before.

After the congregation sang "Silent Night" with the children, the little ones all rejoined their parents. Galen watched as Laney slipped back into the pew across the aisle. *Next Christmas, she'll be sitting here beside me.*

When Galen focused on the front of the church, he wondered why his brothers and Brett had left the wise men's gifts on the altar.

Pastor Dawes gestured toward them. "Wise men and women still bring gifts to the Lord. It's not just something the Magi did on that day when Christ came to earth; it's symbolic of what we still set at His feet."

First he lifted the purple velvet box that was heavily trimmed in golden braid. "Gold. It represents how we honor our heavenly King. It's not just what we give of our finances; it's what we give of our hearts. By yielding to the process of the fiery trials, we allow God to purify and mold us. . . ."

Next, the pastor held up a camphor glass box. Intricate silver scrollwork embellished the cloudy white glass. "Frankincense." He nodded approvingly. "It's appropriate that we've used a white box to represent that gift, because the word *frankincense* actually means 'whiteness.' The bark on certain trees in Persia is slit, and a white juice seeps from the wound in tears that must harden for three months before they're harvested.

"Extremely expensive, frankincense is used as medicine or perfume, but the Israelites also burned it in the temple during worship for its sweet fragrance. Remember, though, that the frankincense comes directly from that tree's wounds and pain. The lesson we learn from this gift is when we worship the Lord in the midst of our greatest sorrows, it is especially sweet to Him. He knows the tears that trickle from our broken hearts, our hurts, and our repentant spirits are our private frankincense, burned on the altar of our lives."

Ma huddled closer. She'd been dabbing at her eyes, but she finally turned her face against Galen's chest and wept in huge, nearly silent sobs. He held her tight and bowed his head.

The pastor went on. "Myrrh is a resin that is obtained the same way frankincense is. Though it's fragrant, the name means 'bitter,' because myrrh tastes acrid. Kept in alabaster, like this urn, myrrh will stay fragrant for more than a century. The bodies of very wealthy people were treated with myrrh before burial. It was also ground up and used in wine to treat pain.

"The wise men took myrrh to Jesus, a fragrant and costly offering; but we see myrrh once again when Christ Jesus refused to accept it as He hung on the cross. Through myrrh, we acknowledge that Christ experienced what it was to be human, to endure the most bitter pain and sorrow."

Galen pulled his handkerchief from his pocket. *This wasn't the sermon I expected, but it's the one I needed.*

Pastor Dawes spoke just a little longer. After a few other insights, he said, "God's greatest gift to us came wrapped in swaddling clothes. Wise men knelt before Him. Angels sang. As for us— we worship and praise Him, too."

The preacher said a fine prayer, and a mere breath after he said amen, the sanctuary door burst open. Ishmael stood in the opening, one hand wrapped around Ivy's arm and the other curled around Galen's rifle.

"Galen O'Sullivan, you low-down, filthy polecat. You done spoilt my sis."

Chapter Twenty

G alen stood and stared at Ishmael in disbelief. "You're mistaken. I've never—"

"Onliest mistake was you thankin' you wouldn't get caught."

Galen shook his head. As he did, he saw Ma's fright and Ethel's scowl, but most of all, Laney's sudden pallor. Anger surged through him. He boomed, "If your sister is in trouble, it's not my fault. I've done nothing. Nothing at all."

Ishmael flung Ivy forward and cocked the rifle. "Ivy ain't no flannel-mouthed liar. She named you as her baby's pa."

Galen glowered at her. She'd lost her balance when Ishmael flung her forward, and she now sat in a rumpled heap on the floor. Rivulets on her less-than-clean cheeks made it clear she'd been crying. She might well be a woman in trouble, but it wasn't his doing. "Tell him. Tell him the truth. You know I'm not—"

"You ain't a-gonna bully my sis." Ishmael raised the rifle. "I'm a-givin' you a choice: either you marry up with her right now or that parson's a-gonna be prayin' over yore sorry dead carcass."

"I have no reason to marry her. None whatsoever."

Ishmael aimed the rifle at him. "Shore you do. 'Tis the onliest way yore a-gonna stay alive and breathin'. Y'all sit yoreselves back down. Thar's either gonna be a weddin' or a funeral here in jist a minute."

My rifle. Ishmael went into my house and got my rifle. The implications behind that were worthy of thought—later. Right now he had to protect his family. Galen edged past Ma and motioned to Colin to scoot them far away as he stepped out into the aisle.

Finally he cast another look at Ivy. He rasped, "We both know—"

"We both know," Ishmael cut in, his voice shaking with fury, "that whilst I worked yore land, you've been visiting my sister."

"I have not." Galen stared back at him.

"I got proof. 'Least five times now you done gone and took a poke full of food to her."

Members of the congregation gasped. Lester's brows formed a foreboding *V.* Eddie Lufe's chin hiked upward and his jaw jutted forward. Brothers and sisters in Christ suddenly stared at Galen with undeserved condemnation.

Disbelief speared through Galen. "I left food for you out of Christian charity—nothing more."

"The part you ain't sayin' is you took somethin' in return."

"I did not." Galen glared at Ishmael.

"First time you e'er saw us, you gave Sis a purdy sack she turned into a bodice. I still got three of t'other sacks you put food in."

Whispers buzzed through the church.

"Them blankets—" Ishmael growled.

"You ruined your blanket fighting the fire. You'd have frozen without the ones Ma sent over."

"I was a fool, a-thankin' you brung 'em to be kind. You was makin' yore bed with my sister. Now yore a-gonna lie in it."

Galen felt Pastor Dawes step up beside him as Josh flanked him on the other side. Only a few moments had passed since Ishmael burst into the church, but it felt like years. Galen dared to look past Josh to Laney.

Her beautiful brown eyes glowed with . . . hurt? With fright? Not a speck of color remained in her cheeks.

Josh growled under his breath, "Don't." He moved to block Galen's view of her.

Don't? Don't look at Laney? Don't marry Ivy? Lord in heaven, what am I to do?

"Yore the parson." Ishmael lowered the rifle as he spoke to the minister. "Start hitchin' 'em."

"Marriage is a sacrament. It isn't to be entered into lightly."

"I ain't gonna stand by and let no man take

my sister lightly, neither. Get on with it."

Galen barked, "I won't abide raw talk—especially in the house of God or in the presence of ladies."

Ishmael's chin rose. "Didn't mean no disrespect, but I aim to take care of my own. Cain't keep a secret what you done. They'd all know soon 'nuff."

"I've not . . . *dallied* with Ivy. I'd never yoke myself—heart, soul, or body—with a woman who wasn't a believer."

"You ruint my sis. No other man's ever gonna want her now, and 'tis yore babe in her belly."

"Ivy can't have a baby." Confusion and fear mingled in Dale's shaky comment. "A lady has to be married to have a baby."

"I'm seein' to it she's married."

"Let's settle this matter in private," Josh said.

Ishmael raised the rifle. "Time's far past talkin'. Make thangs right by her, or else."

Ivy wrapped her arms around Galen's legs and wailed, "Don't hurt him, Ishy!"

Ethel huffed, "You compromised the girl. Marrying her is the least you can do." Several men and women suddenly refused to look Galen in the eyes.

"On the fearsome day of judgment, God will call us all to account for our conduct." The minister looked from Galen to Ivy and back. "Only you know who is telling the truth here."

"I refuse to lie. I won't love and cherish this woman till death parts us."

"Shoulda thunk 'bout that afore now." Ishmael closed one eye and stared down the barrel. "Yore honor bound to provide for my sis and the babe. If'n you don't wanna say a lotta fanciful words, it don't make no nivermind. Long as she's yore wedded wife."

The anger in Ishmael's eyes and set of his jaw made it clear he meant business. *Any chance I had to be happy with Laney is ruined. I can't ever tell her I'd fallen in love with her.*

"I did take food, but that was all." Galen watched as Ishmael's finger curled around the trigger. *I have no choice.* "I promised Da I'd take care of Ma and the boys. I can't do that if you shoot me. Pastor Dawes, I won't defile the solemn marriage vows by speaking them at the altar. Let this serve as my pledge. I, Galen O'Sullivan, am hereby bound by no reason other than my word of honor that I will provide for Ivy Grubb and the child she carries."

His stark words hung in the air.

Pastor Dawes cleared his throat. "Ivy, please stand."

Ivy rose. She teetered for a second, but Galen refused to reach out and steady her. Bracing her hand against the back of a pew, she stared at Galen's chest. "I reckon 'tis my turn. I'm Ivy Grubb, and from now on, I'll be your awful wedded wife. I'll do my best for you and yore kin." Her gaze skidded toward the minister. "Guess that does it."

The pastor heaved a gusty sigh. "May God bless this union. Amen."

Galen stared past Ivy and watched as Ishmael lowered the rifle. "God had nothing to do with it. This was the devil's doing."

Ivy's nails dug into the fancy wooden church bench. All around her she sensed folks whispering to one another as they scooted away and left the Sunday meetin' house. Waves of anger rolled off of Galen O'Sullivan. Ivy couldn't really fault him. But he'd come around in time. That scary-sounding day of judgment the parson talked about . . . well, if it happened, then she'd face it. It couldn't be any worse than what she had to deal with now.

Josh McCain said something in a low voice, and Ivy couldn't understand it—not over the loud thumping of her own heart.

Ain't nobody gonna be happy with me, but I cain't let that matter. I done what I had to.

Finally, she looked up. Galen's brothers were all gone. Of his kin, just his ma remained—she was leaning against the parson.

Galen stomped right past Ivy. Ishmael had lowered the rifle, and Galen yanked it from his hands. "You've got one hour to gather your things and get off my land."

"No!" The word tore from her throat.

"My sis—" Ishmael started.

"Is no longer your concern."

Her legs shook so badly, they barely held her up. Ivy staggered toward Galen. "Please . . ." Only the word didn't come out right. She reached out her hand, but everything tilted and went black.

"She's rousing."

"I couldn't care less. Ma, don't let your tender heart get in the way of good sense. Rattlers aren't half as deadly." The wagon jounced over a rut, then he half growled, "I'll drop you off at the Broken P."

"Nay, son. I'll be goin' home with you and Ivy. Can't say for sure and certain who's going to be needin' me more—you or her. But be there, I will."

"I don't want you there."

"I'll not interfere. On that, you can depend. And I'll give you privacy to say what needs saying. But her brother, Galen-mine—"

The way his mama's voice quavered and died out tore at him. "Don't you be worryin', Ma. Ishmael got what he wanted. He's not about to kill me now."

"I don't want you there alone until he's cleared out and long gone."

The wagon hit a rut, and Ivy let out a low moan. Ma cast a look back at her. "She's wide awake now, she is."

Galen didn't bother to glance back. Instead, he sat ramrod straight and stared ahead.

No one said another word the rest of the way home. Whilst he helped his Ma alight, Ivy gathered up her skirts and jumped down.

"Nay!" Ma curled her hand around Ivy's arm. "You cannot be doing such things. It could cost you the babe."

"But I gotta go pee real bad." Ivy pulled free and rushed off to the outhouse.

Crude. She's crude. And a nonbeliever. And a liar. And pregnant. Wrath pounded through his veins. *And she's my wife.*

"She's many a rough edge, Galen-mine. I'll do my best to smooth them out." Ma bowed her head and went to the house.

Galen unharnessed the horse but left the wagon in the yard. He didn't know what arrangements Ma had made regarding the boys. In a while he'd use the excuse of needing to go fetch his brothers as a way to go to Laney. The shattered look on her face this morning haunted him.

I'll discover who fathered Ivy's babe and break free from her. He strode into the house and climbed the ladder to the loft. A plan formed in his mind: He'd move to the tack room. Aye, he would. During the day he'd pressure Ivy until she confessed the truth; by night, he'd keep such a distance between them, no one could mistake the fact that they'd never shared a bed.

"I'll holp you, ma'am," he heard Ivy say.

Galen tensed at the very first word out of her mouth. He glared down as Ma and that liar stripped Ma's bed. They put a clean sheet on and Ivy pulled one end up to the top of the bed. Ma went to the bottom of the bed and did some kind of fancy moves and folds with the sheets. The liar's side turned into a wadded mess. A thick wool blanket the color of summer grass, then a heavy, colorful quilt topped the bed.

Ma didn't say a word. She just took an embroidered white flour sack and stuffed a pillow into it.

Ivy grabbed the other pillowcase and stared down at it. A daintily embroidered collection of leaves and vines trailed along the opening on one side. "Shore is purdy."

Galen's hands clenched around the loft rail. He could only think of one reason Ma would change the sheets. Under no circumstance would he ever share a bed with Ivy. His words came out as if he were dropping large stones one at a time down onto the floor. "What . . . are . . . you . . . doing?"

The girl didn't even bother to look up at him. "Holpin' yore ma."

The muscles in Galen's jaw twitched. He stomped down the ladder and turned his attention to his mother. Jabbing his forefinger toward the bed, he growled, "That bed is yours. Yours alone. I'll bring in the cot." He cast a hostile glance at Ivy. "*She'll* sleep on it."

His mother nodded. She briefly pressed her hand to his chest, then left.

Galen waited until Ma was out of earshot. In those moments, he couldn't suppress gut-wrenching worry. *What is Laney doing now? Today was to have been so special, and my beloved lass is suffering because of this liar.*

His boots made a solid hammering noise as he paced into the center of the cabin. Folding his arms across his chest, he felt the ring in his pocket. Suddenly the slender circle of gold weighed an unspeakable burden and measured a distance that was incalculable. It branded through the pocket, clear into his heart and soul. The cost of Ivy's lie burned there. "Who is it?" Galen demanded in a harsh tone.

Ivy continued stuffing the pillow into the case.

"Who's the father?"

Cramming one last fistful of pillow into the now lumpy case, she stated, "Yore the baby's pa."

"We both know that's not true."

Ivy dared to look into his blazing eyes. "Yore my husband. Yore the baby's pa."

"I've never even touched you." His gaze raked over her. "And I never will. You'll sleep on the cot—alone. When I bring you to your senses, this so-called sham of a marriage will be annulled."

"What's nulled?"

"Erased. Canceled."

Ivy shook her head. "You cain't do that. I'm yore swore-in-front-of-God-and-man wife."

"Don't you ever invoke the name of God when you don't believe in Him. I'll not have you profane the sacred just to suit your needs."

She hitched her shoulder and brushed her callused thumb back and forth over the embroidered pillowcase. "You done went and give yore word in front of all them folks. Cain't back out now."

Her casual, matter-of-fact assertion galled him. Her name and the embroidery matched: Ivy—something that looked harmless and ordinary but clung to whatever was handy and caused its ruination. Galen yanked the pillow from her arms and pitched it onto the bed.

"We both know I've not wronged you." He glared at her. "That babe you carry couldn't possibly be mine. Who's the father? Who?"

Ivy pretended she didn't hear a word.

Galen crowded closer until he was inches from her face. "Who?"

"I'm yore wife. I—"

"Wife?" His anger blazed brighter. "Make no mistake: You might carry my name temporarily, but you'll never be my wife. Rightfully some other man out there should claim his child. Who is he?"

Ivy's gaze dropped, and she compressed her lips.

"So this is how you repay my kindness? Not once, but twice I allowed you to remain on my land even though you were squatters. I've given you food, provided your brother with a job, and the clothes you wear were made in this very home. Never once have I touched you. Why did you lie?"

She kept her focus down.

Galen took her chin in his hand to force her to look him in the eyes, but she jerked back and turned to the side.

Her reaction took him by surprise. Someone wouldn't flinch and evade that reflexively unless they'd been struck on other occasions—several other occasions.

Wrath twisted to horror. Galen rasped, "I assumed you got yourself into this fix. Am I wrong? Did someone hurt you?"

He curled his hand around her upper arm and squeezed. "Is that it? A man forced himself upon you?"

Eyes cold and nearly as colorless as the ice that once dripped from the thatched roof of their Irish farmhouse stared back at him. No remorse, no shame, no sorrow shone in them. "Don't make no nivermind how I got me a babe. Yore my man."

Her words scorched away the only possible

excuse he might have understood for a desperate action.

"'Tisn't just your soul that belongs to the devil; he owns your heart, too." Galen didn't merely release his hold of her, he yanked his hand away in a move of sheer disgust. "Make no mistake. I'll find out who the father is. Best you come clean now and confess who he is."

"Thar's a hole in the elbow of that shirt of yourn. I cain stitch it up right quick."

Galen stared at her. She'd stolen his future with Laney and destroyed his reputation, yet she thought mending his shirt would mollify him?

"We—" a low, breathless shout came through the still-open door—"had . . . a . . . deal!"

"Ishy!" Ivy ran toward the door.

Galen got there first. He blocked her way out and glowered at Ishmael. "Get off my land."

Ivy stood on tiptoe to peek over his shoulder. Her brother was sweat-soaked and out of breath. She tried to shove Galen out of the way. "He run all the way from town!"

Galen didn't budge.

"We . . . had . . . a . . . deal!" Ishy roared again. He bent forward and rested his hands on his knees. "No moonshine. I'd work for you. Me and Ivy could live on yore land. We ain't trucked in likker. I been a-workin' hard for you."

"You betray me and then you expect me to keep you around? No."

Ishmael's whole body heaved from the effort he'd spent running. Had he been a horse, Galen would have cooled him, walked him, then watered and fed him. But horses were loyal; Ishmael proved himself to be a traitor. Refusing to show any pity, Galen demanded, "Get your gear and clear out."

"Don't you pay him no mind, Ishy. Yore my brother. You getta stay."

"Absolutely not," Galen snapped. He continued to block the doorway. Ivy's attempts to make him budge had no effect. "You and your sister came up with this scheme, but it's the last one you'll ever cook up together. You stuck me with Ivy, but I'm not stuck with you. Get out of here."

"Ishy, don't you go nowhar." Ivy repeatedly poked her finger into the thick muscles of Galen's broad back. "My brother done proved he'll protect his kin. Yore kin now. You ain't got no reason to be a-scairt."

"I'm not afraid." He'd deal with that insult later. "I'm just not a fool."

A loud sound and a sharp cry came from the barn.

CHAPTER TWENTY-ONE

Colin sat in the buckboard with his arm curled protectively around Sean. Dale huddled into Laney's side. Laney wasn't sure—was he shaking or was she?

Hilda patted Sean's knee. "Wait till you see my German tree. It's beautiful. Isn't it, Ruth?"

Ruth sat sideways on the seat and nodded back at them. "I'd never seen one before. Have you boys?"

"No," Colin mumbled.

"I have pretty little trinkets hanging from it. You boys are welcome to look, but no touching." Hilda shook her finger at Dale. "And no taking a cookie off of it until after Christmas dinner!"

Mind awhirl and her world falling apart, Laney let the others try to distract the boys. What she wanted more than anything was to be Galen's wife, but that could never be now. That realization left her wanting to weep for the rest of her life.

"Ruth, I need your help in the kitchen,"

Hilda ordered. "The boys can help Josh unhitch the team and put the wagon up."

Hilda never wanted help in the kitchen. It was her domain; she chased Ruth and Laney out of it whenever they dared to venture in there. Laney understood Hilda was giving her a chance to have some privacy, and she gratefully accepted the gesture.

Laney kept her emotions under control until she got into the house. Once there, she lifted her skirts, ran up the stairs, and slammed the door to her room. Sobs wracked her as she flung herself across her bed.

Anguish swept through her again and again. Hopes and dreams slid into her mind, each to be obliterated by the devastating knowledge that she'd lost the man she loved. He'd never again murmur things to her in that low lilt. They'd not have a houseful of redheaded children together. She wouldn't awaken early to brew him the strong black coffee he relished and feel the sun shine down on them as they walked through the fields of their farm.

Other girls wanted to marry rich and important men. But Galen was rich in what truly mattered—he loved the Lord. He didn't strive to be noticed; he gladly worked hard because he regarded those he loved as the most important priority he held.

But he's married to Ivy.

She cried until her breaths were ugly, jagged

hiccoughs. Turning onto her side, Laney opened her eyes and let out a small cry. There on her bureau rested a small frame. On a walk they'd taken together, Galen had picked a few wildflowers for her. Deep in her heart, Laney had known that day that he had come to see her as a woman—and he wanted her to be his own. She had come home and pressed those flowers, then carefully placed them in a frame. They were the first symbol of a love that would last a lifetime.

Only he'd married Ivy.

Unable to look at that reminder any longer, Laney pushed off of the bed and bit her lip to keep from crying out as she lifted the frame. The drawer she pulled out to hide the pressed flowers in was filled with more reminders of a future she'd never claim. Lengths of fine lawn, linen, the softest cotton, and myriad ribbons as well as yards of lace lay folded there—every last piece carefully selected so she could start sewing a trousseau.

The second-place ribbon she'd won for her grape jelly taunted her. Galen had praised her for winning it—that was the first time he'd shown interest in her instead of going out of his way to avoid her.

The door to her bedchamber shut. Startled, Laney spun around. Ruth rushed across the room, arms open, and Laney fell into her hold. "Tell me it's a bad dream."

"I'm so sorry," Ruth whispered thickly.

"I love him. I thought he was starting to care for me, too."

"We all did." Ruth stroked her back. "But you can't do this to yourself. You can't love him anymore, Laney. He's a married man now."

It wasn't until Hilda pried her from Ruth's hold and mopped Laney's face that she realized the housekeeper had let herself in, too.

"That brother of yours." Hilda shook her head. "I'm not sure whether to hug him or slug him. Bringing the O'Sullivan boys here—"

"They couldn't go home. Not after they'd been looking forward to having Christmas here." Ruth clasped Laney's hand tightly. "And they're too young—they shouldn't be in the middle of whatever's going on over there right now."

"All that's true, but our Laney's heart is breaking." Hilda yanked out the dishcloth she'd tucked in her apron and dabbed at Laney's cheeks again.

"Mr. Josh"—Dale's little boy voice filtered up to them—"I'm wondering if they got lost up there. Your house is so very big!"

His sweet innocence pierced Laney. Until now, she'd gone through most of her life with that selfsame wide-eyed wonder. Suddenly she felt old . . . terribly old.

The boys—I have to be strong for them. They've been through so much. Laney took possession of the dishcloth and scrubbed her face. Then she twisted and stooped.

Ruth and Hilda both grabbed for her.

"I'm not fainting. I'm finding the loop so I can swag up my skirts."

"Why?" Hilda looked completely baffled.

Laney looked at Ruth and nodded.

Ruth gave her a bolstering smile. "She's staying busy."

"Go on down," Laney said. "I'll wash up and be right there." The cold water didn't remove the blotchiness of her skin or the puffiness around her eyes, but Laney smoothed her hair, then pinched her cheeks so they'd be rosy. As she reached for the doorknob, she prayed, "Lord, please give me strength."

Colin seated her at the supper table, then took the chair beside her—both things his older brother should have done.

Is Galen sitting next to Ivy now, sharing a private Christmas dinner?

Josh seated Ruth and brushed a fleeting kiss on her temple as he took his place to her left.

Josh and Ruth never behaved indiscreetly, but the affection they held for one another always showed. Fleeting looks, a brief kiss— those small gestures proved their marriage was satisfying. *I thought Galen was being respectful of me. The most he ever did was hold my hand for a few stolen moments. For Ivy to be with child . . .* Laney feared she was going to be ill.

"Miss Laney?" Dale tugged on her sleeve.

"Hmm?" She tried her hardest to push aside

any thoughts other than what the little boy wanted.

"I can't figure something out. Beef is meat that comes from cows."

She nodded.

"And pork is meat that comes from pigs."

"Yes." She took a small serving of mashed potatoes after placing a dollop of them on Dale's plate.

"And turkey is meat that comes from a turkey, and chicken is meat that comes from a chicken." He sucked in a big breath. "So why don't I ever get the gizzard when we eat pork or beef? I like gizzards a whole bunch."

Laney passed the potatoes to Colin and accepted the meat platter from Ruth. "There's a reason for that." She put a small serving of roast on Dale's plate and an even smaller piece on her own. It was a waste of food to put anything on her own plate—she had no appetite whatsoever.

"You gonna tell me what the reason is? Is it 'cuz I'm the littlest, so the big people eat it first?"

"Oh no." Laney forced a smile. "Cows and pigs don't have gizzards."

"Oh. So Hortense and Mr. Snout don't, and none of the piglets will, either?"

"No, they won't. Only things with wings have gizzards."

Ruth laughed. "Laney, I imagine your Miss Genevieve would be suffering apoplexy about now."

"Who's Miss Genevieve?" Sean licked at his milk mustache.

"A lady who was the boss at the fancy girls' school Laney attended," Josh said, making a face. "She liked lots of fussy rules."

"Teachers at those schools are stiff-rumped, sour-faced biddies," Hilda declared. "I'll bet not a one of them ever gnawed on a juicy rib or had a pillow fight."

"Or went barefoot or dug up worms to go fishing," Ruth added on.

"Seems like *you* should have been teaching *them* stuff." Sean slathered honey on his roll. "They don't know the important stuff about life."

If only life were really that simple!

"Wait. I got a question!" Dale clung to the table on both sides of his plate and looked at Laney with wide blue eyes. "Miss Laney, angels got wings. Do they have gizzards?"

Laney managed to murmur something about asking God when they got to heaven. Her answer seemed to satisfy the little boy. The rest of the meal blurred together. Laney couldn't eat, so she moved the food around on her plate. *What is Galen doing now? He was supposed to be here, but he's with Ivy instead.*

"You boys did a good job eating," Hilda said, bobbing her head approvingly. "Go and take a cookie off the tree—but be careful. I don't want any of my trinkets to get broken."

"Don't worry, Hilda," Josh said as he stood. "We'll be careful."

Hilda leaned back and gave him a baffled look. "What do you mean, *we*, Cowboy?"

"Mr. Josh is a boy." Sean scooted free from the table. "You said us boys could get a cookie. Do we eat the cookies in here or out on the porch?"

"The porch is too cold." Ruth looked at Laney. "Don't you think so, Laney?"

Laney nodded.

"Since it's Christmas, I think it would be okay if the boys ate their cookies in the parlor." Josh pulled Ruth's chair from the table. "Let's all go together. Hilda, stop fussing about clearing the table. Let's all go enjoy your wonderful German tree."

After they ate cookies, Ruth slid her hand into Josh's and gave it a squeeze. Laney's heart twisted. *I wanted Galen and me to have a marriage like theirs—loving and accepting.*

"I've never allowed candles on the tree before, but this year is different." Josh smiled at Ruth. "My wife wanted them, and I've relented."

Sean and Dale clapped their hands with glee.

"I have buckets of sand and water in here," Josh said. "I want everyone to listen to me. If the candles start a fire, you're all to leave. Do you understand me?"

Everyone nodded.

Josh slapped Colin on the back. "I think you're plenty old enough and tall enough to help me light the candles. I know at home you use flint and a striker, but Ruth bought some of these Lundstrom safety matches. We'll start at the top of the tree and light around and down."

As the two set to work, Dale grabbed Laney's hand. Ruth took Laney's other hand and gave it a squeeze. The flame on each candle turned into a golden nimbus. Laney's tears blurred the sight so the entire tree looked like it wore a glowing halo.

"I wish Ma and Galen were here," Sean said, his voice wistful and soft.

"Me, too." Dale tugged on Laney's hand. "Miss Laney, why are you crying?"

She knelt beside him and held him close to her side. She wanted to shelter his beautiful innocence. In the midst of today's tragedy, he was completely unscathed.

"The tree is so beautiful," Ruth said, "I think Laney's speechless."

"Almost," Laney rasped. "It's a wondrous sight."

"I'll never forget today," Sean declared, his voice filled with awe.

Neither will I. Laney swallowed hard.

Dale hitched his arm around her neck and tilted his head so his temple rested against hers. "Miss Laney?"

"Mm-hmm?"

" 'Member on my birthday how I got to blow out the candles on my cake?"

"Yes?"

"I don't think I can blow all these out. Does that mean I don't getta make a wish?"

"Christmas is Jesus' birthday."

Josh finished lighting one last candle.

Dale thought for a moment. "So do we sing 'He's a Jolly Good Fellow' and help by blowing the candles out for Him?"

"Never did that before," Hilda grumbled.

"But nobody's better than Jesus." Dale's logic framed the whole issue innocently, yet profoundly.

"You're right," Josh said as he and Colin stepped back to take in the sight. They all stared at the tree, and then Josh began to sing. After the song, Josh lifted Dale. "You blow out the very tip-top candles. The rest of us will help, too."

One by one, they extinguished the candles. Wisps of smoke trailed upward, momentarily battling the scent of the evergreen. The light was gone, leaving only charred wicks on melted candle nubs. *Like me. The love-light in my life can't burn brightly. It barely shone before being snuffed out. Oh, Galen . . . why?*

Dale wiggled in Josh's arms. "That was fun. Can we do it again?"

Josh set him down. "No. Some things are special, so you only do them once."

Like getting married.

"Or once a year," Ruth added.

Sean reverently touched a glass star hanging from the tree. "Next year, we'll bring Ma and Galen."

And Ivy. Laney bit the inside of her cheek.

"And now for a special surprise!" Ruth looked to Josh. "I can't wait anymore."

"We getta eat another cookie?" Dale touched one of the big sugar cookies Hilda had baked. Hanging from the boughs by scarlet ribbons, they looked more than tempting.

"No. A different kind of surprise." Josh motioned for them to all be seated.

Laney froze. The handkerchiefs she'd embroidered for Galen, the dress for Mrs. O'Sullivan—all of the special gifts would be drawn out from their hiding place. She looked across the parlor and mouthed to Ruth, *I can't bear this.*

Ruth came right over and pretended to straighten Laney's cameo. She whispered, "Don't worry. Josh took care of things."

After they'd all taken places, Josh lifted the tablecloth that hung from beneath the tree clear down to the floor. "In church, Pastor Dawes spoke of gifts at Christmas. I think there are some gifts here, too."

Ruth had selected a different book for each of them. Sean and Dale received wooden ball-and-cup toys. Josh made a big deal over how Colin was growing into manhood and presented him with his first tie. Hilda had made an apron for Ruth and another for Laney; they gave her a new skirt and shirtwaist.

"Hmm. What could this be?" Josh squatted down and peered beneath the table.

"What?" Sean tilted his head.

"Maybe you and Dale had better drag it out. It's under there pretty far."

The boys grunted and tugged until they pulled out a wooden box. "Wow, it's heavy." Dale looked at Josh. "Betcha it's for you."

"Actually, Ruth gave me this pocket watch this morning. Isn't it a beaut?" Josh showed it to the boys. They admired the handsome cover.

"The fan that belonged to my mama was broken," Ruth said softly as she opened a beautiful ivory-and-silk creation. "Josh found one just like it. I'll always treasure it."

"Oh, Josh." Laney looked at her brother. "That was so thoughtful of you."

"Ruth? Laney?" Hilda acted confused. "Do you know whom that big box is for?"

Josh stroked his hand across the top and let out a low, appreciative whistle. "Cherry wood. Smooth as silk. I guess we ought to open it. When we see what's inside, maybe we'll know who's supposed to get it."

"Okay!" Sean scrambled to unfasten the latches. Dale was more of a hindrance than a help. Josh helped them open the lid.

"It's gotta be for you, Mr. Josh." Sean

reached in and touched the wooden handle of a tool.

"I don't know. I already have plenty of tools. What does this say up here?" Josh ran his forefinger across bright red lettering on the inside of the lid.

Colin read aloud, 'Geo'—that's short for George—'Parr's Juvenile Tool Chest.' " He straightened up and shot Josh a disbelieving look. "Those are real tools, but they're for boys!"

Josh chuckled. "Yep. They sure are. I think they're just the right size for your little brothers. What do you think?"

Sean and Dale whooped. While they took out the tools and admired each one, Josh handed a leather sheath to Colin. "A young man needs his own knife."

Colin's ears and neck turned red, but his delight was unmistakable.

Awhile later, Laney watched as Josh and Colin carried crates out to the wagon. Gifts for Mrs. O'Sullivan, Ivy, and Ishmael were inside. Laney wasn't sure whether the gifts for Galen were with them. After this morning, Josh might have kept those things out. *I still want Galen to have the handkerchiefs. No, maybe I don't. I'm not sure.*

Staying busy had helped a little—but now the boy's exuberance and innocence gave no respite from reality. Laney melted onto the settee.

Sean giggled. "Lookit what Dale did!"

Laney motioned to him. "Dale, come here."

"I didn't do nothing."

"You buttoned your coat funny. Here. I'll help."

Dale drew closer and whispered loudly, "'Member at the fair how Hortense liked the cookies? Mr. Josh said Miss Hilda wants to leave the rest of the cookies on the tree for a few days. When you come on Friday, do you think you could bring one for Hortense and another for Mr. Snout?"

"No," Hilda blurted out.

"Why not?"

"Laney's going to be very busy for the next little while," Ruth said.

Dale shook his head. "Laney and me are partners. She told me we got a 'sponsibility to each other. Partners don't slack off or give up. Never, ever. No matter what. That's what Miss Laney said. And Miss Laney comes every week to check on our business. She'll come—won't you, Miss Laney?"

Laney clearly remembered telling him that. *But I never once imagined these circumstances.* Laney looked into his big blue eyes. *His eyes are just like Galen's.*

"You don't have to bring cookies." Complete trust shone in his features. "You don't even have to bring cookies for me or Ma or my brothers, either. So you can just come and visit me and Hortense and Mr. Snout."

"I . . ." She tried to smile. "I'll do my best."

"I knew you'd come!" He threw his arms around her. "You're the bestest partner ever!"

Josh tickled Dale's sides and pulled him away. Squatting in front of the giggling little boy, he said, "Laney's going to need some extra time to do some things. If she can't make it over, I'll come. You can show me, and I'll be sure to tell her what a great job you're doing."

"Like when Sean does the dishes an extra night 'cuz Colin has to study?"

"Exactly." Josh straightened up. "A family works together and helps out."

Sean heaved a loud sigh. "I wanted Laney to be family. Now we're stuck with Ivy."

Laney didn't speak. Couldn't. The pain she'd tried so hard to hold back crashed over her in relentless waves. Her eyes swam and her nose tingled from the tears she tried not to shed.

Colin cleared his throat loudly. "That tool chest is huge. Are the both of you boys thinking you can carry it between yourselves?"

With that distraction, Josh and Colin managed to steer them out to the wagon. Ruth remained behind. She started to embrace Laney, but Laney pushed away. "I can't go. You know I can't. Please go along with them. Let me know how—" she took a choppy breath—"how everyone is doing."

"Laney, you matter more than they do."

She shook her head. "I need time alone.

Mrs. O'Sullivan—she might need another woman." As soon as she spoke the words, Laney cringed. *She has Ivy now.*

"I understand what you mean. I'll go and make sure Josh behaves himself." Ruth gave her a quick hug and dashed out the door. "Wait! I'm coming, too!"

Laney raced upstairs, peeled out of the dress that was supposed to enchant Galen, and shoved it into the bottom of her wardrobe. Every stitch she'd sewn had been filled with hope. She never wanted to see that dress again.

After changing into her riding skirt, Laney slipped down the back stairs and out to the stable. Toledo had occurred to be there. He'd been in church that morning; he knew what had occurred. "I'll saddle up a horse for you."

Laney dipped her head in acknowledgment. In a matter of minutes, she was racing across their land, but she knew she'd never outrun her heartache.

CHAPTER TWENTY-TWO

I t ain't busted, but it shore is nasty," Ivy declared.

Galen flipped the hem of Ma's gown back down to cover her ankle. He'd come to the same conclusion as Ivy, but having her volunteer her unsought opinion grated on his already-raw nerves. "Ma, hold on to me." He looped her arm around his neck.

"Ishy, run ahead and git the tin bucket of water outta the springhouse."

"This is a bunch of nonsense," Ma protested. "I can walk."

Galen ignored her and carried her back to the house.

"I'll wrap it up in a cold water towel. 'Twon't get so swoll up thataway." Ivy dashed over to the bed. "Mr. O'Sullivan, you lay her down here, and I'll tuck a pillow 'neath her foot. Mrs. O'Sullivan, ma'am, don't mean you no disrespect, but I aim to peel off them stockin's of yourn."

Galen stepped away from the bed and turned his back. Judging from the way Ma's ankle had already started to swell, her stocking needed to come off. Ma never made an issue out of being the only female in the family; she managed to bathe and dress when the boys were otherwise occupied. Had he needed to, Galen would have pulled off her stocking; but since another woman was present, it seemed better to let Ma keep her modesty. *Even if it is Ivy.*

Ishmael rushed into the house. "I brung the pail, sis. Water's real nice and cool. I cain hie back to town if'n you need me to fetch the doctor."

"That's not necessary," Ma said in a firm tone.

"Doc cain't do nothin' more'n what we'll do," Ivy stated with great certainty. "I got me some willow bark in a cigar box. I'll bile up a tea that'll holp you feel loads better."

"Miz O'Sullivan—" Ishmael set the pail beside his sister and patted Ma's shoulder with an awkward gentleness—"I spied a nice straight sycamore branch t'other day. I'll fetch it back and carve you a walkin' stick right away."

"She's a short dab of a woman, Ishy. Only make it up to yore hip."

"Ishmael is leaving." Galen enunciated the words in low, forceful tone.

Ivy stopped wringing the dishcloth. The only sound in the cabin was the steady drip-

drip-drip of water back into the bucket. Carefully, she draped the cloth over the rim. With measured steps, Ivy went to the cupboard and pulled out the metal sheet Ma used for baking cookies. She covered it with a folded towel, eased it beneath Ma's foot, then wrapped the cold cloth around her ankle.

It wasn't until Ivy straightened back up and turned to her brother that Galen noticed tears slipping down her gaunt cheeks. Ishmael unashamedly dragged his sleeve across his own eyes, then held her tight. She clung to him, so he shifted her to the side and kept her in the shelter of his arm as he crossed the room and out the door.

Galen turned back toward Ma. Tears rained down her face, too. "If you're hurting so, I'll go fetch Doc."

She shook her head. "All they have is each other."

"He changed that behind a shotgun today." Galen rubbed the back of his neck. "There has to be a way out of this. Laney—"

"Laney is Josh's sister. You've been saying she's a pest for a long while."

Galen frowned. "Ma, you know good and well things changed."

"And they changed again today. You cannot look back, son. You must look ahead." Ma tried to scoot up higher in bed and grimaced. He leaned over and helped her, then stayed close as she wrapped her arms around his neck. "Galen-mine, tell me you never made a pledge to Laney. You didn't yet, did you?"

"Not in so many words, but my intent was clear."

"We all hold her dear, and 'tis understand-able—you wantin' her for your bride. Words can't hold the sadness of setting her aside, but 'tis what you must do. The lass is young yet, Galen-mine. You've said so yourself often enough. With you married, she'll realize 'tis time for her to set aside a youthful fancy."

"She's a woman, not a child." Galen straight-ened up. "I made the mistake of not realizing it sooner. I'll not dismiss what we feel for each other."

"You're a married man now. Honor demands you set aside other thoughts and dreams. You must dedicate yourself to the woman who shares our name now."

In some ways, Ma was right. *By spending time with Ivy and pressing her for answers, I can discover who the father is and still have the mar-riage annulled. Then I'll be free to wed Laney.*

Ivy's sobs and Ishmael's half-whispered words filtered in on the stiff winter breeze. ". . . write. Someone read to you . . . Best . . . needs his pa."

Ma's hand slipped over the quilt and her fin-gers laced with Galen's. "The baby deserves to know his uncle."

"Ma, 'tis sentiment speaking. Not half an hour ago, you worried Ishmael would try to do me harm."

"Nay, son." Her head moved from side to side on the pillow, and Galen wasn't sure whether it was from pain or that she disagreed with what he'd said. "You mistook my meaning. I didn't fret that he'd hurt you; I worried for what you might be tempted to do to him."

"Never once have I done a man harm."

"I know." She let out a pained sigh. "But this is different. A man embarrassed before others and made to do something against his will— that's a dangerous man."

Galen stared at her.

Ivy's sobs filled the silence. Galen didn't feel a single scrap of compassion for her. *She did this to herself. The last thing I'll do is allow her brother to stay. They conspired to do this. Without him, she'll break faster and identify who the father is.*

"You're angry, son, but don't make them suffer."

"Angry doesn't begin to describe—"

"'Be ye angry, and sin not,'" Ma quoted from the Scripture. She raised her voice. "Ivy! Ishmael can stay."

Galen's clenched his jaw and fisted his hands.

"Ma'am?" Ishmael's voice sounded unsteady.

"You heard me." She didn't look away from

Galen. "You're hardworking. That's not changed. Life goes on."

Respect for his mother kept him silent, but only just barely. Galen stared at her.

"I'll go muck the stable right now! Sis—she'll gather up eggs. You won't be sorry!"

Ivy and Ishmael left the porch. Galen half growled, "How could you—"

Ma held up a hand to silence him. " 'Tis already hard enough, this predicament. Ishmael only did what he had to, to make things right."

Disbelief iced Galen's spine. With exaggerated slowness, he splayed his fingers and pulled away from her touch.

"The sooner you own up to this, the better things will go. We'll all make the best of it."

"You think I've been with her." Galen stomped out of the house and straight to the barn. Ishmael had just grabbed the shovel. "You."

Ishmael turned around.

Galen stabbed his finger in the air to punctuate his words. "From now on, all decisions and orders come from me. You can stay—but only by my rules. You and your sister stay apart. Unless I'm there, you can't speak to her. Not one word. The first time I catch you breaking that order, you're out of here."

Ishmael leaned on the shovel. "If'n you say so."

"I say so." An old saying ran through Galen's

mind. *Keep your friends close and your enemies closer.* His eyes narrowed. "I'm moving to the tack room. You'll sleep there, too. Clean it out."

———— ◆ ————

Once Laney rode off and no longer had an audience, her restraint shattered. She couldn't help herself—she was drawn to the edge of the Broken P where their land ended . . . and the O'Sullivans' began.

Countless times she'd come here and dismounted. Sitting on the split rail fence, she'd faced Galen's home and dreamed of the day when she'd be his bride. In the past weeks, she'd come to hope—even believe—that the Lord had answered her prayers and she'd soon be Galen's wife.

She stayed atop the gelding as memories flitted through her mind—of how Galen's callused hands folded and his voice took on a stillness whenever he prayed. The way his chuckles could grow into a delightful belly laugh. The sureness in his hands as he worked with horses, the way he always stomped his feet in a right-left-right sequence to knock the mud off his boots on rainy days. Myriad details swamped her, driving home how she'd completely lost her heart to him . . . and how she thought he'd lost his heart, as well.

But he'd married Ivy.

The fence was no longer a flimsy barrier

between them that would come down in a short time. It now represented something entirely different. It might as well be a brick wall. Her dreams lay in tatters on her side; his future rested with Ivy. And there was going to be a child.

Ivy had been married in church, wearing the green dress Laney not only gave the material for, but also helped stitch. *All this time I've tried to be her friend, but she was stealing the man I love. And now she's carrying his baby.*

Things Galen had said and done now came back and took on a completely different meaning. *It feels awkward, but I'm asking you to be kind to Ivy. . . . I want her to feel welcomed. . . . I can't explain it now. It's . . . well . . . complicated.* Though he loved ribs, he'd given Ivy his whole one and been satisfied to eat the remainder of Laney's. In church today, he admitted he'd been alone with her—taken her food and blankets, too.

Laney wept until her eyes no longer teared, but her heart continued to ache with an emptiness she knew would never be filled. At some point, she had turned loose of her reins, and her gelding wandered where he willed. Finally, when he stopped, Laney became aware of her surroundings again.

Trees grew in clumps here along the roadside. The road followed a serpentine path along the dips and swells of the foothills. From her vantage point, she could see only this small stretch of the dirt road. Where it started and ended would be a complete mystery to someone who didn't live in the area. Less than a mile away, the earth suddenly dropped into an unexpected ravine.

I used to know where I was going. Now everything has fallen away. What will I do?

The wind shifted direction and grew far stronger. Her gelding turned and shook his mane. Sensing his restlessness, Laney used light pressure with her knees to direct him to an outcropping of rocks. Once there she slid off, gathered the reins, and decided to walk. *I can't go home yet. I can't.* In the past, when she'd needed advice, she'd gone to Mrs. O'Sullivan. *That's impossible now.*

Laney heard a noise in the distance and led her horse farther from the road. Though she couldn't see anything, she knew it would be Josh and Ruth returning from the O'Sullivans'. She didn't want to talk to them just yet.

Harnesses jingled and wooden wheels made a gritty, lumbering sound over the dirt road. "Whoa."

Laney stepped back into shadows.

"I know I saw her." Worry strained Ruth's voice. "She doesn't even have a wrap, Josh."

"Laney Lou," he called, using his pet name for her—the one he'd crooned to her in the dark the night he came to tell her their mother had died, the one he'd boomed with joy the day she'd come home from finishing school. His tone held nothing but loving concern.

That fact undid her. Tears filled her eyes again. *I thought I'd cried myself out. I don't want anyone to see me like this.*

"C'mon, Laney Lou. Let's go home." Josh now stood less than a foot away.

Laney squared her shoulders and blinked back tears. "I'll ride along behind you."

"Ride in the wagon with Ruth. I'll follow on Juniper."

"You're arguing with me?"

"Even if I agreed to let you ride, Ruth wouldn't stand for it." A rakish smile tilted one corner of his mouth. "You know I'm right." He took the reins from her.

When they reached the wagon, Ruth scooted over and Josh lifted Laney to sit by her. Ruth opened one side of her shawl as if to make half of a set of angel wings, but she patted something in her lap. "This is yours."

Laney shuddered. Made of the finest cashmere, the caramel-and-beige shawl looked wonderfully warm and soft. She compressed her lips to tamp down a cry and merely shook her head.

"It's from Josh and me. Mrs. O'Sullivan's been keeping it for us so you wouldn't find it." Ruth let her own shawl slide down her back and wrapped Laney in the gift. "You're half frozen! Josh, we need to get home."

"The wagon's not budging until you cover up, yourself."

"Oh honestly." Ruth huffed, yanked her shawl into place, and flicked the reins. "Laney, has your brother always been this bossy?"

"Ruthie?" Josh didn't sound perturbed in the least.

"Now what?"

"You're going to drive those poor horses crazy and get nowhere until you release the brake."

Laney tried to smile.

Once they got underway, Ruth called out, "Josh, ride on ahead and ask Hilda to put on some tea. Your sister and I are both chilly."

Josh rode off.

Ruth kept her focus on the horses. "Laney, I'm sure you'd want to know that Mrs. O'Sullivan—"

"Please, Ruth, don't say another word. I can't bear it."

The short ride back home remained painfully silent. Ruth halted the wagon by the kitchen door. Josh came out of the house and helped her down. As he set Laney on the veranda, he didn't turn loose of her. "I want you to listen to me. It's not right for you to visit the O'Sullivans."

"I couldn't"—she shuddered—"go over there. Not now. Not ever."

Chapter Twenty-three

"Y ou young'uns need to get to bed." Ivy stood just a few feet inside of the barn. The kerosene lantern gave off a white light that made her hair look like a dozen tangled spider webs.

"Awww," Sean glanced at the lopsided stool he'd been building, then looked at Galen. "Do we have to?"

"Yeah, Galen." Dale stopped banging a nail. "Can't we stay up awhile?"

Colin didn't stop whittling from his perch on a bale of hay. "It's Christmas."

That's a perfect excuse. I can make the boys happy and at the same time I'll be putting Ivy in her place.

"It bein' Christmas, that cain be yore gift to yore mama—obeyin' her with a gladsome heart 'stead of draggin' yore feet," Ivy replied.

"Ma wants us to go to bed, or you do?" Belligerence tainted Sean's voice.

"Since yore mama wants it, I do, too."

"Ma sent you out here?" Colin's eyes narrowed.

"Shore did. She cain't very well come after you, what with her ankle all swoll up."

"Go on in," Galen told the boys. "Be sure you put your tools away first."

A few short minutes later, the boys headed toward the house. Ivy hadn't budged an inch.

Galen turned his back on her and checked the latches on each stall so the horses would be secure through the night. He'd already finished his work here. Normally, he'd go on in and use the time to read from the Bible and pray with his family.

Tonight he didn't want to go in. He'd spent the afternoon recalling each and every minute he'd spent with Laney. She'd been like a sunbeam—warm and gentle during some of the darkest days of his life.

"Mr. O'Sullivan."

Ivy's soft, twangy voice grated on his nerves. Galen thought about ignoring her. Instead, he wheeled around and glowered.

"I wanted to say thankee for letting my brother stay on."

"That was Ma's doing, not mine."

As if he'd said nothing, Ivy went on, "I ain't niver slept on a 'bove-the-ground bed. Thankee for carryin' that cot inside."

"Ma hurt herself trying to reach that cot for you."

Ivy wrapped her arms around her ribs. "I reckoned 'twas so. I'm dreadful sorry, and I tole her so. Don't you worry none, though. In a handful of days, she'll be right as rain. Ain't nothin' gonna go undone whilst she's laid up. I'll do it all."

Galen stared at her. *She might well be speaking the truth, but she lied today and it cost me my sweet Laney. Now I'm stuck with this woman—her hair a fright, her dress askew, her speech whiny.*

Unaware of his thoughts, Ivy tacked on, "In the church, I promised to holp you and yore kin. All you gotta do is say how."

"The only help I want from you is a confession that you've lied and the child isn't mine. This sham will be over, and you can go." He dared to take a step closer. "You made a bad choice in using me as your mark. I don't have money to pay you off."

She wagged her head from side to side. "I ain't a-lookin' to get no money. Don't wanna go noplace else."

"Well, I don't want you here. I don't want you."

Ivy hitched her right shoulder. "Pa didn't want me, neither. Didn't keep me from cooking for him and tendin' his rheumatiz. You'll see— I'm useful."

"If I wanted a useful woman, I'd hire a maid or a cook!"

"You jist said you got no money." She shivered.

Galen scowled. "You don't have the sense God gave a flea. Even Dale knew to put on a jacket."

"That Dale—he's a smart one." She bobbed her head. "Then thar's Sean—full of life. And Colin—pert near a man now."

"My brothers are none of your concern."

"Thar my kin now."

"Saying something doesn't make it a fact. You can talk all you want, but I won't agree with a liar."

"Yore hungry."

He made no reply. Talking to Ivy was impossible. If she didn't like what was said, she ignored it or changed the subject. It didn't matter that she was right about his brothers or right about his being hungry. He'd refused to sit at the supper table and eat the Christmas meal the McCains brought. He had no appetite, and he certainly didn't want to share his table with Ivy and Ishmael.

"When yore of a mind to come on in, I set food in that warmin' box atop yore mama's stove."

"I'm not coming in." He stared at her.

The ponderous *clop-clop-clop* of a weary beast drifted into the barn. A moment later, Ishmael led his mule inside. "Brung ev'rythang, Boss." A mere breath later, Ishmael's expression changed. "Didn't know you was here, sis."

"She's going inside. Now."

"I got your bed set up in the tack room, jist like you tole me to."

Ivy's brows knit, and she turned to Galen. "You moved yore bed out here to the tack room?"

Color suddenly flooded Ishmael's face. He looked back and forth from Ivy to Galen. "Sorry. Didn't realize. It's yore weddin' night. 'Course the both of you wanted privacy," he mumbled to his boots.

"Never." Galen folded his arms across his chest. "As soon as your sister identifies the father of her child, she can go to *him*."

"Sis ain't goin' nowhar. Best you know that." Ishmael shoved the mule's nuzzle away when the animal began to seek affection. "You spoke your vows."

"I vowed to provide for her and the child. If it means I scrape up money each month and send it to wherever she and her lover are, I'll do it."

Ivy leapt between them and wound her arms tightly around Ishmael. "Don't, Ishy. Please don't."

Ishmael pried his way free. "For true, I'm tempted to bash my fist into yore ugly mouth, Boss. But I ain't a-gonna. I give you and yore ma my word that I wouldn't cause no troubles."

Galen let out a rude snort. "You've already

caused more trouble than I could handle in ten lifetimes."

"You cain go on blamin' ev'rybody 'cept yoreself if'n it makes you feel better, but that don't make 'em responsible."

"Tell that to your sister." Galen turned to her. "Your brother knows he cannot be with you or speak to you unless I'm present. I—"

"Now that thar's the craziest thang a body e'er said." Ivy gave him a peeved look.

"I don't mind, sis." Ishmael wrapped his arm around the mule's neck. "A man's gotta right to say how thangs go in his home. I tole Boss we'll foller his rules."

Ivy still looked disgruntled, but she shrugged.

"Yore thangs are wrapped up in the blue bundle," Ishmael said, tilting his head toward the travois. As Ivy stooped to get them, Ishmael asked, "Boss, d'ya want Muley to spend his nights in the pasture or here in the stable?"

Galen studied the beast. He'd never seen a sorrier animal. Its ribs stood out in stark rows. "What have you been feeding him?"

"He forages." Ivy cupped the bundle of her belongings to herself and said proudly, "Hard-workin' animal, thar. And he don't cost you nuthin' at all to feed. I reckon yore plow horse is a-gonna get scairt you might not need him no more."

Ishmael cleared his throat. "Betwixt Muley

and that plow horse of yourn, we'll be able to plow and harrow a field in half the time. I could clear another field or two as winter stretches on. Come spring, you'd have yoreself more land to plant."

"Don't go making plans for too far into the future." Galen eyed Ivy's bundle. "Take those things inside."

"G'night, sis." Ishmael turned loose of the mule and hugged Ivy.

I'd rather deal with the mule than with the marriage. Galen's stomach rumbled. He stood his ground, and Ivy scurried off.

Ishmael pulled another meager bundle from the travois. "Don't know whether yore mama's a-gonna want these here thangs. Ain't much, but I reckon it niver hurts to have 'nother pot or knife. 'Specially with two wimmin at the stove, extry gear might come in handy."

Galen stared at the battered pot.

"Ain't much to look at, but Ivy shore cooked up a mess of good food in it." Ishmael grinned. "Better the gal be purdy and the pot ugly than t'other way round."

Galen gritted his teeth. No use antagonizing the man. Making the best of this situation was going to test his mettle. "Stick him in the far stall."

"Yessir."

Galen stomped into the house, and his mouth started watering right away. The tempting aromas of Hilda's cooking filled the cabin.

Colin sat on the edge of Ma's bed. Dale and Sean both cuddled her from either side. "Where is she?" Galen demanded.

"Ivy went to the necessary." Ma's head dipped, and she rested her chin on Sean's head.

Galen nodded curtly and turned so he could see out the window. If Ivy dared to go toward the stable . . .

"We waited for you."

Colin brought Da's Bible to Galen. Just last night, Galen had read the Christmas story to them. He'd stopped immediately after the shepherds paid homage to the Christ child. Galen refused to take it. "You read tonight."

"Okay." Colin went back to sit by the lamp beside Ma's bed.

Ivy came into the house. Everyone stared at her. She let out a nervous laugh. "Chilly out thar. Sore chilly."

"We read from God's Word each night, Ivy," Ma said, motioning to her. "Sit quietly and listen."

Colin read the passage, and Sean wrinkled his freckled nose. "It doesn't say there were three kings. Our song said, 'We three kings.'"

"And a grand song 'twas." Ma smiled. "I suppose we think there were three wise men since they brought three gifts."

"Galen wasn't 'round when Mr. Josh brought us home. He hasn't seen his gifts yet."

Dale wiggled next to Ma. "Do we get to stay up and watch him?"

No. He opened his mouth to refuse the request, but something about his baby brother's innocent enthusiasm struck Galen. At the church, his brothers and mother had been terrified. This would allow them to end the day with a scrap of fun and a good memory. "Sure."

"They're in the crate under the table." Ma said the words so quickly, Galen suspected she feared he'd change his mind.

"I'll fetch 'em for you." Ivy popped up.

Galen's glower kept her pinned to her cot. He turned back to his brothers and made a point of rubbing his hands together. He'd keep Ivy on the fringes and try to shield his brothers from her influence and presence. "Oh, so you boys were hiding the crate from the McCains from me, were you?"

"We weren't hiding it." Sean peered at him. "I know better hiding places than under the table."

"Do you now?" Galen quirked a brow.

Sean straightened up. "Yes, and Dale, don't you dare tell them where."

" 'Course I won't. I'm good at keeping secrets. No one would ever think to look—"

"Galen-mine," Ma interrupted Dale, "I didn't want the lads to stay up so late. Best you fetch that crate."

" 'Twill be fun to see what's in it!" Ivy said.

Galen fought the urge to react to her at all. He dragged a bench out of the way and hunkered down to pull out the crate. "Our Galen, don't peek at it under there!" Dale called out. "We want to see, too!"

"Of course you do." Galen tugged the crate and rose in one fluid move. Setting the crate on the bench so they could see, he mused, "Either there's something heavy in here or I'm turning into a weakling."

"We all got books."

"Shh, Dale." Sean reached over Ma and poked his little brother. "Don't ruin his surprise."

"This doesn't look like a book to me." Galen drew a pair of britches from the crate.

Ma nodded. "And they're brown. They won't be showing the dirt much."

Colin set aside the Bible. "Mr. Josh bought them when we all got so grubby at the fair. I told him brown's your favorite."

"And we helped him pick out the shirts, too!"

"Dale . . ." Sean huffed.

"It's not ruining the surprise. He can see them, can't you, Galen?"

He draped the britches across the table. "Sure and enough, I can see a fine white shirt here." He started lifting the first store-bought shirt he'd ever received. "And there's another beneath it!"

"You needed a new Sunday-best shirt. Whilst I ironed the one you have, I saw the elbow's about gone on it."

Galen nodded and drew out the other shirt.

"It's blue, just like Dale's."

"Aye, Colin. It surely is."

"Miss Laney picked it out. She said it matches our eyes." Dale opened his eyes wide. "Our *handsome* eyes."

Colin cracked his knuckles. "So what book did you get?"

Bless him, Colin is trying to help me through this. He's striving so hard to grow and stretch into manhood.

"Indeed, son. What book did Ruth choose for you?"

Galen solemnly laid aside the blue shirt and lifted not one, but two books. "My, my. The new *Farmer's Almanac* and my own copy of *The Animal Husbandry Guide.*"

"You won't have to be riding over to the Broken P to read their guide anymore." Ma's voice held an undertone.

Galen put the books down on the table with exaggerated care. Ma was underscoring how things would change. Anger flashed through him again—at Ma, for not having faith that he'd conducted himself above reproach; at Ishmael, for forcing him into a sham of a marriage; but most of all at Ivy, for telling the lie that broke dear Laney's heart and ruined his life.

A bit of white caught his attention. Galen peered at the bottom of the crate. Lying in the bottom were three handkerchiefs. All were white, but each had been painstakingly monogrammed in a different color. A green one, a brown one, and a blue one—all evidence of Laney's heartfelt sentiments toward him. He dared to run his rough finger over the delicate, impossibly tiny stitches. She must have spent hours on them, designing a different style for each of the three monograms.

He'd known she couldn't read until last year. Josh had subtly orchestrated things so Laney never had to reveal her secret. Following Josh's lead, Galen had never let on that he knew. But Laney had learned—and the letters she'd embroidered on the handkerchiefs were more than mere pictures. They were proof of her triumph.

But they're saying something even more. Here's absolute proof right before me that she more than returns the feelings I hold for her—'tisn't a mere fancy on her part, but an abiding love. She waited these years for me to see we were meant for each other, but I took too long. Now we'll never be together. She's a lass whose heart and soul are finer than the stitching she did, yet a vile lie now keeps us apart. My poor little Laney.

"Thar's sommat else in that crate," Ivy said as she craned her neck. "I can see a scrap of white."

Galen dumped everything in atop the handkerchiefs. He refused to reveal the sentimental gift Laney had made for him. "I'm done, Ma. The lads ought to be going to bed now."

Someone yawned and Ma said, "You boys have stayed up late enough."

The sound of Ma giving them good-night kisses pulled Galen back to the bitter reality of how life went on. "Off to bed with you now."

"We didn't have our prayer." Colin didn't budge.

"It's my turn." Dale folded his hands and waited for the others to do the same. "Dear Jesus, thank you for being the Christmas baby. Thank you for all of the presents today. Please keep us safe and warm and well. God bless Ma. God bless Galen. God bless Colin. God bless Sean. God bless me, too."

And Lord, please bless and be with Laney.

"And God bless Ivy. Amen."

CHAPTER TWENTY-FOUR

Tap-tap-tap-tap. "Laney?"

Even before Ruth called her name, Laney knew it was her sister-in-law. Dear, exuberant Ruth—only she could knock like a frenzied woodpecker.

Ruth didn't wait for an invitation; she came on in. "I saw the light on under your door." Relief sketched across her features. "Oh good. You're reading the Bible."

Laney nodded.

Josh sauntered in. He acted as if he was casually following his wife, but Laney knew better. They were worried and had this all planned out. "What passage were you reading?" he asked.

"Genesis." Laney pressed her hand to the open pages. "Where Laban tricks Jacob, and Jacob ends up married to Leah instead of Rachel."

Josh's features went taut. "Nonetheless Leah was his wife, Laney. She bore him several sons."

"But he still loved Rachel, and it wasn't his fault that Leah was his wife."

Ruth came over and sat on the bed. She laid her hand atop Laney's. "But this isn't Bible times. Men can't have more than one wife."

"Whatever feelings you and Galen had for one another have to end." Josh's hand curled tightly around the bedpost. "He's a married man with a child on the way."

"But it's not his child," Laney asserted. "I'm ashamed of myself for thinking even for one minute that it might be. It's not his. I'm sure of it."

Josh and Ruth exchanged a look.

Laney gasped. "You can't think it is! Josh, you're his best friend. You—of all people— should know he wouldn't have . . . have . . ." Her voice died out.

Josh's face remained grim. "In the end, it doesn't matter whether he fathered the child. It's still his baby, and Ivy is his wife."

"What if Ivy and Ishmael lied and there's no baby at all?"

Josh shook his head. "It's rare you see any-one that livid. Ishmael is normally mild-mannered."

"Ivy's still lying."

"She might be." Ruth wouldn't meet Laney's eyes.

"Might?!" Laney felt a second flash of sur-prise, then indignation.

Ruth started brushing her thumb back and forth on the back of Laney's hand. "Laney, you know I've struggled with all of the silly rules of society. Being proper isn't easy for me, but even I know a man shouldn't ever be alone with a woman. Galen admitted he's been alone with Ivy on more than one occasion." Ruth winced. "And he even gave her a blanket."

"He was showing Christian charity."

"He showed poor judgment." Josh shook his head sorrowfully. "Galen acknowledged seeing her alone, and that's compromised her. She's in a fix now, and almost no one else knew she existed."

Laney stared at her brother. "You can think whatever you want. You can believe whatever you please. I know the man I love. Galen wouldn't ever . . . indulge. He's an upright man."

"Even upright men sin on occasion." Josh's voice ached with sadness.

"Laney, you must listen to us." Ruth stopped rubbing Laney's hand and squeezed her arm. "You just called Galen the man you love. That cannot continue. He's married to Ivy. Regardless of the tenderness you hold in your heart for him, he's her husband. It's wrong for you to nurture any feelings. It's . . ."

"Adulterous," Josh finished.

Their words hit Laney with devastating impact. She could scarcely breathe.

"As for Ivy—even if we assume she's told a

lie . . ." Ruth still held on to Laney. "She's not a Christian, Laney. She doesn't have the same sense of morality we do."

"Which is why it's so very wrong to condemn Galen!"

"Laney," Josh heaved with a gigantic sigh. "They're married. Deciding who's to blame isn't going to change that fact. It doesn't matter."

"Doesn't matter? Oh, Josh. I'm so disappointed in you. You know Galen's character. You're supposed to be his friend."

Josh's gaze held steady. "I am his friend. The length and quality of that friendship is the only thing that's keeping me from tearing him limb from limb for hurting you."

"You're more important to us," Ruth declared.

"But this isn't a situation where you have to choose between us."

Ruth slid her hand back down and curled her fingers around Laney's. "Josh taught me that I didn't have to be perfect for him to love me. Can't you see? Instead of expecting Galen to be flawless, Josh is accepting that this is the way things are for Galen. Just because you care for someone doesn't mean they're always right."

Josh sat at the foot of her bed. "You're reading about Jacob. Don't forget, Laney—he cheated Esau from his birthright. It's a reminder that even though a man might do something wrong, God can still use him for mighty works."

Laney slowly shut her Bible. "But think about Leah. She knew Jacob wanted Rachel, but Leah played her part in her father's deception and trapped Jacob."

"Look how sadly that turned out," Ruth said quietly. "Jacob never wanted Leah. She always knew he didn't want her. Ivy was humiliated by being dragged into church today. Everyone knows she's sullied. Galen married her, but Ivy can't possibly ever forget that he didn't want her."

"Galen's rejection isn't what should upset her; don't you see? Whoever the real father is— that man is the one who spurned Ivy and left her in this predicament. Galen didn't care for her; he cared for me." Laney dared to add, "I love him, and I'm sure he loves me."

"The best thing you can do is stay away." Josh gave her a stern look.

Tears filled her eyes. "Now, more than ever, Galen needs to know I believe in him."

"I'm so sorry, Laney. But Josh is right. You can't go over there. At least not for the next week. Things need to settle down."

"A week!"

Ruth nodded. "You'll see him at church. I know you've grown accustomed to seeing him every other day—"

"Ruth." Josh's voice carried a warning.

"Sweetheart, pretending otherwise is only going to make it difficult for Laney to accept this." Ruth stroked Laney's arm. "I know you dreamed of one thing, but it isn't to be. What we're going to do is pray for God to bring along the man He wants for you."

"I couldn't possibly ever love another man."

Josh rose. "It kills me knowing you're heart-broken. But, Laney, don't make this any worse."

"It couldn't possibly be worse!"

"You're wrong." He took Ruth's hand and tugged her from the bed. "You're too distraught to see how even the most innocent of actions on your part would cause others to make supposi-tions about you."

"I don't care what other people think. I spent years worrying over that. I was miserable. I have to live by my convictions and answer to the Lord—not to anyone else."

"If you won't think about yourself, think about Galen, then." Her brother didn't back down in the least. "He's on mighty shaky ground in the community now. The last thing he needs is for you to give everyone reason to gossip about how you're stealing away the attention and affection a man owes his wife. I'm serious, Laney. For everyone's sake, you have to let at least a week go by before you so much as step foot on his land."

"Pray about it, Laney." Ruth leaned over and brushed a kiss onto her cheek. "We will, too."

They shut the door behind them. Laney set her Bible on the nightstand and blew out the lamp. As she curled into a ball of misery, tears started flowing again. Her prayer consisted of only one word. *Why?*

Ivy sat on the edge of the cot and stretched. She hadn't slept much last night. Part of the problem was that the cot was so soft. After a lifetime of sleeping on a pallet on the ground, her body couldn't quite get used to this floating feeling.

A few times she sneaked over to be sure Mrs. O'Sullivan's leg stayed up on a pillow. Ivy wanted to scoot her cot right next to the bed, but the ladder to the loft was in the way. It felt so lonely, though, sleeping with so much space between her and everyone else. She and Ishy had started out sharing a womb, then a cradle. Never once in her whole life had she spent a night away from her twin. *Well, I hope Ishy got more shut-eye than I did.*

Cool air sneaked through the hole in the elbow of her nightshirt. A nightshirt. That's what Mrs. O'Sullivan had called it last night when she'd given it to Ivy. She had been surprised to learn Mrs. O'Sullivan slept in a floor-length blue flannel nightgown. Imagine, folks having special clothes just to wear to bed!

Pushing back her tangled hair, Ivy rose. Her stomach lurched, but she steadied herself with a few deep breaths. Her being sick on a morning was what had made Ishy suspicious.

Cain't be sickly. Work's gotta be done, and I ain't lettin' my husband thank I'm a sluggard. The nightshirt billowed around her knees as she tip-toed across the floor and out the door.

A few minutes later, she reentered the cabin. Galen stood over at the stove, building up the fire she'd banked the night before. "I'll see to that," she whispered as she went over to him. "And I'll brew you coffee straightaway."

Galen's gaze raked her from head to foot.

Ivy curled her bare toes under. She'd been in too much of a hurry to put on shoes.

His voice came out in a low hiss. "What are you doing in my shirt, and where have you been?"

Having to whisper in the morning wasn't anything new. Pa always slept later, so she and Ishy often used muted tones. "Yore ma give this to me to sleep in. And I went pee." She flashed him a smile. "Seems I'm doin' that a lot these days."

His jaw hardened. "I won't have it. No, I won't. It's indecent for you to be seen like this, and it's vulgar for a woman to discuss bodily functions."

"Won't nobody see me but kin. Vulgar—cain't say I know that word, but you asked me whar I went." She took the coffeepot over to the pump.

Galen snatched the pot from her. "Get

dressed before my brothers see you."

She hitched her shoulder and walked toward the peg where she'd hung her dresses. Today was a work day. She'd wear her flour sack dress. By the time she slipped into the dress, Galen had jerked the drawer from the coffee grinder and dumped the entire contents into the coffee-pot.

"That coffee's gonna be strong 'nuff to pull a plow through a field of rocks." She sat on a bench and hiked up her skirts so she could put on her boots.

Galen yanked her skirt back down. His left eye twitched as he stared at her. "You'll behave modestly in my home."

"I ain't showin' nuthin. Jist need to lace up my boots." She wrinkled her nose. "Don't know why yore all het up. Ever'body gots legs, and ever'body pees."

"A lady doesn't show her ankles—let alone her calves or knees." The words sizzled out of him like water drops on a hot skillet. "When you use the necessary, you don't have to announce it."

"Then don't ask me whar I went." She doubled over and tried to wiggle her foot into the boot. Finding the laces and tying them blindly rated as ridiculous, but no use telling that to him. Pa had his peculiarities, too—like using a branch only if it pointed a certain direction.

Gonna have a few rough days till he settles

down and gets used to the notion that I'm his wife. Niver saw him mad afore, and he's got a fearsome look in his eyes. I'll jist bide my time. Gotta make thangs work out. My babe's countin' on me.

As she tied her second boot, Ivy whispered, "D'ya want johnnycakes or eggs for breakfast?"

"The only thing I want is the truth so I can be free of you."

"We shore got us a fine flock of layin' hens."

"*We?*" He almost shouted the word.

"Huh?" Mrs. O'Sullivan bolted upright. Pain pulled at her features.

Galen shot Ivy an accusing look, but he softened his voice to a coaxing lilt. " 'Tis early yet, Ma. Go on back to sleep."

Mrs. O'Sullivan rubbed the sleep from her eyes. "If 'tis early, you'd best be telling me why I'm already smelling coffee."

Ivy didn't want to have to confess that she'd managed to make her husband shout at her their very first morning together. "Eggs—I decided on eggs for breakfast. I know jist how you like 'em. I'll have 'em right quick." She snatched the wire egg basket from the table and started to make her escape.

" 'Twill be cold out there," Mrs. O'Sullivan called. "Borrow my shawl."

"Oooh." Ivy blinked back a sudden rush of tears. "Yore offer warms me straight through."

" 'Tis pure foolishness to catch a chill when you can avoid it—especially when you're carrying a babe. I expect you to be mindful of that."

"Yes'm. But first we'll wrap yore shawl round you, and I'll holp you go—" Ivy caught herself—"to the ah . . . necessary."

"I'll carry you, Ma." Galen plucked the shawl from a peg beside the door and took it to the bed.

"There's no need, Son. Ishmael carved me a fine cane."

"It's too soon for you to walk."

He shore does have a mulish side. But he's my man. Gotta back him up. "Ishy didn't mean for you to start a-usin' the walkin' stick jist yet." Ivy clutched the egg basket close. "He brought it in so's he could measure it. He'll have to cut an inch or more off'n the bottom so's it'll fit you. E'en after he cuts the staff down a mite, he'll need time to smooth the whole thang down. Cain't have you gettin' no pickers in yore fingers."

Galen slipped the shawl around his mother and picked her up. "Plenty of work needs doing. Ishmael won't get to that for a few days."

Ivy opened the door as he drew closer.

Mrs. O'Sullivan rested her head on her son's shoulder. "Ivy, the pot with the dented side—"

"The one what we melted wax in for toppin' the jelly jars?"

"Aye, 'tis that one. First thing each morning, I put it on the stove so Galen and Colin will have hot water for shaving."

"I'll tend to that straight off." While they were gone, Ivy quickly filled the pot and set it on the stove. Galen clearly wanted his mother to rest, so Ivy straightened the bed and folded back the blanket and quilt. She folded the blanket she'd used and tucked it beneath the pillow on the cot.

Real beds. Her babe would grow up in a real house and sleep in a real bed. He'd have a nice thick blanket and plenty to eat. Best of all, he'd get to go to school and learn to read. She pressed her hand to her flat belly. *Whatever it takes, young'un, I'll see to it you don't want for nuthin'.*

Galen rummaged through the box below the tool bench.

"Whatcha lookin' for?" Dale bent forward and blocked Galen's view. "Wow!"

His baby brother's misbuttoned shirt and morning-rumpled hair were a sight. He'd scrambled down the loft ladder minutes earlier. Delighted to hear that Ivy was doing his chore of gathering eggs, he'd tagged along with Galen to the barn.

He turned and showed Galen his newfound treasure. "Lookit these really long bolts!"

The bolts were just as flimsy as they were long. Galen didn't even recall where they'd come from. *With that fancy toolbox, the boys are going to be scrounging for all sorts of things.* Galen slowly ran his thumb down one of the bolts. "Pretty interesting, huh?"

"Yeah! Can I have 'em?"

"It does a man no good to have things just for the sake of having them. Do you know what you'll use them for?"

"Boss? Breakfast is ready."

Galen shot to his feet. Dale dropped the bolts and grabbed for his hand.

"You dropped sommat thar, pardner."

Dale's voice shook. "You're not my partner. Miss Laney is."

"That's a fact." Ishmael walked toward them.

Winding his free hand around Galen's thigh, Dale blurted out, "He gots a knife, Galen!"

Chapter Twenty-Five

The knife is in the sheath." Galen modulated his voice carefully, but he glowered at Ishmael. *He planted fear into the hearts of my young brothers, and it'll be a crop I have to weed for days to come.*

Ishmael dropped down onto his knees, then

sat back on his heels. Resting both hands on his thighs, he said, "I ain't yore pardner, Dale. What I am now is yore brother."

"Nuh-uh!" Dale's little fingers squeezed two of Galen's with desperate strength. "You're not. None of us brothers would ever wanna shoot another."

"'Yore right that I was sore mad at Galen. But that was afore we was brothers. We had us a big problem, but he done sommat what made thangs right. He up and married my sis, and now thangs're all better. And when they married up, well that made you and me brothers."

"You're not gonna try to shoot him again?"

"Nope. Niver."

"And you won't use your knife on him?"

"Nope."

Galen rasped, "There you have it."

"Or the ax?" Dale persisted, his voice insistent and desperate. "Or a club or a log or a—"

"Not a thang. Niver ever. Cross my heart." Ishmael started to trail his finger across his chest.

"Don't do that! It's bad." Dale turned loose of Galen. "Ma won't let us do that."

"S'pose you could explain that to me?"

Dale stooped to pick up the bolts. "Dunno why. But Ma thinks it's important. Betcha Galen knows. He's smart."

"Boss?"

A million thoughts buzzed through Galen's mind. Ishmael was right—they were now brothers-in-law. Not that Ishmael could claim any lawful relationship to anyone else in the family, but explaining that to his little brothers might prove confusing, and mentioning it to Ishmael would rip away the "protection" of his being "kin." *Letting him stay here in the stable—Ma was right. Best I know where he is and allow him to think we consider he's part of the family.*

Ishmael had been good about reassuring Dale, too. That counted for something. From his standpoint, he'd done what he had to in order to fix a problem. Holding a grudge would make it far harder for Ma and his little brothers. *'Tis a bitter truth, but I'm going to have to swallow my pride.*

Galen cleared his throat. "Drawing an *X* on your chest is making the sign of the cross. Jesus died when men nailed Him to two pieces of wood that formed a cross, so that's like you're swearing by His name."

"If'n that Jesus feller died, then what does it matter? He ain't a-gonna hear what we say."

"Ishmael!" Giggles bubbled out of Dale. "Jesus didn't stay dead."

"Breakfast is getting cold!" Sean hollered from the porch.

"I'm gonna show Sean my bolts!" Dale raced ahead.

"I weren't jawin', Boss. Yore kin now. Ain't no danger of me causin' any harm." Strain pulled Ishmael's features tight.

"It's going to be a long time before my family gets past their fears."

Ishmael let out a mournful sigh. "Don't doubt that sad fact. Wisht now I'da thunk awhile on it. Soon as I knowed Sis was in trouble, I saw red. Niver been het up like that afore."

"If you so much as look or sound threatening ever again, you'll be gone. I won't have it."

Ishmael dared to scowl straight back. "I 'spect thar won't be no need for me to get het up e'er again. A man treats his wife good. Long as yore good to Sis—" He stopped. "Yup. That's all I want."

"This isn't about what you want."

"Pa always said a man's gotta take care of hisself 'cuz ain't nobody a-gonna holp him out. 'Twas foolish of me to set aside that teachin' jist on account of you talkin' 'bout bein' a Christian."

My own ma thinks I'm guilty. Why would I expect him to think otherwise? Ivy's lie is making everyone question both my character and my Christianity. Part of the time, I'm sure he conspired with her over this debacle; the other part, I think Ivy's done it alone. But I can't take any chances.

"I reckon I cain't blame a Christian man for settin' aside his scruples to catch hisself such a prize."

Galen folded his arms across his chest. "Ishmael, my relationship with God is more dear to me than anything or anyone. This is the last time

I'm going to say anything about this situation to you. My heart is clean, and I'm not ashamed of anything I've done."

A slow smile lit Ishmael's face. "That's a fine way of lookin' at it. You made thangs right, and ain't no way you oughtta be 'shamed. You got yoreself the purdiest gal around, and yore 'spectin' a babe." He slapped Galen on the back. "Chow time."

"Go on ahead. I don't have much of an appetite."

Ishmael chortled softly. "So Ivy's mornin' sick and yore lovesick. I'll jist tell her yore savin' up room for an extry-big lunch. That'll keep her feathers from rufflin'."

Alone in the stable, Galen stared back down at the box of odds and ends. A small length of clothesline lay coiled up in the corner. He needed it and a blanket to make a pull-across screen. Ma could explain to Ivy how she needed to cultivate modesty.

Lord, I barely slept last night. Woke up this morning hoping it was all a bad dream, but Ishmael was snoring like a bear on the other side of the tack room. That was bad enough. When Ivy traipsed into the cabin, barefoot and wearing my shirt this morning, it all hit me again. I don't know why you're letting this happen. All I did, it was in your name. Simple Christian charity. You've got to break me free of this. I love Laney, yet I'm unequally yoked to Ivy. I need your help.

Laney took a deep breath as Josh slowed the horses and brought the carriage to a stop in the churchyard the Sunday after Christmas. She rested her hands on her brother's shoulders as he lifted her down.

"Careful," he warned.

Resolve quickened her pulse. "Trust me."

Folks milled around outside the church, and as Galen and his brothers rode up, a strained silence descended. "Why's everybody staring at us?" Dale asked in a piercing voice.

Laney stepped forward. She modulated her voice carefully. "Staring is rude, Dale. I'm sure no one would do that on purpose. I've been worried about your mother, though." *Dear mercy, that didn't come out the way it ought to have.* Laney quickly added on, "Ruth and Hilda have both mentioned their concern, as well."

Ethel piped up, "I saw Galen come fetch the doctor on Christmas. How's that bride of yours doing, Galen?"

The gossip intentionally twisted the conversation. Incensed, Laney injected a matter-of-fact tone into her voice. "I'm sure Galen's wife is concerned about Mrs. O'Sullivan, as are we all." It took every scrap of poise she could muster to say the words *Galen's wife*. She refused to stand by and remain silent.

Ruth stepped up beside her. "The fact that

Ivy stayed home in order to help your mother deepens our concerns, Galen."

"Doc said it'll be another week till Ma's up and walking well." He gave them a polite nod. "I'll be sure to tell the ladies you asked after them."

"Please do."

"Ma and Ivy'll be here for church next week." Colin stood by his brother in a move of support.

"Good thing." Lester elbowed the man standing next to him in. "Some folks need to get religion or brush up on what they have."

Galen's jaw hardened.

Josh's voice went steely. "We all have room to better our walk with the Lord. Stopping your own walk to pick up stones and throw them at someone else . . . well, we all know what Christ said about being blameless before we cast stones."

Tension crackled in the churchyard. Wanting to change the topic and still show her support, Laney smiled at Galen. "Hilda, Ruth, and I plan to come over for our usual Friday sewing time unless you send word otherwise."

"Miss Laney," Dale said as he tugged on her skirts, "when you're there, you can visit our pigs."

"Pigs?" Ethel's scoff sounded remarkably like a snort.

"Yep. Pigs," Dale boasted.

"Yes. Dale and I are partners." Laney fought the urge to glare at Ethel and smiled down at Dale instead. "He's doing most of the work, though. We're raising pigs."

"Since when?" someone asked.

Before she could respond, Dale did. "Since I won the greased pig catch at the fair!"

Greta Newman skipped over. "He told me all about it! Dale said sooo-eee, and the pig ran straight to him, and they named him Mr. Snout."

Sean elbowed his way into the yard. "And guess what? There are going to be babies."

Dale turned on his brother. "You weren't s'pose to tell! It was a secret."

"No use trying to keep secrets like that." Bart Winslow's laugh sounded downright mean. "Time brings 'em to light."

"Speaking of time"—Laney caught herself almost yelling, so she softened her tone—"the service ought to be starting soon." Dale and Greta chased around, but Josh escorted Ruth and Laney toward the church.

Galen stood at the steps. He looked so grim Laney's heart almost broke. She kept track of how closely folks followed her and dared to whisper, "By comparison, Ethel's conversation skills make her look like a famous chef."

Galen's eyes glinted for a second, so Laney knew he'd heard her. *Waiting until Friday to tell Galen that I believe him won't be easy, but at least he knows I support him. That'll have to be enough for now.*

As soon as church ended, the O'Sullivans left. Laney didn't blame them. They'd come to worship, and Galen faced condemnation and cruelty from the people who knew him best.

Laney stood with Hilda and Mrs. Newman as they discussed the merits of lard versus butter in piecrust. Ethel nosed in. "Nothing's better than olive oil for pie crust. Since Lester refuses to order oil through the mercantile, I have to make do with bacon drippings."

"Hilda's bucket of lard took first place at the fair," Laney said, wanting to put an end to the mundane conversation.

"Laney, dear," Ethel tutted. "You're such a sweet child. You have something nice to say about everyone—even when it's not warranted. Why, after the way Galen O'Sullivan broke your heart—"

"Laney does bring out the best in us all." Ruth whipped open her new fan and fluttered it. "Ethel, just before we went into the sanctuary, she made a comparison, and your cooking came out favorably."

Ethel beamed.

Laney took the opportunity to change the conversation. "Ruth, I believe I overheard Mr. Maltby mention that the Basquez brothers have decided to relocate to San Francisco."

Mrs. Newman nodded. "It's true. Mr.

Maltby mentioned it to my husband."

"Rick Maltby!" Ethel pressed a hand to her bosom. "That's it! Laney, you could do far worse. He'd be a steady provider."

Laney tried to redirect the conversation. "Ruth, wouldn't the Basquez brothers' shop be an ideal location for the library?"

"Absolutely!"

Mrs. Newman drew her shawl a bit closer. "That would mean you'd be able to open the library far sooner. Greta's learning to read, so we're anticipating visiting often."

"When we were in Sacramento, Ruth bought a wide variety of children's books. Dale and Sean helped select them—"

"Those O'Sullivan boys." Ethel shuddered dramatically. "If you knew what was good for your little Greta—"

"Greta enjoys playing with Dale," Mrs. Newman said with a smile. "It's so nice for her to have a friend her very own age."

"They were darling together on Christmas morning, weren't they?" As soon as Ruth spoke, she grimaced and shot Laney a forgive-me look.

A young woman came over. "Aunt Ethel? Are you ready to go home?"

"In a minute, Myrtle."

"We need to get going, too." Hilda craned her neck. "Ruth, where did that husband of yours go off to?"

322

"Pastor Dawes is speaking with him and a few other men."

Myrtle tacked on, "It's probably about that awful Galen O'Sullivan. I hope the elders take a stand and vote him off the board of deacons."

Laney's blood ran cold. "Galen has served this church faithfully."

Myrtle gave Laney a pitying look. "That's so nice of you to say—especially after he practically jilted you at the altar."

"For that no-account white trash girl," Ethel spouted.

"Perhaps you ladies should write a book for Ruth's library." Laney forced herself to laugh, though she wanted nothing more than to weep. "This ability you have to concoct a story is very entertaining. Galen O'Sullivan never spoke a word of love to me, yet you already had us at the altar. I'm sure Ivy and I will giggle over that when she and I sew together later this week."

"Let's go." Josh's curt words warned Laney that things hadn't gone well at the impromptu meeting.

On the way back home, Ruth pulled her shawl close about her shoulders. "After today, I'm not sure why we worried about you, Laney. You are a born diplomat."

"I don't care if she's a diplomat. She's going to have to be careful," Josh muttered.

"She was killing 'em with kindness," Hilda harrumphed. "I just wanted to kill 'em."

———— ◆ ————

"I don't need anything from you," Ethel's brother snapped as he stood on the back steps of the Copper Kettle on Monday morning. Stubborn lines plowed furrows across his forehead.

"I see." Pride kept Galen from saying anything more. Someone from the O'Sullivan farm had been bringing milk, butter, and eggs to town twice a week for a good long time. Colin had delivered them last Friday, and there hadn't been a problem. Galen knew precisely why the owner of the town's only diner tacked on "from you." He'd judged Galen and found him guilty.

Ivy's done this. She's destroyed my good name. Galen drove on. Once he reached the mercantile, Lester appeared in the back doorway. "I've butter, milk, and eggs aplenty," Galen announced.

Lester wiped his hands on his long green apron. "Prices are changing."

"Are they, now?" Galen shoved back his hat. "Why would that be?"

"War's coming. Things get more expensive."

"I suppose so," Galen said. "Well, I'm sure Ma won't mind you paying her a wee bit more for her eggs and such."

"Less. I'm offering less. To offset the higher prices on some things, I have to reduce the cost of others. It's a business decision."

Galen clamped his jaw shut and nodded, knowing they needed every last cent. Through clenched molars, he said, "I'll take what you're offering."

"All I want are two of your cans of milk . . . and the eggs? Five dozen will do."

The quantities Lester had just given amounted to about two-thirds of his normal order. Galen turned away and lifted the first milk can.

Galen unloaded while Lester stood back and watched. Other folks kept an account at the mercantile, but Da refused to. He'd always insisted on paying ready cash. If they didn't have enough for something, the O'Sullivans did without until they could save up. Never before had Galen given much thought to the practice—it was Da's way. Now he felt glad he owed nothing to Lester.

Lester shoved the egg money across the wooden counter, then pulled the feather duster out and started to dust a spotless display. He'd always handed the money to Galen—and the slight was intentional. Galen picked up all but one cent. He left it on the counter for the only thing he'd buy today.

Lester always saved the broken candies from his jars. Whenever he had them, he'd slip a few to Galen or Ma to give to the boys. When he didn't have them, he apologized and promised to have something the next time. He'd not said or done either this time.

Galen opened a jar. The stick of candy he removed made a loud snap in the silent store as he broke it in half. Galen tucked both halves into his shirt pocket and walked out. Ma and Colin—they would have to endure some of the hardships Ivy's lie caused, but Sean and Dale were mere lads. Galen knew he couldn't shield them from all of the ugliness. Yesterday's moments in the churchyard showed folks were going to speak their minds. But in this one way, Galen knew he could guard their hearts. He didn't have the penny to spare, but he'd bought the candy anyway. His brothers' innocence was priceless.

On the road back home, he spied Josh coming toward him. Josh drew nearer and pulled his wagon to the side of the road. "Galen!"

Galen halted his own wagon. The slosh of milk in the milk can and a full egg basket gave testimony to what had occurred in town. Bitterness swept through him. *Ivy—she's to blame for this.*

Josh had to notice the contents of his wagon. He asked, "How'd you know Hilda wanted me to pick up eggs today?"

"I didn't. You have a henhouse."

Josh grimaced theatrically. "Don't remind me. Ruth was um . . . chicken tending—"

"Chicken tending?"

"That's what she calls it." Josh shook his

head. "She read somewhere that oyster is good for hens."

"Oyster shells."

"I'm not quite sure whether the book omitted the word *shells* or if Ruthie forgot that small detail. She saw a couple of cans of oysters in Lester's store."

"Cans!" Galen rolled his eyes. "Much as she reads, I would have expected Ruth to know better. Food wasn't made to be stored in metal cans. It goes bad or makes folks deathly ill."

"Since chickens peck the ground and eat bugs, Ruthie decided they're hearty enough to eat anything."

"Oh no."

"To hear my wife tell it, the chickens considered those canned oysters a delicacy. She told us all about how much they enjoyed them." Josh thumbed back his hat. "The long and short of it is, she's roped Toledo into digging a chicken grave."

"Just how many hens did you lose?"

Josh looked like a man who'd been pushed to the limits of his wits. "All but two."

"That's truly a shame. And your wife—her being a city girl—she thought of those hens as pets."

"She named them." Josh studied the toe of a boot. "My wife eulogized Henrietta's fine plumage. She's reminded us how Melody and Harmony always clucked in unison. On key."

Galen could just imagine Ruth doing that. Under other circumstances, he'd have gotten a great laugh out of it. But things were different. "Laney—"

"Laney's taking Ruth on a walk so they can gather flowers for the grave." Josh stared him in the eye. "Laney's no longer your concern."

The words cut deep. Galen knew Josh spoke honestly, but the truth was a bitter one.

"My sister had high hopes of being your bride; now she's grieving the loss of all her dreams."

Josh's words tore at him. "I wanted *Laney* for my wife."

"Ivy is your wife. We can't change what's happened. Life goes on."

"That's it, then?"

"That's it? Hardly." Josh's voice went harsh. "I have a heartbroken sister who steadfastly believes in your innocence. She cries herself to sleep every night, yet when she prays, she prays for you and Ivy to have a sound marriage."

A groan of pure anguish rumbled through Galen. He'd wounded the woman he loved, yet she still believed in him. She even held him up to the Lord and asked for him to be blessed.

Josh's eyes flashed. "Don't ever speak a word to her of how you felt. Her dreams are shattered; don't steal her dignity, too."

"I only want the best for Laney. I'd never do anything to cause her pain. You've my solemn promise not to speak to her of the tender love I hold—" Galen stopped. Forcing himself, he corrected, "I *held* for her."

Weary as an old man, Galen climbed down from his wagon and transferred the eggs to Josh's. Josh climbed down, too.

"The last thing I want to do is track down a flock of laying hens that are for sale in the middle of winter. Think you can talk Colin into bringing by eggs a couple of times a week on the way to school?"

"Aye."

Josh paid him for the eggs. "I'm still bound for town. The Basquez brothers are moving to San Francisco. Ruth thinks their vacant shop would be ideal for the library."

"That, it would."

Josh grasped Galen's upper arms. "Life has changed, but my friendship for you and the love of God are still yours."

" 'Tis good to know." Galen didn't bother to summon a smile. It would have been a false one. God's love wouldn't change, but Galen knew beyond a doubt that the friendship he held most dear would never be the same. Nor would the love of his life ever be his.

CHAPTER TWENTY-SIX

G alen never spoke to me regarding marriage," Laney said to the mirror. She'd been practicing that phrase for days now.

The words were honest. She strained to think of other truthful things she might say—to Ivy or anyone else. In half an hour, she'd be going over to the O'Sullivans' for the first time since . . . since . . .

"Galen and Ivy were married." Laney could barely form the words. She shuddered and strove to concoct something that wouldn't reveal her deepest feelings about the tragedy. The debacle. The horrible mistake. Ivy's trap was sprung. . . . *Lord, I don't know how I'm going to get through this. Please grant me the words at the right time. I can't let any of my feelings for Galen out. He's a married man now. I have to respect that Ivy is his wife—even if she accomplished that in a vile manner.*

"Laney?"

Unsure if her voice would be steady, Laney resorted to, "Hmm?"

Ruth traipsed in. "When Josh went to town on Monday, I asked him to pick these up for us." She plopped a few items onto Laney's bed. "We need to take a gift to the O'Sullivans. It'll be from our whole family."

"Yes. That would be proper."

"Mrs. Earnest—isn't that name gallingly right for a woman who owns a finishing school?" Ruth didn't wait for an answer. "Well, anyway, Mrs. Earnest said propriety is the best defense for a young lady's dignity."

Laney nodded as she glanced at the aprons, dish towels, and hot pan holders.

"I can't believe it!" Ruth shot her a disgruntled look.

"They're very nice," Laney said.

"I really can't believe it!" A smile tugged at Ruth's mouth. "Don't you think for a single minute that I'm oblivious to the way you and Josh keep a tally of how many headmistresses I've mentioned. Well, you're sworn to secrecy about that one, Laney. So help me, if he ever finds out exactly how many finishing schools gave up and sent me home in utter disgrace, I'd be mortified."

"Josh would love you no matter how many there were."

Ruth shoved back one of her corkscrew curls and managed to dislodge another in the process.

"All true loves are invariably forced to endure at least one great trial."

My true love will only face one trial—that we'll never be together at all. Laney sighed.

"All true loves are invariably forced to endure at least one great trial," Ruth repeated under her breath as she started folding one of the aprons.

"That doesn't sound like something you'd say. You're more practical than philosophical."

Color flooded Ruth's cheeks. "Someone I once knew was fond of that phrase." Ruth shook her finger at Laney. "And if you have the smallest dab of loyalty, you won't ask me who that woman was."

"Another headmistress?"

Looking thoroughly peeved, Ruth tugged on one of the apron strings and managed to turn the lopsided bow into a knot. "I was reading an article about a detective agency called the Pinkertons."

"Ruth! You know how I adore those dime novels. Don't spoil it by telling me anything more!"

"It's not fiction—the Pinkertons are real. They guard people or investigate for a price. The way you keep trying to discover all about the string of schools I shamed myself at, I think you could apply for a position with the Pinkertons."

Laney stared at the wedding gift she'd

stacked so neatly on her bed. "The only mystery I want to solve is determining who the father of Ivy's baby is."

"Laaa-neeey." Ruth stretched out her name and gave her a reproachful look. "Hard as this is, you have to let go of your dreams and find a new future. God is faithful—He has someone special in store for you."

Laney gave no response. Ruth was encouraging her to do the honorable thing. Galen's mother once told Laney something, and those sage words filtered through her mind. *Just because something's right, that doesn't make it feel right. More oft than not, 'tis the difficult path we must take when we follow where God leads.*

"Well!" Ruth rubbed her hands together. "What did you plan to sew today?"

Laney didn't want to look at any of the lengths of cloth she'd bought for the trousseau she'd never need. "I don't know."

"I thought maybe, if you're not set on any particular project yet, we could hem bandannas for all our cowboys."

Relief flooded Laney. "That's a good idea. Toledo's bandanna looks ready to disintegrate."

"Remember that blue material we thought to use for Hilda's dress? Since it's flawed, it'll work for bandannas, don't you think?"

"Ruth!" Hilda's bellow from the kitchen sounded inordinately perturbed.

Ruth groaned, "Now what did I do?"

Hilda stomped up the stairs, muttering every step of the way about cowboys wanting to die.

"I don't think she's mad at you," Laney whispered.

"Will wonders never cease?"

"Ruth!" Hilda clomped into Laney's room. "I don't care if you're newly wedded. If that husband of yours steals another one of my coffee cakes, I'm going to make you a widow."

"Now, Hilda." Ruth patted her shoulder. "You should be flattered that all of the Broken P's cowboys love your baking so much, they pester Josh until he relents."

Hilda didn't look in the least bit mollified. "I used apple-pear butter in this one!"

"And my husband took it?" Ruth shouted in outrage.

Hilda nodded. "I tracked it out to the barnyard. Eleven cowboys all standin' 'round, crumbs in their mustaches and on their shirts—and every last one complained he hadn't gotten his fair share! Josh skulked away before I reached him, but when I do—"

"Josh ran away?" Ruth demanded. "Like a naughty little boy?"

"And he took the cake pan with him." Hilda adjusted her apron. "If I weren't such a lady, I would have chased him down and whomped him on the head with that very pan."

"When we get home tonight, I might hold him down so you can do just that." Ruth pouted,

"I can't believe he took my apple-pear coffee cake."

Dreading going to the O'Sullivans', Laney figured she could delay their departure. "We'll wait while you make another, Hilda. We don't want to go to the O'Sullivans with empty hands."

"I'll sift together all the dry ingredients and put them in a jar. When we get there, I'll add one of Kelly's jars of apple-pear butter." Hilda brightened at her clever solution. "Yes, that's what I'll do. You girls be ready in ten minutes."

All the way to the O'Sullivans', Ruth praised Hilda's solution for replacing the coffee cake. Hilda wasn't modest in the least about the situation. They were so busy congratulating themselves, Laney was sure they didn't notice how quiet she remained.

Walking into the O'Sullivan house had always been a joy, but this time, Laney did so with a heavy heart. She let Hilda and Ruth precede her—partly out of deference, partly because she knew once they were inside she'd have to join them, but also because she needed one last moment to steel herself.

"No, no. 'Tisn't half as bad as you imagined," Mrs. O'Sullivan said as Hilda and Ruth exclaimed over her injuries. The minute Laney entered, Mrs. O'Sullivan spread her arms wide. "Now, then, there's our Laney!"

In all of the times she'd been here, Laney

had learned a little quirk. The O'Sullivans some-times tacked on *our* in front of someone's name. It was a special endearment—but one reserved only for family. Never before had Galen's mother used *our* with Laney.

The moment was so bittersweet, Laney blinked back tears. Mrs. O'Sullivan used that as a way to let her know she was still welcome and loved—but Laney knew deep down that it also meant that she'd never truly be one of the O'Sullivan family.

Laney went over to the rocking chair and embraced the woman she'd once dreamed of having as her mother-in-law.

Holding her tight, Mrs. O'Sullivan whis-pered, "Courage and faith. They'll bring you through."

Laney squeezed her back and nodded. As she slowly drew back, she looked at the woman's foot. "Are you healing well?"

"Aye. I'm staying off it. 'Tisn't half as swol-len as just a few days ago. You'd think I'd suf-fered an amputation for all the fuss everyone's kicking up."

The coffeepot clanged down onto the stove. "I reckon we'll want some coffee later on," Ivy said. "All t'other times we've sewed, we've nigh unto drained the pot twice over."

"I brought over a coffee cake—or at least the fixings for one." Hilda put the quart jar on the table. "Josh ate the one I'd already baked. Kelly,

I'm adding in some of your pear butter and some lard."

"Oh now, Hilda. Why don't you go on and use a jar of apple-pear? I know 'tis your favorite, and we'll all be sharing it."

"What a wonderful idea!" Ruth grinned at Hilda.

"If Kelly insists . . ." Hilda bustled over to the cupboard to grab a jar.

"Is there anything I can do for you?" Laney asked as she tucked a blanket across Mrs. O'Sullivan's lap.

"Nary a thing."

Ivy watched as Hilda cut lard into the dry ingredients and dumped in the apple-bear butter. "You put some of that special bakin' powder in thar so's to make that rise up?"

"Yes." Hilda nodded. "It's a vast improvement over saleratus."

"Mrs. O'Sullivan says that selfsame thang."

She calls her Mrs. O'Sullivan? I would have called her Mother *or* Mama. Laney's eyes met Galen's mother's. Understanding flashed between them.

"Laney and I decided to make bandannas out of this length of blue cotton." Ruth dumped the fabric onto the table.

Ivy frowned. "I recollect you a-sayin' you got blue 'terial for a dress."

Ruth spread the fabric out on the table. "My housekeeper from back home used it to help pack some of my things that I shipped here. I just folded it up without paying any attention. Once Laney and I decided to use the fabric, we discovered an ugly flaw running through half of it."

Laney couldn't remember which way the woof and warp of fabric went, but at the mill, something must have gotten into the loom. It tangled and broke threads, and though the remaining threads spread and tried to fill in the gap, the remaining length of cloth still couldn't recover from the loss. *Like me. Ivy ruined the fabric of my life, and—*

"Whoa." Ivy squinted at the flaw. "That's a cryin' shame."

It is, and I've cried plenty.

Ruth chewed on her lip and coaxed a wrinkle out of the material. "I think we can cut around it."

"That's right clever." Ivy bobbed her head and smiled directly at Laney. "Yup. It shorely is clever of you."

She's Galen's wife, and as much as it galls me, I'm going to have to be neighborly. It's not just rude, it's un-Christian to treat her badly. Laney managed to rasp, "A dress would have been much nicer, but the Broken P's cowboys could use new bandannas."

"Sometimes," Mrs. O'Sullivan said slowly, "you have to change plans and make the best of what you have."

"I—" Laney caught herself. "Ruth and I are doing the best we can."

She's here. Galen quickened his pace.

Ishmael chuckled. "After you et such a big breakfast, yore still hungry?"

Making no reply, Galen hastened up the steps and opened the door. *There she is. My Laney.* He stared at her like a thirsty man leaning over a well for the next bucket of water.

Laney turned toward him. Her face brightened and her big, beautiful brown eyes lit with joy.

"So that's why you was a-hurryin' to get here, Boss." Ishmael sniffed. "Sommat smells downright sinful good. What is it?"

Galen stepped inside, and Ishmael followed. Laney's cheeks went pale in that instant. The happiness sparking her features faded just as fast. She dipped her head and turned away as she mumbled, "Coffee cake."

"Hilda jist took it outta the oven." Ivy started pouring coffee. "C'mon in and take the load off yore feet."

Laney scooped a long length of cloth from the table.

"Here. I'll help you fold that." Galen grabbed a portion.

She gazed up at him, a tumult of emotions brimming in her eyes. Galen looked down at her. *My beloved lass. 'Tis you my heart beats for, but 'tisn't allowed.*

Her chin lifted ever so slightly, as did the corners of her mouth. Courage and her faith in him came through as loudly as if she'd shouted the very words.

I love you, lass. That'll ne'er change.

Tears began to form. Quickly ducking her head, she pretended to search for the corners of the blue material they'd been holding between them.

"I must have grabbed the middle." Galen cleared his voice. His fingers brushed hers, and warmth streaked through him. *I gave Josh my word not to rob her of her dignity. Honor demands too much of me . . . the grudging words of a sham marriage and the letting go of a true love.*

"I'll take it," Laney said, gently tugging the fabric from him.

Galen knew she meant far more than the outward meaning held. He pressed it all into her arms and for one last sweet instant, he slid his hand over her small, soft one and squeezed. Letting go—really letting go—was the hardest thing he'd ever done.

CHAPTER TWENTY-SEVEN

I used to love Sunday, Galen thought as he headed toward the house. He dreaded subjecting Ma and his brothers to the possibility of another churchyard scene. In one sense, he had to admit he'd brought condemnation down upon himself by "compromising" Ivy. He'd tried to show simple Christian charity and not bothered to examine how others might misconstrue his actions. He'd meant well, but his motive didn't count. It opened his integrity to suspicions. *But Ma and the boys—'tisn't right that they should suffer.*

His "wife" would accompany them to church today. Whether she wanted to or not wasn't important. As an O'Sullivan, she'd go— and Galen made that point clear last evening when she balked at the notion.

Ma passed Galen in the yard. "Ishmael said if his sister's going to worship, he will, too. I ironed his shirt."

"She should have done that, Ma."

" 'Tis a good thing, the fact that they're coming to worship. Think on that."

Colin came out of the house, biting into a hard-boiled egg. A small red spot on the angle of his jaw tattled that he'd cut himself shaving. "I'll harness the horses."

"I already did." Galen's stomach growled. "Go on ahead and drive the wagon out here. The air has a bite. Throw a couple of blankets in the back."

"Aye, that I will."

Galen went inside and grabbed a wedge of cheese from the table. On Sunday mornings Ma usually left what she called hand-to-mouth food on the table. With everyone jostling at the washstand and hurrying to get chores done before leaving for church, they'd grab a slice of bread or coffeecake, a hard-boiled egg, cold rashers of bacon—whatever was available.

"Hey!" Galen scowled at the cot. "Get up."

Everyone else was almost ready to go, but Ivy still burrowed beneath her blankets. Irritated, Galen raised his voice. "You're going to church. Get up!"

He looped his string tie over his head and sawed it back and forth to slide the narrow black strip under his collar. Only half paying attention to his own reflection in the washstand mirror as he tied it, he stared at the image of his unwanted bride pretending to sleep.

Her eyes scrunched shut, and she pulled the

blanket more snuggly around herself.

Galen knew from the past week and a half that she was a light sleeper. Ma said Ivy got up during the night to check on her, and if one of his brothers climbed down the ladder in the middle of the night to go to the outhouse, Ivy always whispered to them upon their return. With Ma's ankle all rooked up, Ivy also rose every morning to get coffee and breakfast going. She could pretend all she wanted, but he knew she was awake.

"Sean. Dale." Galen's little brothers had been standing by the table, shoving food into their mouths while watching Ivy defy him. *This is the last thing I need.* "You boys put on your jackets and go get in the wagon. Colin's bringing it around now."

Dale stared longingly at the cheese. "After I put on my coat, Galen, can I put a wee bit of cheese in the pocket?"

"Aye. But be quick about it."

Once his brothers were out the door, Galen's boots rang out his anger as he crossed the plank floor. He stooped over and clamped his hand on her shoulder. Jostling her, he grated, "You're going to church."

She made a small mewling sound.

"Get up!" He shook her again.

The crazy woman bolted upright, and the abrupt move made Galen let go and back up a step. "It's well past time—"

Ivy got sick all over the front of him.

Galen let out a bellow.

"Son?" Ma asked as she opened the door.

He let out a gusty sigh as he started to strip out of his shirt. "Go on to church."

"The boys can wait a few minutes while I help—"

"No, Ma." Galen's nose wrinkled. "By the time we wash off the stench and clean up, church'll be half over. No use in all of us being late. Go on ahead."

"Brew her some tea, son. 'Twill settle her stomach."

Galen nodded.

"Sorry," Ivy muttered. Her head hung down, but he could see she was as white as his old church shirt. When he'd seen her in it before, Galen hadn't noticed how the "nightshirt" hung on her—she practically swam in it. She sat on the edge of the cot with her legs spraddled wide. Knobby knees stuck out, but she'd tucked her toes way back beneath the cot to keep them clean. She'd made almost as big a mess of herself as she had of him.

"Go on behind that curtain and toss out your shirt. I'll fill the tub so you can clean up."

She started to nod, but abruptly stopped.

Galen stepped back—just in case. A minute later she pulled shut the privacy curtain he'd put up the morning after she'd lied her way into his life and house.

He yanked off his boots and Sunday-best britches. Stripped down to his heavy white cotton, winter balbriggans, he figured he was decent enough. His pants and shirts were out in the tack room. No use putting on a change before he cleaned up her atrocious mess, anyway.

"Mr. O'Sullivan," Ivy's soft twang traveled to him, "fillin' a tub ain't necessary. If'n you give me a pot of warm water, 'twill be all I need."

He banged the last large pot down onto the fourth burner of the stove. Water splashed, dampening his sleeve. "Water's already heating."

"If'n you step outside," she said in a thready whisper, "I cain come out and clean up my puke."

Though sorely tempted, Galen didn't accept the offer. She'd probably get near the disaster and add more to it. "Just stay put."

Cleaning the floor tested his mettle. In all the months Da was sick, it hadn't bothered Galen one bit to mop up after him. *This shouldn't be any different. But it is.* Galen wanted to open the door to air out the cabin, but he couldn't. The last thing he needed was for that troublesome woman to catch a chill. Once he finished the floor, he frowned.

"I told you to toss out the shirt."

"I'm cold," she said in a tiny voice.

"Why didn't you say something?" Irritated, he grabbed a towel and shoved it toward the spot where the blanket screen and wall met.

Cloth rustled, and a bundled knot of cotton slid beneath the blanket. "Thankee. I'll wash up them clothes of ourn straightaway."

Galen shoved her shirt into the same tin pail he'd used to hold his shirt and britches, then set it out on the porch. When he turned back around, she'd started to come out. She let out a squeak and ducked back behind the curtain.

"What do you think you're doing?!"

"I thunk you was gone 'way."

He gave no response. Instead, he pumped water into the tub they'd used just the night before for their Saturday baths. Ma had shared her lily-of-the-valley glycerin soap with Ivy. The whole rest of the evening, Ivy had cooed over how pretty it smelled. Galen carried the partially filled tub over near the curtain. "Water's not hot enough to add yet. Just stay back there and wait."

"Okay."

Her voice came out sounding odd. Sorta faint. Galen frowned. "You're not getting swoony, are you?"

"N-no."

"You're still cold?" He could scarcely imagine why. With the stove burning as it was, the entire cabin felt plenty warm enough to him— far warmer than the tack room. When she didn't answer, he persisted. "Are you cold?"

"This towel you give me—'tis a nice, thick'un."

He could hear her teeth chattering, but she wasn't complaining. Galen stared at the curtain, then a movement caught his attention. The curtain missed hitting the floor by a few scant inches. Galen noted how she stood on one foot, then the other. The woman was a bother.

He grabbed the chamber pot from beneath the bed and slid it under the curtain. "I'm going to the tack room to grab some clothes. Don't come out from behind there."

"Yes, Mr. O'Sullivan."

For all the times Ma had done the laundry, Galen couldn't say exactly how she did it. While Ivy bathed, he stayed outside and rinsed their clothes. Ma used lye soap for laundry. He knew that. Galen couldn't be sure just how much to use, but since the stench permeated the garments, he figured this situation called for a generous amount of soap. He chopped a whole bar into chunks and added it to the washpot. By the time he added water, suds were everywhere.

He built a fire in the fire ring and hung the pot over it. He knew it would take a little while to boil. In the meantime, he'd do some of his Sunday chores.

Sundays were the day of rest, so they only did essential chores. On a farm, that still amounted to a fair load. He saw to the animals, then as he crossed the yard, he spied Ivy by the laundry. "What are you doing?" he roared.

Using a bucket, she splashed more water onto the fire beneath the pot. "Fire's too hot."

"It can't possibly be too hot."

She glowered. "Ain't you niver heared that a washpot niver boils?"

"A *watched* pot never boils." He grabbed the bucket from her. "A *wash*pot is supposed to."

"Yore talkin' in riddles."

Galen took the paddle Ma used to swish stuff around in the pot. His britches looked fair enough, but he decided to let them soak a little while longer. After all, they were thicker cloth. Next, he fished out a dish towel—or at least he thought that's what it was. Hastily, he let go of it and sought his new store-bought, Sunday-best shirt.

"How come's my nightshirt gone dark?" Ivy leaned forward and frowned.

"It's not your nightshirt." He stared in disbelief at the splotchy mess.

"Well, shoot. What'd you do to yore good shirt?"

Galen flopped the shirt over a nearby stump. Turning, he glowered at her. "I won't abide foul language."

"What in tarnation did I say now?"

Sure his molars were going to crack any minute from the way he constantly gritted them together, he stared at her. "Shoot is a thinly veiled reference to what you do in the outhouse."

"Oh, for cryin' in a bucket. Ever'body knows shoot is what a gun does. Yore a-getting splenacious for nuthin'."

"Just because you think you have a plausible excuse, that doesn't make that crudity acceptable. Don't use it again. As for *tarnation*—"

"Oh bother. If'n yore gonna have a conniption o'er shoot, I cain jist imagine what sorta tale you'll spin o'er that'un."

"Hell."

Her jaw dropped. "Mr. O'Sullivan, you jist cussed!"

"No, you did." He glowered at her. "*Tarnation* means 'hell.' I'm trying to let you know what those sayings you have mean. Everyone else is fully aware of what they stand for. As long as you bear my last name, I won't have you darken it by using obscenities."

"You don't hafta git het up. Ain't my fault you Christians got all sorts of funny rules. I'm already foldin' my hands and closin' my eyes when you pray. Seems awful silly to keep telling God yore glad for the grub and askin' Him to bless yore loved'uns. If'n He's God, don't seem like He'd need you to be reminding Him mornin', noon, and night.

"And Dale tole me no crossin' our hearts. But we ain't s'posed to swar 'bout tellin' truth."

"You wouldn't know the truth if it trampled you!" Galen shoved the paddle into the washpot and stepped close to her. "Who sired the babe?"

She compressed her lips into a thin, blood-less line.

His eyes narrowed. "Do you even know who the father is? Is that it? How many—"

She slapped him and wheeled around.

Chapter Twenty-Eight

Galen grabbed her arm and jerked her back. In one moment he was both livid and relieved. She had no right to strike him, yet the outrage behind her action indicated she hadn't been with several men.

"I ain't no tart!"

"Give me his name."

"Don't matter who he was. Yore my man now."

He snorted derisively. "I'll never be your husband."

"I got yore name."

"But you'll never have my heart or share my bed. Your sins and lies will catch up with you. When they do, I'll be free of you." She hadn't relented when he made demands, so Galen shifted tactics. He slowly turned loose of her and toned down his voice. "Give me his name. I'll go easier on you. The lawyer in town owes me a favor. He'll help you."

She stepped to the side and grabbed the paddle. Inspecting the first item she drew out of the washpot, she sighed. "Ever'thang's spoilt."

Hoping she was softening and needed a moment to gather her resolve before she confessed, Galen waited in silence.

"I recollect yore ma sayin' she dyed her dresses all black. If'n she still gots some of that dye, we cain darken ever'thang so's it's black all over and not spotty. Reckon don't make no diff'rence what color none of this stuff is."

He stayed silent.

"Ain't niver seen bubbles that was gray and black. Thar's a powerful lot of 'em, too."

His patience started fraying. A discussion over laundry didn't matter. All he wanted was her confession—nothing more, nothing less.

"Reckon the onliest thang this wash water's good for is them hogs of Dale's. Soap'll take care of any worms they might have."

"Don't give it to them. Dale takes his partnership seriously. None of us is interfering with the hogs."

"Ain't right for me to have a fav'rite, but if'n I did, lil' Dale'd be the one. Sommat extry special 'bout that'un."

"His innocence makes us all love and protect

him. He doesn't understand why folks are treating us differently now."

"Diff'rent?"

Was she that oblivious? Galen stared at her. "A man's word is his bond. By naming me as the father of a child outside holy matrimony, you destroyed my integrity. It's changed everything."

"You ain't meanin' to tell me all them good Christian folks who spout off 'bout the forgiveness of God are holding this 'gainst you and yore family. What kind of deal is that? God's s'posed to forgive them, but they take account of other people and condemn 'em?"

"That's exactly what I'm saying. Forgiveness is granted when we confess our wrongdoings. I won't lie. I won't say I wronged you in hopes of garnering forgiveness. Your lie gave my family, my church, my friends and neighbors—the very people I depend on for my livelihood—cause to doubt me."

Galen took a deep breath. Perhaps if he let her know just how bad things were, she'd understand what a mess she'd made of matters. Maybe then she'd relent and confess. "When my da was alive, it took both of us to keep up on all the chores. Then when he got sick and ailed so long, I couldn't plant as much. Money has always been tight, but in the last months, it's been strained worse than ever."

"Then 'tis right fine you havin' me and Ishy to work 'longside you. We'll holp you plant thrice as much, and you'll be livin' high off the hog in a season or so. That, and the money you get from the Pony—"

"The Pony Express is in arrears with what they owe me, too. I haven't been paid by them for months now. I can't count on that money," Galen gritted. She'd dismissed his concerns without batting an eye. "Every cent we got from eggs and milk—they mattered. Some of my regular customers aren't buying them from me now." He added on, "Your lie is costing my family far more than we can afford."

Telling her those truths wasn't easy. Da once spoke of how some Christians were so busy being "fruit inspectors" that they didn't see how they'd stopped producing fruit and become rotten themselves. Several of the upstanding members of the church and community hadn't given him—their Christian brother—the benefit of the doubt. They'd judged and found him lacking honor. The cost would follow him forever.

Speak the truth, woman. Now that you know the facts, speak the truth.

She shrugged. "Cain't do nuthin' 'bout what other folks say or thank. Gotta jist keep plodding, one foot a-front of t'other."

"All you have to do is admit you lied. You don't even have to reveal who the true father is. Just admit I'm not the child's sire. Then you and your brother could leave and live however you want."

"Don't wanna live noplace else." Skimming off a pile of dark bubbles, she added, "You jist said yore word is your bond. That bein' so, yore bound to me."

His throat ached with the need to shout at her. Galen almost gave in to the temptation, but something held him back. "You expect me to be honorable, but your lie dishonored me. Everyone I care for—from the woman I love clear down to my baby brother—is forced to bear the cost of the wrongs you've done."

"You give me time. I'll make it up to 'em."

He gave her a scorching look. "Impossible."

"Ruth, did you want to have a table and chairs," Laney asked as she surveyed the room, "something along the line of a dining set, or were you thinking of something more like a study with wing-back chairs?"

"Both!" Ruth scanned the now-empty tailors' shop. "I didn't imagine the Basquez brothers' shop was this large. Isn't it wonderful?"

"Yes." Laney watched Rob Price as he rapped his knuckles on a wall. Ruth had persuaded Laney to look at the promising library space with her and the carpenter first thing Tuesday morning.

"Mrs. McCain, this partition is too flimsy to remain. It served its purpose to form a storeroom, but getting rid of it would free up a lot of space."

Ruth bobbed her head. "Good. I'm glad. But there's a bench in there. Can you detach it?"

"I'll take a look." Rob rocked from heel to toe and back. "Where were you planning to put the bookshelf?"

"Bookshelf?" Ruth gave him an appalled look.

"You surprised my sister-in-law," Laney hastily explained. "Ruth is dedicated to making this an outstanding library. She's acquired a considerable number of books."

Seemingly unfazed, he said, "I'll make a book*case* instead. Maybe four feet . . ." He watched Ruth's face. "Five—no? Six feet wide."

"I'll need at least eight of them. Maybe ten."

"Ten."

Oblivious to the shock she'd served the carpenter, Ruth mused, "As the library grows—"

"Mrs. McCain, it's nice to hear how you want to expand; but you said you wanted to open as soon as possible. I can build bookcases as you need them."

"Perhaps I should be more flexible." Ruth tilted her head a little.

Relief flooded Mr. Price's face. "I'm glad you saw reason."

"A dozen of them, four feet wide, would permit me to rearrange as I need to."

Laney took pity on the carpenter. "Mr.

Price, perhaps I should have been more specific about how many books Ruth has obtained. Ruth, I've lost count."

"So have I."

"Two hundred?" Rob sounded incredulous.

"Oh no. No, no, no." Ruth's brow puckered. She always did that right before she spoke her mind.

Laney jumped in before Ruth said something she'd regret. "The number hovered at five thousand before I lost track."

"Five thousand?!" He raked his fingers through his hair. "Are there really that many books written?"

"The library is in my dear mother's memory. You didn't expect me to skimp, did you?" Ruth didn't wait for him to answer. "Of course you didn't. Now that that's settled, I've decided to have everything made of oak."

"I'll have to order the lumber."

Looking thoroughly disgruntled at that news, Ruth huffed, "That's going to mean I can't start bringing the books in by Friday."

"Friday? No." Rob shook his head. "No, you won't. As a matter of fact, it'll take a few months to get this place ready."

"Months!" Ruth whipped out her fan and started fluttering it. Josh had once privately confessed he could tell just how upset Ruth was by how fast and furiously she fanned herself. He'd come up with what he called his "three-beat rule," where whoever was nearest was supposed to swipe Ruth's fan once she'd managed to smack herself with it three times.

"Ruth," Laney said as she stole the fan, "it's better to have everything done perfectly at the outset than to have to shut the library down once your patrons are counting on you."

"But it only took Toledo one day to double the size of the chicken coop." Ruth didn't reveal to Rob that she had recently poisoned all of her feathered pets.

"Bookcases are a far cry from chicken coops," Rob growled.

Ruth fished up her sleeve for a hankie.

Laney handed hers over. Mr. Price probably thought Ruth was upset over the bookcases—which she was—but Laney knew she had to change the topic. Once Ruth started in eulogizing her pet hens, they'd never get anything done. "I'm sure Mr. Price will work diligently. Mr. Price, Ruth and I discussed having a half-dozen small chairs for children."

Rob smiled at her. "How charming."

"You're too kind."

"And a little table, too. Over by the children's books." Ruth regained her composure. Within moments she'd decided they needed white-painted tin ceiling plates and a librarian's desk.

The carpenter pointed out details and asked questions. Laney tried to fade into the background, but Ruth and he kept asking her questions.

Ruth waited until Rob went to the other side of the partition, then she waggled her brows and silently mouthed, "He likes you."

Laney pretended not to understand her and turned to the front of the building. "Have you decided what to do about the window?"

"You sound as if you have some suggestions." Ruth drew closer. She whispered, "Mr. Price is a good man, Laney."

"Yes, he is." Laney glanced down and realized she'd started wringing her hands. Clenching them together tightly, she whispered, "But he reminds me of Josh."

"That's quite a compliment."

"Yes, but . . ." Laney shuddered. "There's a difference between how *you* think of Josh and how *I* think of him. You think of him as your man; I think of him as a brother."

"Oh." Ruth's eyes widened and she added, "Ewww!"

"Is something wrong?" Rob popped out from behind the partition.

Laney would rather perish than let him know what they'd been discussing.

"There's an enormous bug here in the corner."

Laney looked at where Ruth pointed. She didn't have to pretend to shudder when she saw the cockroach.

Rob approached them. "I'll get it. Spiders,

bugs, snakes, mice—you ladies aren't supposed to handle such things." He took a quick look and chuckled. "It's dead. I'll sweep it out of here."

As he did so, Laney whispered, "When we're done here, I'm going to buy chocolate at the mercantile. You get a piece for getting me out of this."

Ruth's eyes twinkled.

When the carpenter returned, he cast a smile at Laney. "If there are any more of those, just call me. I'll handle them."

"The window . . ." Laney knew she was babbling, but she couldn't help herself. Galen made her feel comfortable and confident. He had a calming way about him. Rob Price, Eddie Lufe, Rick Maltby—they were all fine men. Christian men. Single. But not a one of them made her heart skip a beat.

"The window?" Rob squinted. "Is there a crack or something? If there is, I can replace it."

"Nothing's wrong with it. Other than it's being filthy. Once it's cleaned, though, Ruth, we need to take advantage of it."

"Take advantage? How?"

Glad she'd already thought about some possibilities, Laney blurted out, "Either place the table and chairs here to take advantage of the light, or perhaps display some books there."

"Display books?" Rob grinned. "I'm not sure I see the logic behind that. Folks know a library is going to have books."

Galen never made me feel stupid.

"Displays?" Ruth chewed on her lower lip and blinked. "Oh! What a magnificent idea! I could feature something different each month. Biographies, mysteries—"

"But if you stick all of them in the window, what's left for folks to borrow?" Rob shrugged. "I suppose you could keep a list of folks who want to borrow those books when they're available once the display is over."

"I'll do that, too!"

Laney smiled at Ruth's enthusiasm. "It would be fun to have a globe and maps—maybe a compass, too, and do a travel and geography display."

"Ah! Now I see." Rob nodded. "A pickax and a pan, and you could do California history." His brows knit. "I don't suppose that's really history. The gold rush started only a decade ago."

"We could expand it to do a Western theme." Ruth beamed at Laney. "What props would we want for the display?"

"We could place a table there and use bandannas or a horse blanket as a tablecloth. We could have a variety of Western-type books and have a child's picture book open in the center. If we added a pair of spurs and a hat to the pickax and pan, it would balance the arrangement."

"Children's books!" Ruth gave her a hug. "Oh, I love that idea! We'll make a point of having books of all levels—that way, everyone will know they can find something to read."

"So let me make sure I'm getting all of this straight." Rob took the pencil he'd been wearing behind his ear and pressed a slip of paper against the wall. "You want six children's chairs." He scribbled on the paper.

"And a pint-sized table," Ruth added.

Without turning around, he continued, "You want six adult chairs and a dining table—square or round?"

"Rectangular." Ruth smiled. "Let's make it ten chairs."

His pencil came off the paper. "Just how big do you want that table?"

"I'm an absolute dolt when it comes to those things." Ruth looked at her. "Laney knows all of those little details that make life go so much more smoothly. How much space?"

Wait a minute. I thought you understood I don't want you to match me up with this man. "I don't know about library tables. When dining, you plan for thirty inches for each place setting."

"Speaking of which," the carpenter said as he folded the paper and crammed it and the pencil into his shirt pocket, "why don't you ladies do me the honor of joining me for lunch at the Copper Kettle?"

"I really don't think—" Laney began.

"Actually, it *is* lunchtime." Ruth smiled at her, then at the carpenter. "We'd adore having a meal with you."

Laney brushed by Ruth and whispered, "Eat a lot. You're not getting a single bite of the chocolate I buy at the mercantile!"

CHAPTER TWENTY-NINE

Mr. Darlden opened the door to the diner and bellowed across the room, "Ruth, Laney? I brought your guest on over. Lefty and Jeb're loading her trunks onto your wagon."

"Hello," the young woman said in a velvety southern drawl once she reached their table. "I'm Miss Amanda Bradley."

Ruth's mouth was full, so Laney spoke. "It's a pleasure to have you, Miss Bradley, isn't it, Ruth?"

Ruth nodded.

"Please, though, feel free to call me Laney. Women in the West tend to become friends so rapidly, formalities are unnecessary." Laney turned slightly to the side, where Mr. Price had come to his feet. "And this is our town's finest carpenter, Mr. Robert Price."

"How lovely to make your acquaintance."

Amanda accepted the seat Mr. Price pulled out for her. "Thank you, sir."

Ruth swallowed and leaned forward. Her lips didn't move as she whispered, "Sandwich."

Miss Bradley glanced at their plates. All three of them were eating sandwiches, and Laney hoped her sister-in-law's friend would take the hint.

Ethel smoothed her apron as she pattered out of the kitchen. "I heard Mr. Darlden. Where did he go? Oh dear. Well, well, Ruth. Who's your little friend, and where is she from?"

"Miss Bradley is undoubtedly thirsty after traveling, Ethel."

"After traveling, I was positively parched," Laney chimed in as Ruth picked up her sandwich to take another bite. "Ethel, would you be so kind as to bring her a cup of coffee?"

"Of course. Of course." Ethel didn't leave, though. She took a sweeping look at Miss Bradley's clothing. Though rumpled and dusty, it was made of the finest material and lace. Laney didn't doubt for a second that the cook could probably guess within ten cents what it cost. Greed lit her eyes, and she called in a much-too-cheery voice, "Myrtle, be a dear and bring out a cup of coffee." She turned back to Miss Bradley. "You'll want to meet my niece. I'm sure she'll love meeting you, too. Any friend of the McCains is certain to charm us all."

Amanda managed a polite smile.

"It'll be lovely to cook for a young woman of distinction. Today's special is—"

"I'll order for the young lady," Mr. Price said.

"But she hasn't heard about my stewed rabbit and prunes."

Myrtle came out of the kitchen. She carried a cup and saucer, but the look on her face was anything but reassuring. "Did the tea and coffee get mixed up?"

"No, they didn't." Ethel whisked the beverage from her niece and exultantly placed it on the table. "Gourmet coffee. That's what it is. There. Have a taste!"

"I don't believe I've ever had coffee with such an aroma."

Laney grimaced. Amanda stated a fact that no one could deny. If Laney had her way, she would never again smell such coffee, either.

"Travel is ever so difficult on a gentle lady's constitution." Laney reached over and smoothly robbed Amanda of the cup. "I wasn't thinking clearly when I requested the coffee. Tea. Yes, tea." The strikingly beautiful girl nodded her head. Laney suspected the glint in her eyes was gratitude. "Plain. Unless you'd like a touch of honey, Miss Bradley?"

"How thoughtful of you. Tea would be best." She sighed in relief, then added to Laney, "And do call me Amanda."

Ethel squared her shoulders. "Tea and an order of stewed rabbit and prunes."

"A sandwich, Ethel," Mr. Price said in a firm tone.

Ethel beamed. "You'd like another sandwich?"

"No, the young lady would appreciate one."

"Yes, she would!" Laney daintily picked up part of her own sandwich. "Do forgive me for eating in front of you, Amanda, but nobody makes sandwiches like Ethel. Every time I come here, I just have to have one!"

"Please do go ahead and eat."

"I'll get that sandwich." Ethel headed for the kitchen door. Just as she reached it, she paused. "Laney, you never said how good my fricasseed chicken was. Remember taking it home when you returned from the fair?" Ethel started back toward their table.

"I couldn't possibly forget it."

Ruth smiled. "And your chocolate applesauce cake, too. There wasn't a single scrap left of it that night."

"Myrtle, make Miss Bradley a sandwich." Ethel plopped down beside Amanda. "You must tell me all about yourself."

"She's so travel weary, the poor dear." Ruth shook her head. "Amanda, please don't feel obliged to entertain us."

"Indeed," Laney agreed. "When I made the

trip back here, all I wanted was a cup of tea and a comfortable bed."

Clearly grateful for their excuses, Amanda nodded.

By unspoken agreement, Ruth and Laney took turns trying to shield her from Ethel. Ethel seemed to think she should dominate the conversation. She didn't stay on any topic very long, but that was due to the way Laney, Ruth, and Mr. Price redirected what smacked of gossip.

Drooping with weariness, Amanda ate her sandwich when it arrived and remained quiet.

Once she finished, Mr. Price walked them to the wagon. "I'll drive," Ruth asserted. "Laney, you can ride in the back with Amanda."

"Oh no. I insist upon driving. You keep her company."

Ruth gave her an exasperated look. "Laney, your friend is wilting. She needs you."

"My friend?" Laney's face puckered in confusion. "She came to visit you!"

"No, I thought she was a friend of yours from school." Ruth and Laney both turned their attention on the stranger.

A shudder wracked Amanda as she stared at them. "My cousin, Yancy Bradley, made the arrangements. I'm supposed to be a companion to Miss Elaine. I have the letter from Mr. Joshua McCain in my valise."

Mr. Price muffled his laughter with a cough. "I thought only the aged or the infirmed required companions. Miss Laney, which are you?"

Amanda's voice shook as she half whispered, "You're Miss Elaine."

"Yes, I am. There seems to be a misunderstanding. My brother sent out an inquiry regarding a companion for me almost two years ago."

What little color Amanda had left seeped away. "Two years ago." She'd echoed the words in a hopeless tone.

Ruth and Laney exchanged looks. Ruth slipped her hand into Amanda's. Laney took the other side.

"Do you enjoy reading?"

Amanda looked at Ruth. She didn't know Ruth's predilection for concocting schemes, so Laney was sure Amanda considered the question completely out of place. Manners demanded she reply, so she murmured, "I *adore* books."

"Isn't that just like the Lord?" Laney squeezed Amanda's hand. "He knew we needed a librarian."

"Bye!" Ivy stood on the porch and waved. The McCains had been in town the day before and were kind enough to pick up a few necessities and the mail for them.

"We'll see you on Friday," Mrs. O'Sullivan added. After the women from the Broken P drove off, Mrs. O'Sullivan sighed.

"Yore ankle naggin' at you?"

"Only a little. I'm not complaining, though." She leaned on the cane and walked back into the house. "The good Lord above surely blessed me with fine neighbors."

"Them vittles they brung—'twas nice of 'em."

"Laney and Ruth were concerned Sunday. I shouldn't be surprised that they came over today. They're very thoughtful young ladies."

Ivy grimaced. "Wisht I woulda done sommat with the laundry. Hated havin' 'em see how my new weddin' towels and the shirts got spoilt."

"We cannot dwell on that. What's done is done." Mrs. O'Sullivan sank into the rocking chair and propped up her foot.

Ivy started a fresh pot of coffee. "That 'Manda gal said sommat sorta like that. Didja know her cousin's a low-down polecat? He showed up on her doorstep, sayin' he would holp her with the plantation since her daddy up and died. Didn't take long afore he was runnin' the place and acting all biggety. Robbed her of ever'thang that her daddy left her, then sent her here to work. If'n my kin sent me off on a wild goose chase, I'd go back and get even."

"Vengeance belongs to the Lord. It's not for us to seek retribution." Mrs. O'Sullivan picked up her Bible.

"D'ya mind if'n I go stretch my legs?"

"Not at all." Mrs. O'Sullivan looked up. "Ivy, 'tis okay when we're alone, but you'll need to be mindful when others are about us—the words *ankles* and *legs* aren't used. 'Tisn't proper for a woman to refer to her body."

"I'll try to remember me that." Ivy left. As she walked along, she mumbled, "Don't know what the fuss is all 'bout. Ever'body gots ankles and knees and legs. Pretendin' they ain't thar's jist silly."

Wandering along, Ivy thought about the afternoon. Miss Ruth . . . well, she was a hoot. The woman didn't mind laughing out loud, and she didn't seem in the least bit worried over how clumsy she was. Everybody liked her just fine. But she was rich.

Laney and Amanda—they were two peas in a pod. Ivy had watched them all afternoon. They smiled a lot, but their teeth didn't show when they did. When they laughed, they raised a hand in front of their mouth. Their voices were as soft as their hands. They used dainty manners and never once struggled to handle all those yards of skirts they wore.

Reckon they're 'shamed of me. Betcha Galen and his ma wisht he woulda married someone like them. 'Manda wasn't here yet, but they woulda been thrilled to pieces for Laney to have their name and live beneath their roof. Galen said he loved a gal. Was it Laney? No. Cain't be. She woulda tole me. We're friends.

Ivy hiked up her skirts and climbed up onto a boulder. As soon as she settled in, she looked down at her skirt and frowned. The other women sat with their knees pressed together. Everything about them was different. They pinned up their hair, never rolled up their sleeves, and quietly pattered about. *Feller's gotta want a purdy lil' gal like Laney—not a straggle-haired, rough-spoken, boot-clompin' gal whose baby ain't his.*

She pressed her knees together.

Since Sunday, Galen had been avoiding her. Ivy couldn't blame him. If she hadn't puked on him, he wouldn't have ruined his shirt. She'd been just as glad that he'd kept his distance. All day Monday and most of today, Ivy had kept reminding herself she'd done what she had to for the sake of her baby.

Learning that the church folks suddenly treated him different—that surprised her. Even if he was the father—well, one little slipup shouldn't be cause for such a hullabaloo. Wasn't like any of them was perfect. Knowing now that they even made life hard on little Dale . . . well, that left Ivy feeling lower than a gopher in the bottom of his hole.

She looked down again. In just those few moments while she'd been lost in thought, she'd started spraddling again. *I trapped Galen into this marriage. Cain't back out of it. What I'm a-gonna hafta do is turn into a gal he ain't shamed to have by his side.*

This Friday, she and Mrs. O'Sullivan were going to the Broken P to sew. If Laney was really, truly as sweet as the store-bought chocolate candy she shared today, maybe she could help. Ivy figured she had nothing to lose.

———•———

"'Morning, Miss Elaine." Eddie Lufe held his hat over his heart as he stood outside her door on Thursday afternoon, revealing carefully pomaded hair. Wave upon wave of bay rum accosted Laney.

She grabbed her hankie from her sleeve just in time to catch her sneeze. "Excuse me."

"God bless you."

"Thank you, Mr. Lufe." She tried to summon a polite smile. "What a surprise to have you drop by."

"Is that Eddie Lufe?" Hilda trundled over. "C'mon in. Don't just stand there. But wipe your feet first."

"Yes'm."

Under other circumstances, Laney knew she'd be tempted to laugh at the sight of a hulking man deferring to her scrappy housekeeper. Only this wasn't funny in the least. She sensed exactly what was going on. "Am I to assume you have something baking in the kitchen, Hilda?"

"I always do." Hilda nudged Laney. "Take

the gentleman into the parlor. I'll bring refreshments in a moment."

"Please have a seat, Mr. Lufe." Laney swept her hand in the general direction of the parlor. "I'm sure you'll excuse me while I go invite Amanda and Ruth to join us."

"No!" Hilda cleared her throat. "They're going to the cottage to work on the library books. I sent pie along with them."

"Pie?"

Laney plastered on a smile. *Eddie would have been just as happy to come eat as to see me.* "Hilda is a wonderful cook."

"So is Laney." Hilda rearranged her apron bib. "Between me and Kelly O'Sullivan, we've brought our Laney along to the point that she can cook with the best of us. Why, she even took second place at the fair for her grape jelly."

"You don't say!"

Hilda bobbed her head. "And with the grapes you brought over from your very own vines!"

"We took jars of the jelly over to Mr. Lufe, Hilda. Don't you remember? But I'll be happy to grab a few more from the pantry."

"Isn't that just like you, Laney? You just go sit down with Eddie. I'm sure the two of you will find a lot to talk about."

Unable to come up with a reasonable excuse to avoid the man, Laney breezed past him and into the parlor. Though she usually preferred the settee, Laney was afraid Eddie might try to sit beside her. She tamed her hoops and sat on a small chair.

"Your pianoforte is lovely." Eddie sat in the chair her father had always used. It creaked loudly. "Do you play?"

"Only badly." Laney shrugged. "Ruth is the talented one. She plays divinely."

"I'm sure you must have other talents."

Hilda raced in, a tray in her hands. "Oh yes! Laney is quite the artist." Laney strongly suspected the housekeeper had arranged this visit and had the refreshments ready in the kitchen. Ignoring Laney, Hilda set the tray down on the coffee table. "She painted that picture over the piano."

"Did you now?" Eddie stood. "I'll have to look at it more closely."

"Laney also did the flower arrangement. She learned all of those things at her finishing school. Not only that, she helped Kelly O'Sullivan out in her flower garden."

Laney automatically accepted the teacup and saucer Hilda thrust at her. She gave Hilda a dirty look, though. Hilda sounded just like a horse trader, talking up all the selling points of a nag he wanted to unload. *The next thing I know, she's going to talk about my teeth.*

"The arrangement . . . it is beautiful." He tilted his head and closed one eye. "And the picture . . . I feel like I am right there, in that landscape. The details on the little flowers at the very bottom are very realistic."

"Thank you."

Hilda made an impatient gesture at her and mouthed, "Be nice."

Laney stiffened.

Unwilling to let the unfortunate visit come to a quick end, Hilda motioned Eddie back to his chair and served him the tea and an enormous slice of pie. "I believe Laney will plant a flower garden here at the Broken P come spring if she hasn't gotten married."

Pain slashed through her so mercilessly, Laney dropped her fork.

"Don't fret over that," Hilda said as she swooped and picked it up. "I'll fetch another."

"No need, Hilda." Laney clenched her hands in her lap. "I don't seem to have much of an appetite."

"She eats like a bird," Hilda told Eddie.

Eddie smiled after swallowing the biggest bite Laney ever saw someone take. "Between the two of us, we make up for each other. You're small and I'm large. You eat little and I eat lots."

Laney managed a sickly smile. It seemed as if the visit dragged on interminably. When Eddie ate her slice of pie as well as his own, Laney grasped at straws. "Why don't I ask Hilda to send a slice of pie home with you?"

"No, no. But I will be happy to come again soon. And when the vines hold ripe grapes, I will be sure you have as many as you want."

"How kind of you." Laney walked him to the door and leaned against it after he left. The clock showed he'd only been there for forty-five minutes, but it had seemed like an eternity.

Laney marched into the kitchen. "Hilda, don't you do that again."

"Do what?"

"Try to play matchmaker! It was . . . horrid." A tingling behind her eyes warned Laney she was about to burst into tears.

"There's nothing wrong with a neighbor happening by."

"Fine. Then from now on, when a neighbor who happens to be a bachelor comes to pay a visit, you can entertain him."

Hilda made a sour face. "That would be rude, and you know it, Elaine Louise."

"It's no worse than you trying to foist me off on Eddie!"

Hilda came toward her and patted her gently, just as she had when Laney was a little girl. "I know this is difficult, but you have to move on. The next time, it won't be so hard."

Laney's jaw jutted forward. "There had better not be a next time."

"You don't have a mother, so I'm going to step in and have my say. You can't pine for Galen. He's a married man. There's no use wishing it wasn't so. Eddie Lufe is a good Christian man. So is Robert Price. Either of them would be happy to marry you in a heartbeat. Eddie's got more money, but Rob's better looking."

"I don't care about their money or their looks." Laney shook from head to toe. "I won't marry someone I don't love. I can't."

CHAPTER THIRTY

The next day Laney sat in the parlor again. Only this time Mrs. O'Sullivan and Ivy were there for an afternoon of tea and sewing, and of course, Ruth and Amanda and Hilda were there, as well. Yesterday with Eddie had been embarrassingly awkward, but this—it was a hundred times worse. The girl who had ruined Laney's future with her vile lie sat there on the footstool near Mrs. O'Sullivan, just as Laney used to sit by her own mama.

Unbearable as it all felt, Laney knew she had to endure it. "I do so admire your dress," she told Amanda. "The plaid is exquisite."

"Thank you. A very dear woman and her daughter back home insisted upon giving it to me as a going-away present."

"The wool must be nice and warm. It's quite cool today," Mrs. O'Sullivan said before taking a sip of tea.

"Laney, won't you reconsider about that pink wool dress?" Ruth turned to Amanda. "It's the exact same shade as your silk. It never fit me correctly, and Laney is convinced she looks atrocious in anything pink."

"I bet Laney'd look good in a burlap bag." Ivy took a loud slurp from her teacup. "I'm doomed to wear dreary browns. It's this hair of mine."

Laney caught the sly look Ruth cast to the side and said in utter surprise, "Ivy?"

"Huh?" A wary look crossed Ivy's features.

Ruth leaned back and looked at Ivy. "Yes, Laney, I think you're right. Ivy would look beautiful in it. What are we waiting for?" She popped to her feet. "Come on, Ivy! Amanda and Laney, you, too."

"These young girls." Hilda gave Mrs. O'Sullivan a knowing look. "They're always up to something. You girls go on and have your fun. Kelly and I are going to sit by the fire and sew."

As they walked up the stairs, Laney wondered what her sister-in-law was up to. Ruth came up with more schemes than anyone Laney knew. *I don't want to be a part of this one.*

"Mama was sick for a long time," Ruth explained to Ivy. "I had nothing to do other than read to her or sit and sew while we talked." She sighed. "Making her happy was all that mattered to me, so I stitched gown after gown. I didn't realize just how many I had made until our old housekeeper shipped them all out here."

"The blue one you gave me is among my favorites," Laney said.

"Before you go in here, you all may as well know it's a mess. I have dresses everywhere." Ruth opened the door to her bedchamber.

"You shore do," Ivy exclaimed as she stared at the piles of dresses.

"I'm sorry," Amanda gushed. "It's my fault. You took them out of the wardrobe from my room."

"They were hanging in there because I don't ever wear them. Amanda, there's a striped one in here somewhere. . . . Anyway, I want you to try it on."

Amanda stopped so abruptly, Laney almost ran into her. "You planned this!" Laney charged.

Ruth laughed. "Of course I did. If they don't fit anyone today, I've resolved to find new homes for them. It's wasteful for them to just take up space."

"You'd jist give away clothes?" Ivy looked as shocked as she sounded.

"I'm sharing with friends." Ruth gestured to the nearest pile. "Let's see what fits!"

Jealousy speared through Laney. *It's bad enough Ivy stole the man I love. Now I'm supposed to help her charm him?* "Why don't I go back downstairs and you can come model what you like best?"

"We'll be here until noon tomorrow if you don't stay and help," Ruth submitted. "Well, maybe actually suppertime tomorrow. I'm probably more of a hindrance than a help. Laney, will you find the pink one for Ivy?"

Heart aching, Laney started searching for the dress. *Why is Ruth doing this to me? Lord, why are you doing this to me?* Laney yanked the pale pink wool dress from the middle of a pile. The stylish gown must have used fifteen yards to form the voluminous skirts that would drape over hoops. Other dresses slipped and slithered to the floor.

"That'un's like the ones all y'all got on." Just as fast as Ivy's smile started, it faded. "Much obliged, but I cain't wear that thar dress. Mrs. O'Sullivan tole me I'm not s'posed to talk 'bout thangs, but if'n I tried a-wearin' that, ever'body *see* them thangs!"

"Dear mercy, don't we all just dread and fear that?" Amanda stooped to clean up the mess. "All it takes are a few tricks and most of the problems never arise."

Ruth started laughing. "You'll never believe what I've done so I don't have to worry about windy days."

"What?" Laney couldn't help asking.

"Look at the inside of the hem."

Laney upended the dress and searched through the yards of fabric. "Buttons? They can't be heavy enough to make a difference."

"Look at this." Ruth gathered her skirts until the hem slid up over her petticoats and hoops. She flipped up the hem to show little cloth packets every foot or so.

"What's in them?" Amanda asked.

Ruth unbuttoned one and handed it to Ivy.

"Buckshot!" Ivy hooted. "If'n I didn't see it with my own eyes, I'd swar you were pullin' my leg. Oops. Weren't s'posed to use that word. But ain't this jist the beatenist thang?"

"Don't any of you ever tell a soul about this." Ruth sighed. "I'm afraid Josh already has enough on his hands without half of Folsom knowing his wife is daft."

"You'd be lucky 'twas only half." Ivy made a jerky shrug. "Thar ain't nobody for miles round who don't know what a mess I am."

"My dearly departed papa had a word of wisdom about such people," Amanda put in, resting her hand on Ivy's arm. "The very people you most want to impress are the least likely to be your friends. Those who matter care the least about things and most about your heart and soul."

"I reckon yore pa must've been a far sight nicer'n mine." Ivy sounded wistful as she added, "Too bad he ain't here to set a few people straight."

"Oh, but my heavenly Father can." Amanda scanned the room. "Ivy's going to need hoops, Ruth."

I didn't realize Ivy worried about what other people thought. I've spent so much of my own life feeling that way. I was so sure we were different, but we're not. Laney's chest felt so tight she could scarcely breathe. *I should befriend Ivy. She's a neighbor and she's Galen's wife. I should show God's love to her.*

A short time later, Ivy stood in the middle of the room and stared at her reflection in the cheval glass. "Ain't I a sight?"

"Here," Laney said as she fluffed Ivy's sleeves into perfect order. As much as it hurt to release her dreams for a future with Galen, she had to. If by helping Ivy she could make his future better, it was the right thing to do. Laney stepped back as her gaze swept over the girl. Ivy bit her lip in uncertainty, and Laney again felt a pang as she realized Ivy desperately needed reassurance. "You look marvelous. The pink goes beautifully with your coloring."

Amanda added, "The style is very flattering."

Ivy patted her rough red hands across the front of the hoops. "I reckon thar's 'nuff room 'neath all this to handle when my belly gets all swoll up."

A wounded sound tore through Laney before she could stop it. She pressed her hand to her mouth. *Lord, I'm trying so hard, but it hurts so bad.*

"I done it again, didn't I? Opened my big trap an' said sommat wrong."

Ruth took hold of Ivy's hands. "When you and I are alone, we can speak about that. Amanda and Laney aren't married. It's considered improper for a woman to say much about being in the family way."

"I didn't know you were in a delicate condition," Amanda said softly.

"Well, you do now. Cain't see as why 'tisn't okay to talk 'bout me expectin' a babe. I got hitched in the church, and my brother was totin' a shotgun to make shore it happened." Ivy shook her hands free from Ruth and gestured wildly. "Ever'body's gossipin' 'bout it. Seems to me like a load of nonsense. Afore Christmas, all them church folk talk 'bout baby Jesus. Since then, I reckon all they've jabbered 'bout is the babe I'm a-carryin'."

Can you blame them? Laney thought. *There's no denying what you did was wrong. And how can you expect people not to talk when you interrupt the Christmas service with a shotgun wedding?*

"The only thing to do is look ahead," Ruth said. "We cannot change the past."

"That's so true," Amanda agreed. "Clinging to the way things used to be or how we thought they should have turned out is such a temptation. It's hard enough to let go and face our own futures."

"That's dreadful nice of you. Wisht them other folk was of the same mind. Beats me how churchified folk claim to love ever'body, but then they turn 'round and give the O'Sullivans a hard time."

It's been even harder on Galen.

Ivy looked at her reflection again. "I'll wear this here dress you done give me, and I'll go to Sunday meetin'; but I'd rather et that horrible-awful food at the diner than get cozy with them vipers what're warmin' the church benches."

Vipers. The word stopped Laney cold. It was ugly . . . but honest. *I'm one of them. I've let the poison of bitterness and anger slither through the depths of my soul.* Tears blurred her vision. "I'm sorry."

"Aw, now." Ivy wrinkled her nose. "You gals're different. You and Ruth here was my friends back when I first come. Yore standin' strong on the side of the O'Sullivans—still come a-callin' and even brung a weddin' gift." Ivy twisted to the side. " 'Manda, if'n it bothers you I got a babe in me afore I got hitched, I reckon I'd 'preciate hearin' so now."

In that instant, Laney felt a bolt shoot through her. She wanted to shield Ivy from any further hurt.

"Being with a man before you were married wasn't right." Amanda's words came out slowly.

Laney stepped closer and reached for Ivy's hand.

"Just because that's a sin I haven't committed doesn't mean I haven't done many things wrong myself." Amanda slid her hand atop Laney and Ivy's. "I'd be wrong to judge and condemn you, because I want God to forgive me and forget my transgressions."

"Don't know what them trans-thangs are, but I won't thank bad of you, neither."

While Ruth helped Amanda try on a dress, Ivy tugged Laney off to the side. "I gotta ask you sommat. Will you learn me?"

"What do you want to learn?"

"I wanna read."

The longing in Ivy's eyes tore down the last stone of resentment in the wall of Laney's heart. She'd humbled herself the same way, wanting the same exact thing from Ruth. *Amanda's right. Ivy sinned with a man and has told a horrible lie, but I've been guilty of other sins. It's God's place to forgive or seek vengeance, not mine.*

"I wanna read and pick up some of them fancy manners." Ivy's jaw lifted. "But don't you worry none. If'n you don't wanna—"

Laney wrapped her arms around Ivy. "Of course I'll teach you!"

Ivy started laughing. "I thank you'd best git on with learnin' me how to deal with this dress. Both of ourn 're pitchin' up in the back. Bet we look like two tom turkeys!"

"Oh no!" Laney turned loose, wheeled around and theatrically pushed Ivy behind herself.

"What's a-wrong?"

"If we look like turkeys, we're in trouble! Don't you remember? Ruth has buckshot!"

———•———

Later that afternoon, Ma came over and stood on tiptoe next to Galen, looking into the sty. "The new sow's settling in well, is she?"

"Yeah." Laney had shown up without warning yesterday, leading the sow by a rope. Dale was thrilled, and Galen couldn't ruin their fun. Having an additional breeder would boost earnings considerably, too. "If things took, she'll farrow the first week in June."

"I've been wantin' a moment alone with you, Galen-mine."

"Yeah?" He turned and hitched the heel of his boot on the lowest fence rung.

Ma wrapped her arms around his waist and rested her head against him. "You're hurting, son. I'm ashamed to say I'm part of the reason why. You're a man after God's own heart, yet I questioned your integrity."

Galen held her loosely and said nothing.

"Had you lain with Ivy and fathered the child, you'd have decided to make the best of the situation and swallowed your pride. You've not done so. A man and his wife don't sleep separately, yet you've done just that. Resentment and impatience roll off you, and you've forced the twins to stay apart unless you're present. It all adds up. You've been wronged. Aye, you have, and I . . . son, I made it worse."

Ma looked up at him. Her face was a mask of pain. "You've been trying so hard to comfort us all. Grief makes us strangers to ourselves or it causes us to seek solace. If you think on it, you'll realize our Colin was born nine months after your da and I lost Ian and Thomas." Tears filled her eyes and slipped down her careworn cheeks.

" 'Twas no sin, you and Da finding respite together."

Ma barely took a breath. "You're in the right there, but 'twas faulty of me to believe you might have taken license and lain with the lass. Deep in my heart, I know you couldn't have, and I'm askin' your forgiveness for ever imagining otherwise."

Galen looked off in the distance. It cut him to the core, how Ma had doubted him. Laney alone believed in his innocence. An entire lifetime of integrity had crumbled due to Ivy's falsehood. But holding a grudge against Ma—he couldn't. He loved her too much. Her face reflected true remorse. Galen heaved a sigh and tightened his hold. "I forgive you, Ma."

"We'll have to have faith that God will redeem all of this."

"I can't see how." He turned loose of her.

"I've lost the woman I love, friends have forsaken me, Da is gone, and money's never been tighter. Whatever the Lord wants to come out of this, I can't say."

"Ishmael and Ivy are going to church. Surely that's a glimmer of good in the midst of it all."

"The dirt under my nails proclaims me to be a farmer." Looking at his hands, then the land about them, Galen added, "I know full well even though the ground is prepared and the seed is sown, it doesn't always sprout."

"The babe, Galen—he'll grow up in a godly home. Even if Ivy and Ishmael never turn their hearts to the Lord, we'll surround the child with God's love and Word and trust that it will not return void."

He nodded.

"Something happened at the McCains' today."

Anger streaked through him. "Now what did Ivy do?"

"I'm not sure exactly who did what. A young woman's living with them now—Miss Amanda Bradley. She came from South Carolina in response to the inquiry Josh made for a companion for Laney."

Galen started. "What?"

"Josh wrote the letter two years ago. Laney doesn't need a companion, but Ruth has hired Miss Bradley to be the new librarian. Hilda tells me Miss Bradley's not said much, but she's gathered the lass has a cousin who's cheated her out of her birthright. Anyway, while Ruth was giving away some of the dresses she never wears . . ."

Galen said nothing. He had a sinking feeling Ivy said or did something that caused a ruckus, though.

"They all came back downstairs in a different gown. Galen-mine, they'd styled Ivy's hair and had her in a fine frock. She looked grand."

Rubbing his forehead, he groaned. "Ma, I'm like any other man—I appreciate a beautiful woman, but her heart matters most to me. Stuffing Ivy into a different dress doesn't make her any less of a liar."

"Aye, you've the right of it there. But that wasn't what startled me most. 'Twas the change in Laney. She's been careful to be proper and polite to Ivy—even though 'twas clear her heart was aching something fierce."

"It's far more than she ought to have done. My dear Laney's heart is broken. It tears at me."

Ma patted her hand over his heart. "But 'tis why I'm telling you this. What prompted the change, I don't know. But when they came back downstairs, Laney was a different woman—not a lass, Galen-mine. A woman. She's promised to teach Ivy to read. Aye, she has. And though I know full well Laney loved you, I believe in my heart she knows 'tis time she set aside the dreams of her girlhood. Life must go on, and the dear is coming to terms with it. I'm hoping that with her coming to that decision, it lifts the burden of her sadness from your shoulders."

"I could never stop loving Laney," he rasped. "And I can't bear the thought that she'll ever stop loving me."

CHAPTER THIRTY-ONE

I apologize." Robert Price came to a quick halt as soon as he'd barreled into the diner. "I didn't mean to interrupt anything."

"Did you bring the plans for the library?" Ruth asked, eyeing the rolled-up paper he held. She'd been patiently waiting for most of January to see them and could hardly restrain herself now that they were finally before her.

"Library!" Patricia Sickenger exclaimed. "How wonderful."

Laney watched the immediate change in Robert. Twice now he'd come out to the Broken P and called on her. Both times Laney had tried to be polite, but she couldn't summon anything other than sisterly affection for the man. Ruth said she understood, but Laney still suspected Ruth simply hoped for a change of heart. Well, Robert's heart had apparently just changed. He looked thoroughly besotted—with Patricia.

Laney seized the opportunity. "Mr. Price, I believe you already know everyone here except for Mrs. Moran's niece. Miss Patricia Sickenger, this is Mr. Robert Price. Mr. Price, Miss Sickenger."

"It's a pleasure, miss."

"Likewise. How very interesting that you're working on such a project."

Laney scooted away from the table. "I do hope you will all forgive me. I have a few errands to run while we're in town. Ruth, please be sure to bring home the plans so I can see them, too. Mr. Price, why don't you take my place here?"

Laney restrained the impulse to skip along the boardwalk. *I should have thought up this solution to the problem before now. Any of the men Ruth tries to match me up with—I'll simply match them up with some other woman they'll find irresistible.*

She decided to celebrate her scheme by buying some chocolate. The bell over the mercantile clanged as she entered. "Miss Laney! To what do I owe the pleasure of your visit?" Lester asked as he wiped his hands on his green apron.

"There are several little things I need."

"Your wish is my command."

"Oh, that southern charm of yours is

unmistakable." Laney could scarcely conceal her glee. "I'll have to be sure to introduce you to Miss Bradley. She's a lovely young lady. I'm sure hearing her cultured South Carolina accent is bound to delight you."

"I wasn't aware your guest was from the South."

"Why yes, yes, she is. And I don't need to tell you how gracious a gently brought-up belle can be. We are so very blessed to have her here. Ruth has convinced Amanda—isn't that a simply divine name?—well, Ruth convinced Amanda to stay as our town's librarian."

"You don't say!"

Laney picked up a slate and slid it into Lester's hand. "I suppose since she'll be in town a fair bit, you'll want to make her feel welcome."

"Absolutely!"

She thought for a moment. "It never even occurred to me. . . . I'm so very embarrassed to confess this, Lester—but you're a single man. It must have been ages upon ages since you've had a big Sunday supper. Why don't you plan on joining us after worship on Sunday? I'll be sure to introduce you to Miss Bradley."

"I'll be there!" He used the corner of his apron to wipe a smudge from the slate. Laney felt certain nothing could erase the smile from his face.

Delighted with how easily her plan was coming together, Laney took three chocolate bars and slid them atop the slate he held. Just as Lester turned to go toward the counter, Laney said, "Wait!" She smiled. "I'm accustomed to providing for Ruth, Hilda, and myself. We'll need one for Amanda, too."

Lester bobbed his head.

Laney reached for another, then paused. "And there's Mrs. O'Sullivan and Ivy and the boys." She walked her fingers down the stack of Fry's chocolate bars. "Dear goodness, I believe I'm about to deplete the better portion of your stock!"

"Go right ahead, Miss Laney. Truth is, once you asked me to stock those chocolate bars, I tried one for myself. It's sort of bitter and sweet all at the same time. The company I've ordered candy from is in the North, so I won't be stocking many of the sweets I have in the past. But these Fry's bars—they're from England. You'd be smart to stock up now."

Laney could practically taste the chocolate. "I don't want to leave your shelf empty."

"Tell you what: I have a whole box of a dozen in the back." He grinned. "If you're worried about my display, you can just buy that box."

She hesitated.

Lester chuckled. "You know you want to." He lifted two of the three bars off the slate and popped them back on his shelf and slid the third into her hand. "And that one is on the house. I'll go get that box now."

"While I select a few little things, could I trouble you to get coffee? Toledo told Hilda they're nearly out of it in the bunkhouse."

"Can't have that! Did you want the Java or the Rio?"

"A pound of Rio for us; three pounds of Java for the bunkhouse."

Lester shook his head. "You McCains are something else. The Java is more expensive than the Rio, but you buy it for your hands."

"They're more than worth it." While he got the coffee, Laney gathered a few tablets and pencils, along with the latest dime novel.

"You might want to look at the fabric," Lester called to her. "The Broken P is one of my best customers, so it's only fair I warn you that with the tensions between the North and the South, I won't be stocking merchandise from any company in the North—not candy, not food, nothing."

"But fabric? Most of what you carry is cotton, and that's grown in the South."

Lester's jaw hardened. "But it's milled in the North. I won't have my mercantile support immoral enterprises."

Instead of getting mired into such a discussion, Laney took his cue and went over to look at the fabric selection. She fingered some buttery yellow flannel. "Two yards—no, three of this, please."

Men's Sunday-best shirts, nightshirts, babies' gowns, and women's small clothes were all made of white cotton. Just one petticoat would take yards! "And I'll take whatever's left on this bolt of white."

Lester held both bolts and waited as Laney selected three more fabrics. He stacked them all on the counter, and Laney stood nearby to choose buttons. Lester started to measure out how many yards remained on the white bolt. "Nineteen and a quarter yards. This is good cotton, you know. Quality matters, and it shows. The first time I saw that tramp, Ivy, she was wearing a flour—"

"Pardon me, *Mr. Pearson*," Laney cut in. "Surely you aren't referring to my friend as a tramp."

"The world is full of women like her—white trash. Sure, she was all frilled up in that fancy pink dress last Sunday, but she's still half cracker, half Jezebel."

"Mr. Pearson!"

Lester shook his head as he started rolling the material back around the bolt. "Don't get me wrong. It's not just her. Galen's every bit as much to blame. His father must be spinning in his grave. If it weren't for Mrs. O'Sullivan and those boys, I wouldn't be conducting business with Galen, either. As I mentioned earlier, I won't have my mercantile support immoral enterprises. How many yards of the yellow flannel did you want?"

"I'm sorry to have put you through the trouble, Mr. Pearson. I won't be making any purchases today."

He gave her a startled look.

Laney carefully set the chocolate bar on the counter and drew her shawl up over her shoulders. "I must also apologize for speaking too soon when I first came in. I won't be introducing you to my friend Miss Bradley. Since the O'Sullivans are always honored guests at the Broken P and I'll be extending an invitation for them to dine with us after church on Sunday, I accept your regrets that you'll be unable to join us after all."

Lester spluttered as Laney walked toward the door. As she reached to open it, he called out, "But what about the coffee and the chocolate?"

Laney turned and looked at him. "Mr. Pearson, I cannot patronize this establishment any longer." The bell tolled as she left.

———————

The baby moved. Sort of like a small tadpole swishing its tail, the sensation came and left just as quickly. Ivy drew in a breath and let it out. *Ever'thang's gonna turn out alright. It's gotta.*

"This is the first time you've been still all

day." Mrs. O'Sullivan tossed a dishtowel over the pan of supper rolls.

"I reckon I've been restless."

"We're caught up on all the chores, and until the supper rolls rise, there's nothing special that needs to be done. I'm going to read my Bible. Would you like me to read aloud?"

"It's nice—right nice—of you to ask, but I thank I'll stretch my legs. Spring's jist round the corner. If'n I tromp about today, I'll be shore to spot the changes in a few weeks."

"Wear your shawl."

"Yes'm." Ivy didn't need to be reminded. She'd never had a shawl of her own. Depending on how the light caught it, the one Laney had given her was either gray or whitish. Pearl colored, Laney called it. Ivy whispered that pretty description to herself as she shut the door.

She'd wear the shawl now, but once the babe came, she'd wrap him up in it, and folks would all see what a fine baby she had and what a good mother she was. By then, she'd be a woman Galen would be proud to have at his side, and he'd take to the child and love it like it was his own.

Ivy had it all planned out. She'd learn the highfalutin manners like how to use a napkin and sit with her knees together. She'd practice at fixing up her hair so it looked all proper-like. By spending time with the gals from the Broken P, she'd even learn how to talk good and not say the wrong things like *doggone* and *legs*. Most important of all, she'd learn to read. If she could read from his Bible, that would make Galen happy. She was sure of it.

Back when Pa didn't let her go to school, Ishy would scribe letters in the dirt. Laney drew them on a paper for her and taught her a song so she could recollect them in order. Ivy didn't want to get the paper dirty, so she'd carefully folded it and kept it in the pocket of her wedding present apron. Now that she was far from the house, she sat on the boulder she'd taken a liking to and pulled out the page.

For a moment, Ivy stared in wonder at the beautiful paper. Stationery, Amanda called it. 'Twas a sight to behold—two perky little finches sitting on a dogwood branch that went across the top. She'd wanted to show it to Ishy, but that wasn't easy. Galen still demanded she and Ishy not be alone together. At mealtimes, Ivy sat side-by-side with Ishy and tried to share all the things they'd stored up to tell each other.

Galen insisted on paying Ishy. It wasn't much, but Ishy said since he was getting fed better than he'd ever et and had a roof o'er his head, he reckoned that was worth plenty. Ishy—he was working harder than ever. Ivy knew why, too. He didn't want to give Boss a reason to kick him out.

Ishy didn't know Galen wasn't the baby's father. That was the one and only lie Ivy had ever told him. *I don't want him to ever find out the truth.*

Shoving aside all of those thoughts, Ivy concentrated on the paper. She held it in her left hand with her right pointy finger hovering over each letter as she started singing, "A-B-C-D-E-F—" She stopped. "Mr. F, you look like Mr. E, but the bottom done fall offa you."

Over and over, she sang and studied. Suddenly a shadow fell over her.

CHAPTER THIRTY-TWO

I've been looking for you," a man said in an oily voice.

Ivy shivered as she looked at the black-haired man who used to bring corn for the still.

"Where's my money?"

"I ain't got no money, mister."

"Then where's the corn whiskey?"

Ivy gave him a wary look. "Ain't you been thar? The whole thang blowed up. Weren't a drop left."

"That's all a little too convenient. I won't be cheated."

He stepped so close, the reek of whiskey and cigar smoke made Ivy want to be sick. "Mister, ain't nobody cheatin' you. The whole thang burnt up. Pa died."

"You owe me."

More than anything, Ivy wanted to crawl off the back of that big old rock, roll it over this awful, wicked man, and run away. He was too big and powerful for her to succeed, so she squared her shoulders and gave him the meanest scowl she could concoct. "Yore trespassin'. Get off my man's land."

He laughed. Just as quickly, his expression changed. As he dashed away, he called over his shoulder, "I'll see you again!"

"No!"

"Hey! You!" Galen shouted. By the time he reached Ivy, the other man was gone.

Ivy slumped forward in relief. Shivers of reaction left her feeling weak. In his day, Pa had hooked up with more than his share of shady characters, but that man made all the others seem mild. He had the meanest eyes she'd ever seen. Ivy knew beyond a shadow of a doubt that he'd keep his vow to return.

Galen grabbed her shoulders. "Is he the one? He's the father?"

She shook her head. She needed Galen's

strength and protection. Instead, he was hurling accusations at her.

"Give me his name."

Ivy tried to wiggle free from his grasp, but she didn't succeed. "Dunno. Johnson. Smith. Take yore pick."

"This has gone on far too long. Who is your lover?" His eyes narrowed, and he let loose of her shoulders only to grab for the paper in her hands.

Ivy tried to keep it out of his reach.

"Did he sign his love note?" Galen's tone shook with rage. He finally managed to get his hand on the page, but she still didn't let go. As a result, the page tore.

"Now look what you went and did." She stared in dismay at the jagged remnant in her hand.

Galen looked at the page, disbelief making his jaw go slack.

Ivy took the larger part of the paper from him and put the pieces back together as best she could, then painstakingly folded them along the same lines. Tucking the page into her apron pocket, she wanted to howl at how he'd ruined something so precious and important.

"Stop messing with that and give me his name."

"I already tole you," she snapped. "His name was Johnson. Or Smith. Or whate'er other notion he took a mind to call hisself. He brung corn, and Pa give him some of the likker."

"I'll find out who he is. He said he'd be back, and when he is, I'll annul our so-called marriage and send you packing with him."

Ivy shouted at him, "He ain't interested in me. He wants nuthin' but corn likker!"

"I don't want you, either!" Galen bellowed back at her. "Nothing's going to change that."

His words hurt, but Ivy refused to tell him so. "You got me anyhow." She sat so straight, her back nearly snapped. "Ain't nuthin' a-gonna change that, neither."

———•———

"'Ye shall walk after the Lord your God, and fear him, and keep his co-mm-and-ments,'" Dale said, sounding out the long words, "'commandments and obey his voice, and ye shall serve him, and cleave unto him.'" He looked up from the Bible and smiled proudly.

"You did a fine job," Ma praised him.

Galen had been reading ahead in the Bible, and on occasions when he knew one of his little brothers could manage the words, he'd ask them to read aloud to the family. "Aye, our Dale. I'm thinkin' if Da were here, he'd be thrilled to know you were studying God's Word."

"One of these days, sis, yore a-gonna be reading that good." Ishmael took another loud slurp of coffee. "Shore 'nuff, you are."

"I was practicin' my letters today." Ivy's

hand slid down to stroke the pocket of her apron.

Ha. That's quite an excuse, Galen thought. *Is there no end to the lies that woman tells? She isn't dressed like a scarecrow anymore, and her hair isn't a rat's nest, but all she has to do is open her mouth and suspicions swamp me. Once a liar, always a liar.*

"That passage talked about the commandments. I know all ten of the commandments," Sean declared and then proceeded to list them.

Colin clapped little Sean on the back. "That was real good, but what about the eleventh commandment?"

"There are ten, not eleven!"

Colin took the Bible from Dale. He turned the pages and pointed. "Here in John thirteen. Read these two verses."

"'A new commandment I give unto you, That ye love one another; as I have loved you, that ye also love one another. By this shall all men know that ye are my disciples, if ye have love one to another.'"

"How'dya like that? Thar really are 'leven of them commandments." Ishmael set down his mug.

Ma reached over and tucked a pin back into the braid Ivy now wore wrapped around her head. "If you think about it, the new commandment actually covers the others. If we love the Lord and serve Him with all of our heart, His love will flow from us to everyone else."

Ivy twisted and clasped Ma's hands in hers. "I don't put much store in thar bein' a God like you do. Ma, you're like them words Sean jist read. Like that Samaritan feller, too. The love you got in yore heart's always comin' out of yore hands or yore mouth."

"That's one of the sweetest things anyone's ever said to me."

Galen stared at them. *Ivy called her Ma, and Ma didn't even bat an eye. When did that start?*

"If'n ever'body who said he was a Christian was as big-hearted as you and Laney and Ruth and even that 'Manda gal, I reckon nobody could build churches big 'nuff to hold all the folks thunderin' in through the doors."

Dale tugged on Ishmael's sleeve. "I asked Jesus in my heart when I was a little boy. It's really easy. You could do it, too."

The room went still. Ishmael rested his hand on Dale's narrow shoulder. "Some thangs you decide with yore head, and some thangs you decide with yore heart. Decidin' whether to foller God—well, I reckon that's a dreadful important choice. Till I'm shore in my head and my heart, I ain't gonna do nuthin'."

Dale scooted closer and gave Ishmael a hug. "If you change your mind, you can let me know. Da showed me how to pray so I could give my heart to Jesus. I can show you."

"That's a fine offer. I'll tuck it into the corner of my mind."

Dale burst into giggles. "You can't have a corner in your mind. Your head is round, not square!"

"Hey, did all y'all hear that? Dale here says I'm not a blockhead."

Ma laughed. "Tomorrow's a school day. You boys need to be in bed." After she said a prayer, Sean and Dale went to bed. Colin sat at the table to finish reading something for school. As Galen followed Ishmael out the door, he heard Ma ask, "Ivy, would you like to recite your letters for me now?"

Hours later a lantern glowed in the corner of the stable. Galen sat with his back against the post on which it hung and stared at the thirteenth chapter of Deuteronomy. The fourth verse that Dale had read earlier in the evening kept nagging at him. *Ye shall walk after the Lord your God, and fear him, and keep his commandments, and obey his voice, and ye shall serve him, and cleave unto him.*

When a passage wore on his nerves, Galen knew there had to be a reason. He took it step by step. *I'm walking. I'm fearing. I've kept the com*— He halted. The truth glared back at him. He'd been following the letter of the law, but not the spirit of love that Christ commanded. He'd fostered resentment in his heart. The admission hurt. As if that wasn't enough conviction, the next phrase hit every bit as hard.

Obey his voice. "Lord, I've been so busy telling you what I want and need, I haven't listened. I don't know what your will has been."

Ye shall serve him, and cleave unto him. Galen's guts twisted. As a man of God, he was called to obedience. "But with Ivy? I treated her with kindness in your name, Lord, and that's what got me into this mess. If I go easy on her, I'll never find out who the father is, and I'll be stuck with her forever."

He wrestled with God through the night. As the lantern flickered a few last times, Ishmael opened the door and squinted out at him. "You okay, Boss?"

Galen slowly rose to his feet. "Call me Galen, Ishmael. We're brothers."

Laney had to pause for a moment before making her way down the aisle in the sanctuary. It seemed awfully dim in the building compared with the bright March sun outside.

"After you, Miss Laney." Eddie Lufe swept his arm in a gallant motion.

Laney flickered what she hoped passed for a civil smile and subtly compressed her hoops so she'd fit between the pews. Ruth had somehow managed to orchestrate things so Laney wasn't sitting with her, Josh, Amanda, and Hilda. Well, to be fair, maybe it wasn't Ruth's fault. Maybe it was Hilda's. Toledo was sitting next to their housekeeper. *I don't know how they did this to me, but I'll find out so it doesn't happen again.*

Eddie dropped down next to her, and the whole pew shuddered from his hulking frame. Laney felt a small flare of gratitude that she'd worn her widest hoops. They forced him to sit more than a yard away.

Josh turned around. "Laney, be sure to invite Eddie to supper today. I've already asked Toledo."

She gave her brother a chilly look and whispered back, "It's not polite to talk in church."

Hilda announced over her shoulder, "I'm serving ham."

"And apple pie," Ruth tacked on.

They're all in this together.

Eddie chuckled. "You can be sure I'll be there. It couldn't get any better than this."

It couldn't get any worse.

Ivy leaned across the aisle. "Us O'Sullivans're a-comin', too. I'm bringin' sauerkraut!"

It got worse. I didn't think it possible, but it did. Since the day Hilda learned everyone in the household hated sauerkraut, the dreadful dish hadn't been served.

Pastor Dawes stepped to the pulpit and gave a greeting, then instructed, "Please stand with me and sing, 'Come, Ye Disconsolate.'"

Much to her relief, Eddie picked up *The*

Sacred Melodeon. Laney reached to take one, as well, but to her astonishment, there wasn't another where it belonged. Eddie pressed the hymnal into her hands. "You use this, Miss Laney. I know the words." The pianist played a few introductory notes.

Eddie's voice was every bit as robust as his build. He started right in. "Come, ye disconsolate, whatever the language."

Laney stared at the page and wondered at how he'd twisted "where'er ye languish" into his version of the lyrics.

Oblivious to the literary license he took, he continued on, "Come to the mercy seat, fervently kneel. Here bring your wounded hearts, here talk in English. . . ."

Here talk in English? It's supposed to be "here tell your anguish." But two lines ago, he'd changed languish *to* language. *Oh, I'm in terrible trouble. Eddie Lufe's singing is starting to make sense to me!*

As soon as they got home, Hilda ordered, "Laney, go put another place setting on the table for Eddie."

Ivy leaned toward Laney. "Thangs're all backward here. Cain't make no sense of 'em."

"You're not the only one," Laney said in a wry tone.

Amanda tied on an apron. "What's backward?"

"All them years I thunk the servants done

what the master said. Hilda bosses ever'body round."

"Hilda, did you hear that?" Laney raised her brows.

"Elaine Louise, go put that on the table. Supper's going to be ready and Eddie won't have a place to sit!"

"What about Toledo?"

"Ruth saw to that this morning."

Eddie sat beside Laney. Watching all of the other men seat a lady, Ishmael stepped over and handled Amanda's chair. More astonishing, though, was that Toledo seated Hilda. And if that weren't enough, Galen seated Ivy. By the time Josh finished the prayer and they started passing around the bowls and platters, Laney felt confident no one could see how off balance she felt.

"It's nice to see a lady who appreciates good food," Eddie commented, smiling at her.

Laney smiled back—just to be polite.

Ruth and Hilda both started cackling like geese. Laney promised herself that as soon as their company left, she'd give them an earful for landing her in this mess. She accepted the ham platter from Colin and couldn't figure out why he was looking at her so strangely. She took a small, ladylike slice of ham. The serving fork hovered over her plate as she stared at the food beneath it in horror. While musing about the uncomfortable situation, she'd taken not one, but two heaping spoonfuls of sauerkraut!

"Oh, mercy." Once the words slipped out, Laney scrambled to say something so Ivy's feelings wouldn't be hurt. "I'm in a dither today. Look what I did. I can't possibly eat even a quarter of this. I'm going to break just about every rule of etiquette I've ever learned and give this to Mr. Lufe because I know he'll enjoy it."

"Laney! You wouldn't!" Ruth exclaimed. Mirth danced in her eyes.

"We're all friends here." Eddie motioned to Laney. "You go right on ahead."

Laney finally put the slice of ham on her plate, but she first used it to scoot all the sauerkraut to one side. She tried to think of a topic of conversation to get the attention off of herself. "The discussion about the North and South out in the churchyard is enough to strike fear into even the stoutest heart."

"Galen and me were readin' newspapers at the same time." Ishmael shook his head. "The same day that Lincoln feller did that in-inag . . . well, when he swore to be the president back a couple weeks ago, the Southern folk come up with a new flag."

"Inauguration," Colin provided. "I've been studying government at school. The teacher has me keeping track of which states want to secede and which are remaining in the Union. I've been surprised at some of the decisions. I've had to redraw the map several times now because of who's seceding and joining the Confederate States."

"Tennessee surprised me. I thought they'd go with the Southerners," Josh admitted.

"They still might," Toledo said. "It's a volatile situation."

Laney's ploy worked far better than she'd hoped. The men all started comparing opinions and information as she merrily scooped all but a very tiny bit of the sauerkraut onto Eddie's plate.

"Texas siding with the South surprised me." Galen passed the butter to Ivy, even though she hadn't asked for it. "I thought Sam Houston would have had the clout and persuasive ability to sway them otherwise."

"Thankee, Galen."

Laney's breath hitched. Galen was attending to Ivy as a man would treat his wife. Then, Ivy called him by his given name instead of Mr. O'Sullivan. The moment was bittersweet—two people she cared for were making a life together.

"Sis and me—we been through Texas. You coulda pushed me o'er with a feather if'n they'da gone North. Men thar are scrappers. Jefferson Davis is gonna get plenty of fighters from Texas." Suddenly, Ishmael frowned. "Miss 'Manda, you come from South Car'lina. Yore homeland's bound to be in the midst of the battlin'. I shoulda thunk afore I opened my trap. Didn't wanna cause you no more worries than you already got."

Amanda set down her fork, but Laney could see she'd not eaten a bite. "I'm afraid I'm torn in two, just like our nation. On one hand, I feel the States ought to have rights; on the other, I recently came to the decision that slavery is wrong."

"Why don't we find a different topic?" Laney tried not to shudder even though she knew her ham had absorbed some of the taste of the sauerkraut.

"Good idea." Eddie waved his fork toward Galen. "With the Overland Mail Company taking over the mail contract, do you think there'll be less need for the Pony Express? The *Contra Costa Gazette* says part of the Overland's route is using the same line and ferries as the Pony."

A glance at Eddie's plate left Laney agog. He'd nearly inhaled every last bite of the sauerkraut. She watched in amazement as he used his fork to fold a piece of ham the size of her palm in half and shovel it into his mouth in a single bite.

"Can't see why the mail would make a bit of difference." Hilda poured more milk for Sean. "Mail moves like molasses; the Pony runs like water. Anything important or urgent will come by Pony."

Toledo nodded. "The election news is a perfect example of that. What used to take several weeks or even months now can come in ten or eleven days."

"The eastern portion of the Pony seems to be running more smoothly." Galen grimaced. "The *Daily Evening Bulletin* ran an editorial earlier this month that pointed out how several deliveries on our end have been behind schedule."

"It shore ain't on account of yore relay." Ivy bobbed her head once to punctuate her comment. "You and Ishy got the fresh horse rarin' to go. Ain't been a single time a rider come through and had to wait."

"With the transcontinental railroad and the telegraph both underway," Josh said carefully, "do you think they'll have any effect on the Pony, Galen?"

"As Hilda said, the mail moves like molasses and the Pony runs like water. But trains and telegraphs are like the wind. Once the railroad goes through, it'll be faster, safer, and cheaper for people to ride to the West coast than to traverse the Oregon Trail. I hold no doubt that once the telegraph is completed, the Pony won't be needed any longer."

"Well, if'n 'tis so, we'll have us three extra horses—fine horses," Ivy said.

"Yeah!" Dale agreed.

"Nay," Galen said, offering his brother a sad smile. "The beasts belong to the company."

Laney took advantage of a lull in the conversation. "I think the rest of the sauerkraut ought to go to our company!" She passed the bowl to Eddie.

"It's the best I've ever had. Doesn't anyone else want some, too?"

Josh, Hilda, and Ruth all nearly shouted their denials. Laney hastened to say, "We all know how much you enjoy it. Of course we'd like you to have it."

Eddie hesitated. "Toledo, how about you?"

"No, thanks. I'm sure Ivy's a fine cook, but sauerkraut never agrees with me." He motioned to Eddie to eat up. "Men, the sheriff tells me there's still a thief in the area."

"Bold, too." Eddie shoveled his fork under a pile of sauerkraut. "Broke into the mercantile Thursday night while Lester was sleeping upstairs."

"Betcha he uses that as 'nuther excuse to hike the prices on thangs." Ivy made a face. "I cain't read no more'n my letters, but I know my numbers jist fine. Both times I been in thar, he's tole me prices are a-goin' up. I seen his sign. He's askin' twelve cents for a dozen eggs, but he's only payin' seven cents for 'em."

"Ma, he's always given you nine cents a dozen," Sean said.

Mrs. O'Sullivan hitched her shoulder in a move that didn't fool Laney into thinking that it didn't matter. "Aye, he did, boy-o. But things change."

"And they're changing again," Laney declared.

"Yes, they are." Ruth sounded completely

sure of it. "And Laney's going to tell us all how."

"We all loved Hilda's German tree at Christmas."

"It was a fine sight," Toledo agreed.

Eddie gawked at Hilda. "You had a tree? We used to do that back home when I was a little boy."

Dale's eyes grew huge. "You used to be a little boy?"

"Ja." Eddie's robust laugh filled the room. He turned to Laney. "So what is this plan of yours?"

"Hilda said there's a German tradition of coloring eggs for Easter."

"Mama would boil the eggs with onion skins to make the shells turn a beautiful yellow," Hilda explained. "That was the color she did most. But sometimes we'd have other colors, too. She'd draw a cross on them after they cooled." Hilda's wrinkles radiated happiness. "We'd roll the eggs on the grass or down a little hill because Mama said it was like the stone rolling away from Christ's grave."

"What a lovely tradition," Amanda commented.

"Dunno much 'bout that grave stone a-movin'," Ishmael said, "but shore sounds like a heap of fun for young'uns to do that."

"Exactly!" Laney declared. "I'm buying every last egg you O'Sullivans have for the next two weeks. I'm paying ten cents a dozen, and we're going to make them the most beautiful eggs anyone in the county ever saw. On Easter Sunday we'll take baskets full of those eggs to church so everyone in the congregation can take home their very own."

"If you use cherries or beets, the eggs will be pink." Eddie grinned. "I remember those best of all. If I keep this secret, will you make some like that?"

Ivy burst out laughing. "Mr. Lufe, I cain't holp thinkin' yore still a boy deep down inside."

"I've got plenty of beets." A sly grin tilted Hilda's mouth.

"Ahhh, beets." Eddie's voice left no doubt that he loved eating them, too.

Laney and Ruth helped clear the table as Hilda cut wedges of pie. In the kitchen, Ruth leaned close to Laney. "You have to admit, Eddie's a nice man."

"I never said otherwise." Laney gave her sister-in-law a telling look. "He'd be nicer for someone else."

"Oh, I don't know . . ." Ruth's eyes glinted. "You'd never have to eat sauerkraut again."

"Or beets," Hilda added.

"I seriously doubt that. He'd probably want them alternating every other day."

"Laney, you have to give him a chance." Ruth gave her a stern look. "Don't think I didn't notice how you paired up Robert and Patricia."

"They're head over heels in love. You can't deny that." Laney set all the dirty silverware in the empty sauerkraut bowl. "I'm so happy for them."

"Enough about them," Hilda said as she slid a big wedge of apple pie onto another plate. "It's time you stopped pining for Galen."

Laney looked from Hilda to Ruth. "Galen and Ivy seem to be . . . better. Weeks ago, that would have devastated me. Now, I can truly say I'm glad for them."

"Well and good." Hilda waggled the knife at Laney. "You're the one we need to pair up, and Eddie's the finest bachelor in these parts."

Laney was tempted to mention that Hilda had said the same thing about Lester and Robert, too. After Laney had explained what Lester had said about Galen and Ivy, no one bothered to promote him as a prospective suitor anymore. And as besotted as Robert was with Patricia, his name no longer came up in Ruth and Hilda's chronic nagging that they euphemistically called matchmaking.

The housekeeper continued, "You have to overlook Eddie's talent for slaughtering hymns. Every man has his flaws."

"He's easy to talk to and well read." Ruth showed the single-mindedness of a cranky toddler eyeing the candy jar in a mercantile. "I bet you could bring up any subject, and he'd have something remarkable to say about it. You go right on out there and see if it's not so."

A few minutes later, Laney had eaten two

small bites of pie. Eddie ate his whole slice in three. He eyed her plate. "Are you already full?"

She set down her fork. "I've eaten enough."

"No use letting it go to waste." Eddie grabbed her plate. Once he polished off her pie, he leaned back in his chair. "I read the most fascinating thing the other day."

Ruth jerked her head to the side a few times, silently urging Laney to show interest in his comment.

Laney relented—because it was the polite thing to do, not because Ruth would hound her for the next fifty years if she didn't. Turning toward Eddie, Laney asked, "What did you read?"

He leaned forward and rested his elbows on the table. "You know how progressive England is."

Laney nodded. Something about England might be interesting. Anything other than war and robberies would make for pleasant conversation.

"Well, they've been building water closets with plumbing in all the newer buildings for the past five years . . ."

He's discussing the necessary at the table?!

". . . and many actually have water flow that causes them to flush."

"Oh my," Amanda said in a very small voice. Someone else gasped, but Laney wasn't sure who.

Encouraged by what he obviously interpreted as awe, Eddie brought one forearm down and banged the table with his palm. China and silverware jumped. "Such convenience! What do you think of that?"

"That's . . . very—" Laney turned to glare at Ruth—"*remarkable.*"

Chapter Thirty-three

I promise I won't puke all o'er the front of you."
Galen arched a brow. "I figure I'm safe. You wouldn't dare be sick all over that Easter frock Ruth gave you."

Ivy fussed with the hoops. "Ain't none too shore 'bout these thangs," she told Mrs. O'Sullivan. "I'm ascairt I'll move wrong and all them church-folk'll get a long gawk at all them parts I'm s'posed to pretend I ain't got."

"Remember what Laney taught you: glide, don't gallop. You'll be fine." Ma tugged Ivy's shawl up higher and nodded her approval. "We're ready. Colin, once we're in the wagon, bring Dale out to me."

"Aye, Ma."

"I'll tote Sean," Ishmael volunteered.

Galen looked over at the boys sleeping on Ma's bed and grinned. They'd stayed up most of the night in the stable, watching as Hortense farrowed. Ruth had given Dale a children's book on animals, and he'd tested everyone's patience by quoting the page on pigs. He'd told Laney they could expect eight piglets, seeing as it was Hortense's first litter. Maybe ten if they were lucky. Hortense exceeded all expectations and had twelve.

In the wee hours of the morning, when Sean could be convinced that Hortense was done and Dale felt certain his sow and every last piglet were fine, Galen brought the boys back to the house. Ivy surprised them by having hot chocolate ready. When they were done, she'd had the boys wash up and put on their Sunday best pants. Ma let Sean sleep on one side of her and Dale on the other. Now Ishmael and Colin would help the lads put on their shirts and shoes, but Galen fully expected them to doze the entire way to church.

As soon as Galen lifted the ladies into the buckboard, Ishmael rolled Sean into the back and Ma cradled his head in her lap. "Colin," Ivy whispered, "gimme lil' Dale." She didn't lie Dale down. Instead, she kept him across her lap and tipped his head onto her shoulder. A momentary frown sketched across her features. With her free arm, she tugged off her shawl and laid it over his baby brother. Ma straightened the end of it so the shawl completely blanketed Dale's curled-up body.

Galen stripped out of his coat and slid it around Ivy's thin shoulders.

"Oh!" Ivy gave him a startled look. "Thankee."

"Can't have you getting sick," he said gruffly.

Colin looked at the bed of the wagon. If he tried, he could fit back there, but the expression on his face nearly shouted his thoughts.

Galen gave him a good-natured shove. "It'll be a tight fit, but the three of us men can sit up front."

While Colin scrambled in, Ishmael brushed by and said in a low tone, "Yore gonna be a real good daddy."

Galen fought the urge to bellow a denial. What good would it serve? He couldn't help keeping track of time. Exactly three months and one week ago, Ivy had ensnared him with her lie. Never once did she show the least sign of relenting and telling the truth. Whoever got her into this mess was either long gone or so hardhearted that he wasn't likely to step forward now and claim a woman almost five months gone. Or the man was already married.

Daddy. The word hit him hard. Until now he'd been so angry at Ivy, he'd not thought things through. *I'm married to her. I didn't sire that babe, but 'tis legally mine.*

420

Lord, you know the man whose heart most needs to be touched today. I'm leaving it in your hands.

During the service, they sang "Sinners, Dismiss Your Fear." Ma had asked Pastor Dawes what hymns he'd planned for today, and she'd spent the last week teaching Ivy and Ishmael the lyrics. For all the musical talent Ivy lacked, Ishmael counted double his fair share. To her credit, Ma didn't flinch once, even though Ivy stood on her other side and butchered the notes.

Between Eddie Lufe and Ivy, we have the wrong notes and the wrong words.

"Christ, the Lord Is Risen Today" came next. Ivy and Ishmael thoroughly enjoyed blasting out *Alleluia* at the end of each line. The congregation took Communion, and Pastor Dawes read from Matthew. "The angel said to the women, 'Fear not ye: for I know that ye seek Jesus, which was crucified. He is not here: for He is risen, as he said.'"

He preached about how Christ had endured so much and how very dear the price of salvation was. The message was simple, yet profound. Leaning over the podium, Pastor then said, "I want you all to notice something. In this verse, Jesus had told them what would happen, but they were all so busy with what they thought and planned, these believers didn't harken back to what He'd said."

Interesting.

"Those women went to the tomb to tend to burial matters; God gave them the wondrous mission instead to meet an angel and go proclaim the good news. The daily obligations and the ordinary demands of life pull at us. We figure we've got a handle on how things are supposed to be.

"In Gethsemane, Jesus knew what lay ahead. He even asked God to let the cup pass from Him; but He chose to be obedient and endured the worst torture. He did it because He knew submitting to the will of God would bring about redemption.

"We have to roll back the stone to our hearts and souls. What God wants for us, what He plans for us is far above what we could ever dream or expect—but we'll never know unless we die to our selfish plans and desires and allow Him to do as He wills.

"Children . . ." Pastor Dawes motioned. Sean and Dale scooted out into the aisle, and Greta Long and her cousins, Sophia and Olivia, slipped out to join them. Laney and Ruth had gotten to church early and placed ordinary wire egg baskets filled with yellow, pink, blue, and deep mahogany dyed eggs behind the piano. The pastor handed the children those baskets. They in turn carried them down the aisle and passed them down the pews. Galen took a pale yellow egg.

"These eggs represent the stone that sealed

the grave. Each has a cross on it. Jesus sacrificed himself for you. You can hold fast to what you have, or you can relinquish everything to the Lord by rolling the stone away and giving Him free rein to do as He wills with and through you."

This egg is the color of Ivy's hair. Lord, before I came I prayed for you to touch the heart of the man who needed to be touched the most. I was so sure it was the baby's father; it wasn't. It's me. I have to surrender my dreams and wishes, don't I? You're asking me to roll away the stone in my heart and accept that Ivy is my wife.

Slowly, he unclenched his fingers and let the egg tumble into his other hand.

The congregation sang, "Angels, Roll the Stone Away" as the benediction. As people left the church, Ishmael took Dale by the hand and didn't budge. He frowned at Galen. Galen raised his brows in silent inquiry.

"What 'bout the hitchin' post?"

"Hitching post?" Galen couldn't imagine what he meant.

Ishmael pointed to the altar. "That thar hitchin' post. Ain't that whar he hitches brides to grooms?"

"Yes. But no one's getting married."

"But that's whar he hitches folks to God, too, ain't it? Only the parson didn't stand up thar and give the invite."

"The altar is always open, Ishmael. Did you

want to dedicate your heart to Christ?"

"Yup. Dale here tole me he'd holp me when'er I decided I wanted to do it." He looked over Galen's shoulder. "I'd 'preciate it if'n you'd take Sis on outta here. We've always done ever'thang together, but I reckon this is sommat a man does on his lonesome."

The pale yellow egg in Galen's left hand took on a new significance. Galen had relinquished his wishes and now witnessed the unfolding of God's plan. In dying to the dream of Laney being his mate here on earth, Galen now gained a brother for eternity. "Ishmael, take Dale on up to Pastor Dawes. They'll be happy to hitch you to Jesus."

———————

Laney sat out on the front porch early in the afternoon on Monday, reading a dime novel. Amanda and Ruth had both read it and agreed it was among the best they'd ever read. Turning the page, Laney had to agree.

"Miss Laney . . ."

She jumped. "Oh! My. Mr. Lufe! You surprised me."

He stood on the step and looked a little sheepish. "Sorry. I get like that when I read, too. Must be a good book."

"It is. If you like something with adventure and a little mystery in it, you'll have to check it out of Ruth's library once it opens." Laney closed the book and handed it to him.

Eddie read the title and nodded. "I'll remember. Best I hand it back now, though. I'm always tempted to read the last page, just to be sure things work out. Nothing like reading a whole book only to have them leave me hanging until the next one. I can be patient about a lot of things, but . . ." He shrugged.

Laney laughed. "It's cheating to read the last part, but I did that recently myself. It was for the same reason."

"Did it ruin the book or did you still enjoy reading it?"

She thought for a minute. "I can't truly say. The book wasn't very good, so I'm not sure if reading the ending first really spoiled it." As he handed back the book, Laney remembered her manners. "Would you care to have something to drink?"

"No, thanks. I just dropped by to let you know I haven't forgotten about bringing you grapes. I checked the vines myself the day before Easter. They look healthy, so I'm counting on a bumper crop."

"That's kind of you, Mr. Lufe."

"We're neighbors. Have been for years. I'd take it as a favor if you'd call me by my given name."

For being such a massive bear of a man, he had a gentle side. Hope and warmth shone in his hazel eyes. *I don't love him. I don't know if I ever could. But I have to let go of my dreams. It would be wrong for me to mislead him, though.* "We are neighbors, and you've become a friend of my family. I suppose it would be okay, Eddie."

A big smile lit his face.

Before he could say anything, Hilda tromped out of the house. "Laney, who are you talking— Well, as I live and breathe! Eddie! Nice to have you come by. Isn't it nice, Laney?"

She nodded. It was nice. Sort of. Not romantic, but friendly.

"The eggs at church yesterday—they were such a good idea," Eddie told Hilda. "I chose one that you colored with beets. I think Laney must have drawn the cross on it. It was very fancy. Beautiful."

"We ought to do it again next year," Hilda declared.

"Traditions are important. They feel good in here." Eddie tapped his chest. "I've already decided to have a tree in my house for Christmas this year. Knowing you've been doing that made me think how sometimes the old ways are best. Of course, just about the time I think that, I ride the train and decide the new things are better."

After he left, Laney remained on the porch and stared at the cover of her novel. *Lord, I don't know anymore. I don't know what to think or where you are leading me. The old dreams, of being Galen's wife—I don't think they'll ever go away. I know you are blessing his marriage with Ivy, and it makes me happy and sad all at the same time. Is Eddie right? Do I need to just decide the new things are better and deny what my heart still says? Can my mind truly change my heart?*

"Cain you b'lieve all these here clothes?" Ivy asked her brother as she plucked off a wooden pin and folded the shirt it had held to the line. "Mondays, I wanna pinch myself to be shore I'm not dreamin' thangs up. Woulda niver 'magined us havin' more'n the rags on our backs." She put the shirt in the basket Ishy was holding.

"You looked right purdy in that Easter dress yestermorn."

Ivy fought the uncomfortable suspicion that Galen and Ishmael were cooking up a plot to talk her into doing what the parson called "seein' the light." Ishmael went and got hisself religion, and then today at breakfast Galen suddenly announced that Ishy and she could talk to each other whenever they wanted to. Ivy didn't want her twin to start in on her, so she tried to steer the conversation away from church. "Yup. Bakin' flour-built bread and gettin' to wash and iron a big ol' heap of clothes—them don't seem like chores to me. The washboard pert near sings while I rub the dirtiest spots 'cross the ribs. Makes me think back to old Mendel Grisson back home, how he'd play a washboard and a jug at the same time."

"You got yoreself a sharp memory, sis."

"I shorely do. The blankets ain't dry yet. Last time I was tryin' to dry blankets, they took 'most all day."

"Back when we was in the tent?"

"Uh-huh." She laughed as the wind pushed a slightly damp blanket against her. "Grass was still wet from the rain we had the night afore. Soon as I spied them blankets Galen left layin' on the grass, I spread 'em o'er the shrubs."

Ishy turned to push the blanket away from her so she could reach the last shirt. "The blankets from Galen."

"Yup."

"And it rained."

Ivy put the last shirt on top of the others in the basket and gave it a satisfied pat. "Uh-huh."

Ishy dropped the basket, and the shirt bounced out into the dirt.

"Now, why'd you go and do that?" Ivy hunkered down to pick it up.

Ishy stared down at her. "You tole me Galen gave you them blankets."

She nodded as she rose and shook out the shirt.

"But you jist said soon as you spied them—"

Ivy realized she'd let down her guard and not kept her story straight. "'Course I spied 'em." She scrambled to make everything right. "Galen set 'em down so he could give me a hug."

"And they got wet."

Relieved, she nodded. "It rained the night afore. 'Member?"

Quick as could be, Ishy's hands shot out and curled around her arms. "They wouldn't have soaked through. Not thick blankets like that—not from bein' on wet grass for a few minutes."

At the same time fear was chilling her spine, heat was rushing to her face. Ivy forced a laugh that sounded strained even to her. "We sorta got busy and forgot 'bout them."

Her twin's grip tightened and his eyes narrowed. "You lied to me. You told me Galen brung them blankets to the tent."

"He did." She pulled free. "Later on, he did. B-but they was wet. Sore wet. So I put 'em on the shrubs. To dry out."

"A minute ago, you tole me you hung 'em on the shrubs soon as you spied 'em."

"I did. When me and Galen come back outta the tent."

"But that still means he didn't carry them to the tent. You keep a-changin' yore story." Ishmael raked his fingers through his hair. "You lied to me. I cain't believe it. Sis, you ain't niver lied to me afore."

"I ain't lying. You cain't blame me if'n I don't 'zactly recollect them piddlin' details. A gal in love pays attention to her buck, not to them other thangs."

Ishy let out a long, shaky breath. "Makes sense. Wonder if'n the babe'll wind up with that mark he gots on his shoulder."

"Same as the one on Sean's? Could be. Hadn't thunk on that yet." As soon as the words were out of her mouth, Ivy wanted to grab them back. Ishmael's face went whiter than a Sunday-best shirt, and she knew she'd said something wrong.

"Boss ain't got no mark on his shoulder." Every last word came out in a hushed roar. "He ain't the one what done this to you."

"He is, too!" she insisted emphatically.

Once—just once—Ishy's head wagged from one side to the other. His face went stone cold, and then he walked away.

"Ishy!" Ivy wasn't sure whether she whispered his name or called it aloud, so she called again in desperation. "Ishy!" He didn't turn around. No matter how bad things had ever gotten, she'd always had her twin. *I've lost him. What's he gonna do now? What am I gonna do?*

Chapter Thirty-four

B oss?"
Galen slapped the trunk of a tree. "Blossoms everywhere. It'll be a bumper crop of cherries this year."

Ishmael shifted his weight uneasily. "We gotta have us a talk. I did sommat real bad."

Galen didn't say anything. He waited for Ishmael to continue.

"You ain't the one," Ishmael said in a hushed tone. "That babe . . . ain't yourn."

"No, it's not." Galen stared at him.

"Sis was talkin' jist now. Her story kept a-changin'. Li'l thangs—but them thangs don't add up." Anguish painted his face. "She tole me yore the daddy, and she ain't niver lied to me afore. I believed her. I done made you marry up with her."

"Did Ivy tell you who the real father is?"

"Nope. And she ain't gonna. My sis, she could teach Muley a thang or two 'bout bein' stubborn. She still says yore the pa." Ishmael swallowed hard. "I wronged you. I grabbed that shotgun of yourn and hitched you to her. Folks, they all thank bad of you. I done ruint yore good name. On account of me, yore saddled with Ivy and another man's get."

So now what do I do, Lord?

"I'm sorry." Ishmael hung his head. "What I done—ain't no fixin' it."

Galen reached over and rested his hand on Ishmael's shoulder. "You've come to me, man-to-man. You've swallowed your pride and confessed your part. I can't hold you responsible for what you didn't know."

Ishmael blurted out, "That's dreadful big of you, Boss."

"Ishmael, I do forgive you for what you did."

His head shot up and his jaw dropped. "I . . . you . . . Boss, I don't 'spect you to. You was good to me and mine—you give us chance after chance when we didn't deserve none. Ain't right what I done back."

"God forgives us, Ishmael. You're my brother in Christ. It wouldn't be right for me to accept the Lord's forgiveness, then turn around and hold a grudge against someone else when they sought my forgiveness."

"Yore tryin' to be like God. That's why you give us all them chances, ain't it?"

Nodding his head, Galen said, "Christians try to be as much like the Lord as we can. We aren't perfect, Ishmael. We make plenty of

mistakes—and we have to live with the consequences."

"But yore the one what has to live with the
consequences, and you didn't do nuthin' a-
wrong. What're you gonna do 'bout Sis?"

"I don't have an answer for you." Galen
leaned against the tree trunk. "I'm torn. At first,
I admit I was livid. My plan was to force Ivy to
tell me who the father was. Once I did, I was
going to break free from the marriage."

Ishmael grimaced. "Cain't say as I blame
you."

"I've had to set aside the plans I made before
all of this happened. I'm not the only one who
was hurt by this."

" 'Twas a time when I thunk you was jist
bein' mannerly to all the gals. Now that I been
round you more and seen the way other bucks
act round women, 'tis plain to me that you'd set
yore cap for La—"

"Stop right there." Galen stared straight
through him.

"I could go talk to her."

"No."

Ishmael looked down and scuffed his toe in
the dirt. " 'Spite all this, that gal's been terrible
nice to Sis."

That's my sweet Laney. "The Bible tells us to
return kindness for evil and do good for them
who hate us. I've been slow to do that. I've not
been . . . gentle with Ivy."

Looking up, Ishmael sighed. "You been better than good to her. Thar at the beginnin', I didn't wanna leave on account of bein' ascairt you'd hurt her."

"I'd never do that."

The corners of Ishmael's mouth tightened. "I know that now. Yore ma and brothers—they've all taken a shine to Ivy, too. Yore ma—least I could do is tell her—"

"She knows I'm not the father."

"And she still tole Ivy to call her Ma?" Ishmael rubbed his palm over the scar that had formed on his forehead. "You O'Sullivans is pure hickory. I fear it's gonna be mighty hard for me to get o'er this with Sis. Her and me—we always holped each other and stood up for each other."

"You still love her, Ishmael. You hate what she did, but you don't hate her."

The strain in Ishmael's features lightened a little. "True." Cramming his hands into his pockets, he leaned forward a little. "I wanna hear all 'bout the angel-feller what come."

"What angel?"

"You know—Parson said angels come and give folks messages. Coupla times in church, whilst he was a-sermonizin', he tole all 'bout it. I recollect when you tole me 'bout the Christmas baby, that God sent His angel to talk to Joseph on account of Mary carryin' a babe that weren't his. Betcha God Almighty sent that 'zact same one, tellin' you—"

"I haven't seen an angel, Ishmael."

"No?" He looked downright disappointed. In the next instant, his features twisted. "I gotta ask you sommat. If'n no angel tole you to keep the babe, what are you fixin' to do?"

"Put your fears to rest. That babe will grow up under my roof, and he'll be loved." The breeze sent a shower of cherry blossom petals into a snow-like flurry.

"Didja see that, Boss?" Ishmael's eyes widened in wonder. "Looks like a million tiny angel wings fluttering round about us. Weren't truly angels, I know, but shorely did settle my heart."

Galen nodded. It was a fanciful notion, but he had to agree that after this conversation, he felt more at peace. "One last thing, Ishmael."

"Yeah?"

"Don't call me boss. I'm your brother."

———◆———

Something was wrong. Laney couldn't put her finger on it, but the way Ivy had been blurting out things and sounding a little too jovial over the last few days left Laney sure something was amiss.

"Tell 'em, Ishy. You heared all 'bout it whilst you was in town."

"You know more?" Amanda turned to him. "Please do tell us what happened."

"The Bensons' place was the one what got robbed. The missus was outside at the washtub and Mr. Benson was out in the fields. Mrs. Benson heared her babe a-cryin' and went inside. Found a mess all o'er. She done swiped her young'un outta the cradle and run to get her man."

"Cain you 'magine that?" Ivy shoved her hands into the pockets of her apron.

"How terrifying!" Amanda shuddered.

"Miss 'Manda—" Ishmael glanced at her, then addressed the toes of his boots—"I know you been a-spendin' lots of time out thar in the li'l cabin, gettin' all the books organized and ready for the library, but maybe you oughtta not be on yore lonesome till the sheriff catches that varmint."

He's sweet on her! Laney fought to keep her surprise hidden. *I'll bet that's what's happening. Ivy knows her twin likes Amanda, and she's trying to play matchmaker!*

"Ishmael, that's an excellent point," Laney said.

Amanda said in a whispery drawl, "It's so kind of you to be concerned about my welfare." Her gaze dropped as a slight blush filled her cheeks.

Laney and Ruth's gazes met. Ruth blurted out, "Amanda and Ishmael—" She caught herself before she said anything more.

"That's a wonderful idea, Ruth!" Laney

linked arms with Ivy. "Ishmael, since I'm going
to work with your sister on her reading this
morning, I'll be staying here in the parlor.
Amanda was planning to go over to the cabin.
Since you've pointed out that might not be wise,
would you mind going to the cottage and bringing back a few boxes of books?"

"Shore. I cain do that."

"I'd appreciate that no end." Amanda gave
Ishmael a charming smile. "It would be a shame
for the library's opening to be delayed."

Ruth made a shooing motion. "Amanda,
why don't you go show Ishmael which boxes
you'd like him to bring?"

"I'm not sure I should."

Laney understood Amanda was worried
about the propriety, but she intentionally pretended to mistake Amanda's meaning. "Ishmael
will see to your safety. I have every confidence
in him."

"I'd die afore I let anythin' happen to you,
Miss 'Manda."

"How gallant of you." Amanda looked at
Ruth. "Won't you come with us? Surely there's
a box you'd like."

Ruth laughed. "I'd be more of a hindrance
than a help. You've gone through so many, I'm
not sure where anything is anymore. I hope
you'll all excuse me. I have a few things to see
to." Ruth left the room.

"I've been hearin' 'bout these books,"

Ishmael said, looking at Amanda. "Got some good ones?"

"Amanda," Ruth enthused, "I think Ishmael should be our first library patron. You could recommend a book or two, and he could borrow them now."

"Yore the very first one, Ishy!" Ivy nudged him. "I reckon that's a right fine honor."

"Miss 'Manda, are you too busy to holp me choose a book? Won't put my nose outta joint if'n 'tis a bad time."

"It seems a terrible waste for those books to languish in boxes when someone could be enjoying them. If you don't mind my practicing on you since I've never been a librarian, I'd appreciate working with you."

"Well, thar you have it!" Ivy beamed at her brother.

Ishmael cleared his throat. "I only got a bit o'er three years' book learnin'."

"That's three times what President Abraham Lincoln has had." Amanda folded her hands at her waist. "With only one year of schooling, he's still a remarkably well-read man."

Once Amanda and Ishmael had left, Laney squeezed both of Ivy's hands. "I think they like each other!"

"'Manda cain't holp herself. Ishy's strong and handsome. What with her bein' all on her lonesome, 'tis understandable that she'd want a man to lean on."

438

"We'll play Cupid!" Laney said, practically jumping up and down. "Yes, that's what we'll do."

Ivy's face fell. "I ain't niver played games afore."

"You and I are going to play matchmaker for Amanda and your brother. When you're trying to spark a romance between two people, it's called playing Cupid."

"Reckon that's a better way to spend this time of ourn than me tryin' to read. I ain't doin' too good at it."

"Nonsense! You're doing well. You're sounding out words already." Laney drew Ivy toward the table where she had paper, pencils, and a book waiting. "Besides, your lessons are going to give us all sorts of excuses to have Ishmael and Amanda work together."

"Don't see how."

"We'll have to ask them to find a book they think you'd enjoy and would be able to read."

"So we'll be killin' two birds with one stone."

"You've taken leave of your senses!" Hilda half shouted from the kitchen.

"Now, Hilda," a low voice rumbled in response.

Laney and Ivy started toward the kitchen.

"I have to be twice your age, Cowboy!"

Laney stopped so suddenly, Ivy bumped into her. A voice Laney recognized as Toledo's said slyly, "You are nowhere near eighty-four."

"Of course I'm not!" Hilda paused a

moment, then croaked, "You are not forty-two."

"Sure am. And if you happen to be a tiny bit older than I am, so what?"

Ivy and Laney turned toward each other with their eyes wide open. Ivy opened her mouth, and Laney promptly held a finger up to her lips.

"The kitchen is spic-and-span, and lunch isn't for a couple hours," Toledo declared. "Now are you going for that stroll with me?"

Hilda spluttered. A moment later, the kitchen door clicked shut. Complete silence reigned. Laney opened the door from the dining room to the kitchen and peeked in. "She went!"

"Could you b'lieve that?" Ivy shook her head.

"I think it's wonderful!"

"I knowed Hilda was a sharp one, but she done went and figured out what half of eighty-four is." Ivy continued to shake her head in wonderment. "D'ya thank if I e'er learn to read, mebbe you could teach me to cipher that good?"

"Of course. But, Ivy, we can't ever let on what we just heard. It was poor manners to eavesdrop."

"Couldn't much holp it, what with Hilda bellering like a wounded moose."

Laney giggled. "Now you have to come over more often. While you're here, we'll be able to play Cupid for Hilda and Toledo, too."

Ivy enveloped Laney in an exuberant hug.

"Yore wondrous smart, Laney. I'm so glad yore my friend!"

Laney hugged her back. Through their voluminous clothing, for the first time, she felt the small mound that proclaimed Ivy's impending motherhood. Even so, Laney patted her back. "I'm glad we're friends, too."

"Let's go."

"Lemme get my papers." Ivy gathered up her things and carefully slid them into a leather case. She bade good-bye to Laney, Ruth, and Amanda, then headed out the door.

Ishmael didn't say a word. He clamped his hands around Ivy and hefted her into the O'Sullivans' buckboard. " 'Bye, ladies. Much obliged for them books."

"I'll enjoy discussing them with you," Amanda said softly.

"Lookin' forward to that." Ishy set the books he'd chosen up on the seat and hopped aboard. With a click of his tongue and a jingle of the reins, he set the rig into motion.

Tension crackled between them as they headed home. Ivy knew it was her fault. She'd lied to him. *But he don't gotta know 'bout the babe's pa. Ain't nothin' good gonna come of it.* Trying to fill the painful silence between them, she ran her hand over the reddish-colored leather case. Burgundy, Laney called it. Laney always had fancy-sounding names for colors—pearl, magenta, burgundy. "Burgundy," she said aloud. "Uh-huh. That's what color this here satchel is. Ain't it purdy? Laney give it to me."

Ishmael barely glanced down at the case in her lap.

"I'm a-keeping all my schoolin' stuff in this." She stopped moving her hand back and forth across the buttery leather and worried the clasp with the edge of her thumb. "I got me a pencil and paper and two books in here. Neat as cain be."

Ishmael nodded.

Please, Ishy, don't be mad at me. "I got me a list of words I cain read now, too."

All he did was nod again.

"Thirty-one words." *Used to be, you'd be tickled that I could read. Don't change.* "I cain read thirty-one words now."

"Good for you." He didn't even look at her or smile. Instead, he looked straight ahead at the horse's rump like he never seen one before.

The buckboard jostled, and the books Amanda had helped him pick out slid. Careful as could be, he stacked them together again.

A thought raced through Ivy's mind, and she laughed with sheer relief. "Yore so busy ponderin' the books you got and how sweet 'Manda is, yore barely hearin' a word I say."

"I heard you."

Chills ran down her back. It wasn't what he

said—it was how he said it. The only time she'd ever heard her twin use that tone of voice was when Pa used to test his patience to the limit. "Ishy, I'm tryin' to make you proud of me."

His head whipped around. "Proud? You lied to me."

"You love me, Ishy. You won't stay mad."

"Might be I won't stay mad, but I'll always be 'shamed of you. Sick-clear-down-to-my-boots 'shamed of you."

His words stole her breath.

"Things was always hard on us. Pa drug us ever'whar and we didn't have nothin'."

"But it'll never be thataway again," Ivy burst out. "Don't you see? We got plenty to et and nice clothes and a real roof and—"

"Warm blankets," he said flatly.

The words hit her like a slap. Ivy winced. She clutched his sleeve. "Ishy—"

"We was twin-borned. We always had each other. You was my pride and joy." He looked at her and shook his head. "No more. I don't feel that way 'bout you no more. 'Cuz of yore lie, I held a shotgun on the onliest friend I ever had. I believed you over him 'cuz yore my sis and yore my twin and you was all I ever cared 'bout."

"Oh, Ishy—"

"You ruint Galen's life."

Her fingers curled more tightly into the fabric of his shirt. "The babe, Ishy. I done it for my babe. So he'll niver be cold or hungry."

His eyes smoldered. "I woulda worked till I dropped dead to get whate'er you and the babe needed."

"And that's 'zactly what woulda happened. Then me and the babe woulda been jist as bad off as you and me always was with Pa."

"Galen—"

"I'll make it up to him. I will. I'll do him proud. Jist you wait and see. My manners and book learnin' should do him right."

"He never looked down on you when you was wearin' your flour sack dress and didn't know yore letters. He was nice to you and me, and this is how you paid him back?" Ishmael's head dropped back as he groaned, "Sis, how could you do this?"

"I'll make it better, Ishy. I will."

"Cain't. You ruint his good name."

"Folks'll forget. Onc't the babe's borned, them gossips are shore to find sommat else to twitter o'er." She let go of his shirt and started stroking the leather case again. "And plenty of folk ain't holdin' nuthin' 'gainst him. The McCains been standin' staunch. You cain't say otherwise. Laney, 'specially. She been a true-blue friend to me."

"Beats me, her keepin' you as her friend."

"Ishy!"

"Galen loved her. She loved him back."

Ivy stared in horror at her brother.

"You done tole your lie and you stole all the

happiness they was set to have. He's saddled
with a wife and a babe what ain't his, and
Laney's heart got broke. You sit here crowin'
'bout the things she does for you, 'bout the nice
thangs you got. Well, I hope yore happy, sis, 'cuz
yore lie bought you those thangs—but the folks
who was the onliest ones who e'er bothered to
holp us paid dear for it. That's right. They paid
with all they e'er dreamed and hoped for."

Shivers wracked her, and she shook her head
to deny his accusation.

"You been making a fuss o'er how somebody's stealin' stuff from the houses round here;
you done worse. What you took cain't be
boughten at a store and put back like nothin' e're
happened."

"Cain't be so. Tell me ain't so," Ivy plead.
"Laney wouldn't be holpin' me, and Ruth
wouldn't give me purdy dresses if'n 'twas true.
They even give me a weddin' gift."

Ishmael's face was grim. " 'Tis the truth."

The satchel slid from her lap, but Ivy didn't
try to catch it. It landed on the board between
their feet.

Ishmael's gaze nearly bore a hole through
her as he demanded, "Tell me who the feller is."

Ivy shoved her fist against her mouth to hold
back a sob.

"You gotta. That's the onliest chance that
mebbe we could set thangs right."

Slowly, she lowered her hand and wrapped

both arms about her ribs. The word stuck in her throat, but she still answered him by shaking her head.

Chapter Thirty-five

I vy, dear, come on inside."

"Yes, Ma." Ivy trudged up the porch steps. Her heart was every bit as heavy as her footsteps. Ever since Ishmael had discovered she'd lied, life had unraveled. Nothing was right anymore. She keenly missed his jaunty smile and soft words of encouragement. Galen—he treated her real fine. He pulled chairs out for her, read aloud to her, even bought material for her to make baby clothes. Every last kind thing he or his ma did made her guilt mount.

Worst of all was Laney, though. Laney still sat beside her and helped her sound out words. She patiently modeled how to move and sit gracefully. When Laney had helped weed the big garden, she'd drawn words in the dirt for Ivy to happen across. Still, every once in awhile, when she didn't know Ivy was watching, Laney would spy Galen and for an instant her eyes would light up. Just as quickly, she'd turn away and get busy doing something else.

I done what I had to. Ivy chanted those words to herself whenever she was alone. *I done it for my babe. Growed-up folks cain learn to get 'long, but a young'un—he cain't holp hisself.* The baby kicked, as if to agree.

"Look who's come by!" Ma thumped the coffeepot onto the stove. "The gals from the Broken P."

Ivy cocked her head to the side. "It ain't Friday already, is it? I lose track of the days."

"No, it's not sewing day." Hilda eyed Ivy's middle.

Ivy fought the urge to shove her hands into her apron pocket and sort of pull the apron out so her belly wouldn't look quite so big.

"Come here," Ruth said. "We wanted to show you something."

"'Kay." Ivy walked toward them and wondered what they were up to. Ruth and Laney suddenly parted, and Ivy saw what had been hiding behind their skirts.

"Not just the cradle, either, Ivy. They've filled it with diapers and baby gowns, too." Galen's ma stood next to her and added, "Silly as it sounds, I'd forgotten just how wee small the baby clothes are. You'd think after rearing all those sons of mine, I'd recall such a thing."

Tears streaked down her face. Ivy tried clearing her throat so she could say something, but she couldn't stop crying.

"Now will you be lookin' at the lass?" Ma wound an arm around her. "Your grand presents left our Ivy speechless."

Laney pressed a handkerchief into Ivy's hand. "I'm sorry we can't stay today, but on Friday, we'll come and have a sewing day."

Ivy nodded. She tried to mop her face, but then she saw the itty-bitty stitching on the corner of the hankie. It was the exact same shade of blue, and the style of the letters embroidered on it were identical to one of Galen's Sunday-best handkerchiefs. In her hand, she held proof of what she'd tried to deny. By giving her baby a home and a father, she'd deprived her friend the love of her lifetime.

The misery didn't abate after the women left. It gnawed at her until Ivy couldn't bear it any longer. The next day, she concocted a reason she ought to go to town. Ishmael and Galen were busy, and Ma needed to do some gardening. Disregarding the warnings she'd been given about the thief, she set out alone for town.

It took all of her nerve, but she finally made a fist and knocked on a door.

"Come on in!" a deep voice called.

Ivy pushed open the door and timidly stepped inside.

"Mrs. O'Sullivan."

Ivy twisted around, horrified that Galen's

mother had followed her. Only she wasn't there.

"Can I help you?" The doctor dried his hands on a snowy towel.

She shut the door and leaned against it. "I ain't good at knowin' stuff. If'n I'm wrong, I want you to tell me straight off."

"That seems reasonable enough."

She swallowed. "Parsons and doctors—they gotta keep a secret if'n a body tells 'em sommat, right?"

"Yes. It's called confidentiality. We can't help people if they're afraid of something and don't give us the full truth. Is there something I can help you with?"

"I ain't got no cash money." Her nose and eyes started to sting with unshed tears. "And the Pony Express ain't been payin' Galen for all his work and for keepin' them horses. Mayhap I oughtta go wait till the parson gets home."

"You can do whatever you feel you need to, Mrs. O'Sullivan. I would like to take a moment, though, and talk to you about the baby."

Her knees started to give way, and she slid down the door as she whispered, "How'd you know that's why I come?"

"Argh!" Galen gritted his teeth against the pain.

" 'Tis a vicious, mean cut," Ishmael announced.

"Aye," Ma agreed. "Doc's going to have to be stitching this together, son."

"You sew every bit as good as the doctor does." Galen jerked his chin toward Ma's sewing box. "Grab a needle."

"Nay, son. Arms are tricky. More important, 'tis your right arm. I'll wrap it up, but you'll be seeing the doctor, and I won't hear otherwise."

Ishmael poked him in the shoulder. "Least you was a-wearin' the shirt you and Sis spoilt when you tried to wash it. Ain't too much of a loss."

"Just rip off the sleeve. No use in my getting blood on another one."

"I'll go saddle up a horse."

"Two horses." Ma gave Ishmael a stern look. "You'll go along to make sure he's okay."

"Cain't rightly do that, ma'am. I give my word to Galen that I'd stay and take care of the relay. It's due through today."

Galen groused at Ma for fussing like a hen and assured her he'd be okay by himself.

"Doc, I feel like ten kinds of a fool for this," he said later as the man examined the wound.

"You would have been a hundred times a fool if you hadn't come in. The cut's right beside a nerve. I'll be able to spare it, but don't be surprised if you can't move your arm well for about a week, because it's going to swell."

Galen nodded glumly. It burned like anything while Doc washed up the cut and stitched it back together. Stupid thing went from his wrist clear up to his elbow. "If Dale didn't put so much store in that dumb pig, I'd turn him into pork chops."

"So it was Mr. Snout, eh?"

Galen gritted his teeth so he wouldn't let on how much it hurt.

"Did you hear about Fort Sumter?" Doc asked as he kept working. "Thirty-four hours of fighting. Thirty-four, and not a man on either side was killed."

"Makes me think it might be God's way of saying He'd rather have His children reason it out instead of fight."

"Things are happening fast. Lincoln declared a state of insurrection and has called up seventy-five thousand troops. Lee refused to lead them and is said to be a possible leader of the Southern army."

"I hadn't heard that. He's from Virginia. Last I knew, Virginia was still with the Union."

"They're not. The day after Virginia seceded, Lee resigned from the U.S. Army. The very next day, Lincoln declared a naval blockade of the Southern ports." Doc continued to fill him in on all of the political happenings.

After Doc wrapped a bandage around the whole mess, Galen asked, "What'll you take for payment?"

Doc thought for a moment. "A favor."

"You're a fair man. I can agree to that. Just name it."

"That you let me deliver your wife's baby."

Galen jolted. "Of course we're going to send for you."

"Good. Good." Doc went to his washstand and started to scrub his hands. "I can't say much, Galen. You know not to ask me questions. All I'll tell you is this: Ivy's very fragile. Treat her with care."

"Is she sick? Is there something I should know?"

"I'll see you at church."

"Don't put me off like that." Galen stared at the doctor. "What—"

"No questions," Doc said, methodically washing each finger. "Just treat her with care and call me when her time comes."

Puzzled by the cryptic advice, Galen went outside. He swung into the saddle and grunted at the pain the jarring motion caused. Having wasted time on this, he decided to take a short-cut back home. He cut across a field and spotted the same stranger whom he'd seen with Ivy. Galen thought to go after him, but something kept him from doing so. He continued on a few hundred yards more and pulled his horse to a halt.

Ivy sat on a stump, doubled over and weeping.

Galen dismounted and approached her.

"Ivy?" He touched her hair, and she flinched. "It's just me, lass. That man—did he bother you? Did he hurt you?"

She looked at him, confusion clouding her teary eyes.

"He's the same one who was with you the time you were studying your letters. Ivy, did he . . . is he . . ."

She wiped away her tears, but new ones replaced them. "Dun-dunno w-w-what you mean."

"A man was here."

She shook her head. "I'm all-all-all on my l-l-lonesome."

She was too upset to lie. Galen couldn't figure out what was happening. Doc hadn't said the half of it when he said Ivy was fragile. *How did I miss how frail she is? She's barely more than a lass.* Galen took her hand in his. Her hand was rough and red and bony. The thing that got to him, though, was how it shook.

He knelt by her. "Ah, lass. You needn't be scared of me. All this time, I've thought you were protecting a lover. That wasn't it, though, was it? When a man hurts a woman, 'tisn't her fault. Whatever happened to you, you're not to blame. You can trust me." He gently raised her hand and pressed a soft kiss on the back of it.

She fell apart. Burrowed into his chest, she sobbed as she finally told the truth.

Galen awkwardly pulled the blanket up to his wife's shoulders and smoothed it in place. She'd wept herself to oblivion.

"I'll have the boys go weed so she can sleep," Ma whispered.

He nodded. "Pray, Ma. Pray."

"That I will."

He went out to the stable. Ishmael was tending the relay pony. "Did the rider come through on time?"

"Yup." Ishmael chuckled and shoved the mustang's nose away from his shirt. "This'un's my favorite. She cain't holp herself. She's gotta get a whiff and try to figger out what I et. I don't make it none to hard on her. Usually, I got me a spot or splash of sommat on the front of me." Ishmael finally turned around. His smile melted. "What's a-wrong?"

"We need to talk." Galen walked out to the pasture, Ishmael following him. The boys would be coming home from school anytime now, and he didn't want them around.

"Boss, did I do sommat bad? If'n I said a bad word, 'twasn't on purpose. You know I'm still—"

"It's not that." Galen slid his left arm around Ishmael. "We need to pray first."

"Okay."

Galen asked the Lord for wisdom and

guidance, for help and healing. When he finished, Ishmael chimed in on the amen. Galen didn't let go. He looked at his brother-in-law and decided the best way to handle the truth was to speak plainly.

"Ishmael, I know who sired Ivy's baby."

Chapter Thirty-six

Ishmael started. "You do?"

"Aye." Galen looked him in the eyes. "Your father got drunk. He—"

"No!" The word tore from Ishmael. He reared back and spun away. "No!" Ishmael walked a few paces away and came back. He'd gone sheet white, and his eyes carried the exact same anguish Ivy's had held earlier. "Oh, no, no, no." Ishmael fell to his knees.

"She didn't want you to know," Galen said quietly.

"She was a-tryin' to protect me, and I shoulda protected her." Deep sobs wracked him. "I shoulda knowed."

Just as he had with Ivy, Galen knelt and

wrapped his arms around Ishmael. Finally, when Ishmael's storm lessened, he raised his head. "I gotta go to her. I gotta. Whar is she?"

"She cried herself to sleep." Galen heaved a sigh. "Let her sleep, Ishmael. Ma's staying with her."

"I gotta talk to her."

"I understand that you do, but not now. I told Ma we'll have the boys bunk down in the tack room tonight. When Ivy wakes up, you can be there for her." Squeezing Ishmael's shoulder, Galen pledged, "I'll be by her side, too. She needs our strength and love."

———•———

"I came to tell you there's been a change in plans." Ruth leaned heavily on Laney.

"I can see why." Laney helped Ruth toward her bed and helped tug off her robe. "You lie back down. I'll get you some tea to settle your stomach."

"Mrs. O'Sullivan's downstairs. She came over with Ishmael, but I'm not letting the two of you ride back there alone. Toledo's going to accompany you."

"Thats fine." Laney drew the covers up on Ruth and checked the positioning of the clean pot beside the bed. "I thought you didn't keep secrets from me."

Ruth opened one eye. How she managed it, Laney couldn't say, but Ruth managed to look peeved. "I wasn't sure. I'm still not positive."

The rattle of china announced someone was coming. Hilda entered, carrying a tray. "Laney, grab your sewing and go on downstairs. You'll go to the O'Sullivans' today. Ishmael will accompany Amanda to town and help her in the library. I'll take care of Ruth. Ruth, I brewed you some tea." Hilda set down the tray and jerked her thumb toward the door.

Laney dipped down, pressed a kiss to Ruth's forehead, and whispered, "You'll be a wonderful mama."

As she walked out of the room, Laney heard Hilda's voice go all soft. "Tea and a soda biscuit will help. I even put apple-pear butter—"

A distressed sound accompanied a flurry of sheets. Laney turned back around.

"You go on. I've got her." Hilda held Ruth's braid to the side.

Laney leaned over the banister. "I'll be ready in a few minutes, Mrs. O'Sullivan."

"Take your time. Hilda gave me a cuppa tea."

Amanda's door opened. She yanked Laney inside her chamber. "Ishmael's going to help me today!"

"So I heard." Laney followed her over to the bedstead. "I'll cinch you in."

"Thank you!"

Laney took hold of the laces and felt a pang. *The first time Galen truly noticed me was the day*

Ruth and Hilda pulled my stays so tight. Now Galen's married and Ruth and Josh are going to have a baby. Amanda and Ishmael are falling in love. Even Hilda and Toledo are courting. There's someone for everyone but me.

"Laney," Amanda squeaked, "maybe not quite that tight!"

"Oh. I'm sorry." She paid attention to the task. "Be sure to wear your ruby combs. If you let one slip out a little, it'll give Ishmael an excuse to admire your hair."

"I will."

"You'll have to tell me all about it tonight!" Laney raced to her room and dressed. Just before she left, she opened a bureau drawer and pulled out a length of lace and momentarily pressed it to her heart. She'd planned to use it as an edge for her wedding veil, but that dream had died. Waiting downstairs in a sugar sack were all of the pieces for a nightgown. Laney had bought the oh-so-pale pink lawn because Galen once had told her to make a pink dress, so when she'd bought fabric for her trousseau, Laney wanted to fashion something in pink. This lace would go on that gown, but Ivy would wear it.

"Leave Ruth be," Hilda said to Laney as she exited her room. "Go on with you now."

Toledo and Josh were out front. Josh helped Laney into her saddle, and Toledo assisted Mrs. O'Sullivan. It would be indiscreet for Laney to mention Ruth's condition, but she needed to say something. She accepted the reins and whispered to her brother, "After this morning, I don't think Hilda's ever going to have to worry about Ruth wanting apple-pear butter."

Josh threw back his head and laughed.

Just before they turned the last corner onto the O'Sullivan spread, Mrs. O'Sullivan halted. "Thank you for bringing us, Toledo. We're fine. I'm sure you have plenty of work waiting for you." She waited until the cowhand rode off. "Laney, I'm needing to talk to you."

Laney detected something in her tone. "Okay." Following Mrs. O'Sullivan's lead, Laney dismounted.

" 'Tis a hard talk we'll have," the woman warned. "And what is said between us can go no further."

"I understand."

"Laney-mine, there was a time I imagined you'd be my daughter. For all the months he ignored you, once my Galen took a good long look and saw the young lady you'd become, he lost his heart to you."

Galen's mother hadn't ever openly acknowledged their budding romance. Hearing her words now made Laney's heart twist. They sat in a patch of grass, and Mrs. O'Sullivan took her hand.

"I was blessed to be wed to my Cullen and bear his sons. Even through his sickness, I cherished each day. My life will never be the same.

On Christmas, you lost the man you loved. You lost the bright future you hoped for and the babies you dreamed of bearing for him. We've both been grieving."

Unable to speak, Laney nodded.

"Proud of you. Aye, Laney-mine, 'tis proud of you I am. To this day, you've let my son know you believed him innocent. You didn't stop there, either. Instead of reviling Ivy, you opened your heart to her. Not a one of us will ever know the cost, but you set aside yourself and reached out to her. Surely God's looking down from heaven and smiling upon you."

Laney pulled a hankie from her sleeve and wiped her face. "It hasn't been easy, but I've been leaning on God and praying for their marriage. Galen's changing. He's become tender with her . . . and I'm glad."

"She needs it more than words can say." Mrs. O'Sullivan drew in a deep breath. "That's why I'm speaking to you. Galen and Ishmael know what I'm going to tell you. Now it'll be just the four of us who know. But for Ivy's sake, Laney, you must hold this in complete confidence."

Laney fought with her curiosity. She wanted to know whatever it was, but she still had to ask, "Would Ivy want me to know?"

"She cannot bring herself to tell you, but she asked me to." In a few stark words, Mrs. O'Sullivan revealed Ivy's deepest secret.

Laney clutched Mrs. O'Sullivan's hand, and they sobbed together much in the same way as they had at Cullen O'Sullivan's graveside. Laney eventually dried her tears and asked unsteadily, "So Ishmael knows?"

"Aye." A shadow crossed Mrs. O'Sullivan's features. "You can imagine how hard he's taking this."

After a short silence, Laney said, "Remember the first time we saw each other after Christmas? You told me courage and faith would get me through. Ivy has plenty of courage, but she has no faith."

"The lack is wearing on the lass. We'll pray for her." Mrs. O'Sullivan stood up. "One last thing, our Laney. I've made it my prayer that God will prepare a man for you. A man worthy of the fine woman you've become. When the day comes, I'll rejoice. But in here—" Mrs. O'Sullivan tapped her heart—"in here, you'll be my other daughter forever and always."

Thud. The bookcase settled onto the gleaming plank floor. Laney watched as the two men slid it into place. "Wonderful! Once we fill those shelves with the books, this is going to be every bit as nice as any big city's library!"

"Magnificent!" Amanda stood back and viewed the shelves.

"It's a sight, I grant you that." Ishmael

grinned. "I'm not so shore you'll ever fill all this space with books, though."

"Piffle!" Amanda giggled at the face he made.

"They haven't seen the bedrooms in the cottage," Laney said to her.

He hefted a crate. "Purdy yeller cottage. You got books in the bedroom?"

"Both bedchambers are filled with books. Amanda's been numbering each crate and organizing things in advance."

Amanda traced her finger over the title of the book in her hand. "There's a shelf for each crate."

Ishmael whistled. "Sounds like a passel of books. Rob, the lil' ladies thank there's a-gonna be 'nuff shelves. Whaddya say?"

Rob Price nudged a shelf into place. "I'm the wrong person to ask. I thought Ruth would need one shelf. Look what this has turned into!"

Clutching a book to herself, Amanda declared, "A haven of knowledge and imagination."

"'Tis a nice way of describin' it," Ishmael said.

Laney shook out a tablecloth and covered the small display table in the window. Amanda and Ishmael were trying to be circumspect, but attraction sizzled between them. With Galen's blessing, Ruth and Josh had temporarily hired Ishmael to help fix up the library in time for the opening. Rob needed the help, but Ruth had urged Josh to get Ishmael involved because it gave Amanda and him a chance to be together. And since Ruth battled morning sickness until at least noon every day, Laney volunteered to come help, also. Today, however, she wished she could just melt into the background.

Ishmael glanced down at the crate he was holding. "Whar d'ya want this'un?"

"I'm sorry!" Amanda gestured. "At the base of the next shelf to your left. Yes, there. It was wrong of me to be chattering when you're holding a heavy crate."

"Weren't all that heavy."

"If it were any larger, I'd have to hire a twenty-mule team to move it!"

Rob chuckled. "Two and a half weeks, and I still can't believe how both of you find new ways to argue over that."

"Now, don't you go embarrassin' Miss 'Manda. Ain't her fault she's so puny she can scarce lift a teacup."

"If that's true, it's a blessing we've had two brawny men to help. Laney's no stronger than I."

"No, I'm not. You men have been a godsend." Laney looked up from the books she'd been arranging around the globe she'd set on the center of the table. "I've been worried we wouldn't finish in time for the grand opening."

"Ruth hasn't been much help." Rob cleared his throat. "That's not to say I'm finding fault.

Since she's had to dash out of church the last two Sunday mornings and Josh can't seem to decide whether to look worried or proud, I assume she'll be indisposed for a little while."

"Thought we wasn't s'posed to say nuthin' 'bout Ruth," Ishmael growled.

Amanda and Laney exchanged a look. Laney wondered if her cheeks were as rosy as Amanda's. She moistened her lips and half whispered, "We won't say anything more."

Rob tapped a piece of molding into place. "Ruth's going to be delighted at the changes we've made. Ishmael, let's go get the next piece from my shop."

"Okay."

Amanda slid the next book into place. "Feel free to leave the door open. It's beautiful out today, isn't it?"

"More beautiful in here," Ishmael murmured as he brushed past her.

Laney pretended she hadn't heard him. "I need to find a block or something to put beneath the globe. It needs to be higher."

"The trunk over in the corner might have something. Perhaps the box the pencil holder's packed in." Amanda started humming.

Laney wove around a few crates and lifted the lid to the trunk. She peeped around the edge. "This thing is huge. If I fall in, you'd better rescue me."

Amanda merely laughed and started putting

books in place on the next shelf.

As Laney stuck her head deep into the trunk, she heard footsteps and a distinct voice ring out, "Ruth truly went the extra mile, didn't she?"

"Hello, Ethel." Amanda's tone managed to sound both polite and firm. "Ruth's been incredibly generous. As you can see on the sign in the window, the library will be opening next Monday."

"I know, dear. Unlike some of the folks hereabouts, I can read. It says May seventh, but I just wanted to take a quick look around. Surely you wouldn't mind loaning me something a little early."

"Your curiosity is understandable, but we won't be checking out books until the grand opening. If you'll excuse me, the men will be back in a few minutes with another bookcase. I'm afraid the space for maneuvering them has become limited."

Laney remained quiet. As the librarian, Amanda was in charge. She'd handled the matter quite nicely. Fearing Ethel would appeal to her if she made her presence known, Laney figured to stay out of sight.

"I'll be gone before the men return. Oh my. Dime novels?" Ethel tutted. "A library ought to have tomes that enlighten and uplift. You and I will have to speak with Ruth. From the day she arrived, that girl has—"

"I don't mean to be rude, but I have considerable work to accomplish."

"Of course you do. And this is such a nice
job for you. Genteel. I've seen how that Ishmael
Grubb has been trailing along after you. We'll
have to find him someone of his own class.
You've been so gracious, but he's so far
beneath—"

Laney pulled herself out of the trunk.

"Mr. Grubb is a fine man." Amanda's voice
trembled with outrage. "The finest I've ever
known. He has more honor than any of the so-
called 'gentlemen' I've met in the upper echelons
of Southern society."

Ethel spluttered.

"A harder-working man doesn't exist, and in
the short time he's been a believer, he's grown
tremendously in the Lord."

"Oh dear. You must be lonesome and home-
sick. You don't want to make a mistake—"

Amanda grabbed a book from a nearby
bookcase. "Ma'am, I have made a mistake. You
shouldn't wait a week until the library opens to
borrow a book, and I know just the one for you.
I believe you ought to read this right away."

"What is . . . I already have a Bible!"

"Then I'd invite you to read Philippians 2:3.
'Let nothing be done through strife or vainglory;
but in lowliness of mind let each esteem other
better than themselves.'"

Ethel smacked the Bible down on the nearest
surface and stomped out.

Laney rose. She would have gone to Amanda, but Ishmael beat her there. "God changes hearts," Ishmael said quietly.

Amanda sucked in a sharp breath. She turned and looked at him with wide eyes and crimson cheeks. "You heard me?"

"Shore did." He reached down and cupped her jaw, his thumb rubbing an arc across Amanda's cheek. "If'n God decides to change a heart, I'm hopin' He changes Miz Ethel's and not yourn, on account of the fact that I ain't niver a-gonna find me a woman half as special as you."

Laney sank back out of sight. The moment a man and woman professed their affection was supposed to be private. *Lord, I'm so glad for them. Truly, I am. But I dreamed of a day when Galen would speak to me of his love. That's impossible now, and my heart won't mend. What am I to do?*

***

"Lookee here at this'un." Ivy tapped her finger on the book she'd borrowed from the library. "Thank I could stitch that on the blanket?"

"Perfect!" Laney handed her a sheet of rice paper. "Here. Notice how you can see through this? Trace the design lightly with a pencil, and then we can transfer the letter to the blanket."

"You'll learn me how to do them fancy stitches?"

"That's all satin stitch. The length widens and narrows is all."

They sat side-by-side in the shade, embroidering. Laney started humming.

"We sung that in church last week, didn't we?"

"Yes." Laney began to sing, " 'Father, whose everlasting love—' "

"Stop right thar." Ivy went sheet white. "You sing and talk 'bout yore heavenly Father. Well, me? I don't want no pa."

Laney felt sick. She hadn't thought about what she'd been singing.

Ivy whispered to the hands she'd knotted in her lap, "You know what mine done."

"And it breaks my heart, Ivy."

"You cain't understand. Ever'body else gots a pa what done 'em proud."

"Not me." Laney's hands knotted in her own lap. "My father was a horrible man. He fooled us all until the very end, but we found out that he was a murderer. He was a liar and a cheat and a thief. He even tried to kill Ruth."

"Yore putting me on."

"It's the truth, Ivy." Laney looked at her friend. "I never speak of my father because I'm so ashamed of what he did. You and I both had earthly fathers who did wicked things. But think, Ivy; we have a second chance because we have a heavenly Father who loves us."

"Nuh-unh. If'n yore God was so good, He

oughtn't have let bad thangs happen."

"He allows bad things to happen, Ivy. We don't always understand why. Just as we have the privilege to be His children, we also are given the choice to turn our back on Him. Good and bad bump against each other. The sad truth is, sometimes innocent people pay the consequences for someone else's wrongs. God doesn't desert us, though. He stays beside us in the midst of those circumstances."

"Well, my circumstances are gettin' the better of me. Cain't see my feet no more. Cain't fit into but two of my dresses, neither." Ivy suddenly threw back her head and laughed until she snorted.

"What's so funny?"

"Me! Jist a year ago, I only had that ratty flour-sack dress. Now I'm wallowin' in the poor-pitiful-me's on account of the fact that I cain only fit into two nice ones."

"Miss Laney!" Dale shouted as he ran up. He held a piglet under his arm. "Galen said if the pigs got out again, we'd be eating pork roast for a month. You gotta help me. You're my partner."

"Go put him back in—"

"Hi, Galen!" Ivy said loudly.

Laney grabbed the piglet and stuffed it beneath her hem.

"I got chores to do." Dale scampered off as Galen drew close.

The piglet snorted.

Ivy promptly laughed and made a snorting sound. "'Tis funny. You have to admit, 'tis."

"What's funny?" Galen asked.

"Ivy," Laney blurted out. "She was just bemoaning the fact that only two dresses fit, but then she realized a year ago she only owned one dress."

The piglet and Ivy snorted in unison.

Galen's brow puckered. "Ivy, I've said all along that you need to go to church, but if you're feeling it would be uncomfortable now, you could stay home."

"I reckon my place is aside you."

The piglet started rubbing his snout on Laney's ankle. She smothered her giggle as best she could. When Galen gave her a questioning look, she pasted on a smile. "Isn't it wonderful that she's coming to worship?"

Galen nodded.

The piglet started to move, so Laney quickly trapped him between her ankles. Afraid Galen wondered what all the motion was about, she leaned forward. "I've managed to get lint all over myself, sewing."

"Me too." Ivy bobbed her head.

"It's a worthy cause." Laney couldn't resist looking at Ivy and explained, "We're doing everything we can for the little one."

Ivy grabbed the tracing she'd made and waved it. "Uh-huh!"

"Are you showing me something or fanning yourself?"

At the same instant, Laney answered, "Showing!" while Ivy said, "Fanning!"

Galen reached up and shoved back an errant lock of hair.

"Laney, did'ja notice how good Galen's arm healed? Cain hardly tell whar he got cut."

Galen didn't give her a chance to reply. His nose wrinkled. "What am I smelling?"

"It's a new scent I'm trying." Laney found another speck of lint as she translated piglet into French. *"Eau de porcelet."*

"I might try it someday, too!" Ivy chimed in.

"Don't." Galen studied the toes of his boots. "You gals go on and enjoy your sewing."

As he walked off, Laney glanced down to see a pink spiraling tail sticking out from beneath her hem. She pointed at it and whispered, "That proves you were right! You can hide a baby under all these hoops!"

Galen didn't look back, but he called, "If that piglet isn't in the sty in five minutes, I'm going to barbecue it!"

———•———

"We still ain't et no pork," Ivy said to Laney as they entered church that Sunday.

Laney winked and compressed her hoops so she could slide into the pew. Ivy didn't make any mention about how Ruth sat by the aisle. Ivy sat across the aisle between Ma, who had the aisle seat, and Galen. She whispered, "Ruth's skin sorta matches her eyes."

"Maybe Laney let her borrow that new perfume," Galen said. He gave his wife a sly look.

Ivy bit the inside of her cheek to keep from laughing aloud. The rest of the service, she barely noticed how Galen and Ma kept trading off and fanning her. The parson was preachifying like he always did, but Ivy couldn't tear herself away from what he was saying. It was like he was talking to her—just to her and nobody else.

John Wall got up and started singing. Chills went up her spine as he kept on singing in a strong, deep voice about amazing grace. Ivy reached over and gripped Galen's hand. He smiled at her.

"Gimme Dale."

Galen dipped down and murmured, "Church is almost over."

She squeezed his hand. "I know! Gimme Dale. I want him." Not willing to wait, Ivy let go of Galen and reached around his back to Dale, who was sitting on his other side. "C'mere, Dale."

Fighting her skirts, Ivy bumped past Ma and dragged Dale along in her wake. Once in the aisle, she pulled Dale in front of her and cupped his shoulders as the song ended.

"Ivy," Galen asked, "what are you doing?"

"You done read it to me. The Good Book

says a little child's supposed to lead 'em. I'm fixin' to go up to the hitchin' post, and Dale here cain holp me jist like he done for Ishy."

"Dale," Pastor Dawes said, "bring your sister to the altar."

Ivy took one step, then halted. "Parson, me hitchin' myself to God—that'll make Laney and Ruth and 'Manda my sisters, won't it?"

"Yes, it will."

"Cain they come holp me, too? And Galen and Ishy and Ma?"

Parson pronounced a benediction and dismissed everyone else, and the people she loved made a big circle around her at the front of the church. After asking Jesus into her heart, Ivy said, "I been thankin' on what I wanna promise God."

"Why don't you tell us what that means?" Galen said.

"When folks get hitched, they both gotta make promises. Jesus promised to take away my sins and live in my heart. So now I reckon 'tis time I speak my piece."

Galen clasped her hand. "You go right on ahead."

"Okay. I reckon 'tis like when we got married."

"But now you're not Ivy Grubb," Laney said softly. "You're Ivy O'Sullivan."

Galen and the parson nodded.

"Okay. God, I'm Ivy O'Sullivan." Ivy

remembered what she'd promised on Christmas Day and changed the words so they'd fit. "From now on, I'll be yore daughter. I'll do my best for you and all this kin I'm a-gettin'."

"Amen," everyone said together.

As they stepped out of the church, Ivy was amazed at how everyone was standing out in the yard. It was almost like they were waiting for her. Folks crowded around her and gave her hugs and said nice things.

Lester from the mercantile stepped forward. "It's good to see Ivy found her way to the Lord and repented of her sinful ways. Galen, did you repent, too?"

"If'n Galen done anything wrong, ain't that s'posed to be betwixt him and God?"

Lester stammered, and Galen pulled Ivy close to his side. "Let's—"

Suddenly she understood what Lester meant. Ivy pushed away from Galen. "I gotta say sommat. All y'all listen here."

Chapter Thirty-seven

"Ivy, no." Galen tried to tug her back.

"I lied. I was sore afraid and I tole a dreadful bad lie." She knew they'd be mean to her, but at least she could right her wrong. "Galen here ain't my baby's pa."

"He's not?!" Ethel nearly shrieked.

Ivy could feel Galen as he stepped close and rested his arm around her shoulders. "But I'm honored to be the baby's daddy."

"A lot of people here have been gossiping and judging." Laney reached out and took Ivy's hand. "All of us are sinners. Instead of judging and condemning, we're called to confess and forgive."

Ivy watched as folks suddenly started moving around and talking. The same people who'd been mean started stepping forward and sheepishly asking for forgiveness. Some of the ladies promised to come help with the baby after it was born.

As the crowd thinned, Ivy dragged Laney off

to the side. "Do we gotta tell ever'body ever'thang we done a-wrong?"

"What do you mean?"

"When we was hidin' that piglet, was that a sin? You tole Galen 'bout yore per-fume."

"I said it was a new scent. Many colognes and perfumes have names that start with *eau de*. Those are French words. I added the French word for piglet. So I was completely honest when I told Galen he smelled the scent of a piglet. If you think we did something wrong, though, we can go to him and ask for forgiveness."

"Nah. We promised Dale we'd holp him. But we gotta 'nother problem."

"What?"

"Them lil' pigs shore are cute. If'n you and Dale decide to go butcherin' or sellin' 'em off, I'm a-warnin' you now not to look 'neath my hem. I'll hide as many as I cain."

"No one would ever look beneath your dress, Ivy. It's simply not done." Laney's eyes sparkled. "We can't allow anyone to discover that we have limbs beneath these hoops!"

"Well, finally. All them dumb rules are comin' in handy."

The porch felt crowded. Laney took another sip of tea and wondered what Miss Genevieve would advise her to do. Lester sat to her right, and Eddie sat on her left. Both had showed up on Monday afternoon without an invitation. Eddie had brought a big fist full of wild flowers. Lester had brought a chocolate bar. They glowered at one another.

Toledo tromped up, pulled off his hat, and wiped his brow. "Laney, I'm going to need your help."

She grasped at the opportunity to get away from the awkward situation. "Of course I'll help. Just tell me what you need."

"Can't you see Laney's already busy?" Lester sounded as if Toledo had swiped the chocolate and sent him home.

Well, maybe that's close to what will happen. Laney smothered a smile. "Toledo wouldn't ask unless it was important, Lester. What do you need, Toledo?"

"Can't say for sure." He shifted his weight and grimaced. "Mostly, I'm going to need help handling Hilda."

Laney walked over to him. Eddie and Lester flanked her.

Toledo cast a look at the house, then confessed, "Someone left the gate open. Coupla cows wandered over to the clothesline."

"Oh no!"

"Oh yes." Toledo's voice sounded funereal.

Laney thought for a moment. As awful as the situation was, it could have been worse. Hilda liked to split laundry into two days; at least today wasn't the day all of Laney and Ruth's unmentionables would be hanging to dry.

Lester cleared his throat. "Well, I need to be getting back to the store. Laney, I have a whole box of those imported chocolate bars in the back room of the mercantile if you want them."

"You've told her that three times already," Eddie said. He gave Toledo a man-to-man look. "He brought her a candy and is trying to sell her more. You'd think she's a hog instead of a pretty woman."

"I'd never insult Miss Laney like that!" Lester's shoulders went back and his chest stuck out. He reminded her of a scrappy little rooster.

"Gentlemen," Laney said in a low tone. "We're all friends here."

"You can all be friends," Toledo said. "But Hilda's another matter. Once she gets her dander up . . ." He rolled his eyes.

"I will help." Eddie managed to sound stalwart. "What do we need to do?"

"If I knew, I wouldn't be asking Laney for help."

Lester strode to the side of the house, gawked around to the back and whistled under his breath. "Toledo, you're going to have to come clean and tell Hilda." He gave Eddie a dirty look, then repeated, "I have to get back to the store. I'll see you soon, Laney."

Eddie perked up. "Come clean. That is what we will do. We will make the clothes come clean.

Laney, you go in the house. While you keep Hilda busy, Toledo and I—we'll wash the clothes again."

Relief eased the worry lines in Toledo's face. "You know how to do laundry?"

Laney stared at Eddie in amazement.

"What is there to it? We'll just have to rinse them, ja?"

"Most of them, probably." The worry lines returned to Toledo's forehead.

"*Gut!* Laney, you go keep Hilda busy."

Laney went inside and found Hilda in the kitchen. From the corner of the window, she could see Toledo and Eddie gathering up shirts and britches. She pulled out the cookbook. "I thought maybe you and I could copy a few recipes for Ivy. Ones she could read. What do you recommend?"

"Where did your suitors go?"

"Lester needed to tend the store. Eddie is . . . helping Toledo with a project."

"That Eddie—he's a hardworking man. Strong as an ox, too. He's a good man, Laney."

"So is Toledo. Well, he's not as strong as an ox, but he's as smart as a whip."

"Don't go trying to—" Hilda's eyes widened. "If that cowboy's so smart, why's he messing with my wash?"

"Now, Hilda, he's trying to make things right." Laney held Hilda back. A second later, her jaw dropped open. She couldn't help it.

Laughter bubbled up from deep inside.

"A horse trough! They're dunking my clean laundry in a stinkin', filthy horse trough!" Hilda's voice rose with every syllable.

"They're good men, Hilda. And they are working hard."

Hilda moaned. "Do you see that? That's how they think to wring out the clothes?"

"Maybe we should go rescue them."

"If you're talking about the britches, you're probably right. If you're talking about the men, never. I aim to sit here and eat a piece of pie and watch the show. You know what they're doing?"

Laney nodded. "Laundry."

"Nope, honey. What they're doing is showing us how much they love us. Ain't often you get a chance to see something like this. Fill your eyes, Laney. And fill your heart. Eddie's a fine man. If that's not proof out there, I don't know what is."

"There we go!" Laney let go of the wheelbarrow's handles. For the past two days, they'd made cherry pies, tarts, canned cherries, and fruit leathers. Everywhere about them, new life abounded. "Just look at this, and it's only part of one day's harvest!"

"The Lord's been generous," Mrs. O'Sullivan agreed as she looked at the heap of vegetables they'd picked. "Ivy, you need to go rest."

Ivy pressed her hands to the small of her back and arched. "Don't mind if'n I do. Ain't feelin' like no spring chick no more."

"You're not an old hen like me, either." Mrs. O'Sullivan gave Ivy a hug.

"Don't talk about chickens around Ruth," Laney whispered as her sister-in-law and Amanda came along with Hilda and the other wheelbarrow.

"We have plenty of time before lunch," Hilda declared. "Let's empty these out and go do some weeding. Ivy's in no shape to be helping with that chore."

"I'll be setting Sean and Dale to weeding when they come home from school. Ruth, Galen's going to town today. I'll ask him to buy you some lemon drops at the mercantile. If you suck on them, they'll help settle your stomach."

"I'd stand on my head in a weed patch if that would work."

"You couldn't possibly do such a thing," Laney said.

"On account of ever'body bein' able to see that you got le-limbs," Ivy tacked on. She looked inordinately pleased that she'd caught herself and minded her manners.

After lunch Laney stayed to work with Ivy on reading and writing. "Here are the sentences I want you to copy today." Laney set down a page with three sentences on it. After each, she'd left sufficient space for Ivy to print them.

Ivy squinted at the first line. "'God is the King.'"

Laney smiled.

Ivy read the next line. "'I am His' . . . uh-oh. That's a fearsome big word."

"Daughter," Laney supplied.

"'I am His daughter.'" Ivy bobbed her head and trailed her finger down to the next line. "'That makes Ivy a pr-prin-cess. Princess. That makes Ivy a . . .'"

Laney watched in delight as the meaning of the words dawned. "Princess," she said together with Ivy. "That's you, Ivy. You're a daughter of the King of Kings."

"You done wrote a story in them three lines."

"I found a passage this morning that I want to share with you. It's so special, Ivy. It'll be worth the work of sounding out the words." Laney turned to the third chapter if Zephaniah. Sliding a bookmark under the beginning of the fourteenth verse, she said, "You start, and I'll help you if you need me to."

Ivy bit her lip and then began. "'Sing, O—'" She grinned. "O is a real easy word, ain't it? Too bad they all ain't that easy. 'Sing, O daughter of Zion; shout, O Israel; be glad and re-joice with all the heart, O daughter of Jer-oos-all-em. Jerusalem. . . .

"'The Lord thy God in the midst of thee is

mighty,'" she continued haltingly; "'he will save, he will rejoice over thee with joy; he will rest in his love, he will joy over thee with singing.'"

"I love those verses," Laney said. "Can you imagine? We're God's daughters. He loves us and takes joy in us and sings over us."

"Makes me wanna tuck them words in my pocket so's I cain take 'em out and read 'em o'er and o'er."

"That's why Christians memorize the Scripture, Ivy. So we can relish God's words." Laney tucked the bookmark into the fold of the Bible. "Those words are God's gift to us." She turned to the frontispiece. "This Bible is my gift to you. See? Your name is right here."

Ivy jumped up and dashed toward the door. "If'n I didn't hafta pee so bad right now, I'd hug you!"

Mrs. O'Sullivan handed Laney a cup of coffee. "That lass—I can't help lovin' her. Because of you, our Laney, she's coming along nicely."

"Isn't it wonderful? Ruth taught me to read, and now I'm teaching Ivy. Some day she'll help that baby read."

"There's a grand thought."

On her way home, Laney let her mare walk as they went toward the bend in the road where she'd ended up on Christmas Day. Going past that spot always hit her hard. *No matter how glad I am for Ivy, it still hurts. God, I keep thinking I've let go of this, but it keeps coming back.*

Lost in thought, it took a moment for her to realize a man had stepped out into the middle of the deserted road. Laney tugged back on her reins. In that instant, she knew she'd made a mistake. The stranger drew a gun.

Chapter Thirty-Eight

Lemon drops. It felt silly, buying another man's wife candy, but Ma swore it would help Ruth. Josh was so grateful, Galen offered to pick up more any time he delivered things to town. Ethel's brother at the Copper Kettle was happy to buy eggs, fruit, and vegetables again, and Lester not only apologized for his behavior, but actually started paying Galen a little more for the eggs and the goods Ma canned.

Today he'd learned that as of July, Placerville would become the Pony Express's terminus. Between now and then, he'd still be losing money by running the relay. Rick Maltby had volunteered to broker some kind of deal with the company, but Galen wasn't holding out any hope of recovering much.

Mulling over matters, he rode around the bend of the path. Seeing a man with a gun drawn on Laney, he shouted, "Hey!"

The stranger wheeled around. As he did, his gun went off. Spooked, Laney's mare bolted. In that instant, Galen's wrath turned to cold fear. Her horse was thundering straight toward the ravine.

He spurred his gelding after her. Even then, she was so far ahead, he feared the worst. *God, spare her. Help me. Help me. Spare her. Spare her.* His heartbeat and the hoofbeats matched the urgent cry of his soul.

The distance between their horses narrowed, but Galen knew nothing short of a miracle would save her. Straining to reach her, Galen hooked his arm about her and jerked her out of her saddle just before his own horse veered to the left and safety. "Are you all right?"

Laney caught her breath, then fretted, "Your arm—did you hurt your arm?"

"My arm's fine."

She slumped against him. Galen held her in place and headed toward the Broken P. "Do you know that man? Have you seen him before?"

"No. But he knew me."

"How?"

"He said—" She shuddered.

Galen tamped down his anger. Laney was already upset enough. "What did he say, Laney? I could see he was talking to you."

"He knows my name. And he knows Ivy and I are friends. He said—" She took a deep breath and confessed in a rush, "He said the Grubbs owe him money. He figured if they wouldn't pay up, Josh would."

"As soon as I get you home, we'll go after that man."

"I think you scared him more than he scared us."

"Impossible." They stayed silent as he took her home. Her perfume drifted up to him. It was the lemony one she'd worn the day he first noticed she was a woman. Ever since Christmas, she hadn't worn it. This was the first time since then he'd noticed her wearing it again. He dismounted and helped her down. Loath to let her go, but knowing he must, he growled, "You should wear that other perfume."

"What?" She gave him a baffled look.

"The oh-you-porcelain one."

Laney walked away from him, but not before she started laughing like a loon.

Galen shouted for Josh.

Josh took one look at his face and came running. Toledo soon joined them. Galen looked over his shoulder to make sure Laney couldn't hear him. His voice shook with fury. "A man just tried to kidnap Laney."

Josh let out a roar.

Galen didn't pause. There was no time to waste. "Laney said he told her the Grubbs owe him money. Since they haven't paid, and Ivy and Laney are friends . . ."

"I'm getting him. When I do, I'll—"

"Turn him over to the law." Toledo clapped his hand on Josh's shoulder. "The sheriff said the thefts started about the time the Grubbs set up the still."

Galen added, "Which is why he thought Ishmael was behind the robberies. Someone willing to moonshine and rob is bad enough, but now he's tried to kidnap. Seeing him with a gun on Laney—"

"He had a gun on my sister?!" Josh's face was bright red.

Toledo's tone went as harsh as his expression. "None of the women will be safe until we catch that man."

"I'm going home to make sure Ma and Ivy are safe. I'll pick up Ishmael. All I have is that one shotgun. Ma can use it. Josh, I want you to loan me two firearms—one for me and the other for Ishmael."

Josh turned to Toledo. "You stay with Ruth, Laney, and Hilda. I'll ride along."

Toledo shook his head. "Boss, I'll keep an eye on things here, but you'd best get Eddie Lufe. He's got a stake in this, too."

Galen took weapons from Josh and rode off. He'd go on this manhunt and get that lowlife. That much he could and would do for Laney. As for Eddie Lufe . . . Galen suppressed any further thought. He was married to Ivy.

———•———

"Laney, you came!" Ivy sat on the edge of the bed and gave her a weak smile.

"You almost got shot once," Ruth half shouted. "The men have been searching for four days now, and they still haven't caught that bandit. What did you think you were doing, coming here alone?"

"I didn't come alone. The minute I came home from town and heard Ivy's in labor, I rushed right over. Besides, that terrible man has to be long gone by now. Josh even said so at breakfast. The men are back to their usual chores—"

"And still carrying a weapon," Ruth tacked on. "I still can't believe you rode over here."

"I made Toledo bring me. Not that it mattered. If anyone tried to stop me, they'd have lost the fight." Laney dragged Ruth toward the door. "I'm representing the McCains now. You let Toledo take you home." Laney wouldn't take no for an answer and pushed her sister-in-law toward the door.

When Ruth turned around, Laney whispered to Mrs. O'Sullivan, "Ruth shouldn't see this yet. It'll scare her. You just tell me what to do, and I'll see that it's done."

Doc arrived. After determining Ivy's contractions were spaced far apart, he declared,

"First labors tend to be significantly longer." He looked around. "Do you have a clock?"

"Nay," Mrs. O'Sullivan said.

"I'm wearing a brooch with a clock on it," Laney said, touching the piece.

"Fine, then. When the pangs are coming three minutes apart, send Galen for me." He patted Ivy's arm and left.

"I reckon thar's no use in me lyin' round the whole livelong day." Ivy rolled off the bed.

Mrs. O'Sullivan gave Ivy an approving pat. "That's right. You stay on your feet. I did with every last one of my birthings, and it made them much easier."

Laney feared the baby might fall out on his head, but she didn't say so. Mrs. O'Sullivan ought to know what she was talking about, and Ivy didn't seem in the least bit concerned.

"You ain't said nothin' 'bout my nightdress," Ivy said as she plucked at the pale pink bodice. "After all that stitchin' we done, you niver saw me in it."

"You're beautiful. Your hairpins might be uncomfortable later. Would you like me to brush and braid your hair?"

"I wanna leave it up. Want my babe to come into the world and have his first look at his ma bein' a lady, not a raggedy moonshiner's daughter."

"You're a daughter of the King of Kings.

Don't ever forget that." Laney knew Ivy loved hearing those words.

"That makes me a princess." Ivy compressed her lips and held still. Finally, she drew in a shaky breath. "Ma, if'n I'm a princess, folks cain't tell me what's proper, cain they?"

"What do you want to do, Ivy-mine?"

"I wanna go sit in the shade under the sycamore and soak my feet in a bucket of cold water."

Mrs. O'Sullivan shrugged. "There's not a reason in the world why you can't do that."

"In my nightdress?"

"As long as you have your shawl around you, it's perfectly proper." Laney winked at Mrs. O'Sullivan. "If you take Ivy out there, I'll bring a bucket and a surprise."

Ivy was delighted when Laney brought her a piglet.

About half an hour later, Ishmael started their way. Laney quickly hid the piglet under her skirts, winking at Mrs. O'Sullivan as she did it.

Ishmael knelt by Ivy. "You farin' alright?"

"Do I gotta choice?"

"I reckon not. I brung sommat to holp keep yore mind offa the pain." He went behind the tree and returned with a burlap bag. "I heard of this, but I ain't actually ever seed one."

Ivy opened it up. A pain cut short her laughter, but when it was over she said delightedly, "A pig in a poke!"

"I'll be back later and collect him."

The one Laney had hidden wiggled his way to freedom. Once he was out, he squealed happily as Laney tickled him between his ears. "Ivy, I think you and I got the best brothers in the world."

"Shore did."

"You lasses have lots of blessings to count." Mrs. O'Sullivan took a ball of yarn and a crochet hook from her apron and started to work.

Ivy looked at the first tiny stitches. "What're you makin' this time?"

"A cap. My own mother kept me company whilst I was laboring with Galen, and she made him a wee cap to wear. I thought 'twould be a grand tradition to continue—making a grandbaby's cap."

"I been thankin' on sommat." Ivy toyed with the piglet's little ear. "On account of me havin' Ishy and Galen havin' his brothers, my babe ain't a-gonna lack no uncles."

"Aye." Mrs. O'Sullivan smiled.

"Ishy's sweet on 'Manda."

Laney laughed. "Amanda's been dancing on clouds ever since we roped him into helping finish the library."

"One of these days, mayhap she'll wind up bein' my sister. Then this here babe'll have hisself a aunt."

"She'll make a wonderful aunt," Laney said.

"Anyhow, I been thankin' 'tain't right for my

babe to hafta wait till his uncles up and marry to get his aunts. Ma here's takin' on my baby as his memaw, and Galen's takin' on as his pa. Laney, it'd make me dreadful happy if'n you'd take a mind to 'dopt my babe and be his aunt."

Laney wrapped her arms around Ivy. "I'm honored."

"'Tis fitting," Mrs. O'Sullivan said as she continued to crochet. "After all, you're sisters in Christ."

Ivy moaned softly. "The pangs—they're a mite stronger from what I 'spected."

"You're doing fine, dear." Mrs. O'Sullivan nearly dropped her crocheting. "Galen's coming. Hide those piglets!"

"Ain't nuthin' a-gonna hide 'neath this here nightgown."

Laney scooped one beneath her skirts and Mrs. O'Sullivan saw to the other. As soon as she straightened up, she started crocheting. "Hello, son."

Galen drew closer, carrying a small crate. "How are you doing, Ivy?"

"I'm sittin' in the shade, a-soakin' my feet like I ain't got a care in the world."

"I thought you might enjoy this." As he set down the crate, a snout popped up over the top. The piglet squealed, and the other two promptly answered back. Galen sat back on his heels. "Laney Lou, did you just squeal?"

"You can't blame me, Galen. Ivy just asked

me to be the baby's aunt."

"'Tis such a delightful thing, son, I'm thinking I might have made a wee sound myself."

The piglet peeked beneath Laney's hem. "Well, look what we have here!" She scooped it up.

Mrs. O'Sullivan set aside her crocheting and caught her own piglet before it ran off. "Indeed!"

Galen drummed his fingers on the edge of the crate. "Ivy?"

"Huh?"

"You don't have to pretend there's a water bucket under your hem."

"I ain't pretendin'." When Galen gave her a dubious look, Ivy hiked up her nightdress. "See? I ain't got no piglet under thar."

Clearly astonished, Galen asked, "Then where's the other one?"

Ivy let out another low moan.

Galen rasped, "Want me to go get Doc?"

When the pain ended, Ivy shook her head. "I ain't a-gonna need him for a long while yet. I want you to go find that piglet. We cain't let our Dale's pets go a-missin'."

Late that afternoon, her shoulder covered with the shawl Laney had given her, Ivy held her baby to her bosom and let out a weak laugh. "You gotta holp me, Laney."

"What do you need?"

"Go tell Galen I lied. Turns out I had a piglet

under my skirts after all."

———•———

"Boss . . ."

Galen let the baby curl her tiny fingers around his thumb. "Yeah?"

Ishmael jerked his head toward the door. When Galen scowled, Ishmael rasped, "This cain't wait."

"I'll be back," he said as he settled the baby in Ivy's arms.

"No he won't." Ishmael strode off toward the stable.

Galen followed him and was surprised to have Ishmael shove the shotgun into his hands. "What is this all about?"

"Don't care that this here horse b'longs to the Pony. I need him." Ishmael swung into the saddle. "I found the thief. You and me are a-gonna bring him low."

Galen saddled up. "Where?"

"You ain't a-gonna believe it."

"Where?"

"I went to go stomp on Pa's grave. I knowed wouldn't make no diff'rence, but it made me feel better. Sis was a-hurtin' to get her baby borned, and 'twas all I could thank to do."

"The thief—"

"That's what I'm a-tellin' you. Jist like in them dime novels Ruth gots—the thief returned to the scene of the crime. He's Pa's ol' partner.

He's set up a still again in the 'zact same place. I woulda jumped him on my lonesome, but I 'membered he gots a partner hisself."

"Good thinking. We'll go in quiet so we have the advantage of surprise."

They halted about seventy yards away from the old site and hitched the horses. Upon coming to the edge of the tree line, Galen motioned to Ishmael.

Ishmael nodded, moving to the left as Galen looped around to the right.

The wind shifted and the sickly sweet smell of corn mash hovered in the air. Galen didn't see any horses. Ishmael had told him only one man was there, and the absence of a mount made Galen think that would still be the case—or that no one would be there. But moonshiners were cagey. They wouldn't be likely to leave the still untended.

The shotgun felt heavy. Galen had used it to hunt, but he'd never once had a need to aim a weapon at a man. The responsibility felt grave, but there was no other way. This man had proven himself to be dangerous. Running a still was bad. Thievery, worse. Breaking into the Bensons' place when the baby was napping there unpardonable; folks got real jumpy over that, but then nothing more had been stolen. They'd mistaken that lull as a sign that the robbers had moved on, and everyone had become complacent—until Laney's attempted kidnapping. This man had to be stopped. Galen tightened his grip on the weapon.

From the corner of his eye, he saw a flash of blue.

He glanced over. Ishmael. A long, slow breath exited his lungs. Ishmael ducked behind a pile of rocks to cover him, and Galen moved forward. He chose his steps carefully. The crackle of dried leaves or the snap of a twig would give him away. As it was, just the sound of the gritty earth beneath his boots sounded loud.

As he drew closer to a shrub, Galen spied a rifle on the ground. *Lord help me.*

He rounded the shrub and stepped on the hand reaching for the rifle. Aiming his shotgun at the black-haired man, he grated, "Don't give me an excuse to kill you."

Ishmael jogged around toward them. He pushed the rifle aside and tied up the man while Galen kept his weapon trained on him.

Ishmael yanked the man to his feet. "Whew. This here feller's been nippin' at the brew."

"Where's your partner?" Galen demanded.

"Who says I've gotta partner?" The man sneered. A moment later, he muttered, "Find him yourself."

He wouldn't answer questions, and Galen didn't want him to shout a warning, so he used the man's own bandanna and gagged him.

"Boss, I'm gonna bust all this up. If'n his

partner comes back and finds him missin', he might set ever'thang afire so's he cain get away."

"Good thinking. But we have to save at least one jug. The sheriff needs evidence that they were brewing liquor."

It didn't take long for Ishmael to destroy the equipment and pour out most of the liquor. Ishmael cast a look at their prisoner. "I got me a bad feelin'. What say we do some trackin'?"

"I have no skill at that."

Ishmael grinned. "I do. I don't usually hunt for two-legged varmints, but I reckon huntin' them ain't a-gonna be much different. We're a-gonna lose our light in 'bout an hour, so I hafta get goin'."

Galen jerked their prisoner toward the tree line. "If the other one comes back, we're not losing this one."

"Whar d'ya wanna take him?"

"Broken P. One of the cowboys can drag him to town." Galen hefted the man and flopped him over his horse.

"I'm used to trackin' on foot. You might as well ride on o'er. From what I see, the footprints are goin' west. Every now an' again, I'll drag a stick a-hind me so's you cain catch up."

"Be careful. Don't do anything till I'm there to back you up."

Ishmael nodded his agreement.

"God go with you."

It didn't take long for Galen to haul his prisoner to the Broken P. He didn't want to frighten the women, so he went the back way and stopped at the bunkhouse. One of the hands was there, so Galen sent him to town with the prisoner and instructed him to bring back the sheriff.

Galen had no more than saddled up again when he heard Josh shout his name. He rode over and rasped, "I sent Felipe to town with one of the thieves. They've been running a still at the exact same place the other was. Ishmael says there are two men, so he's tracking the other."

"Which way did he go?"

"North by northeast. After you make sure the women are safe, you can join up. Ishmael's on foot and is leaving a trail in the dirt." Galen headed out. He'd not gone far when he saw a groove in the earth. His head whipped around, and he saw Ishmael jogging toward the little cottage not far from the main homestead. A heartbeat later, a woman screamed.

CHAPTER THIRTY-NINE

Ishmael charged ahead. Galen spurred his horse to go toward the back of the cottage. He vaulted out of the saddle and burst into the cottage. Amanda stood with her back to the wall. Ishmael and a stranger were fighting for possession of a pistol. They whirled and banged into a window, shattering the glass.

Knowing he couldn't fire the shotgun without endangering Ishmael, Galen shoved the gun into Amanda's hands. "Get out of here!"

Without waiting to see if she obeyed, Galen joined the fray as the men fell to the floor. The assailant fought with a strength borne of desperation. Galen and Ishmael fought to protect the ones they loved. The scuffle probably lasted less than a minute, but it felt like an hour. Galen wrested the pistol away at the same time Ishmael smashed his fist into the man's jaw and knocked him out.

"Boss, it ain't right to kick a man whilst he's down, but I'm sorely tempted."

Galen cast a meaningful look to the side.

"Awww, sugar pie." Ishmael strode over and pulled Amanda into his arms. "Yore safe. Safe as cain be. Here. Gimme that ol' shotgun." He set it aside.

Galen didn't have any rope handy, but the cords that tied back the curtains would do. He hog-tied the man while Ishmael comforted Amanda.

Suddenly Ruth and Hilda burst in. Ruth was holding a tiny muff pistol, and Hilda was clutching a rolling pin. Galen snapped to his feet and swiped the pistol from Ruth. "Does Josh know you have this?"

"I don't carry it up my sleeve anymore," Ruth said, as if that explained everything.

Hilda passed the rolling pin to Ruth. "If that rascal so much as looks like he's trying to get up, you brain him. Galen, where's Laney?"

"With Ivy and Ma."

All of a sudden Ruth focused on him. "Galen, what are you doing here? Your wife is in labor!"

"Not anymore, she's not. We have the prettiest little girl you've ever seen."

"Thankee for comin', Miz Newman. And thankee for the purdy li'l doll you made for my girl."

"Annabelle is beautiful, Ivy. I hope she

brings you as much joy as my daughter brings me."

Laney finished drying the teacups. "Just imagine: someday Greta and little Annabelle will have tea parties together."

"What a sweet thought!" Mrs. Newman peeked into the cradle one last time. "I wanted to come celebrate your arrival, but I can't help myself. Mr. Newman and I are to be blessed again. Annabelle might have a little playmate her own age."

"When yore time draws nigh, we'll come holp you."

A few minutes later, Annabelle let out one tiny squeak, and Ma bustled across the cabin. "There, there," she cooed.

"I'm heating water so she can have a bath," Laney said.

"The both of you are making that baby spoilt as cain be." Ivy leaned back in the rocker. "And you done spoilt me, too. I been lazier than a 'leven-year-old hound dog for the last week."

Ma snuggled the baby on her shoulder and patted her on the back. "Annabelle, dear, tell your mama to enjoy her leisure now. Before long, the tomatoes will be coming ripe, and so will everything else. In a few weeks she's going to wish she could just sit around!"

" 'Member the day we made all that pear butter? 'Twas one of the bestest days of my life. Ruth was a-standin' out on the porch and callin',

'Laney, come meet our new friend.' Made me so happy, thought my heart was bustin'."

"We'll be sure to make pear butter again this year," Ma promised.

Laney put the last teacup in the cupboard. "Who do you think will ask about adding apples to a batch—Hilda or Ruth?"

"Hilda already mentioned it to me," Ma said.

Ivy let out a tired laugh. "And Ruth done asked me—only she said 'twould all be for Hilda on account of the stuff makes her wanna puke now."

Galen came into the house. He stood behind Ma and tapped Annabelle's tiny nose. "Hello, sweetheart. Ma, I'm going to send Colin to town with the vegetables. He's got on those britches you made—the ones you dyed with indigo. Lester's bound to have a fit and decide our Colin's ready to join up with the North just because his britches are blue. Can you talk sense into him?"

"Into our Colin or into Lester?" Ma laughed. "I'm thinkin' they're both stubborn. Have Colin tell Lester we'll be needing paraffin wax so we can make more jelly for him. That ought to sweeten his attitude."

"After Ivy nurses Annabelle, I'll bathe her. Mrs. Long brought over tonight's supper." Laney tested the water on the stove. "Why don't you go to town with Colin? Ruth said she's expecting a new book entitled *Great Expectations* that's all the rage back East. We could read it aloud."

"An' mebbe you could ask the parson what hymns we'll sang in church Sunday. You and Laney cain teach me the words so's I ain't bellerin' out the wrong 'uns like Mr. Lufe."

"You'll still be bellowing—just the right words," Galen teased.

"Yore the one what tole me that Bible verse 'bout makin' a joyful noise. A crow prob'ly wouldn't swap his voice for mine, but I'm a-gonna lift it and sang to God anyhow."

Galen went back out to work and Ma left for town. After Laney and Ivy had bathed Annabelle, Ivy collapsed into bed and fell fast asleep. Her dreams turned wild, and she was aware of Laney touching her forehead and fretting, "She's still far too hot!" She opened her eyes just enough to see Galen kneeling by the bed, praying. It was too hard to keep up with it all, so she kept her eyes closed and slept.

———•———

"Laney?" Ivy's voice was thready.

"I'm here." Laney grabbed a cool cloth and bathed Ivy's face. "Your fever's down. You look much better."

"Ain't sayin' much. Niver looked any good to begin with." Ivy closed her eyes for a few minutes.

"You need to drink. Here." Laney slid her

arm behind the pillow and lifted.

" 'Tis 'nuff. Thankee. How's my Anna-belle?"

"Fat and sassy. Galen tried to change her diaper this morning. You've never seen such entertainment. We'll have to ask him to do that chore more often, just for fun." Laney did her best to sound chipper, but in truth, she was desperately worried. Three days of fighting childbed fever had sapped every last shred of Ivy's stamina. Just this morning Doc had come by, looking grim when he examined Ivy.

"Ma, are you here?" Ivy asked.

"I'm over here, ironing."

"I aim to talk to Laney. What I gotta say, 'tis fittin' that you hear it, too. Mostly, I want you to make Laney listen to me."

"I'll listen," Laney said. "Just don't assume it means I'll agree with you. I'm shamefully stubborn."

"When I lied, I done a bad thang."

Laney gently sponged Ivy's limp wrists with a tepid cloth. "God's forgiven you."

"But I didn't jist lie. I stole." Ivy drew in a shallow breath. "Ishy said so, and he was right."

"Ivy, you'd never steal anything."

"I stole yore happiness," she breathed, tears silvering her eyes. "I stole yore man. I was so scairt, but that ain't no excuse. I just thought Galen was showin' good manners. But after all you taught me, I know 'twas special courtin' manners he used round you."

Lord, what am I to say? Laney used the cloth on Ivy's forehead and cheeks. "Galen's a gentleman. Of course he was kind to me, just as he is to every other woman."

"I feel dreadful bad."

"It's the fever. Once you rest and have your strength back—"

"No. Well, yeah." Ivy opened her eyes. "My body ain't doin' me no favors. But that's why I'm tryin' to get you to listen to me. My heart cain't be at peace 'less you make me two promises."

"You'll get better."

"Annabelle. I love her."

Laney smiled. "I know you do. We all do. She's a darling baby girl."

"I tole the lie 'cause I wanted my babe to have better'n I did. And she will. She ain't gonna be cold or hungry or lonesome. Please, Laney, don't hold it 'gainst her that her mama was a liar."

"Annabelle is my precious little niece. My love for her is as pure as can be. Don't ever worry about that, Ivy."

Ivy closed her eyes and let out a long, choppy sigh. "I seed the love in yore eyes. I know 'tis true."

"So now you can rest easy."

"Cain't. Not till you promise t'other thang."

Laney cast a wary look at Mrs. O'Sullivan.

She put the iron back on the stove and approached the bed. Cupping Ivy's cheek, she said in a loving lilt, "Ivy-mine, Annabelle needs her mama. You need to save your energy and get well."

"I give my heart to Jesus at that hitchin' post in church. If'n He wants me to walk them streets of gold aside Him, I reckon my soul's ready. My heart ain't, though. I cain't have peace yet. I busted up Laney and Galen, and that was a sore bad thang to do. I niver give my heart o'er to Galen. He's been a dreadful fine friend, but 'twas all he e'er was to me."

"Galen has grown very fond of you," Laney said.

"I knowed that. I like him jist fine, too. And I always want him to know that. But I see how Ishy and 'Manda feel for each other and how Ruth and Josh do, too. Me and Galen—we was friends what shared his last name for awhile."

"You still do. When you get better, you and he can spend time together. I'm sure you'll develop tender feelings for each other."

Ivy let out a sigh. "Cain't force a turtle to fly. I ain't a-gonna rest 'less Laney give me a promise that she'll step 'longside Galen and rekindle their love."

In the few seconds Laney struggled to formulate a response, Ivy fell asleep.

Laney sat out on the porch and stared into the distance. Mrs. O'Sullivan stepped behind her. "We don't know what the future holds, Laney."

"Which is why I can't make any promises to her. When she gets well—"

"If a miracle happens, she will. I've seen but one woman recover from her childbed fever."

"Well, Ivy will be the second one."

"Courage and faith. I told you 'twould be both you'd need to see this through."

"I have faith that God can heal Ivy."

Mrs. O'Sullivan curled her fingers around Laney's wrist and turned her. "I had faith that God could heal my Cullen, too. But I had to come to terms with the fact that just because He could and that was what I wanted, it didn't mean it would be so. Faith also means trusting God will act in love."

"But—"

"On Christmas Day, when this all started, we thought nothing good would come of it. We were wrong. Ishmael and Ivy both found salvation. People in our church learned to be more loving."

Laney swallowed and gave no response.

Several hours later, Ivy reached for Laney's hand. "You ain't promised yet. 'Bout Galen."

Laney had prayed and thought hard. She gave the only pledge she could. "If ever there's a need, I'll step alongside of Galen and help with Annabelle."

Galen was wearing the gray-black shirt they'd ruined the day he'd tried to do laundry. When he injured his arm and the sleeve got the ragged rip, everyone else said the shirt was ir-reparable—everyone but Ivy. Mending that rip seemed so important to her. She'd bowed her head over the jagged edges and painstakingly put the pieces back together. Galen under-stood—she couldn't fix what really hurt, but she could repair that sleeve. He'd worn the shirt since then as a sign to her. He'd hoped it would get through to her that with time and care, her heart would mend, too.

Now Annabelle slept in his arms, all wrapped in the blanket Ivy had so painstakingly embroidered for her. He and Ishmael both un-ashamedly wept as Pastor Dawes said a prayer over Ivy's grave.

Back at the house, Laney took care of Anna-belle while Hilda saw to feeding everyone. Over the next week, the ladies from the Broken P came and did everything from washing diapers to canning tomatoes. Doc made up a recipe using Borden's canned milk and molasses so Annabelle would have something to eat.

Then Ma got a sore throat. Gargling with salt water didn't help. Two days later, Ma had scarlet fever. Laney swept into the house, bun-dled up the things she needed, and told Galen,

"I'll send Hilda to care for your mother. I'm taking the three boys and Annabelle to the Broken P. It's for the best."

"If this is catching, Ruth shouldn't be exposed."

"I'll stay in the cottage with the children. You take care of things here."

After two long weeks, Ma was finally recovering enough that Laney and Hilda could bring the boys back home. Galen sat at the lunch table and watched as Laney coaxed Annabelle to drink some milk. In his heart, he knew Ma wasn't strong enough to do that every couple of hours. He cleared his throat. "It's good to have the boys back. They can help Ma and do some chores. Laney, I hate to ask, but can you keep Annabelle a little while longer?"

Laney's shoulders melted. "I'm so glad you asked. I wasn't sure how to offer without offending anyone."

"To be sure, I'm getting stronger," Ma said. "I could mind her."

"Nonsense." Hilda scowled at Ma. "You call yourself my friend, and here you are trying to hoard that baby all to yourself. You'll have a lifetime with her. You're going to share her whether you like it or not."

"I'll take good care of her," Laney said, gazing down at Annabelle. "Truly, I will. If you'd like, I'll bring her over every afternoon so you can hold her."

Ma heaved a loud sigh. " 'Tisn't good for the wee lassie to be out that much. Not with her being so young. I canna be putting my pride before her welfare."

"Then I'll come each day to report on how Annabelle is doing." Hilda walked over to the oven and took out the bread she'd brought to bake.

When they left, Galen pressed one last kiss on Annabelle's cheek. "I wouldn't trust her with anyone else."

Laney gave him a sad smile. "Neither would I."

"I'll be back tomorrow, plowboy." Hilda flicked the reins. "But you send Colin to fetch me if you need me in the meantime."

The next few days passed uneventfully. Ma rested a lot and seemed a little better after each of Hilda's visits. Still, Galen worried. He confessed his concerns to Hilda.

"I'm worried, too. But she's improving. Your mother loved Ivy. I think maybe the grief is making it hard for her to recover any faster."

The next day, Dale ran out to the field. "Galen! Galen—Ma's sick!"

CHAPTER FORTY

I t'll take a month or better before she fully recovers."

Laney shifted Annabelle to her shoulder and patted her until she burped. "We're doing fine here, Galen. Truly, we are. Rheumatic fever is nasty, and your mother needs to rest. Doc said he's seen a few folks get rheumatic fever like this after scarlet fever. He doesn't know why, but Hilda told me Doc said if she doesn't take it easy, she'll relapse and end up with heart problems. We can't allow that to happen."

"You look tired," he blurted out.

Laney raised her brows. "And you think you don't? Galen, Ivy was a dear friend to me. She trusted me with Annabelle. You need to, as well."

He heaved a deep sigh. "I'm free of the Pony now. As of yesterday, the final stop for them is Placerville. Rick Maltby said the Pony's operating at a huge loss and can't pay their bills, so they've agreed to allow me to keep two of the mares to settle their debt. Your brother offered . . . um . . .”

Laney knew that Galen was trying to choose his words carefully. “Josh mentioned you were thinking of building up a stable of horses. He's always praised your talent. I'm glad he offered to loan you our stallions.”

Galen twitched her a smile. “We received a small reward for the thieves we caught. Ishmael and I thought it ought to go toward replacing the things they stole. As it turns out, there was just enough left over to pay for fencing in another paddock and getting a few harnesses. In the weeks ahead, I'll be coming over so Josh can give me pointers so I can benefit from his experience. I'd like to see Annabelle whenever I'm around.”

“Of course you would. She's a precious little girl, Galen.”

“I've been fighting to keep from grabbing her from you,” he said, reaching out as he said the words.

Laney released her. “Have a seat. I'll get you some coffee.”

More evenings than not, Galen stopped by. Ishmael came on the days Galen didn't. Laney teased Amanda that it was hard to tell whether he paid more attention to the baby or to Amanda.

In early August, Galen sank down into a wicker chair. He leaned back and studied Laney as she gently rocked Annabelle to sleep. “It's hard to fathom how clear across the country they're suffering the horrors of war. Reports about the Battle of Bull Run or Manassas are catastrophic. News of that new income tax leads me to believe this isn't going to be the brief spat most of the experts predicted. Man is inflicting grievous wounds on his fellow man, yet here I sit on a quiet summer night and enjoy the sight of a lovely young woman and a content baby."

Laney looked at Galen, not sure what to think of his words. "She is a content little girl. Just this afternoon, Ruth was saying she hopes her baby has such a sweet temperament. Josh nearly choked on his coffee. He predicts if their children are anything like Ruth, he's going to be gray by the time the first one is a year old."

"How did Ruth react to that?"

"She agreed." Laney laughed. "Then she tacked on that if their children take after Josh, he'll be completely gray in six months."

Galen grinned. "Whose side did you take?"

"Neither." Laney waited a beat. "I said if their child inherits even the smallest scrap of each of their dispositions, they'll both be tearing out their hair and end up bald by the time the baby is a month old."

"They're lucky to have you here. You'll be such a help to them when the baby comes. I know how blessed I am for all you've done for me and Annabelle."

"It's been an honor. I promised Ivy I'd help you however I could."

Galen leaned forward and rested his forearms on his knees. "I don't think I ever thanked you for how kind you were to Ivy. Any other woman in your position wouldn't have befriended her."

"I can't say it was easy—especially at first. But Ivy had a good heart, Galen. I grew to cherish our friendship, and I miss her. I'm sorry for all you've gone through. You've endured so much in the past year."

"But God brought me through. Many times, He used you to ease the burden. I sit here now and look at you—all grown up. For so long, I thought of you as Josh's little sister. I was an idiot for not realizing—"

Afraid of what he might say, Laney interrupted. "I really was a pesky little sister, wasn't I? I think Josh despaired of my ever growing up." She pasted on a smile. "In fact, now that I think of it, it's probably a miracle that with me around, Josh and Hilda both didn't yank out every last strand of hair they had."

Galen didn't say a word or respond in any way.

All these months, I've told myself he was Ivy's husband. I've denied the feelings I held for him. It was wrong to have feelings for a married man . . . but he's not married anymore. Panic streaked through her. *I've got to get away from him. If I don't, I'll say something that will embarrass us both.* She rose. "I hope you don't mind my leaving you. I need to put Annabelle to bed."

---·---

"O'Sullivan?"

Galen gave the nail one last smack and straightened up. "Lufe. What brings you here?"

"My love for Laney. It brings me here."

Galen looked at his neighbor. "You love Laney."

"Ja, I do. I would be a happy man to have her as my wife."

"Have you asked her? Have you asked Josh?"

"No." Eddie's chin lifted. "Laney—she is a dear woman. She is kind to me, but she does not feel toward me in the way a woman would love her husband. There is only one man who can hold her heart, and that is you."

Lord can it be true? I know what I want, but is that what you want?

"I have my pride. I cannot ask a woman to marry me when I know she loves another. There was a time I thought if I tried hard enough, I could change her heart, but I cannot. You, alone, can make the difference. So I come to you. If you do not love her, you must tell her. Only then will she be free to see that I could be the man for her."

Longing radiated in Eddie's eyes and voice. Galen knew what he had to do.

"Ma, she's coming home today."

"It's about time. You have no notion how much I've ached to ride over to the Broken P and claim my darlin' lassie."

Galen gave his mother a long, telling look. "I've felt the same way about another darling lassie at the Broken P."

"And what are you planning to do about that?"

"Did I ever tell you what Da said about my knees?"

"Your knees?" Ma looked completely baffled.

"My knees." The memory of his father sharing this snippet of wisdom as they worked together in the fields made Galen smile. "Da told me to save my knees for three things—to pray, to propose, and to play with my children."

"Now, then. That sounds exactly like something my Cullen would have said. So tell me, son—which of those three are you planning to use now?"

"You'll have to wait and see."

They'd barely finished their conversation when Laney and Josh arrived. When Galen went out to the buckboard, he could tell straight off that Laney had been crying. She held Annabelle close to her heart and didn't want to turn her loose even for the moment it took for Josh to lift her down. Annabelle didn't seem any too pleased to be out of Laney's arms, either. She let out a healthy squall. Laney took her back and crooned softly as she swayed. Annabelle hushed immediately.

Josh folded his arms across his chest. "Laney's grown quite attached to Annabelle."

"I don't blame her. I've a fine little daughter."

Ma came to the door.

"Your mother looks like she's planning to keep the baby here now," Josh said.

" 'Tis a fact, she wants to."

"Hello," Laney said in a shaky voice.

"Come on in, our Laney. And bring that precious babe. You and I, we'll have tea. As for Annabelle, well, I have all the makings for one of her feedings all ready."

Laney headed up the steps. "We've been praying for you. Hilda says you're doing much better."

Galen jerked his head to the side in a silent bid for a private discussion with Josh. Once he and Josh were a ways off, Galen didn't waste time. "I was an idiot. Instead of seeing what a wonderful young lady Laney was long ago, I pushed her away. I've kicked myself over that at least thrice a day."

"To my estimation, it should have been at least five times a day."

Galen couldn't read Josh's shuttered gaze. "Just after Christmas, I gave you my word I'd not speak to Laney of my love for her. Release me of that vow, Josh."

Josh didn't say a thing.

"I can't make up for lost time. I'm not wanting her now just to get a woman to tend my child. Josh, I never stopped loving Laney. I know it's soon after burying Ivy, and I mean no disrespect to her memory, but Laney fills my heart. I married Ivy because I had no choice; but this time, I'm choosing, and I'm choosing your sister."

"Are you asking me for Laney's hand?"

Galen shook his head. "No."

"Last time you at least had the manners to ask for her left hand. You're getting old and cranky. Can't you do anything right?"

"I'm telling you I'm marrying her. I'm seeking your blessing, though."

"It's about time."

Galen came into the house. "How are things going?"

"Grand for me, but Laney's heartsick about leaving Annabelle here."

Galen took the baby from his mother and cradled her against his chest. He bowed his head and murmured soft, sweet noises to her. To Laney's surprise, he turned and passed his daughter back to Mrs. O'Sullivan.

"Laney, I'm thinking mayhap we ought to give Ma a little time alone with Annabelle. That way if Ma is feeling tuckered out or nervous, you'll be able to take her back for a day or two. Do you mind?"

"No."

"Fine, then. Ma, I'll just take Laney for a wee stroll."

"Take your time." Mrs. O'Sullivan looked up only long enough to flash a smile at him.

Though he said they'd stroll, Galen took Laney to the stable. "I thought you'd like to see what I'm starting out. 'Twill be a few years ere the horse business turns a profit, but I'm pleased with my stock."

Laney walked along and looked in the stalls. "These two are the ones you got from the Pony Express?"

"Aye. They ride well. Here. I'll saddle up."

"It's not necessary, Galen."

"'Tis a favor you'd be doing me. They're accustomed to being ridden, so I try to take each horse out at least every other day. With Ma being under the weather, it's been two days now."

"Okay."

Galen headed north by northwest, and Laney rode alongside him. "Where are we going?"

"To a little spot. I hope you'll like it." Ten minutes later, he turned to her. "So what do you say?"

Laney patted the mustang's neck. "She rides like the wind. If the rest of your stable is half as spirited and hale, your business venture will be a huge success. Don't you think we ought to get back?"

"This is just where I wanted to be." While saying so, he dismounted.

Laney didn't want to get off her horse. Since the day Galen and Ivy wed, Laney hadn't come back here. Without asking her permission, Galen curled his long, strong fingers about her waist and pulled her down to earth. They stood together by the fence that separated the McCain land from the O'Sullivans'.

"I used to see you up here," he said.

Laney gasped. He'd seen her staring at his farm? He knew how infatuated she'd been?

"At first I'd spy you here and find something to do so I'd be out of sight. Later, I wouldn't set foot outside my cabin without glancing up here to see if I'd catch the merest glimpse of you."

"I haven't come here in a long while."

"But I brought you here for a reason. Actually, three." Galen turned toward her, then abruptly dropped to one knee. "Elaine Louise, I can't fight it any longer. I can't wait another moment. I love you, and I'm asking you to marry me."

People might say it's too soon. He's a widower. But I don't care what they say. "I love you, too, Galen. I'd be happy to be your wife."

He rose and slipped two fingers into his shirt pocket. "Christmas Day, I had such plans." He withdrew a simple band of gold. "Back then, I'd given my heart to you. I'd wanted to slip this band o' gold on your finger and let the whole world know of my love. God had different plans."

Tears filled her eyes.

"Oh, lass. Don't grieve for the time lost. We've a lifetime ahead of us to share."

"They're not tears of regret, Galen. I'm realizing how young we were. Probably too young to appreciate what we almost had. It's been hard, but I wouldn't want it to be any different. For all we've been through, I'll never take even one day with you for granted."

"Hard as it was for me, I always thought 'twas far harder on you."

She shook her head. "And I always thought you were hurting far more. I have a confession to make. Psalm thirty-seven says, 'Delight thyself also in the Lord: and he shall give thee the desires of thine heart. Commit thy way unto the Lord; trust also in him; and he shall bring it to pass.' I claimed that as a promise that God would make you love me. In the end, I learned a bittersweet lesson. I had to give up my own dreams and hopes. I had to trust that His plan would turn out far beyond what I could ever want." Her voice caught with emotion. "It has."

" 'Twas a lesson we both learned." Galen slid the ring onto her finger and looked into her eyes. "The second reason we're here is because I was hoping you'd say yes, and I wanted our first kiss to be here."

Laney shivered in anticipation as Galen cupped her waist and drew her closer. His head dipped, and their lips met. After the kiss, Galen embraced her as if he'd never let her go. *And I don't ever want him to.*

"Laney, there's still one more thing."

She looked up at him. "What?"

Together, they tore down the fence—not the whole thing, but a small part of it. Galen took the tools he had tucked into the saddlebag and, using two of the boards, fashioned a cross that he set into the gap. The summer sun warmed the land and created a shadow of the cross.

Galen stepped back and drew her into his strong arms. "There's not a thing between us, and we're at the foot of the cross. Sunshine or shadow, Laney-mine, I'll be the happiest man God ever made because He gave me you."

Epilogue

Yards upon yards of delicate white silk whispered in the room as the last petticoat fell over the hoops. Laney's heart quickened as Ruth approached the trio with the wedding gown in her arms. It, too, was silk. The iridescence of the fabric and the airy lace made the whole garment shimmer.

"Scoot over just a tiny bit, Laney."

Laney let out a breathless laugh. "There's not much room left. The hoops take up a lot of space."

"I'll see to the buttons." Hilda wiggled closer as the gown fell into place.

As she started fastening the buttons, Ruth tilted the cheval glass. "Look at yourself, Noni! Oh, it's just perfect!"

"It is." Laney eyed the sight before her and blinked back tears of happiness.

"Ohhhh." The breathless sound shivered out of Noni. She reverently touched the lace on the sleeve. "Laney, it's so lovely."

"And you look radiant in it." Laney stepped back and looked at her friend.

"Are you sure you don't mind if I use your wedding gown?"

Laney laughed. "Of course not. It'll be your 'something borrowed.'"

Not long after she and Galen had married, Laney had awakened in the middle of the night to feed little Annabelle. Contentment blanketed her as she thought of her marriage and the double wedding for Toledo and Hilda and Ishmael and Amanda that followed soon after. Everyone but Eddie had someone to love. In the quiet of the night, deep in her heart, Laney knew the Lord would work things out. And in the midst of Laney's prayers, Noni Neubauer came to mind.

Childhood friends in Sacramento, Noni had reentered Laney's life when Ethel had fallen sick and the Copper Kettle hired Noni to fill in. Laney soon invited her to Sunday dinner, while Galen invited Eddie.

Within five minutes of meeting each other, Noni and Eddie had gotten into an argument. Eddie went to the Copper Kettle the next day just to prove he was right. But when he got there, he forgot to give Noni his evidence because she wasn't just cooking—she'd also baked. He ate two orders of lunch, then bought the entire strudel so he'd have some to eat at home.

Everyone in town delighted in watching their courtship. Hilda said Eddie's appetite and Noni's cooking were the only kind of music Eddie could make—and even then, there wasn't much harmony. Noni scolded him for eating too fast but never for eating too much—and she always served him heaping plates. He bellowed at her for something she said, only to be seen tenderly kissing the tip of her burned finger moments later. They were like kerosene and a match—volatile as could be. Galen had secretly commented that since Eddie Lufe owned the most spirited stallion in the county, it stood to reason that he'd wind up with a wife twice as feisty.

Ruth came over and squeezed Laney's hand. "You tease me about my schemes, but this was your doing."

"No, no. The Lord brought Noni to mind. I'm sure it was His will."

"Well, I'm thankful to you and to God." Noni looked at her reflection again. "Eddie's going to be so pleased."

Hilda finished buttoning the gown. "That man would marry you if you wore a gunnysack. He's so besotted, it's a wonder he hasn't gotten a stiff neck from craning it to look at you every second of the day."

Ruth laughed. "If that's not the pot calling the teakettle black! Toledo's that way around you, Hilda."

A quick knock sounded, and then Amanda

slipped into the bedchamber. "Noni, it fits like a dream!" she exclaimed as she admired the gown.

"Only because Hilda cinched me in so tight. Laney's waist . . ." Noni's voice died out.

Laney laughed. "I don't know that my waist will ever be that size again. Galen says he likes me fat and sassy." She sank down onto a chair.

"I'm sorry. I didn't mean to embarrass you." Noni's smile wobbled.

"I'm not embarrassed in the least. I'm thankful the Lord is blessing Galen and me."

Amanda cleared her throat. "Since we're on the subject, Ishmael and I are also expecting. Laney, you haven't said yet what you and Galen plan to use for a name. Ishmael and I would appreciate it if you'd use anything but Ivy. When we have a daughter, we'd like to grace her with his twin's name."

"Of course!"

Hilda sidled out from behind Noni. "Don't you gals go looking at me. I'm too old to be a mama." She tilted her head to the side. "Noni, don't you dare tell Eddie the dress fits. If you do, he's going to haul you off to the parson's today. We'll tell him you need a month."

"He'll never agree. He'll say next week."

"It better be next week." Laney paused as the baby kicked. "I don't want to miss the wedding."

A baby's wail sounded from downstairs.

"Isn't that just like a man?" Hilda tried to

sound gruff, but she couldn't. She adored Kenton. "Ruth, that son of yours is already acting like a man—bellowing the minute he wants something. You'd better go get him. Laney, you go on down, too. Amanda and I will help Noni out of this."

As Laney and Ruth started down the stairs, Laney whispered, "I have to tell you what Dale said yesterday. He watched Ma thump a melon to see if it was ripe, then turned to me and asked if that's how Doc knew when to stay to deliver the baby."

Ruth burst out laughing.

Josh was pacing back and forth at the foot of the stairs. "It's not funny, Ruth. I can't make him stop. He's—"

"Hungry." Ruth hastened down to her husband and son.

Galen knelt on the floor. "Laney-mine, sit down on that second step there."

She suspected why he wanted her to, so she promptly complied.

He set Annabelle down on the floor and steadied her. "Go to Mama."

Annabelle took a few halting steps, then fell. She promptly rolled over, got onto her hands and knees, and crawled to Laney's lap.

"It's a start." Galen's eyes twinkled as he came to sit beside her.

"Well?" Eddie couldn't wait any longer. He

cast a look upstairs. "Does the gown fit my Noni?"

"She needs a little time," Laney said.

"Who're you talkin' 'bout?" Ishmael asked with a grin. "L'il Annabelle or Noni?"

"Both."

Galen wrapped his arm around Laney, pulled her close, and looked deep into her eyes. "The most important things are always worth the wait."

Looking for More Good Books to Read?

You can find out what is new and exciting with previews, descriptions, and reviews by signing up for Bethany House newsletters at

www.bethanynewsletters.com

We will send you updates for as many authors or categories as you desire so you get only the information you really want.

Sign up today!